"TELL ME EVERYTHING YOU KNOW ABOUT THIS FLYING GIRL."

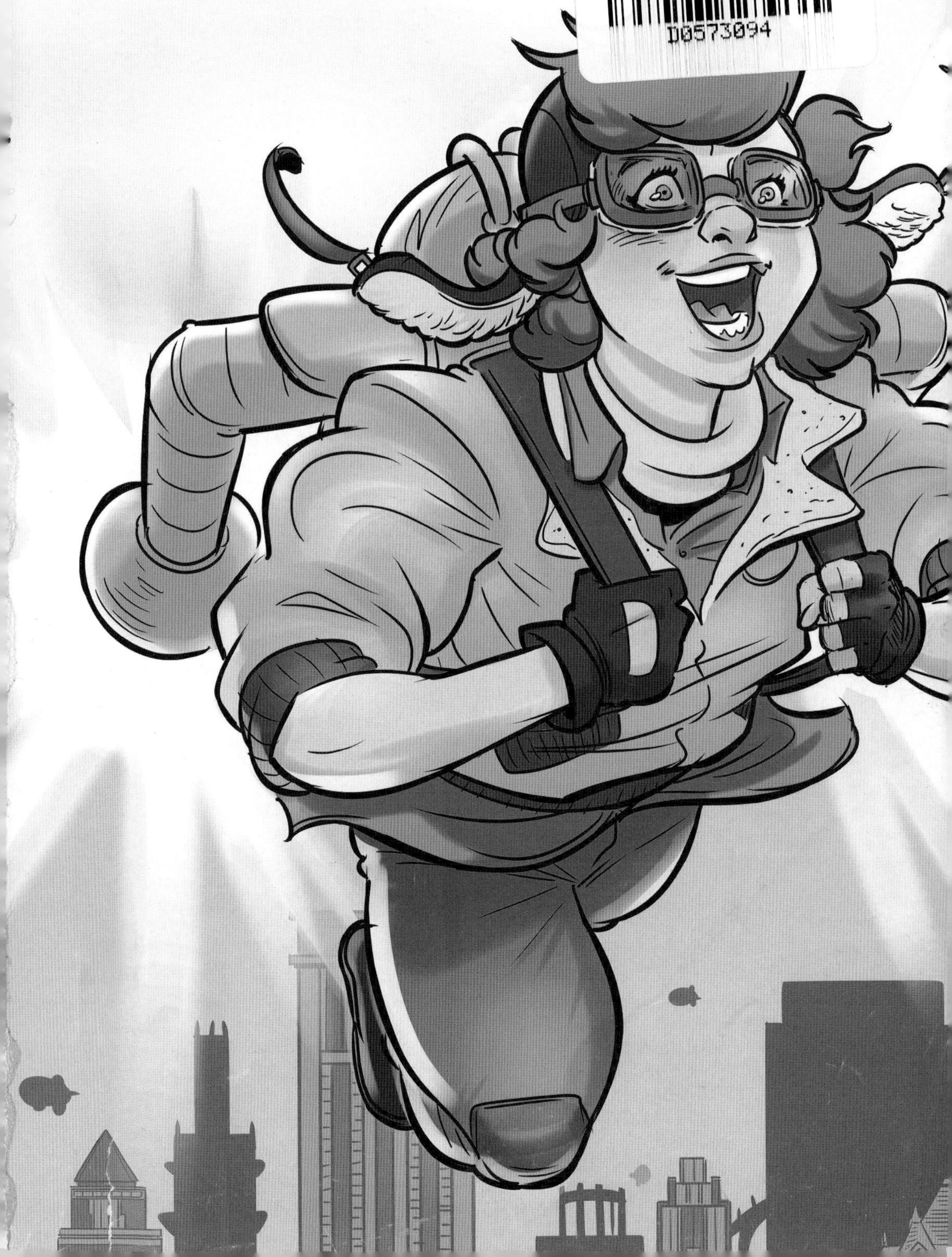

WRITTEN BY:
JASON INMAN &
ASHLEY VICTORIA ROBINSON

LINEART BY:
BEN MATSUYA

COLORS BY:
MARA JAYNE CARPENTER

COLOR FLATS BY:
SARA ALFAQEEH & TORI RIDLEY

LETTERS BY:
TAYLOR ESPOSITO OF GHOST GLYPH STUDIOS

COVER ARTIST (A/B):
BEN MATSUYA

COVER ARTIST (C):
JONBOY MEYERS
WITH COLORS BY:
RYAN KINNAIRD

PUBLISHER/ CEO: BRYAN SEATON • EDITOR IN CHIEF: SHAWN GABBORIN
PUBLISHER-DANGER ZONE: JASON MARTIN • MARKETING DIRECTOR/EDITOR: NICOLE D'ANDRIA
EXECUTIVE ADMINISTRATOR: DANIELLE DAVISON • TEST PILOT: CHAD CICCONI
PRESIDENT OF CREATOR RELATIONS: SHAWN PRYOR

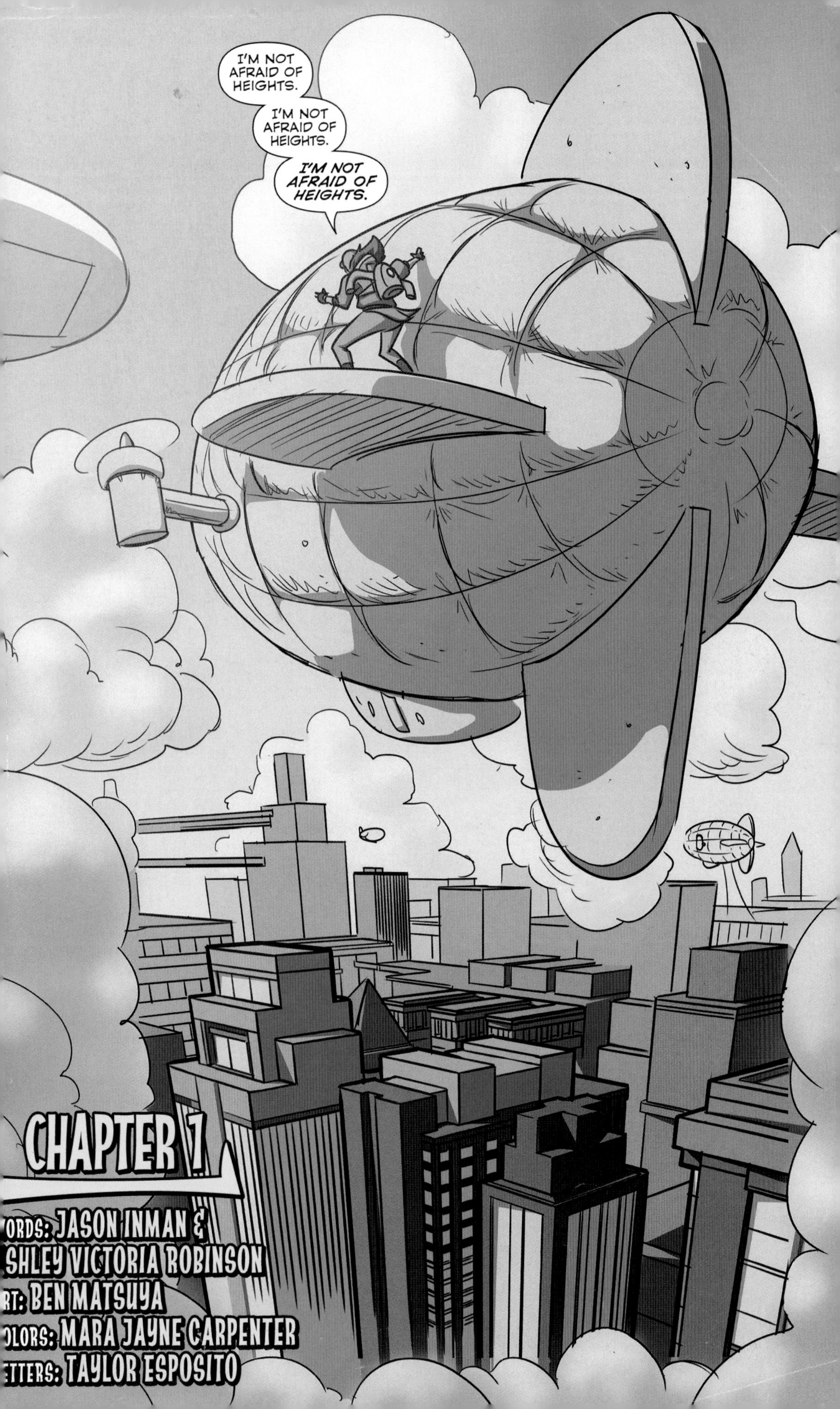

I'M NOT AFRAID OF HEIGHTS.
I'M NOT AFRAID OF HEIGHTS.
I'M NOT AFRAID OF HEIGHTS.
CHAPTER 1
ORDS: JASON INMAN &
SHLEY VICTORIA ROBINSON
RT: BEN MATSUYA
OLORS: MARA JAYNE CARPENTER
ETTERS: TAYLOR ESPOSITO

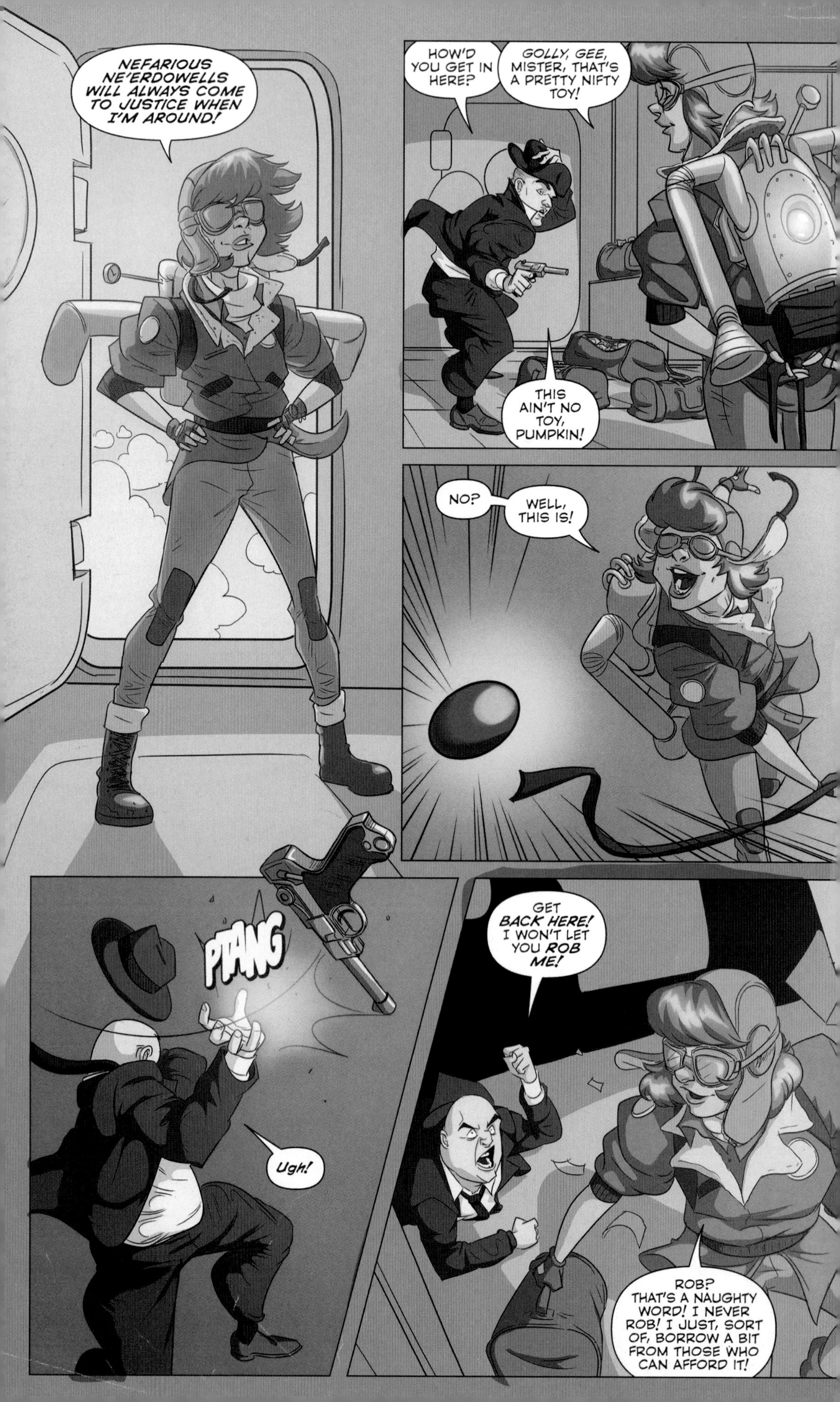
NEFARIOUS NE'ERDOWELLS WILL ALWAYS COME TO JUSTICE WHEN I'M AROUND!
HOW'D YOU GET IN HERE?
GOLLY, GEE, MISTER, THAT'S A PRETTY NIFTY TOY!
THIS AIN'T NO TOY, PUMPKIN!
NO?
WELL, THIS IS!
PTANG
Ugh!
GET BACK HERE! I WON'T LET YOU ROB ME!
ROB? THAT'S A NAUGHTY WORD! I NEVER ROB! I JUST, SORT OF, BORROW A BIT FROM THOSE WHO CAN AFFORD IT!

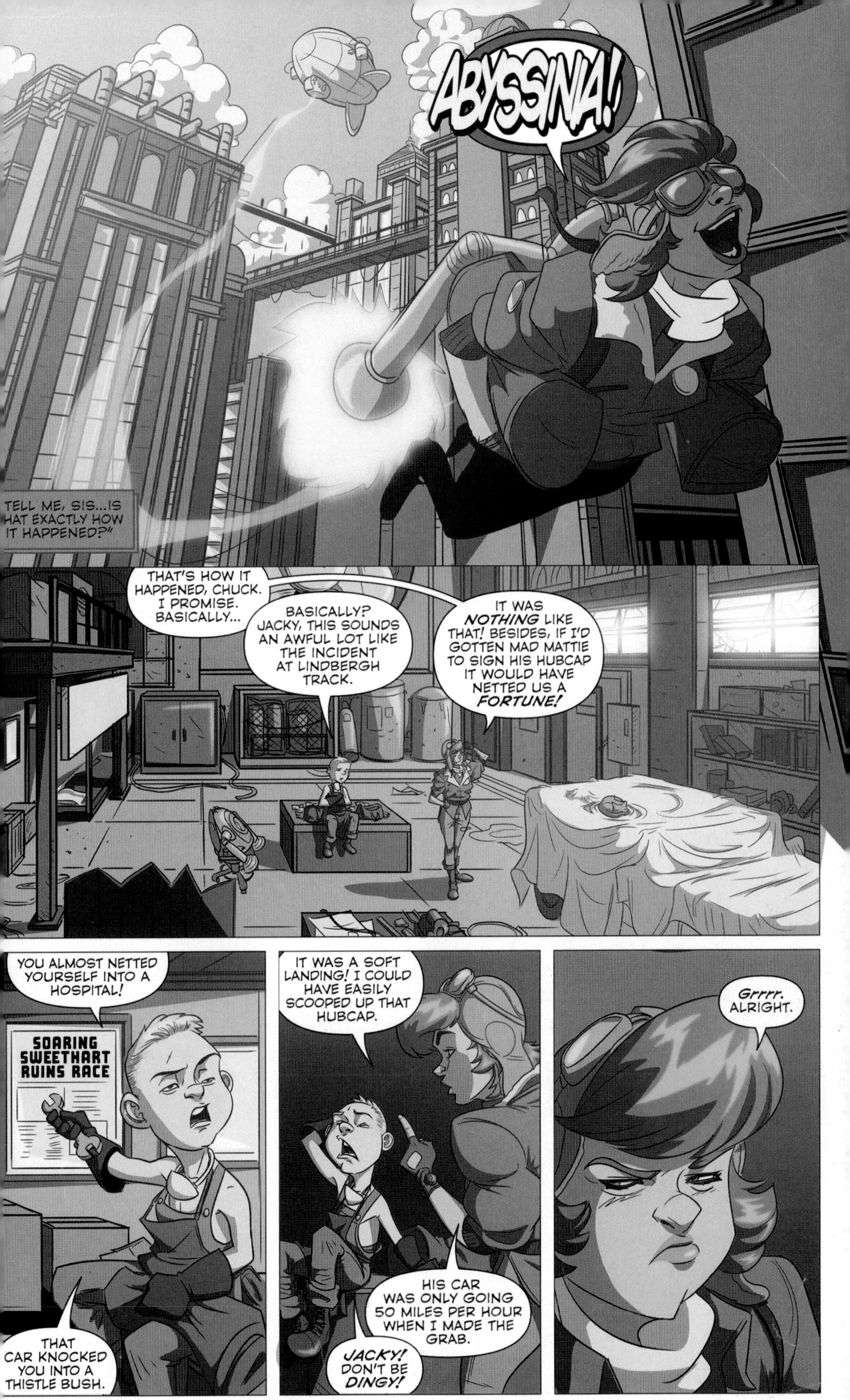
ABYSSINIA!
TELL ME, SIS...IS HAT EXACTLY HOW IT HAPPENED?"
THAT'S HOW IT HAPPENED, CHUCK. I PROMISE. BASICALLY...
BASICALLY? JACKY, THIS SOUNDS AN AWFUL LOT LIKE THE INCIDENT AT LINDBERGH TRACK.
IT WAS NOTHING LIKE THAT! BESIDES, IF I'D GOTTEN MAD MATTIE TO SIGN HIS HUBCAP IT WOULD HAVE NETTED US A FORTUNE!
YOU ALMOST NETTED YOURSELF INTO A HOSPITAL!
SOARING SWEETHART RUINS RACE
THAT CAR KNOCKED YOU INTO A THISTLE BUSH.
IT WAS A SOFT LANDING! I COULD HAVE EASILY SCOOPED UP THAT HUBCAP.
HIS CAR WAS ONLY GOING 50 MILES PER HOUR WHEN I MADE THE GRAB.
JACKY! DON'T BE DINGY!
Grrrr. ALRIGHT.

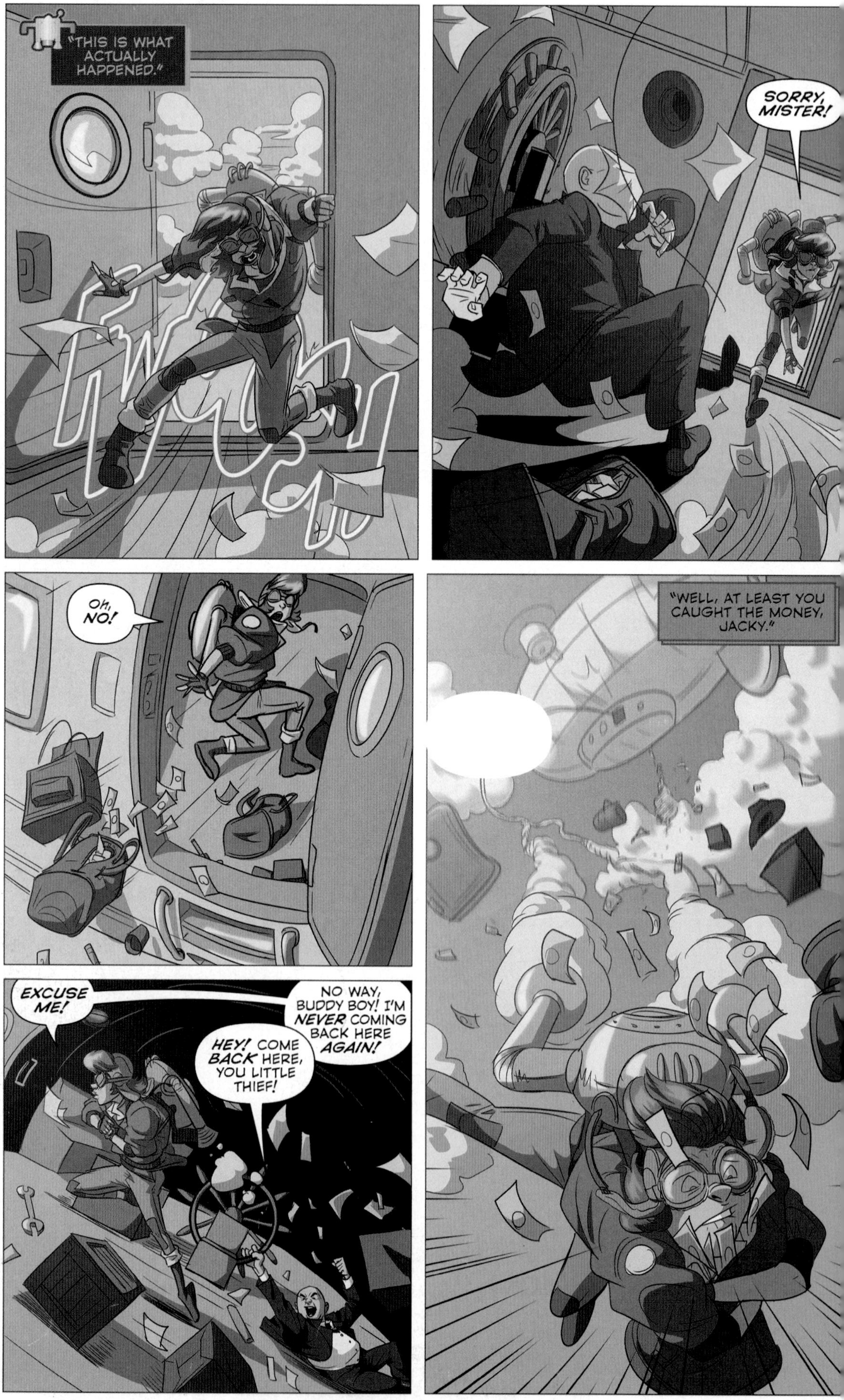
"THIS IS WHAT ACTUALLY HAPPENED."
SORRY, MISTER!
Oh, NO!
"WELL, AT LEAST YOU CAUGHT THE MONEY, JACKY."
EXCUSE ME!
NO WAY, BUDDY BOY! I'M NEVER COMING BACK HERE AGAIN!
HEY! COME BACK HERE, YOU LITTLE THIEF!

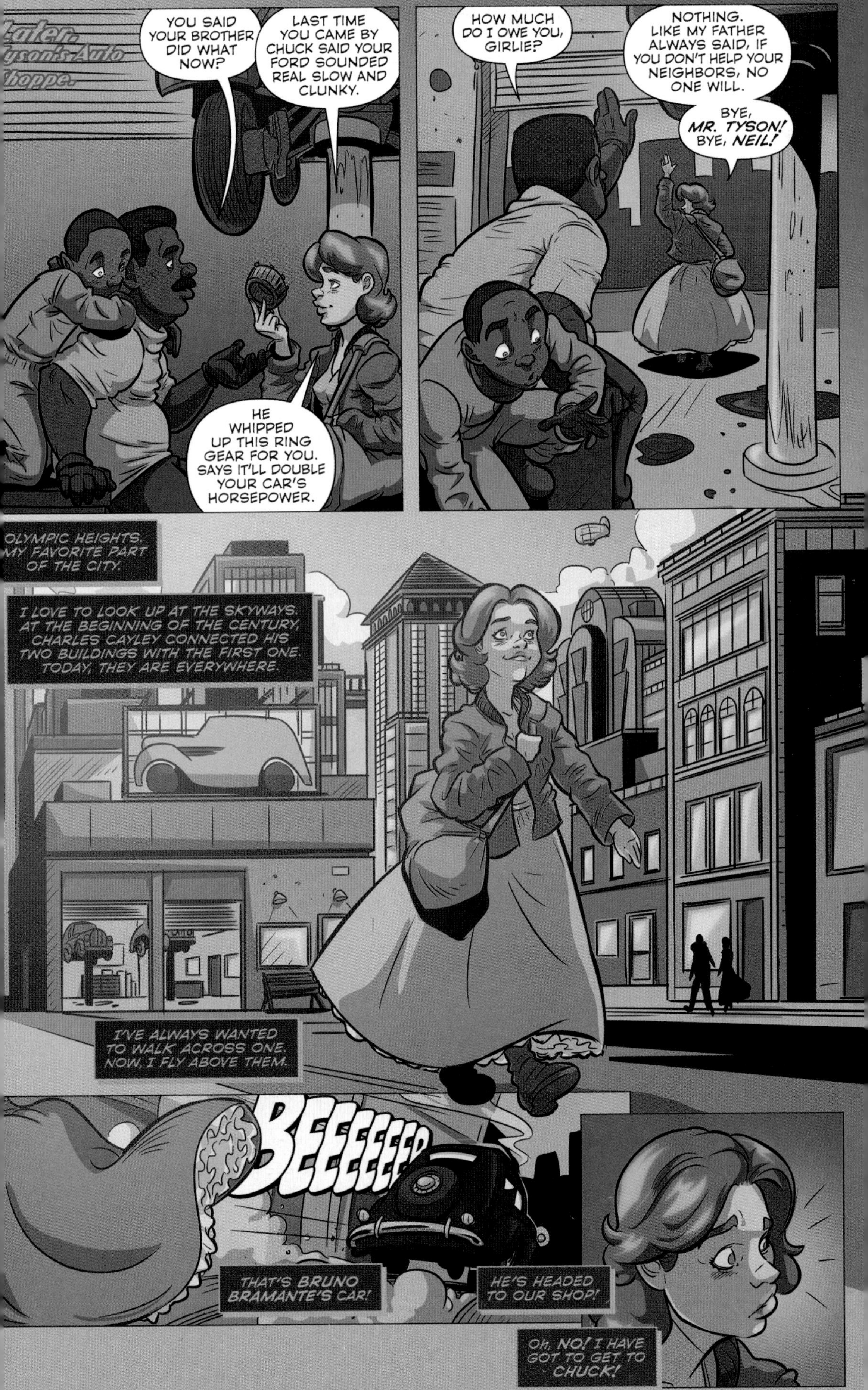
Later.
yson's Auto
hoppe.
YOU SAID YOUR BROTHER DID WHAT NOW?
LAST TIME YOU CAME BY CHUCK SAID YOUR FORD SOUNDED REAL SLOW AND CLUNKY.
HE WHIPPED UP THIS RING GEAR FOR YOU. SAYS IT'LL DOUBLE YOUR CAR'S HORSEPOWER.
HOW MUCH DO I OWE YOU, GIRLIE?
NOTHING. LIKE MY FATHER ALWAYS SAID, IF YOU DON'T HELP YOUR NEIGHBORS, NO ONE WILL.
BYE, MR. TYSON! BYE, NEIL!
OLYMPIC HEIGHTS. MY FAVORITE PART OF THE CITY.
I LOVE TO LOOK UP AT THE SKYWAYS. AT THE BEGINNING OF THE CENTURY, CHARLES CAYLEY CONNECTED HIS TWO BUILDINGS WITH THE FIRST ONE. TODAY, THEY ARE EVERYWHERE.
I'VE ALWAYS WANTED TO WALK ACROSS ONE. NOW, I FLY ABOVE THEM.
BEEEEEEEP
THAT'S BRUNO BRAMANTE'S CAR!
HE'S HEADED TO OUR SHOP!
Oh, NO! I HAVE GOT TO GET TO CHUCK!

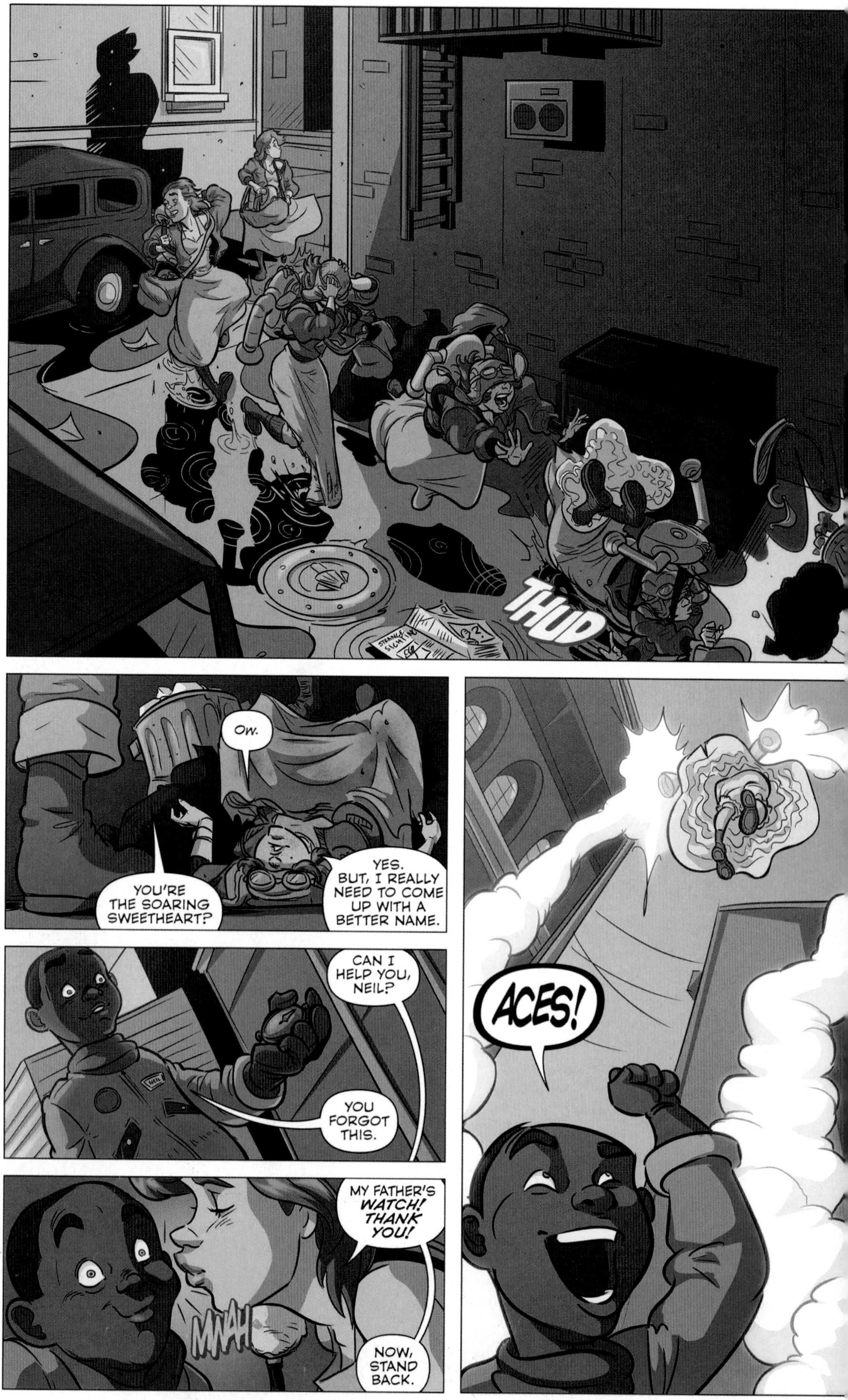
THUD
STRANGE SIGHTING
OW.
YOU'RE THE SOARING SWEETHEART?
YES. BUT, I REALLY NEED TO COME UP WITH A BETTER NAME.
CAN I HELP YOU, NEIL?
YOU FORGOT THIS.
NEIL
MY FATHER'S WATCH! THANK YOU!
MWAH
NOW, STAND BACK.
ACES!

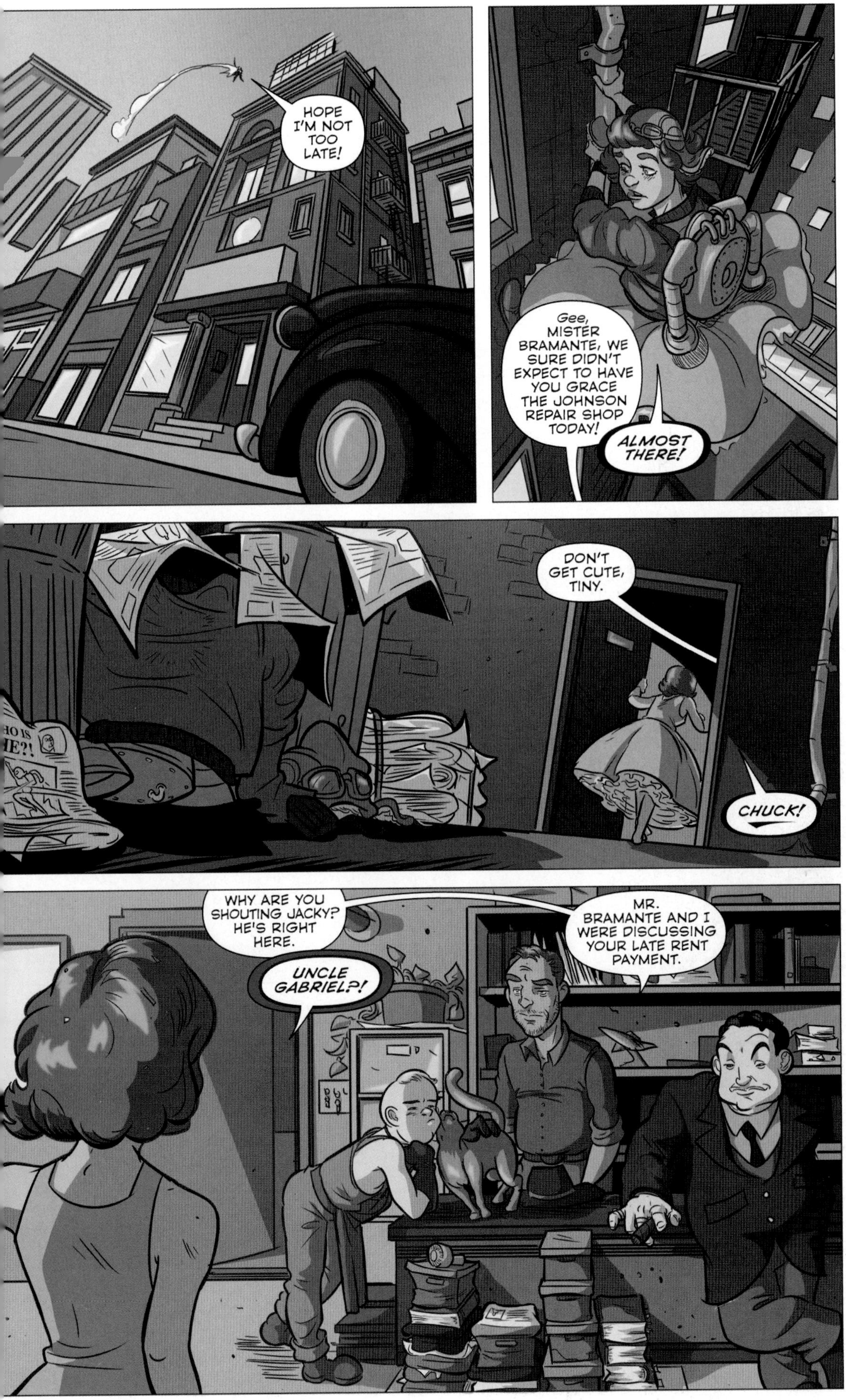
HOPE I'M NOT TOO LATE!
Gee, MISTER BRAMANTE, WE SURE DIDN'T EXPECT TO HAVE YOU GRACE THE JOHNSON REPAIR SHOP TODAY!
ALMOST THERE!
DON'T GET CUTE, TINY.
CHUCK!
WHY ARE YOU SHOUTING JACKY? HE'S RIGHT HERE.
MR. BRAMANTE AND I WERE DISCUSSING YOUR LATE RENT PAYMENT.
UNCLE GABRIEL?!

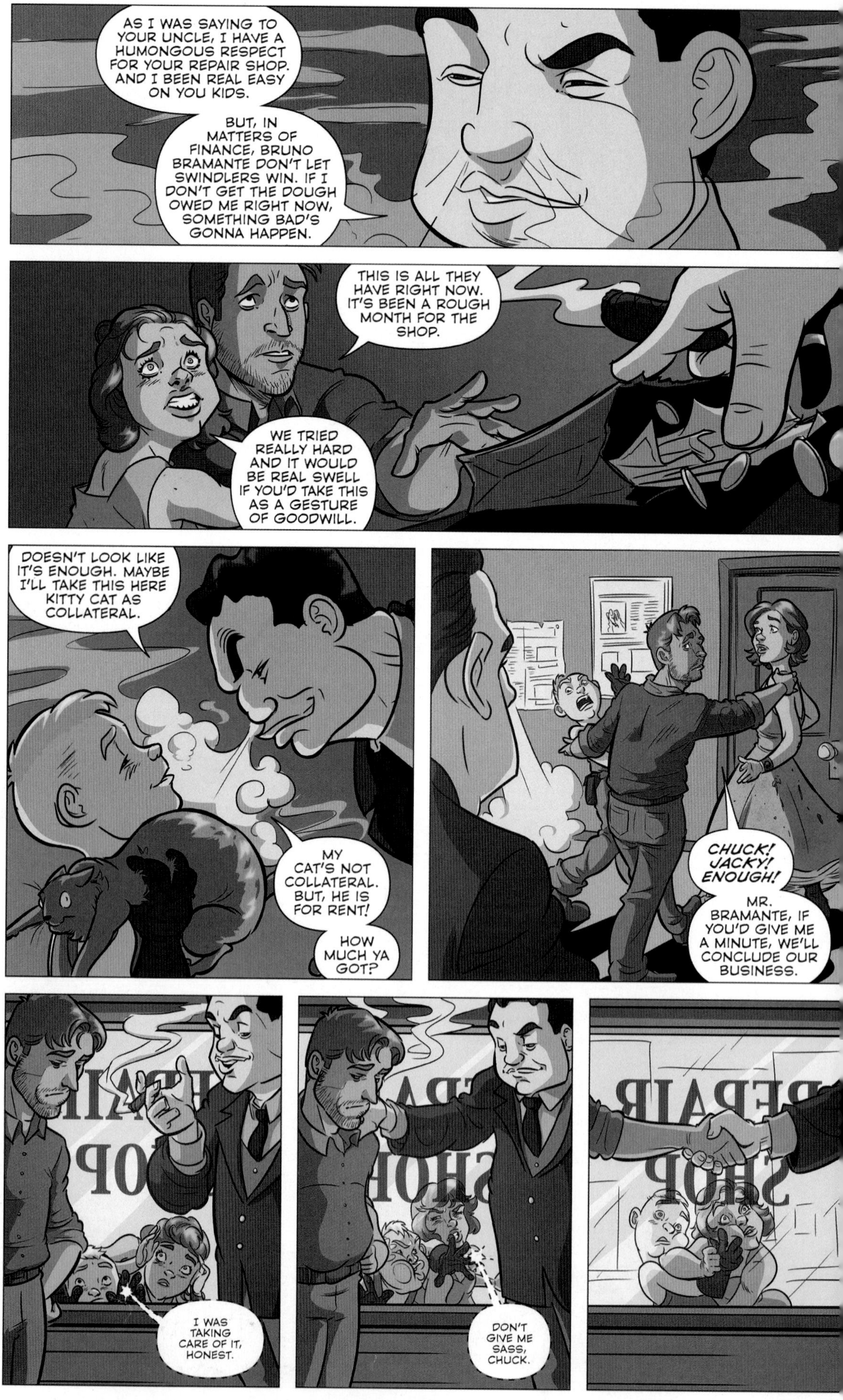
AS I WAS SAYING TO YOUR UNCLE, I HAVE A HUMONGOUS RESPECT FOR YOUR REPAIR SHOP. AND I BEEN REAL EASY ON YOU KIDS.
BUT, IN MATTERS OF FINANCE, BRUNO BRAMANTE DON'T LET SWINDLERS WIN. IF I DON'T GET THE DOUGH OWED ME RIGHT NOW, SOMETHING BAD'S GONNA HAPPEN.
THIS IS ALL THEY HAVE RIGHT NOW. IT'S BEEN A ROUGH MONTH FOR THE SHOP.
WE TRIED REALLY HARD AND IT WOULD BE REAL SWELL IF YOU'D TAKE THIS AS A GESTURE OF GOODWILL.
DOESN'T LOOK LIKE IT'S ENOUGH. MAYBE I'LL TAKE THIS HERE KITTY CAT AS COLLATERAL.
MY CAT'S NOT COLLATERAL. BUT, HE IS FOR RENT!
HOW MUCH YA GOT?
CHUCK! JACKY! ENOUGH!
MR. BRAMANTE, IF YOU'D GIVE ME A MINUTE, WE'LL CONCLUDE OUR BUSINESS.
REPAIR SHOP
I WAS TAKING CARE OF IT, HONEST.
DON'T GIVE ME SASS, CHUCK.

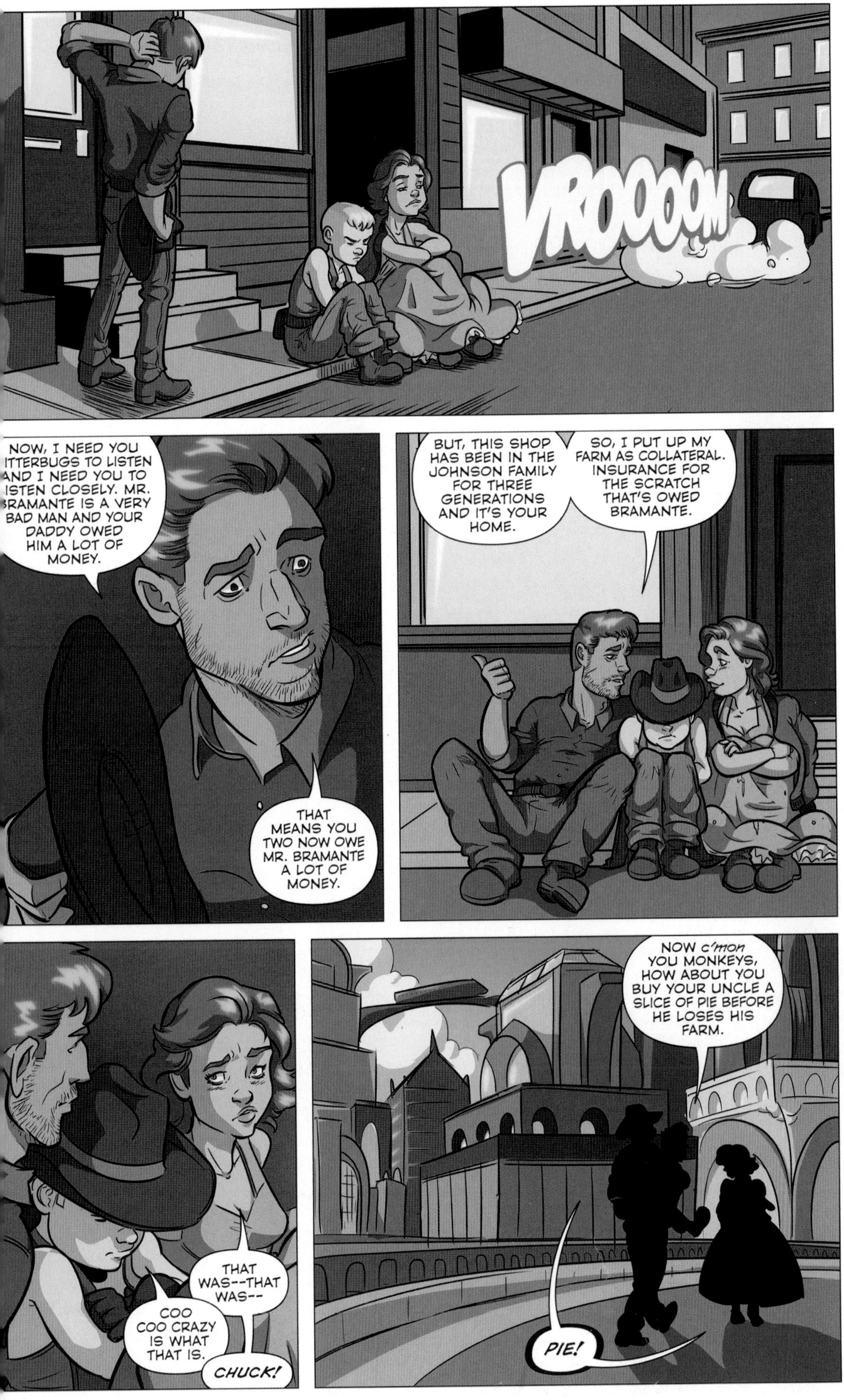

VROOOOM
NOW, I NEED YOU
ITTERBUGS TO LISTEN
AND I NEED YOU TO
ISTEN CLOSELY. MR.
BRAMANTE IS A VERY
BAD MAN AND YOUR
DADDY OWED
HIM A LOT OF
MONEY.
THAT
MEANS YOU
TWO NOW OWE
MR. BRAMANTE
A LOT OF
MONEY.
BUT, THIS SHOP
HAS BEEN IN THE
JOHNSON FAMILY
FOR THREE
GENERATIONS
AND IT'S YOUR
HOME.
SO, I PUT UP MY
FARM AS COLLATERAL.
INSURANCE FOR
THE SCRATCH
THAT'S OWED
BRAMANTE.
THAT
WAS--THAT
WAS--
COO
COO CRAZY
IS WHAT
THAT IS.
CHUCK!
NOW c'mon
YOU MONKEYS,
HOW ABOUT YOU
BUY YOUR UNCLE A
SLICE OF PIE BEFORE
HE LOSES HIS
FARM.
PIE!

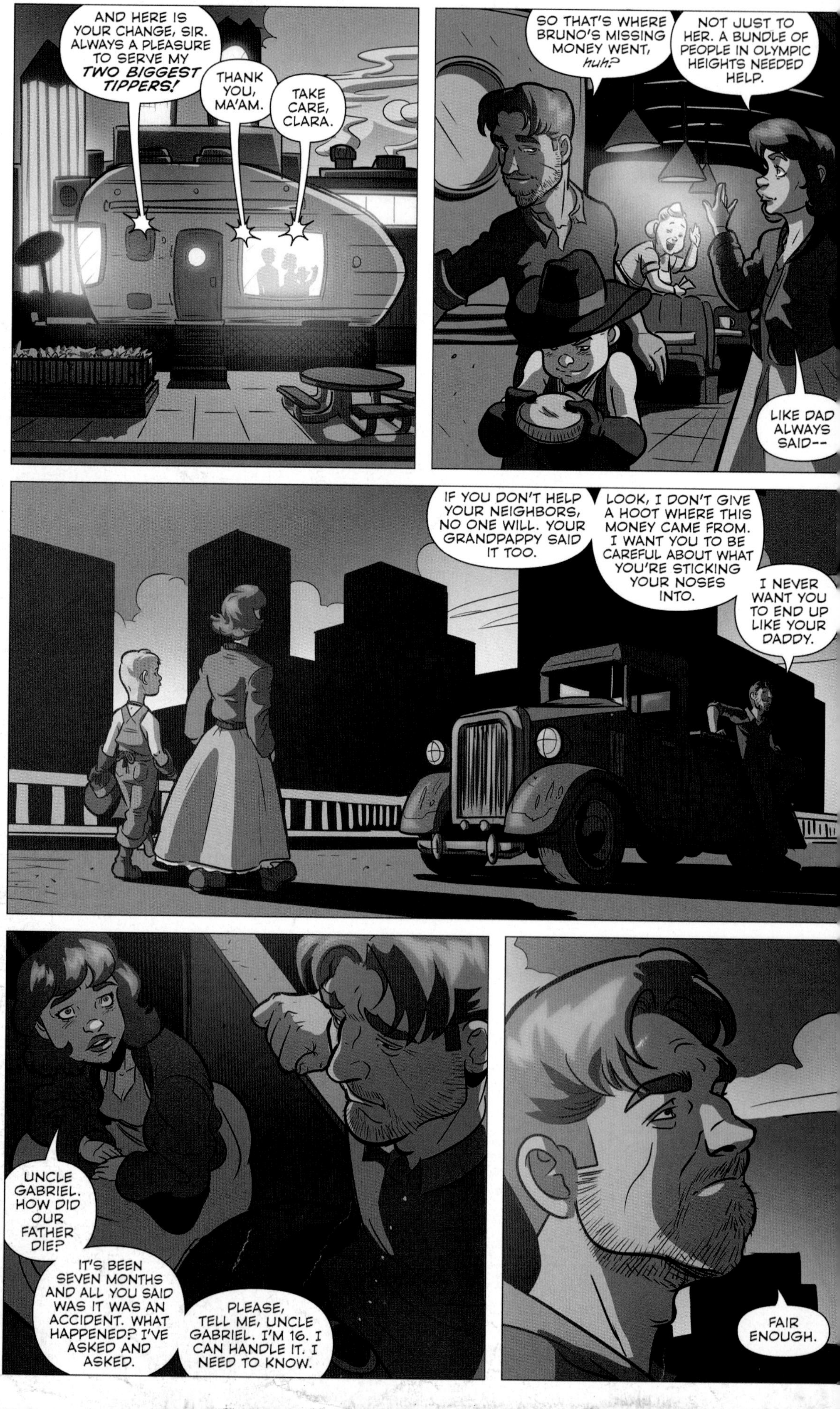

AND HERE IS YOUR CHANGE, SIR. ALWAYS A PLEASURE TO SERVE MY TWO BIGGEST TIPPERS!
THANK YOU, MA'AM.
TAKE CARE, CLARA.
SO THAT'S WHERE BRUNO'S MISSING MONEY WENT, huh?
NOT JUST TO HER. A BUNDLE OF PEOPLE IN OLYMPIC HEIGHTS NEEDED HELP.
LIKE DAD ALWAYS SAID--
IF YOU DON'T HELP YOUR NEIGHBORS, NO ONE WILL. YOUR GRANDPAPPY SAID IT TOO.
LOOK, I DON'T GIVE A HOOT WHERE THIS MONEY CAME FROM. I WANT YOU TO BE CAREFUL ABOUT WHAT YOU'RE STICKING YOUR NOSES INTO.
I NEVER WANT YOU TO END UP LIKE YOUR DADDY.
UNCLE GABRIEL. HOW DID OUR FATHER DIE?
IT'S BEEN SEVEN MONTHS AND ALL YOU SAID WAS IT WAS AN ACCIDENT. WHAT HAPPENED? I'VE ASKED AND ASKED.
PLEASE, TELL ME, UNCLE GABRIEL. I'M 16. I CAN HANDLE IT. I NEED TO KNOW.
FAIR ENOUGH.

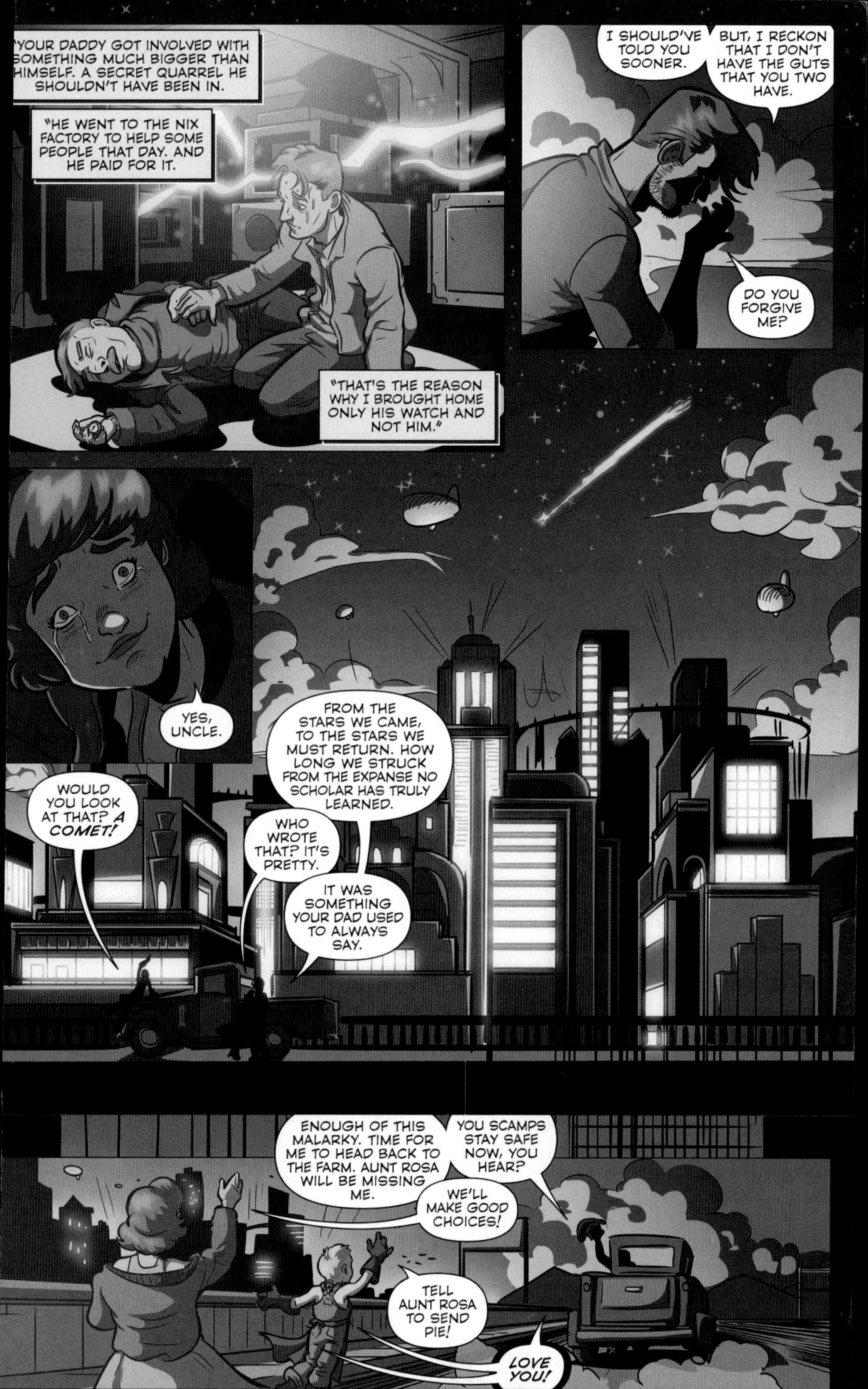
"YOUR DADDY GOT INVOLVED WITH SOMETHING MUCH BIGGER THAN HIMSELF. A SECRET QUARREL HE SHOULDN'T HAVE BEEN IN.
"HE WENT TO THE NIX FACTORY TO HELP SOME PEOPLE THAT DAY. AND HE PAID FOR IT.
"THAT'S THE REASON WHY I BROUGHT HOME ONLY HIS WATCH AND NOT HIM."
I SHOULD'VE TOLD YOU SOONER.
BUT, I RECKON THAT I DON'T HAVE THE GUTS THAT YOU TWO HAVE.
DO YOU FORGIVE ME?
YES, UNCLE.
WOULD YOU LOOK AT THAT? *A COMET!*
FROM THE STARS WE CAME, TO THE STARS WE MUST RETURN. HOW LONG WE STRUCK FROM THE EXPANSE NO SCHOLAR HAS TRULY LEARNED.
WHO WROTE THAT? IT'S PRETTY.
IT WAS SOMETHING YOUR DAD USED TO ALWAYS SAY.
ENOUGH OF THIS MALARKY. TIME FOR ME TO HEAD BACK TO THE FARM. AUNT ROSA WILL BE MISSING ME.
YOU SCAMPS STAY SAFE NOW, YOU HEAR?
WE'LL MAKE GOOD CHOICES!
TELL AUNT ROSA TO SEND PIE!
LOVE YOU!

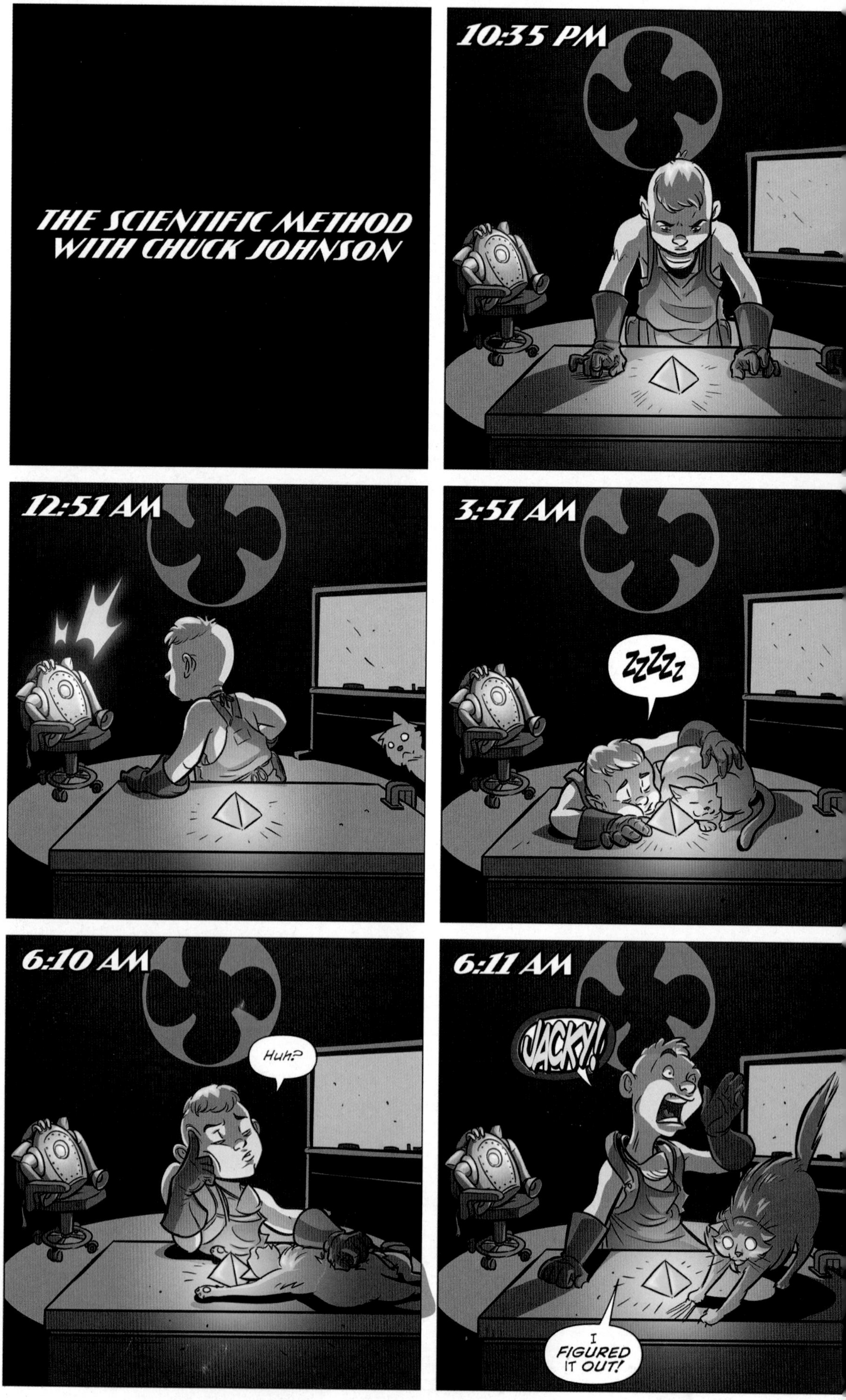
THE SCIENTIFIC METHOD
WITH CHUCK JOHNSON
10:35 PM
12:51 AM
3:51 AM
ZZZZZ
6:10 AM
Huh?
6:11 AM
JACKY!!
I FIGURED IT OUT!

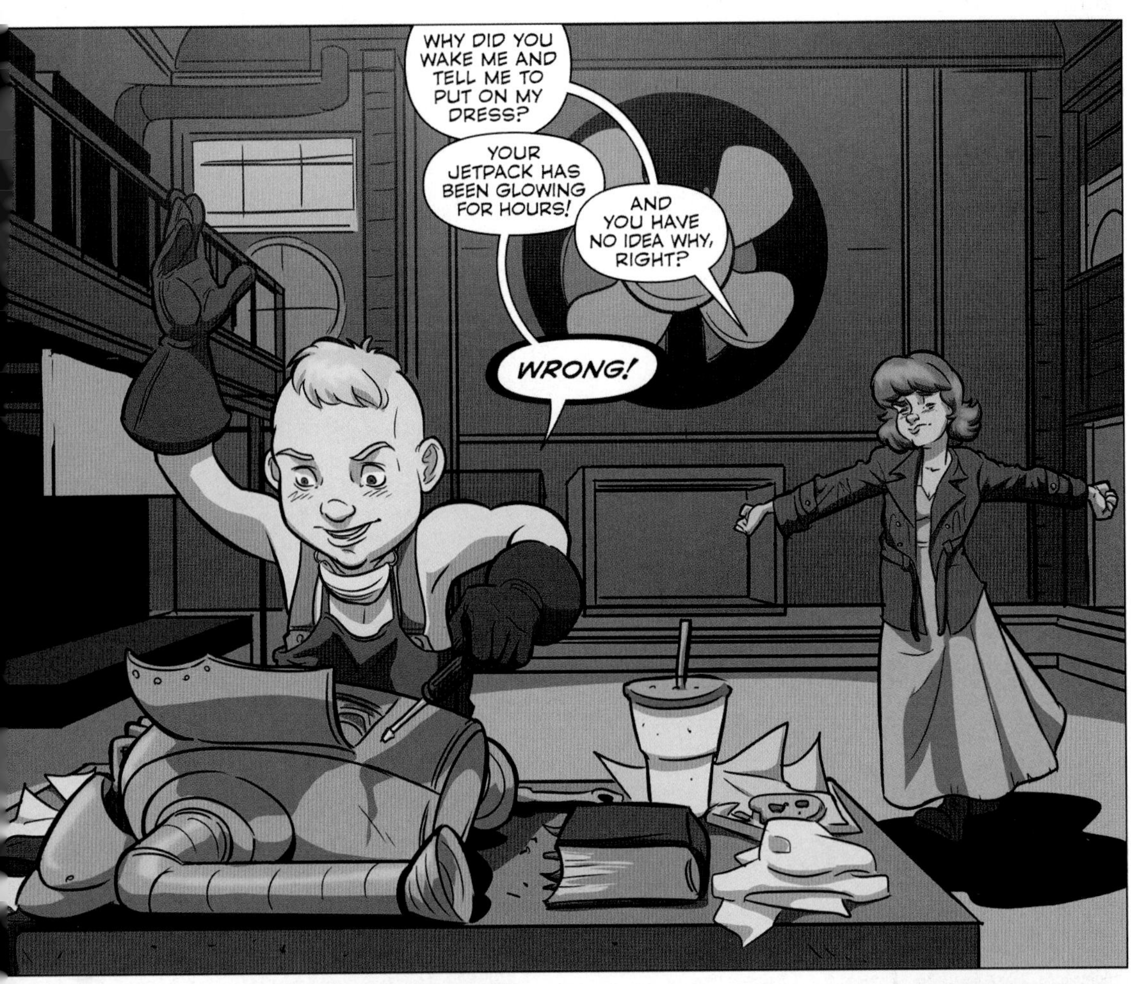
WHY DID YOU WAKE ME AND TELL ME TO PUT ON MY DRESS?
YOUR JETPACK HAS BEEN GLOWING FOR HOURS!
AND YOU HAVE NO IDEA WHY, RIGHT?
WRONG!

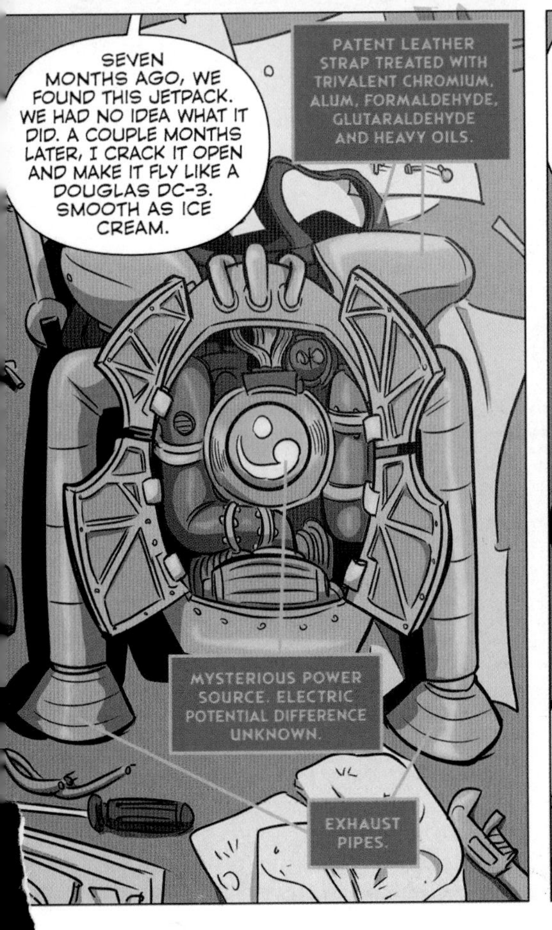
SEVEN MONTHS AGO, WE FOUND THIS JETPACK. WE HAD NO IDEA WHAT IT DID. A COUPLE MONTHS LATER, I CRACK IT OPEN AND MAKE IT FLY LIKE A DOUGLAS DC-3. SMOOTH AS ICE CREAM.
PATENT LEATHER STRAP TREATED WITH TRIVALENT CHROMIUM, ALUM, FORMALDEHYDE, GLUTARALDEHYDE AND HEAVY OILS.
MYSTERIOUS POWER SOURCE. ELECTRIC POTENTIAL DIFFERENCE UNKNOWN.
EXHAUST PIPES.

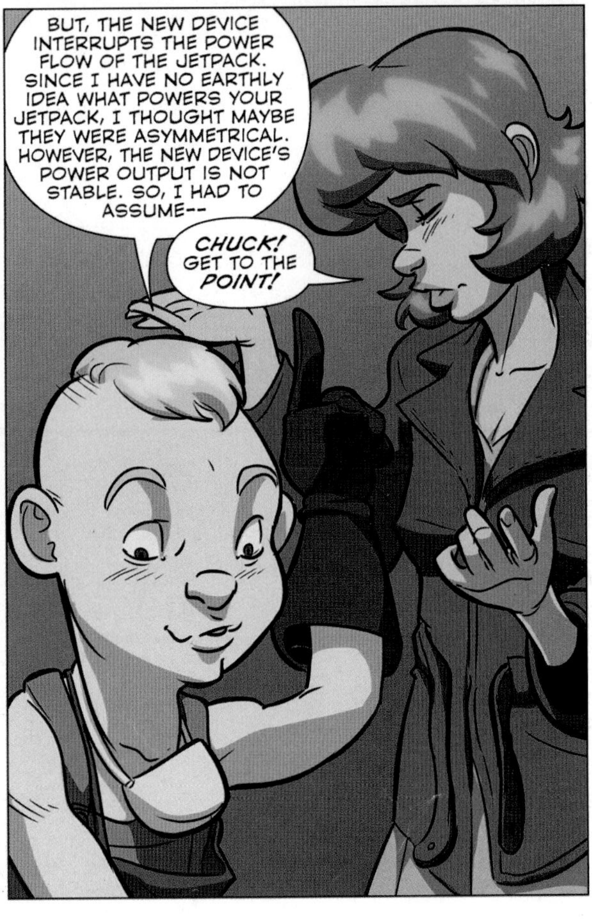
BUT, THE NEW DEVICE INTERRUPTS THE POWER FLOW OF THE JETPACK. SINCE I HAVE NO EARTHLY IDEA WHAT POWERS YOUR JETPACK, I THOUGHT MAYBE THEY WERE ASYMMETRICAL. HOWEVER, THE NEW DEVICE'S POWER OUTPUT IS NOT STABLE. SO, I HAD TO ASSUME--
CHUCK! GET TO THE POINT!

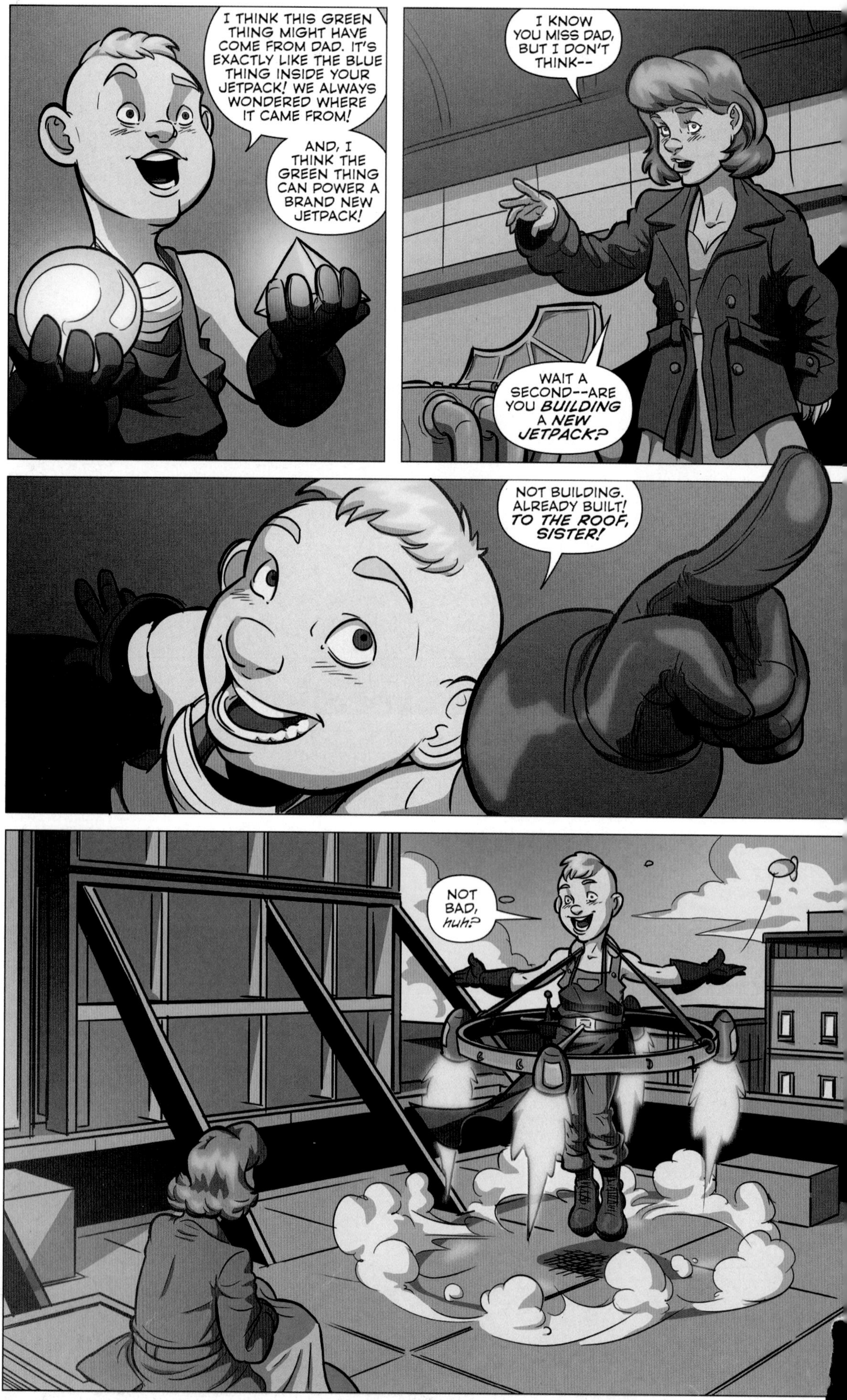
I THINK THIS GREEN THING MIGHT HAVE COME FROM DAD. IT'S EXACTLY LIKE THE BLUE THING INSIDE YOUR JETPACK! WE ALWAYS WONDERED WHERE IT CAME FROM!
AND, I THINK THE GREEN THING CAN POWER A BRAND NEW JETPACK!
I KNOW YOU MISS DAD, BUT I DON'T THINK--
WAIT A SECOND--ARE YOU *BUILDING* A *NEW JETPACK?*
NOT BUILDING. ALREADY BUILT! *TO THE ROOF, SISTER!*
NOT BAD, *huh?*

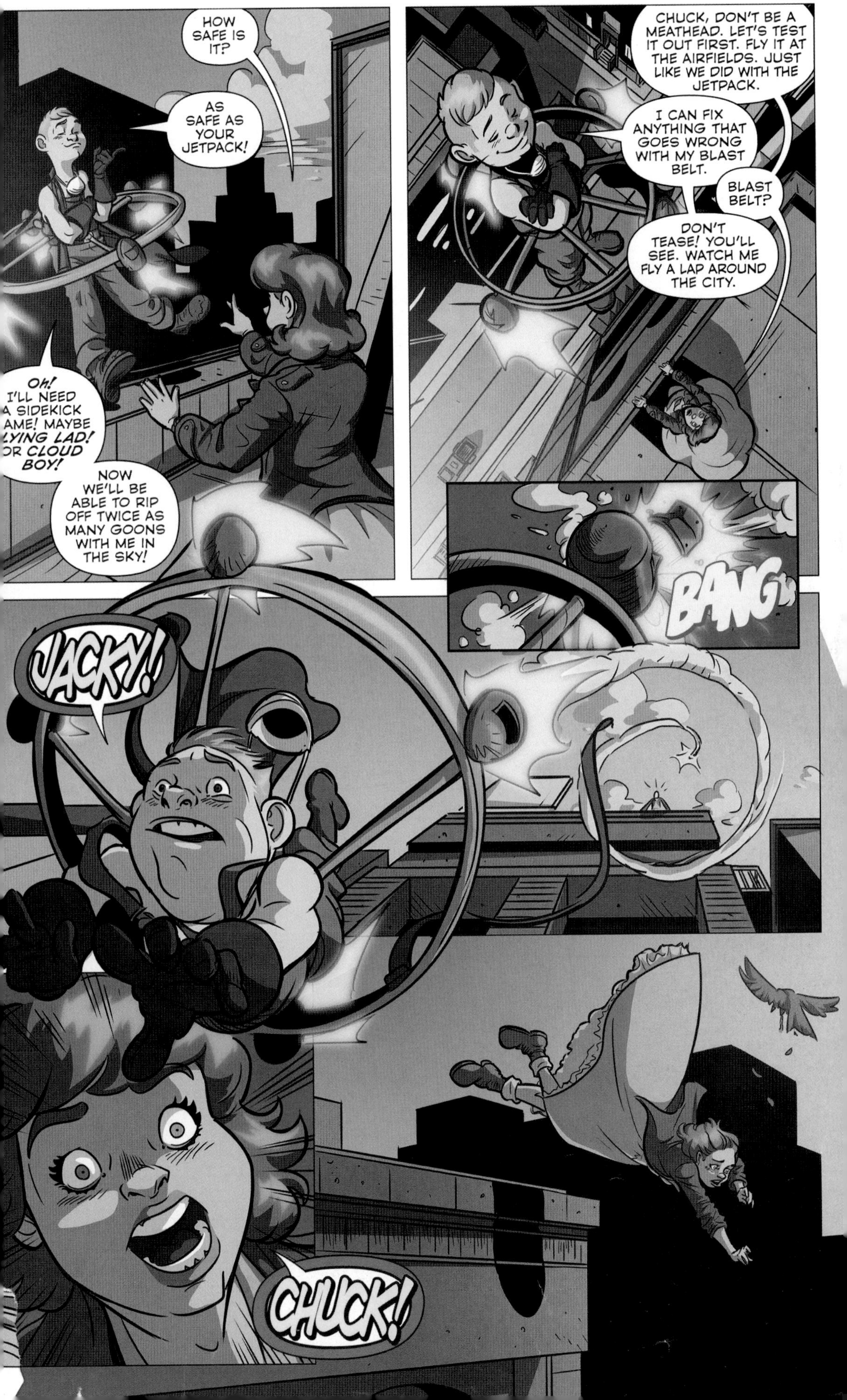
HOW SAFE IS IT?
AS SAFE AS YOUR JETPACK!
Oh! I'LL NEED A SIDEKICK NAME! MAYBE FLYING LAD! OR CLOUD BOY!
NOW WE'LL BE ABLE TO RIP OFF TWICE AS MANY GOONS WITH ME IN THE SKY!
CHUCK, DON'T BE A MEATHEAD. LET'S TEST IT OUT FIRST. FLY IT AT THE AIRFIELDS. JUST LIKE WE DID WITH THE JETPACK.
I CAN FIX ANYTHING THAT GOES WRONG WITH MY BLAST BELT.
BLAST BELT?
DON'T TEASE! YOU'LL SEE. WATCH ME FLY A LAP AROUND THE CITY.
BANG
JACKY!
CHUCK!

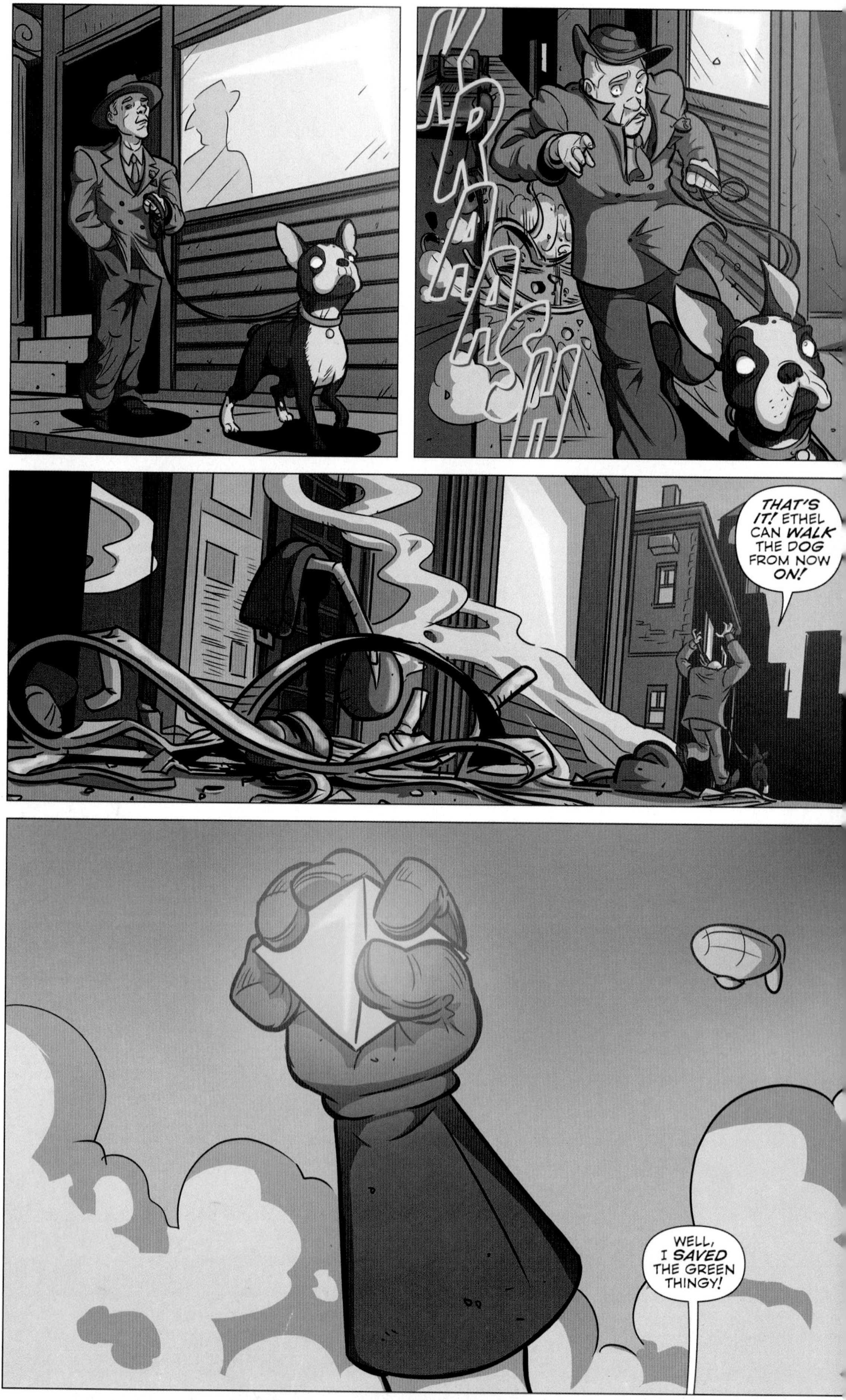
THAT'S IT! ETHEL CAN WALK THE DOG FROM NOW ON!
WELL, I SAVED THE GREEN THINGY!

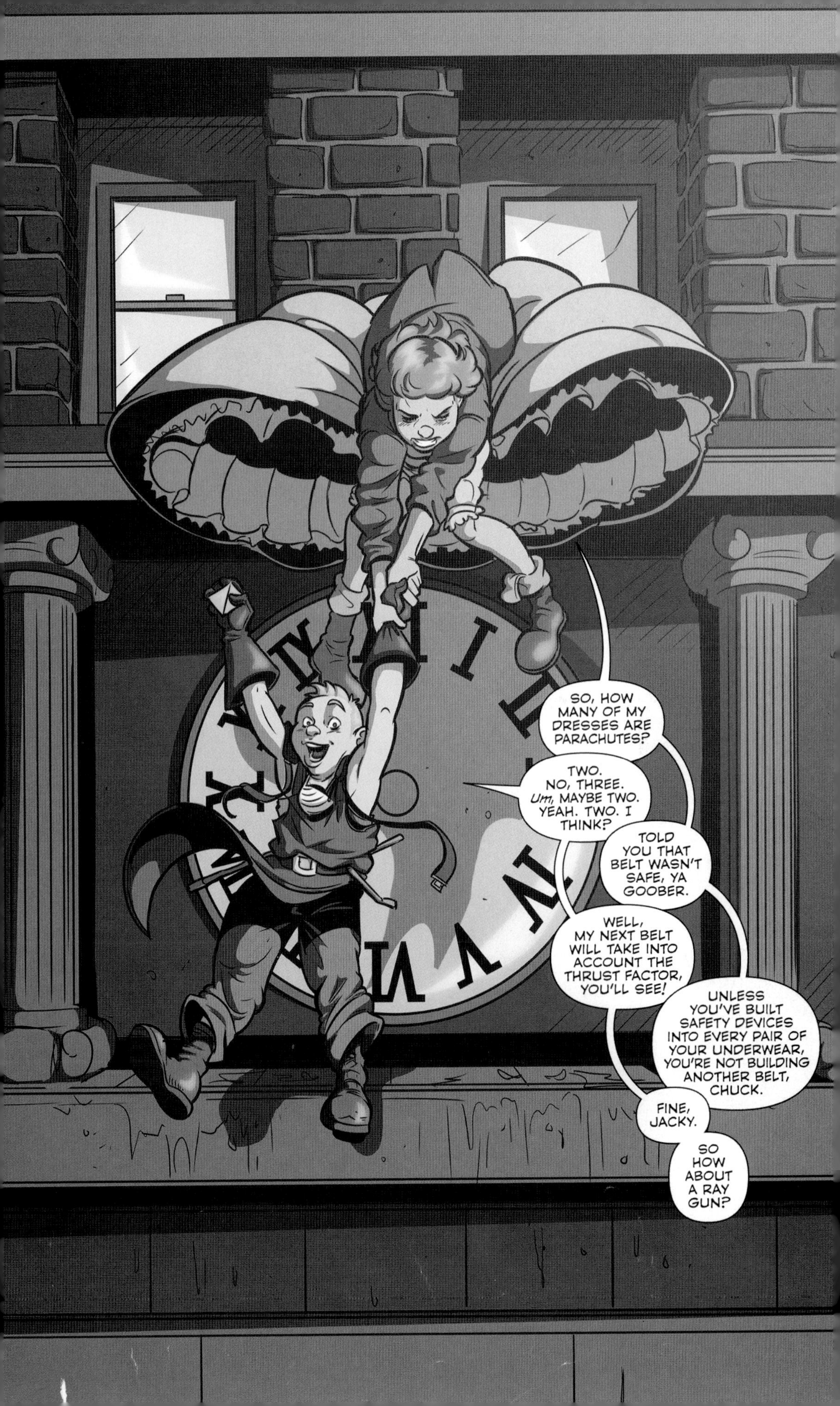
SO, HOW MANY OF MY DRESSES ARE PARACHUTES?
TWO. NO, THREE. *Um,* MAYBE TWO. YEAH. TWO. I THINK?
TOLD YOU THAT BELT WASN'T SAFE, YA GOOBER.
WELL, MY NEXT BELT WILL TAKE INTO ACCOUNT THE THRUST FACTOR, YOU'LL SEE!
UNLESS YOU'VE BUILT SAFETY DEVICES INTO EVERY PAIR OF YOUR UNDERWEAR, YOU'RE NOT BUILDING ANOTHER BELT, CHUCK.
FINE, JACKY.
SO HOW ABOUT A RAY GUN?

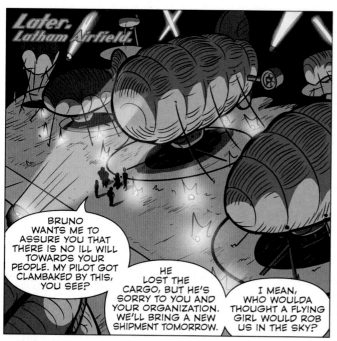

BRUNO WANTS ME TO ASSURE YOU THAT THERE IS NO ILL WILL TOWARDS YOUR PEOPLE. MY PILOT GOT CLAMBAKED BY THIS, YOU SEE?

HE LOST THE CARGO, BUT HE'S SORRY TO YOU AND YOUR ORGANIZATION. WE'LL BRING A NEW SHIPMENT TOMORROW.

I MEAN, WHO WOULDA THOUGHT A FLYING GIRL WOULD ROB US IN THE SKY?

B-ZZZAT

AAHH!

NOW, TELL ME EVERYTHING YOU KNOW ABOUT THIS FLYING GIRL.

To be continued...

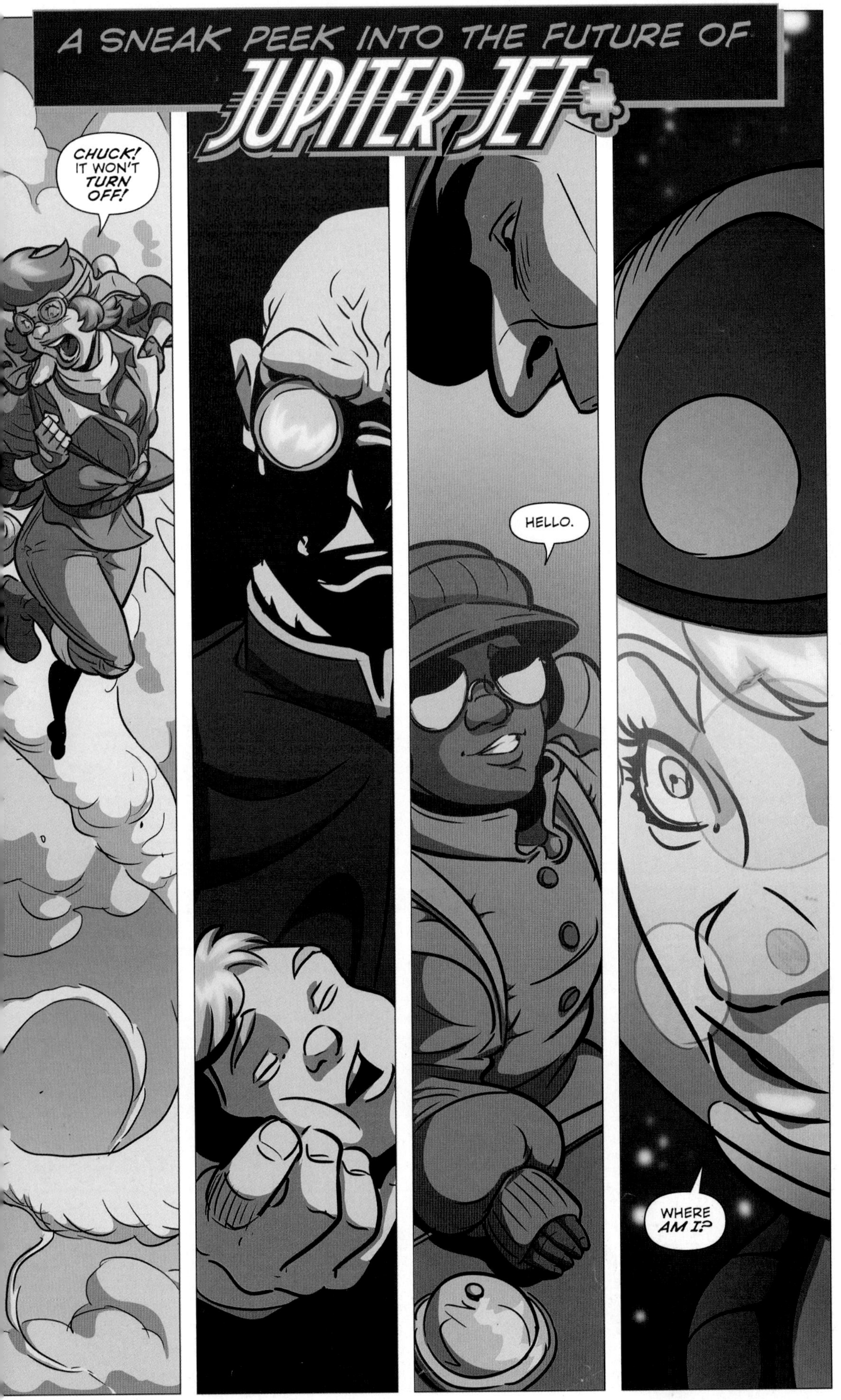
A SNEAK PEEK INTO THE FUTURE OF
JUPITER JET
CHUCK! IT WON'T TURN OFF!
HELLO.
WHERE AM I?

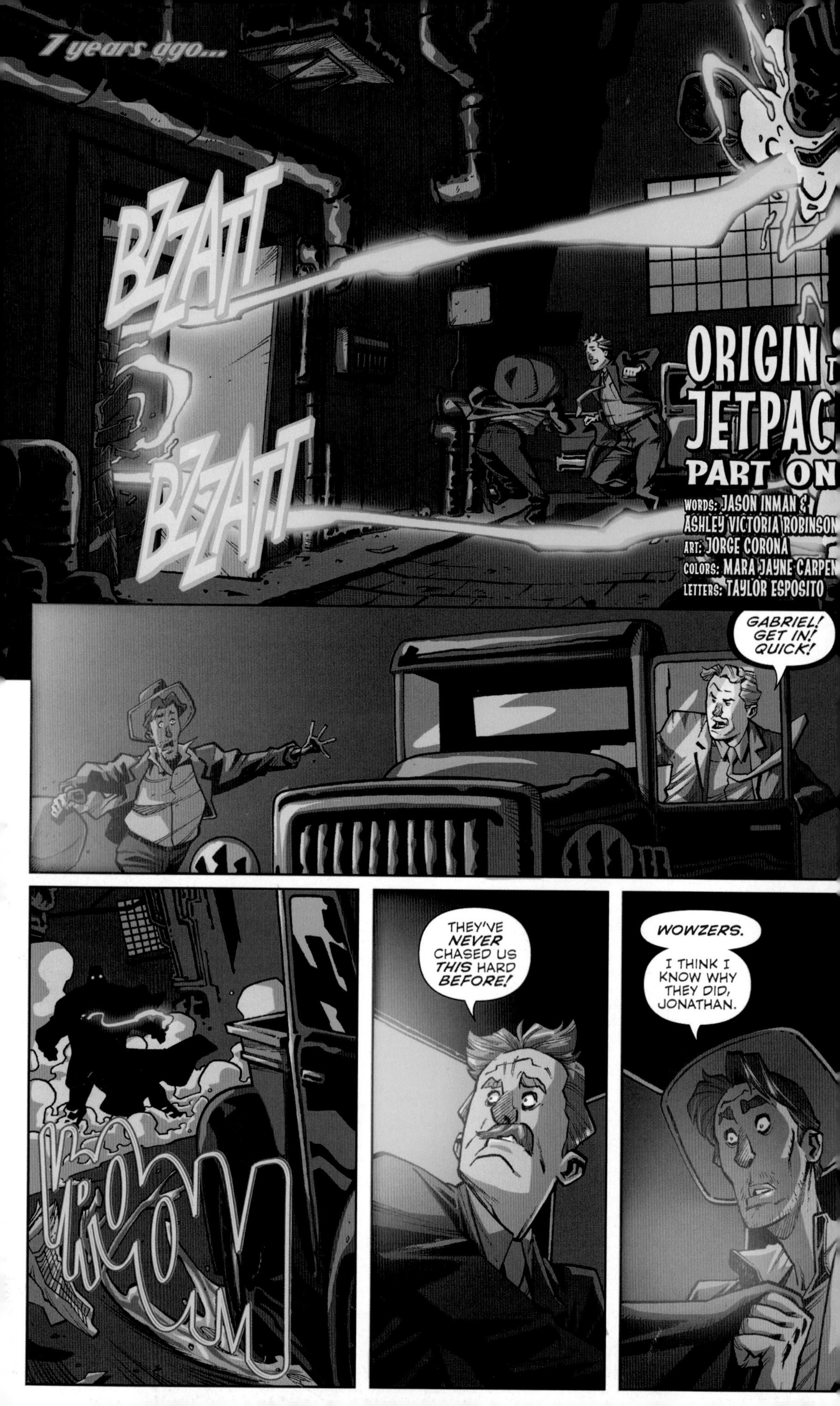
7 years ago...
BZZATT
BZZATT
ORIGIN T
JETPAC
PART ON
WORDS: JASON INMAN & ASHLEY VICTORIA ROBINSON
ART: JORGE CORONA
COLORS: MARA JAYNE CARPEN
LETTERS: TAYLOR ESPOSITO
GABRIEL! GET IN! QUICK!
THEY'VE NEVER CHASED US THIS HARD BEFORE!
WOWZERS.
I THINK I KNOW WHY THEY DID, JONATHAN.

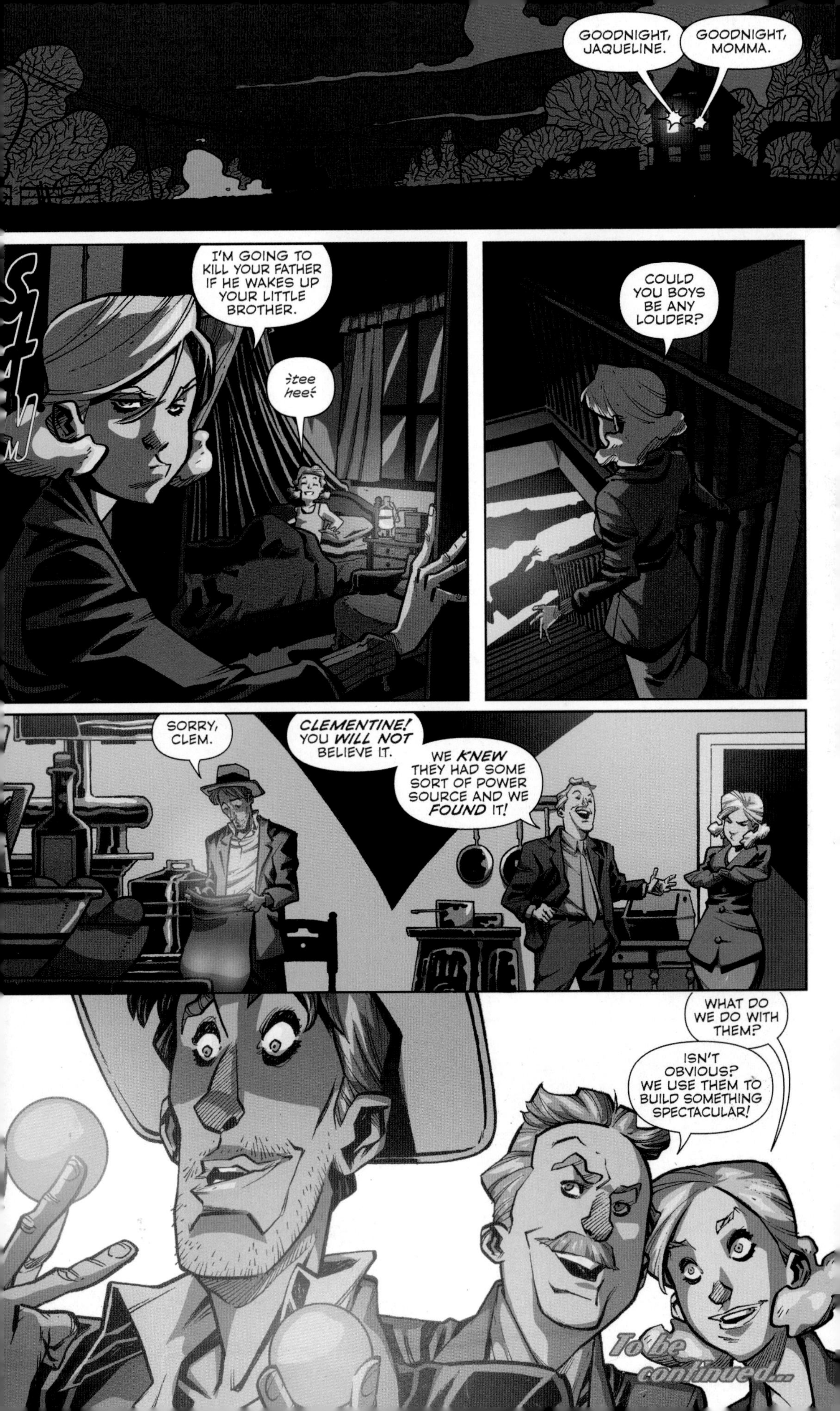
GOODNIGHT, JAQUELINE.
GOODNIGHT, MOMMA.
I'M GOING TO KILL YOUR FATHER IF HE WAKES UP YOUR LITTLE BROTHER.
tee hee
COULD YOU BOYS BE ANY LOUDER?
SORRY, CLEM.
CLEMENTINE! YOU WILL NOT BELIEVE IT.
WE KNEW THEY HAD SOME SORT OF POWER SOURCE AND WE FOUND IT!
WHAT DO WE DO WITH THEM?
ISN'T OBVIOUS? WE USE THEM TO BUILD SOMETHING SPECTACULAR!
To be continued...

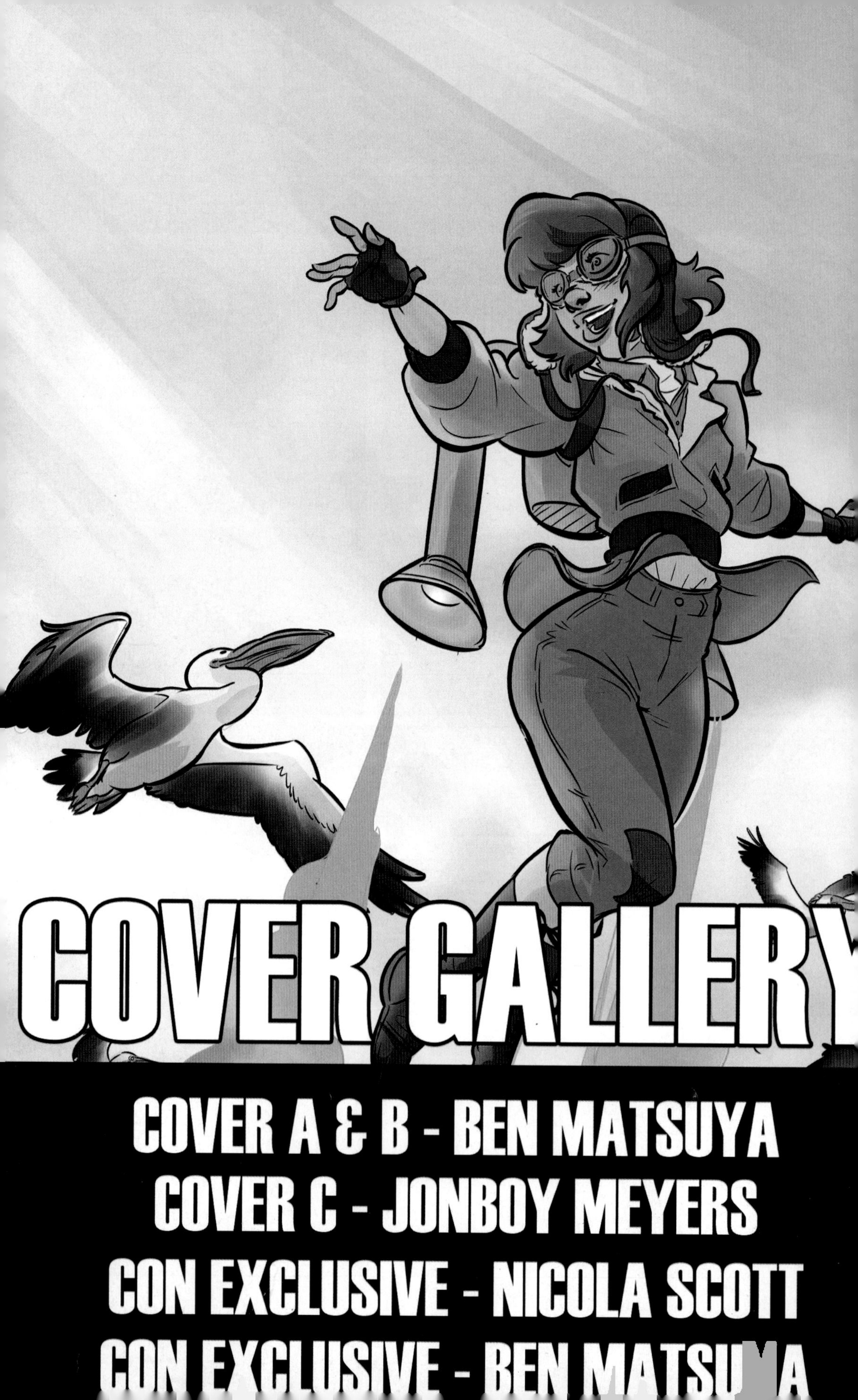

COVER GALLERY

COVER A & B - BEN MATSUYA
COVER C - JONBOY MEYERS
CON EXCLUSIVE - NICOLA SCOTT
CON EXCLUSIVE - BEN MATSUYA

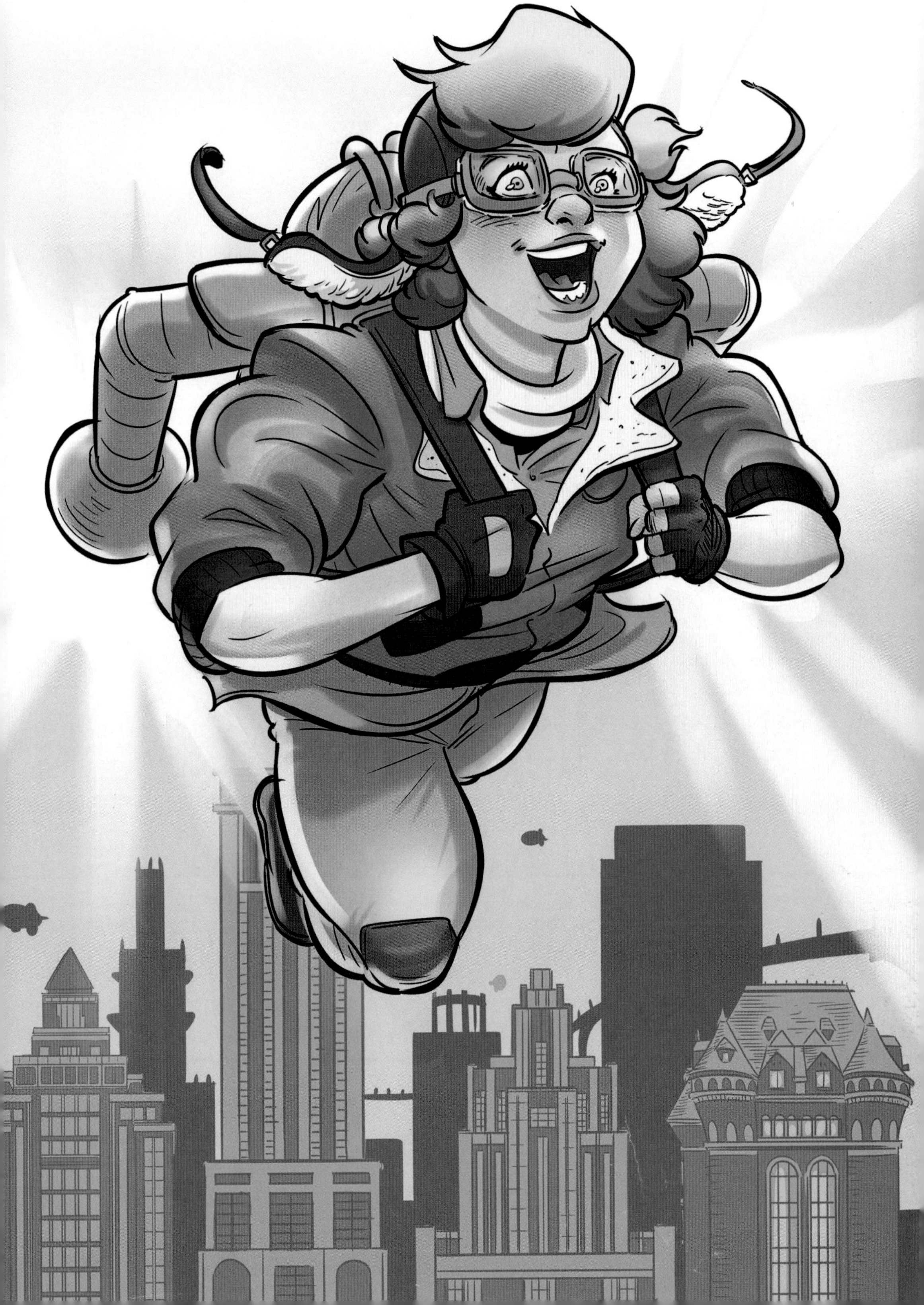

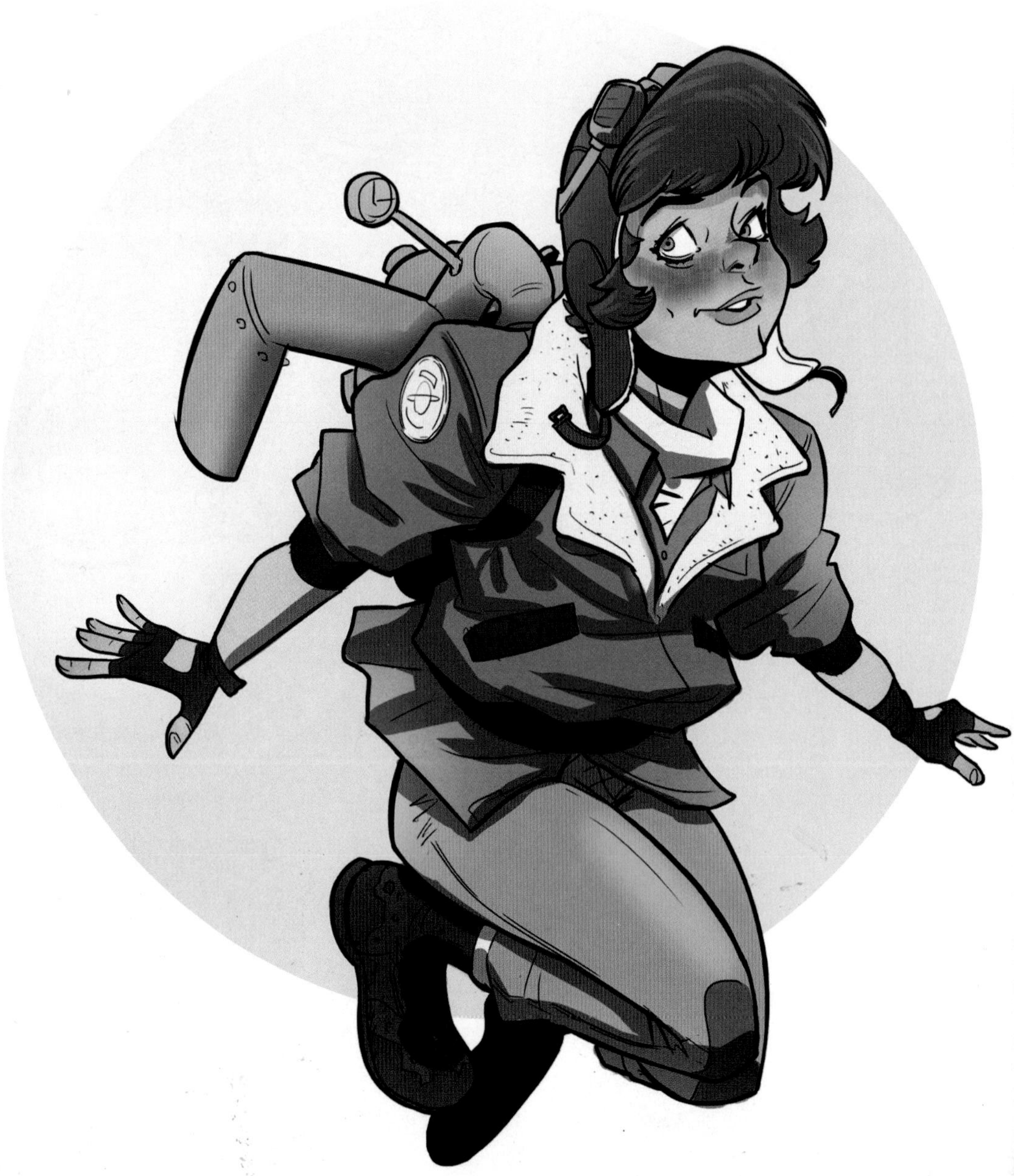

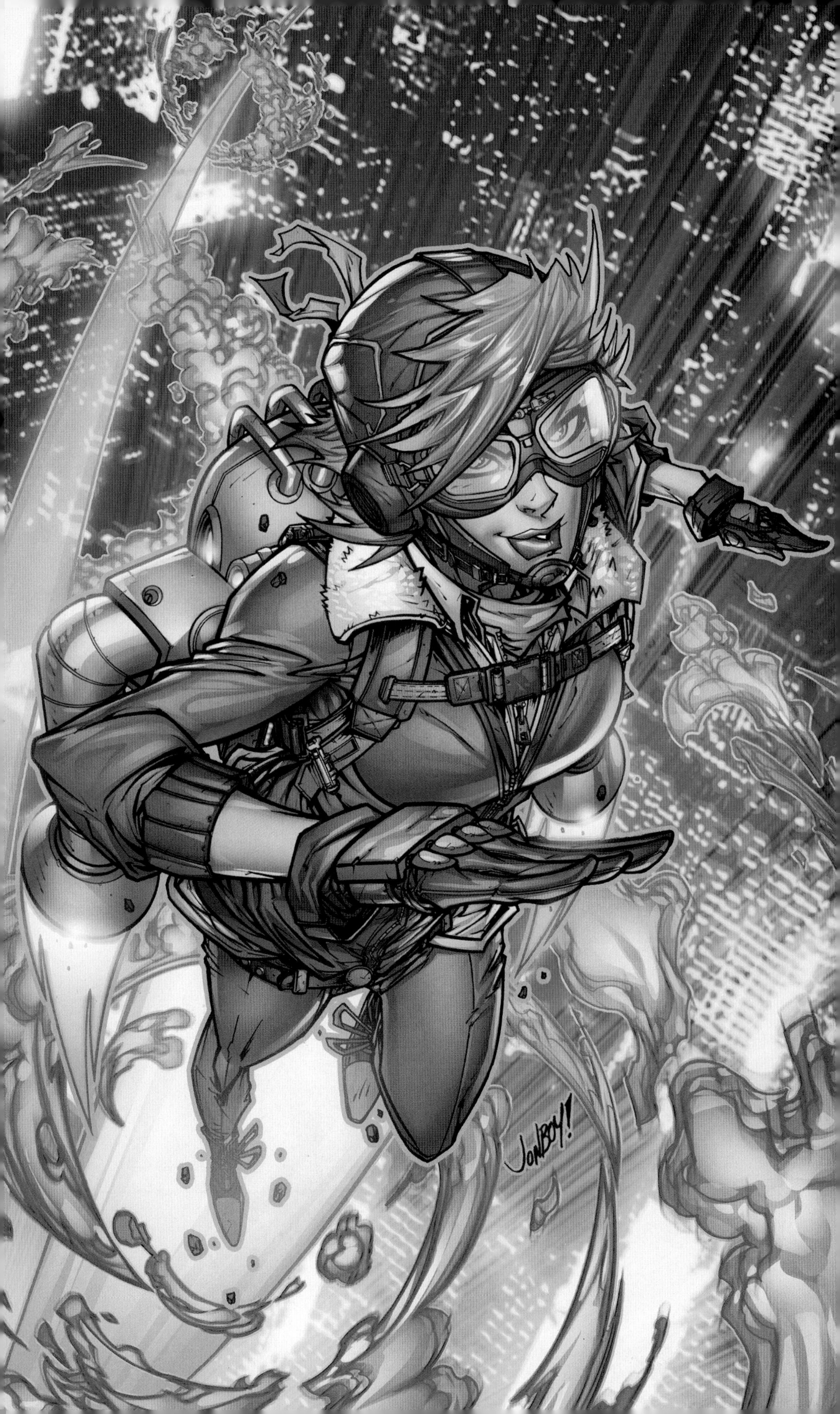
JONBOY!

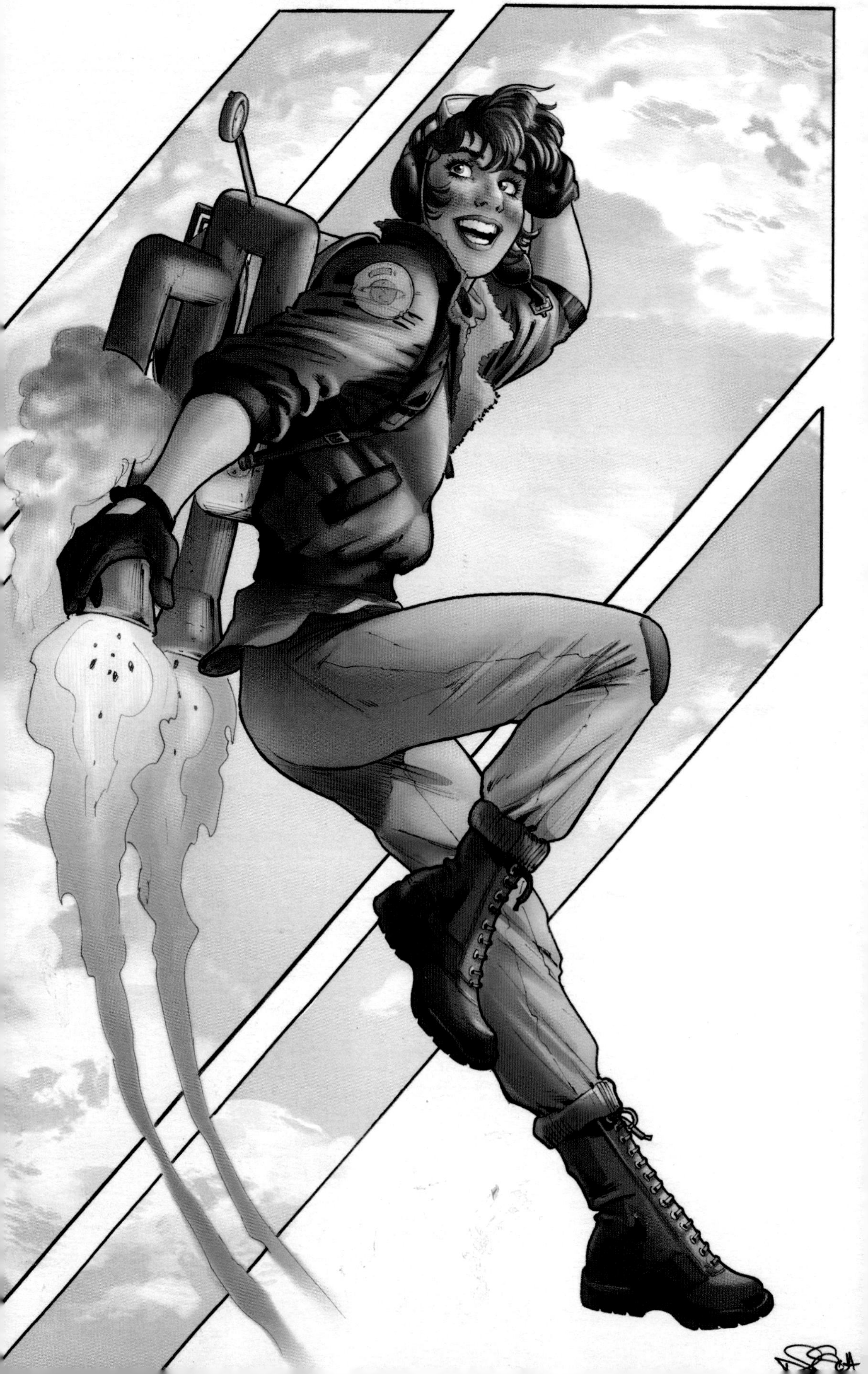

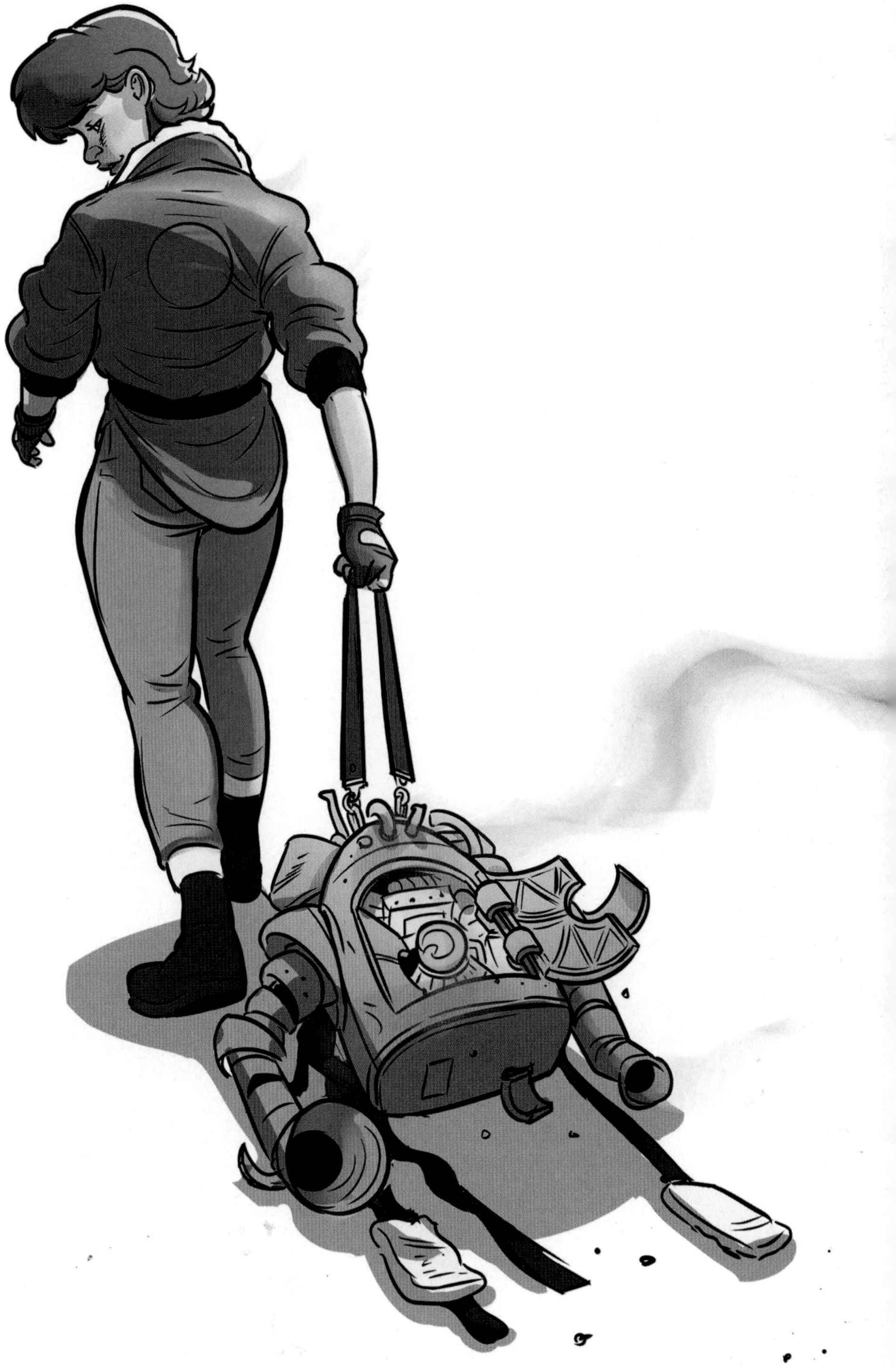

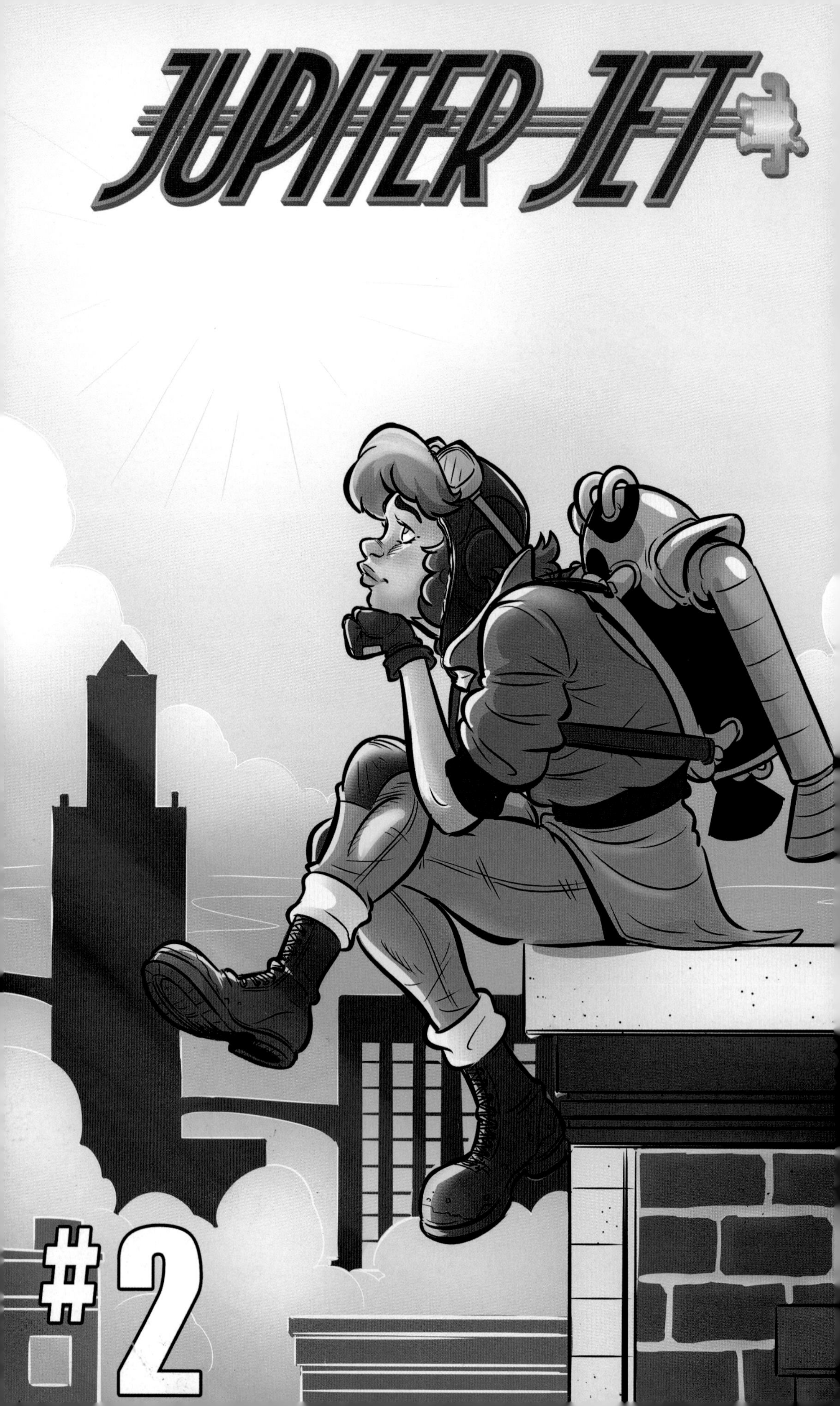

JUPITER JET
#2

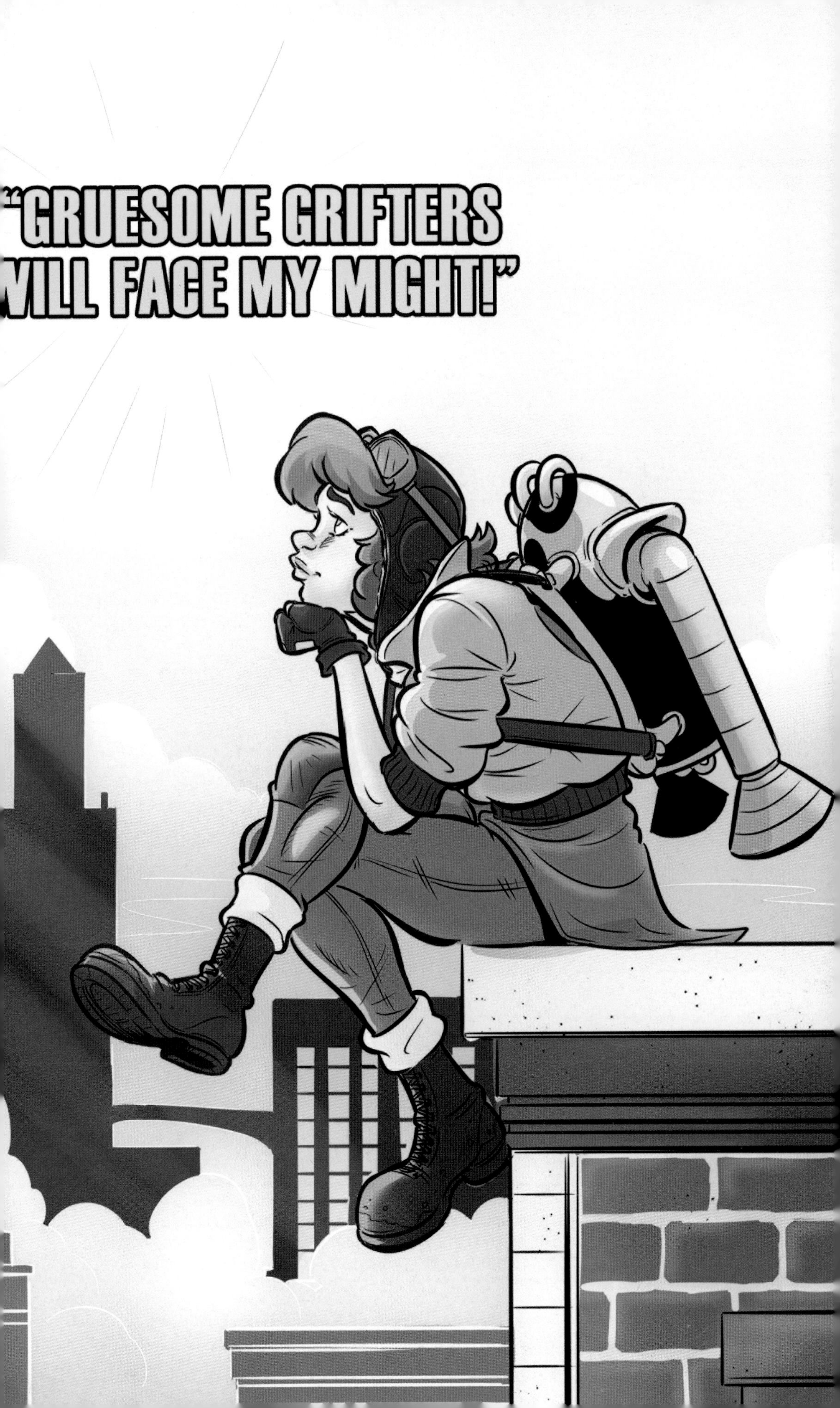
"GRUESOME GRIFTERS WILL FACE MY MIGHT!"

WRITTEN BY:
**JASON INMAN &
ASHLEY VICTORIA ROBINSON**

LINEART BY:
BEN MATSUYA

COLORS BY:
MARA JAYNE CARPENTER

COLOR FLATS BY:
TORI RIDLEY

LETTERS BY:
TAYLOR ESPOSITO OF GHOST GLYPH STUDIOS

COVER ARTIST (A):
BEN MATSUYA

COVER ARTIST (B):
JENN ST-ONGE

PUBLISHER/ CEO: BRYAN SEATON • EDITOR IN CHIEF: SHAWN GABBORIN
PUBLISHER-DANGER ZONE: JASON MARTIN • MARKETING DIRECTOR/EDITOR: NICOLE D'ANDRIA
EXECUTIVE ADMINISTRATOR: DANIELLE DAVISON • TEST PILOT: CHAD CICCONI
PRESIDENT OF CREATOR RELATIONS: SHAWN PRYOR

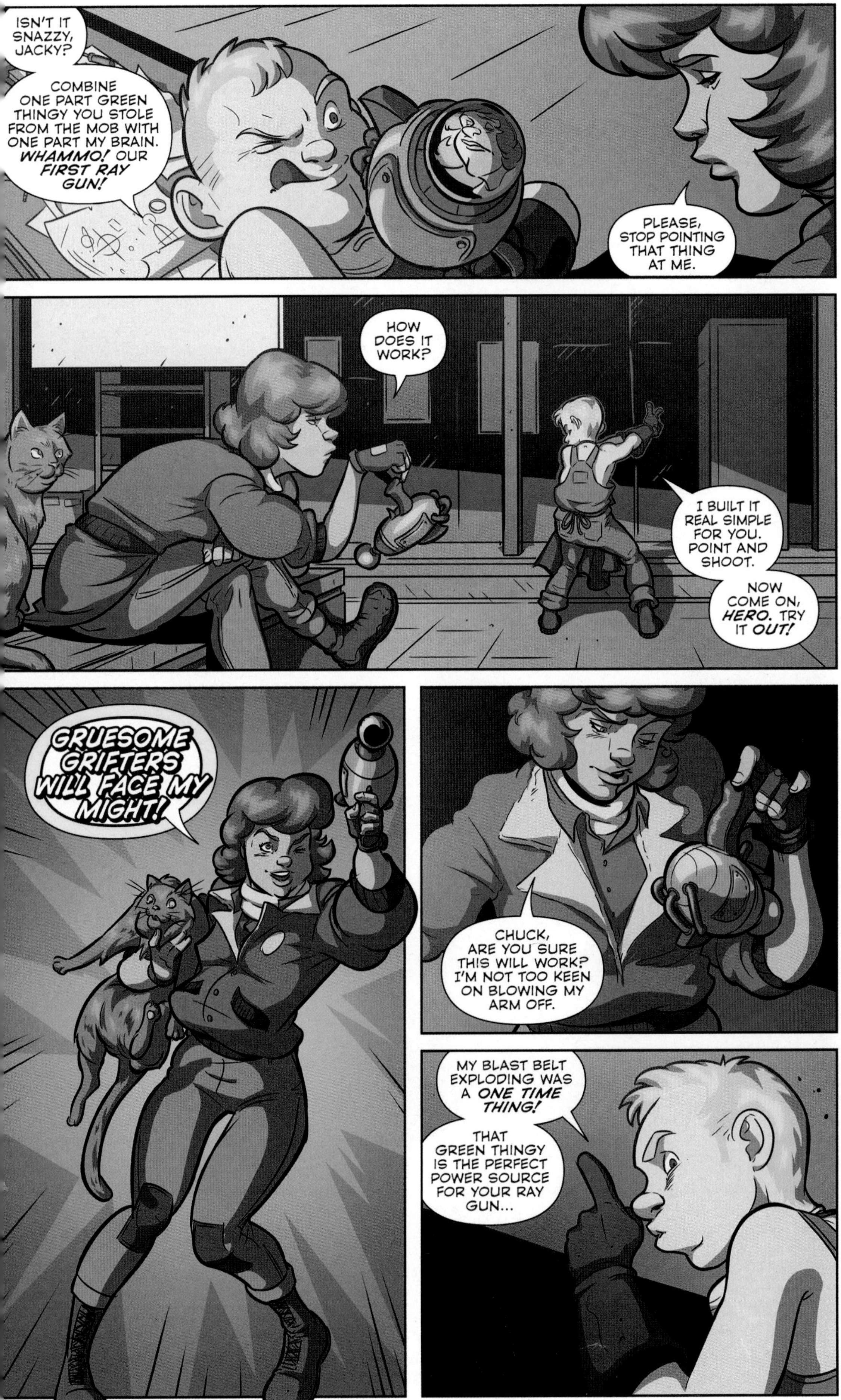
ISN'T IT SNAZZY, JACKY?
COMBINE ONE PART GREEN THINGY YOU STOLE FROM THE MOB WITH ONE PART MY BRAIN. *WHAMMO!* OUR *FIRST RAY GUN!*
PLEASE, STOP POINTING THAT THING AT ME.
HOW DOES IT WORK?
I BUILT IT REAL SIMPLE FOR YOU. POINT AND SHOOT.
NOW COME ON, *HERO*. TRY IT *OUT!*
GRUESOME GRIFTERS WILL FACE MY MIGHT!
CHUCK, ARE YOU SURE THIS WILL WORK? I'M NOT TOO KEEN ON BLOWING MY ARM OFF.
MY BLAST BELT EXPLODING WAS A *ONE TIME THING!*
THAT GREEN THINGY IS THE PERFECT POWER SOURCE FOR YOUR RAY GUN...

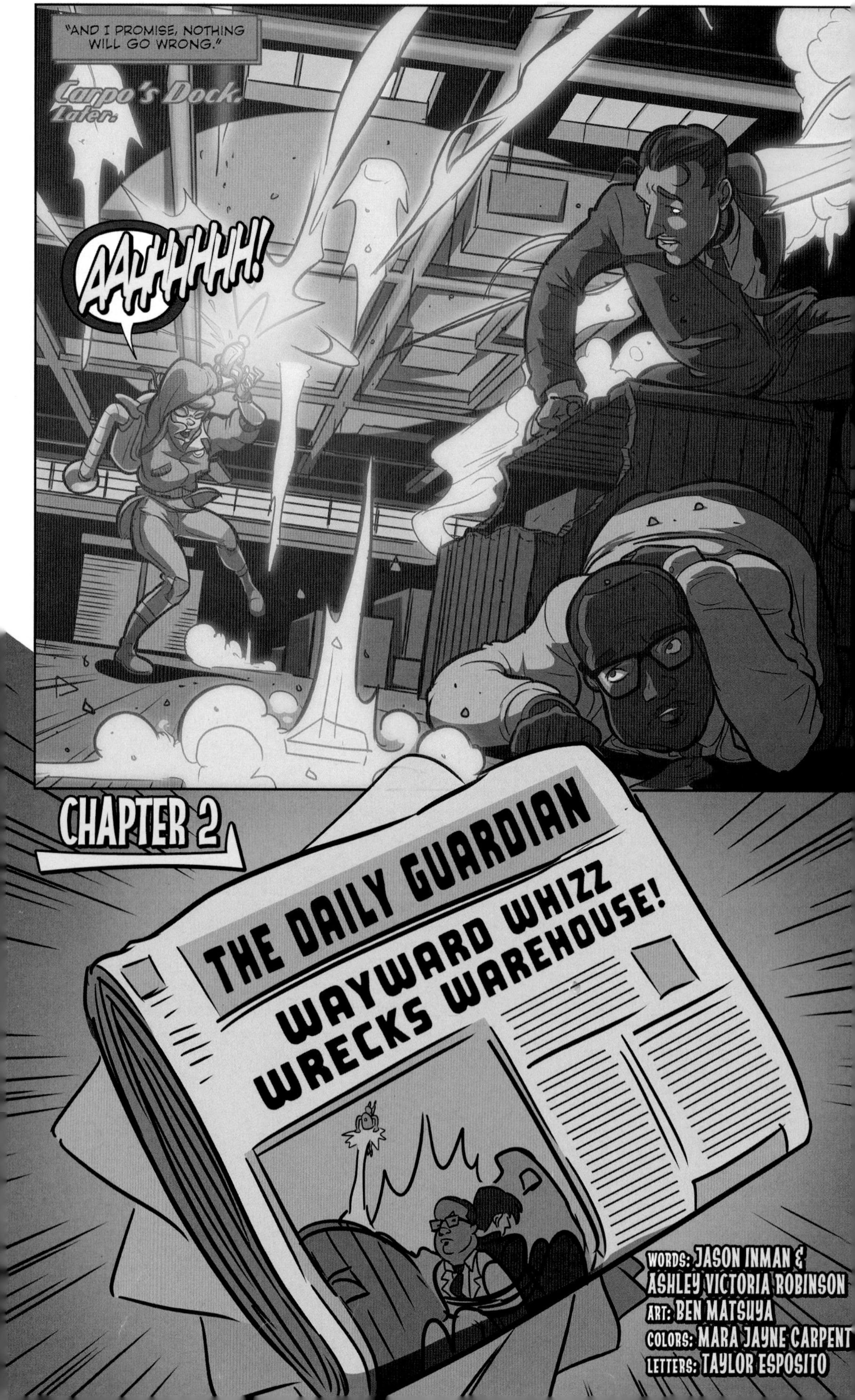
"AND I PROMISE, NOTHING WILL GO WRONG."
Carpo's Dock. Later.
AAUHHHH!
CHAPTER 2
THE DAILY GUARDIAN
WAYWARD WHIZZ WRECKS WAREHOUSE!
WORDS: JASON INMAN & ASHLEY VICTORIA ROBINSON
ART: BEN MATSUYA
COLORS: MARA JAYNE CARPENT
LETTERS: TAYLOR ESPOSITO

HOW COULD I PREDICT HOW THESE TWO *UNKNOWN* ENERGY SOURCES WOULD REACT TO EACH OTHER?!

CHUCK, I *NEED* THIS STUFF *TO WORK!*

Hmmm. MAYBE I NEED TO CREATE A MINI EXHAUST PORT TO VENT THE EXCESS ENERGY THAT BUILDS UP WHEN THE RAY GUN COMES IN CONTACT WITH YOUR JET PACK.

THAT'S EXACTLY WHAT I WAS THINKING?

WHEN I FIX THIS...

"...CAN YOU TRY TO SAVE SOME OF THE MONEY NEXT TIME?"

ANYTHING TO REPORT, CHIEF BEEDLE?

BEAT IT, *NEWSMAN!* NO QUOTE TONIGHT.

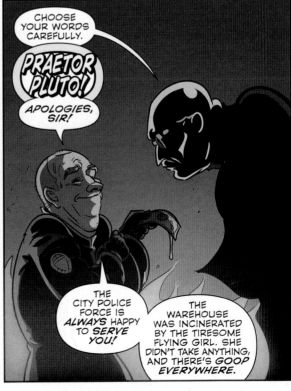

CHOOSE YOUR WORDS CAREFULLY.

PRAETOR PLUTO!

APOLOGIES, SIR!

THE CITY POLICE FORCE IS *ALWAYS* HAPPY TO *SERVE YOU!*

THE WAREHOUSE WAS INCINERATED BY THE TIRESOME FLYING GIRL. SHE DIDN'T TAKE ANYTHING, AND THERE'S *GOOP* EVERYWHERE.

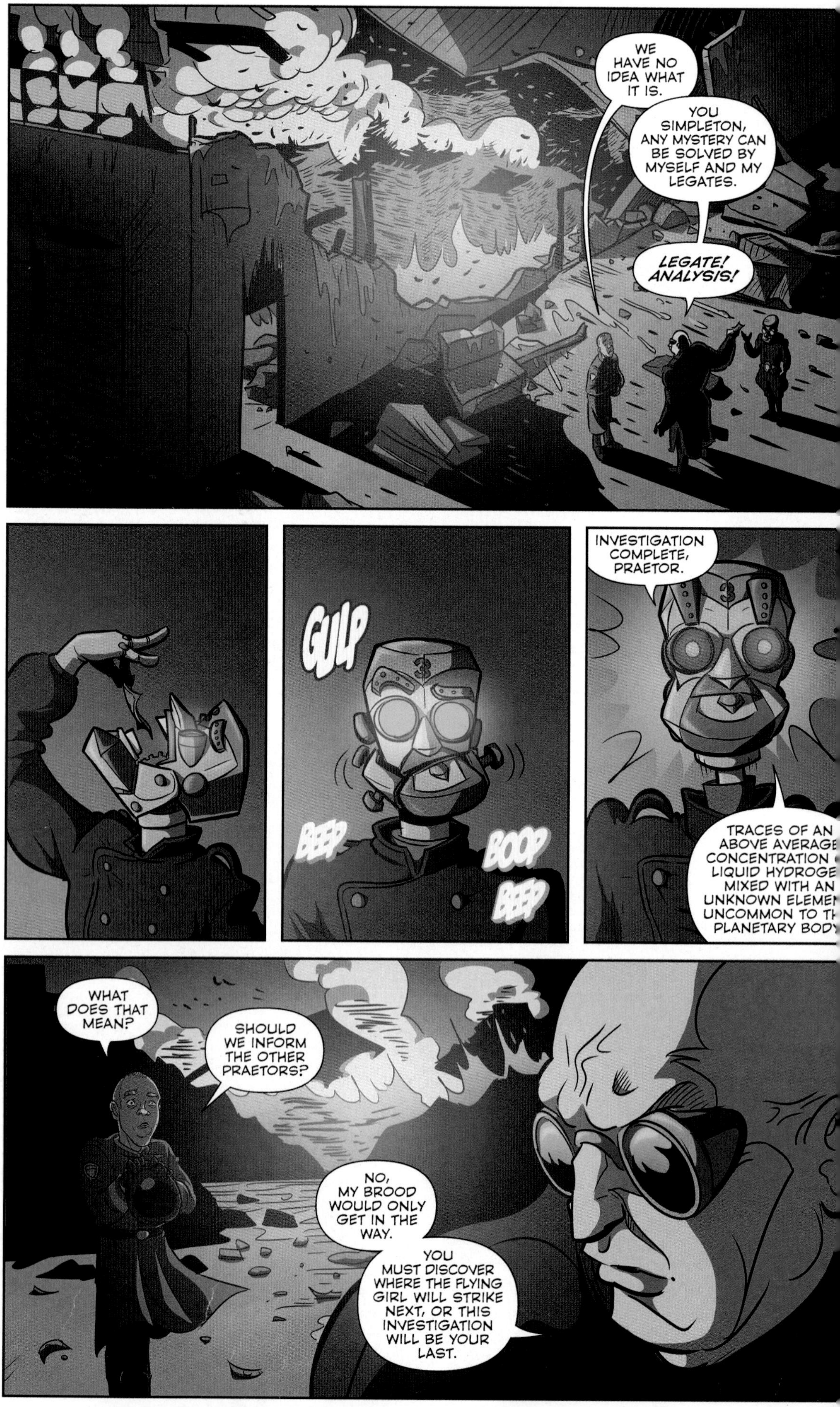

WE HAVE NO IDEA WHAT IT IS.
YOU SIMPLETON, ANY MYSTERY CAN BE SOLVED BY MYSELF AND MY LEGATES.
LEGATE! ANALYSIS!
GULP
BEEP
BOOP
BEEP
INVESTIGATION COMPLETE, PRAETOR.
TRACES OF AN ABOVE AVERAGE CONCENTRATION LIQUID HYDROGE MIXED WITH AN UNKNOWN ELEMEN UNCOMMON TO TH PLANETARY BODY
WHAT DOES THAT MEAN?
SHOULD WE INFORM THE OTHER PRAETORS?
NO, MY BROOD WOULD ONLY GET IN THE WAY.
YOU MUST DISCOVER WHERE THE FLYING GIRL WILL STRIKE NEXT, OR THIS INVESTIGATION WILL BE YOUR LAST.

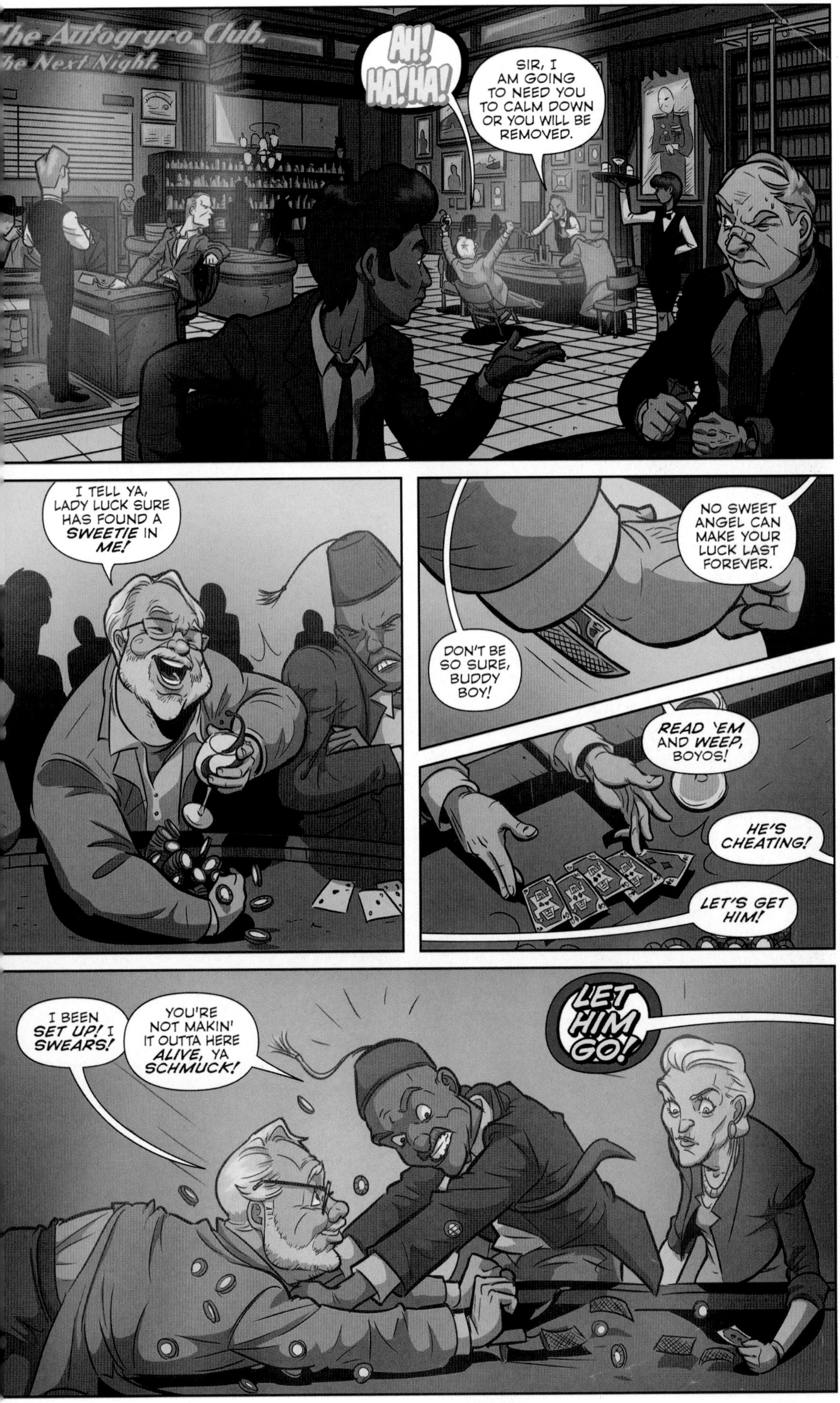

The Autogryro Club.
The Next Night.
AH! HA! HA!
SIR, I AM GOING TO NEED YOU TO CALM DOWN OR YOU WILL BE REMOVED.
I TELL YA, LADY LUCK SURE HAS FOUND A SWEETIE IN ME!
NO SWEET ANGEL CAN MAKE YOUR LUCK LAST FOREVER.
DON'T BE SO SURE, BUDDY BOY!
READ 'EM AND WEEP, BOYOS!
HE'S CHEATING!
LET'S GET HIM!
I BEEN SET UP! I SWEARS!
YOU'RE NOT MAKIN' IT OUTTA HERE ALIVE, YA SCHMUCK!
LET HIM GO!

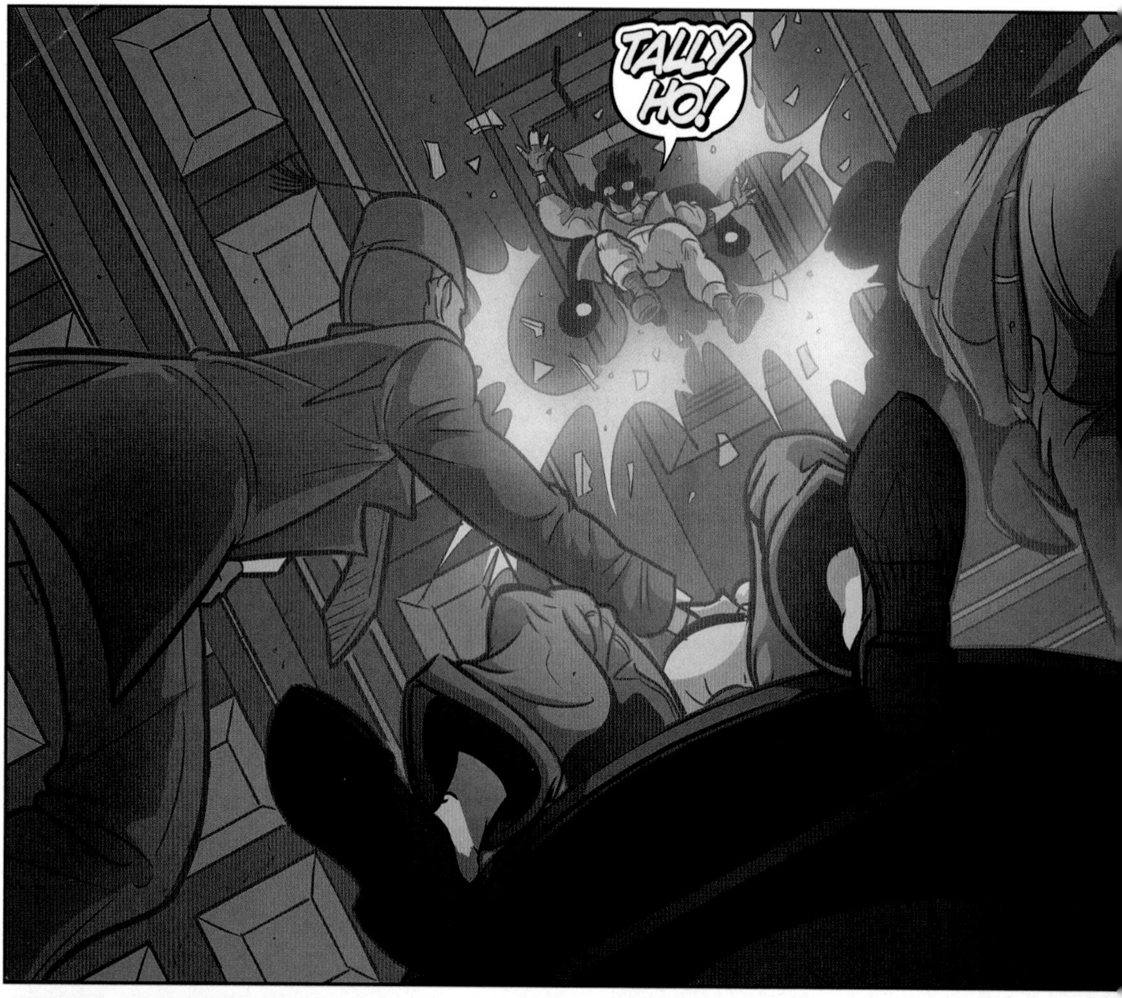
TALLY HO!

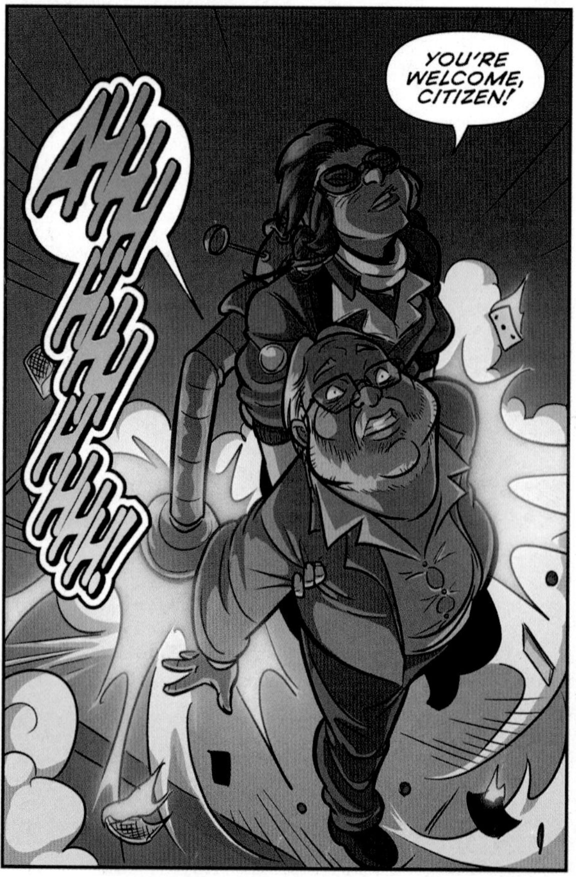
YOU'RE WELCOME, CITIZEN!
AHHHHHHHHH!

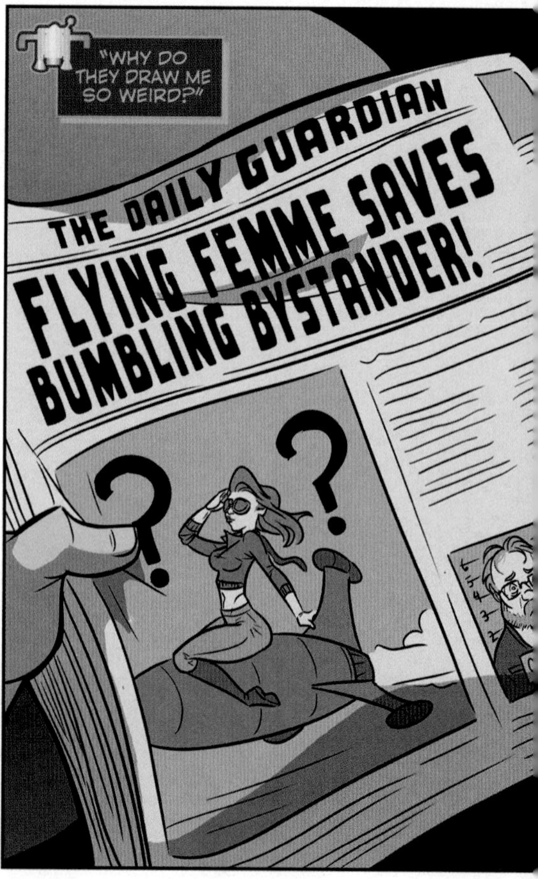
"WHY DO THEY DRAW ME SO WEIRD?"
THE DAILY GUARDIAN
FLYING FEMME SAVES BUMBLING BYSTANDER!

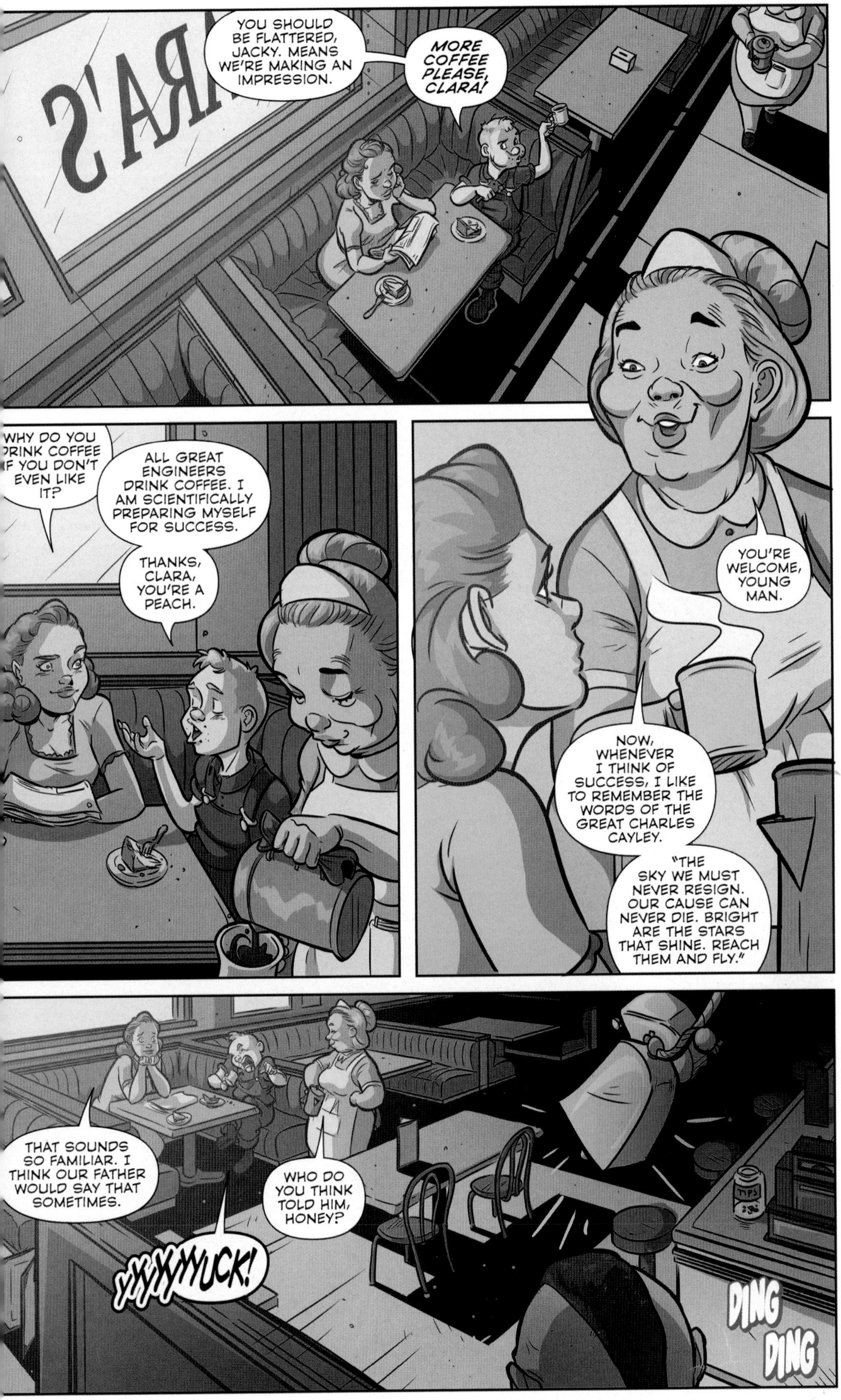

ARA'S
YOU SHOULD BE FLATTERED, JACKY. MEANS WE'RE MAKING AN IMPRESSION.
MORE COFFEE PLEASE, CLARA!
WHY DO YOU DRINK COFFEE IF YOU DON'T EVEN LIKE IT?
ALL GREAT ENGINEERS DRINK COFFEE. I AM SCIENTIFICALLY PREPARING MYSELF FOR SUCCESS.
THANKS, CLARA, YOU'RE A PEACH.
YOU'RE WELCOME, YOUNG MAN.
NOW, WHENEVER I THINK OF SUCCESS, I LIKE TO REMEMBER THE WORDS OF THE GREAT CHARLES CAYLEY.
"THE SKY WE MUST NEVER RESIGN. OUR CAUSE CAN NEVER DIE. BRIGHT ARE THE STARS THAT SHINE. REACH THEM AND FLY."
THAT SOUNDS SO FAMILIAR. I THINK OUR FATHER WOULD SAY THAT SOMETIMES.
WHO DO YOU THINK TOLD HIM, HONEY?
YYYYYYUCK!
TIPS
DING
DING

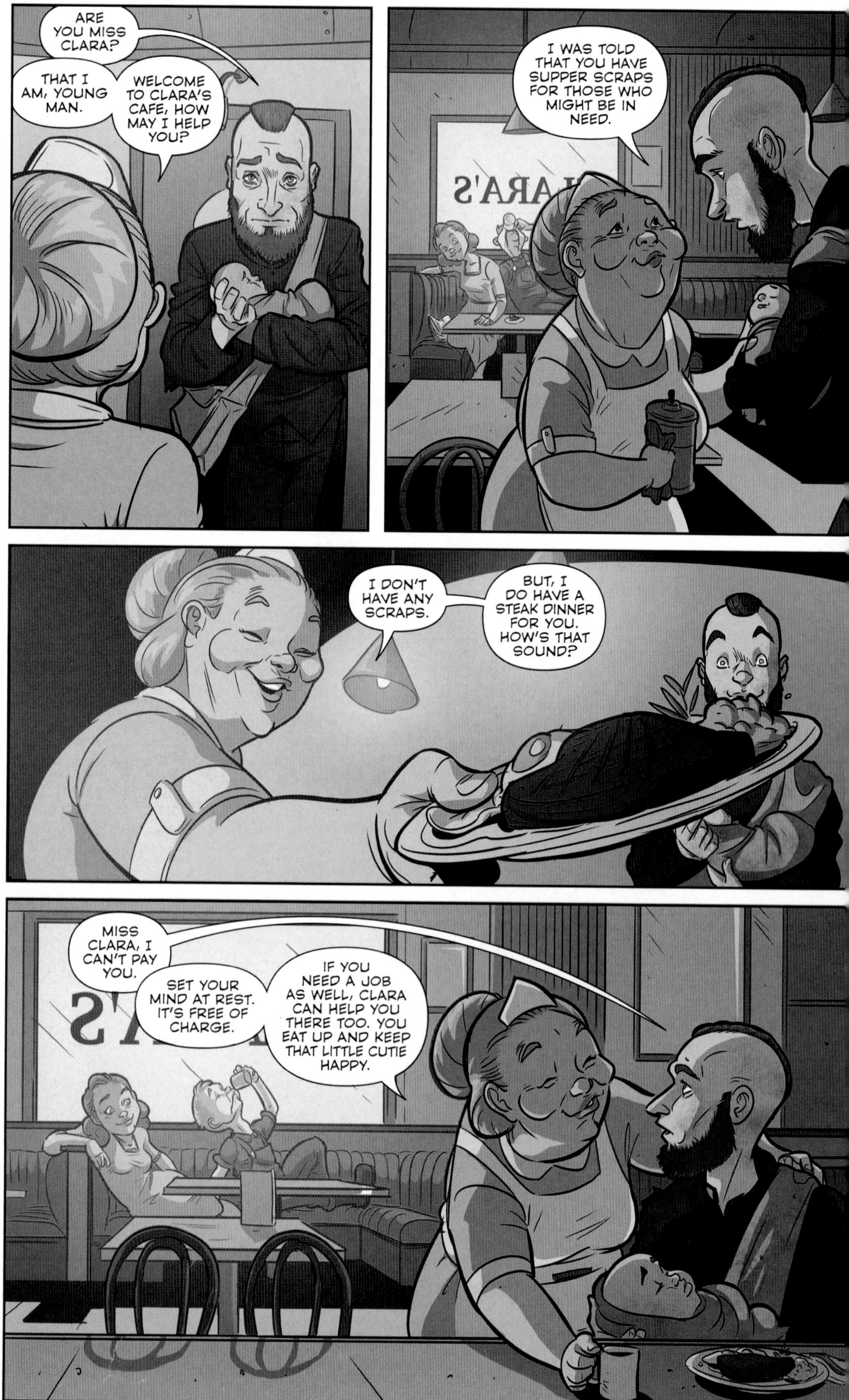
ARE YOU MISS CLARA?
THAT I AM, YOUNG MAN.
WELCOME TO CLARA'S CAFE, HOW MAY I HELP YOU?
I WAS TOLD THAT YOU HAVE SUPPER SCRAPS FOR THOSE WHO MIGHT BE IN NEED.
CLARA'S
I DON'T HAVE ANY SCRAPS.
BUT, I DO HAVE A STEAK DINNER FOR YOU. HOW'S THAT SOUND?
MISS CLARA, I CAN'T PAY YOU.
SET YOUR MIND AT REST. IT'S FREE OF CHARGE.
IF YOU NEED A JOB AS WELL, CLARA CAN HELP YOU THERE TOO. YOU EAT UP AND KEEP THAT LITTLE CUTIE HAPPY.

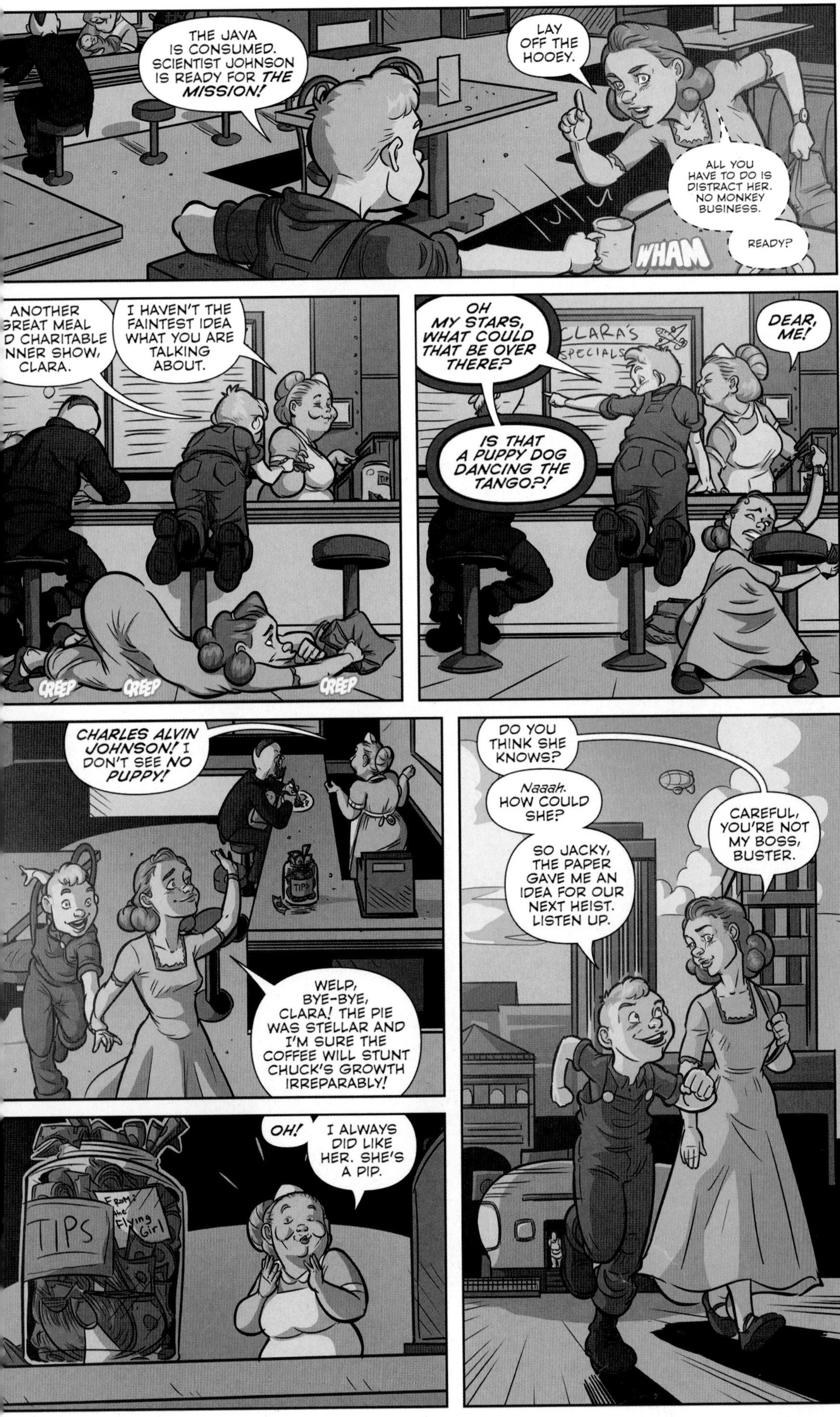

THE JAVA IS CONSUMED. SCIENTIST JOHNSON IS READY FOR *THE MISSION!*
LAY OFF THE HOOEY.
ALL YOU HAVE TO DO IS DISTRACT HER. NO MONKEY BUSINESS.
READY?
WHAM
ANOTHER GREAT MEAL D CHARITABLE NNER SHOW, CLARA.
I HAVEN'T THE FAINTEST IDEA WHAT YOU ARE TALKING ABOUT.
CREEP
CREEP
CREEP
OH MY STARS, WHAT COULD THAT BE OVER THERE?
IS THAT A PUPPY DOG DANCING THE TANGO?!
CLARA'S SPECIALS
DEAR, ME!
CHARLES ALVIN JOHNSON! I DON'T SEE *NO PUPPY!*
TIPS
WELP, BYE-BYE, CLARA! THE PIE WAS STELLAR AND I'M SURE THE COFFEE WILL STUNT CHUCK'S GROWTH IRREPARABLY!
OH!
I ALWAYS DID LIKE HER. SHE'S A PIP.
TIPS
FROM the Flying Girl
DO YOU THINK SHE KNOWS?
Naaah. HOW COULD SHE?
SO JACKY, THE PAPER GAVE ME AN IDEA FOR OUR NEXT HEIST. LISTEN UP.
CAREFUL, YOU'RE NOT MY BOSS, BUSTER.

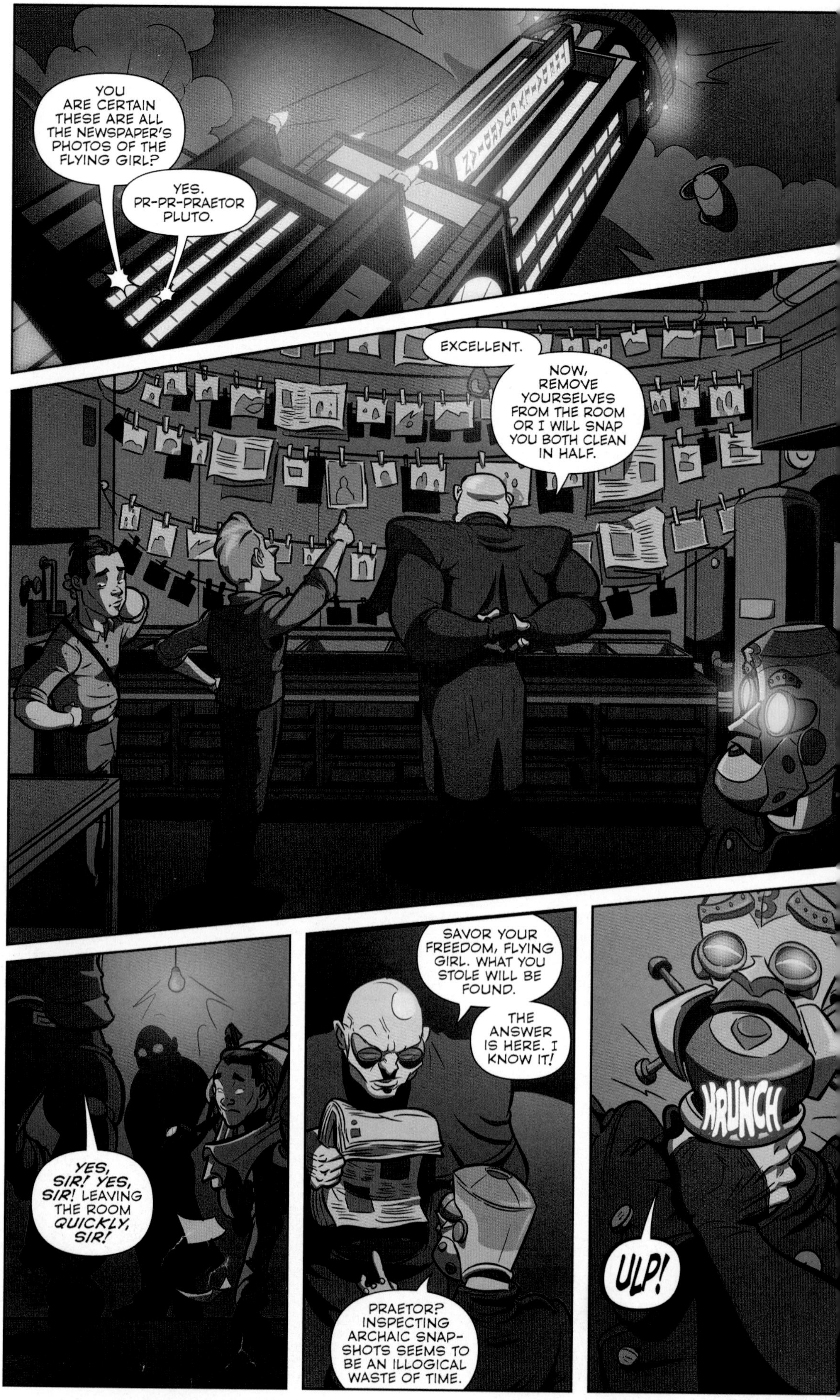

YOU ARE CERTAIN THESE ARE ALL THE NEWSPAPER'S PHOTOS OF THE FLYING GIRL?
YES. PR-PR-PRAETOR PLUTO.
EXCELLENT.
NOW, REMOVE YOURSELVES FROM THE ROOM OR I WILL SNAP YOU BOTH CLEAN IN HALF.
YES, SIR! YES, SIR! LEAVING THE ROOM QUICKLY, SIR!
SAVOR YOUR FREEDOM, FLYING GIRL. WHAT YOU STOLE WILL BE FOUND.
THE ANSWER IS HERE. I KNOW IT!
PRAETOR? INSPECTING ARCHAIC SNAP-SHOTS SEEMS TO BE AN ILLOGICAL WASTE OF TIME.
KRUNCH
ULP!

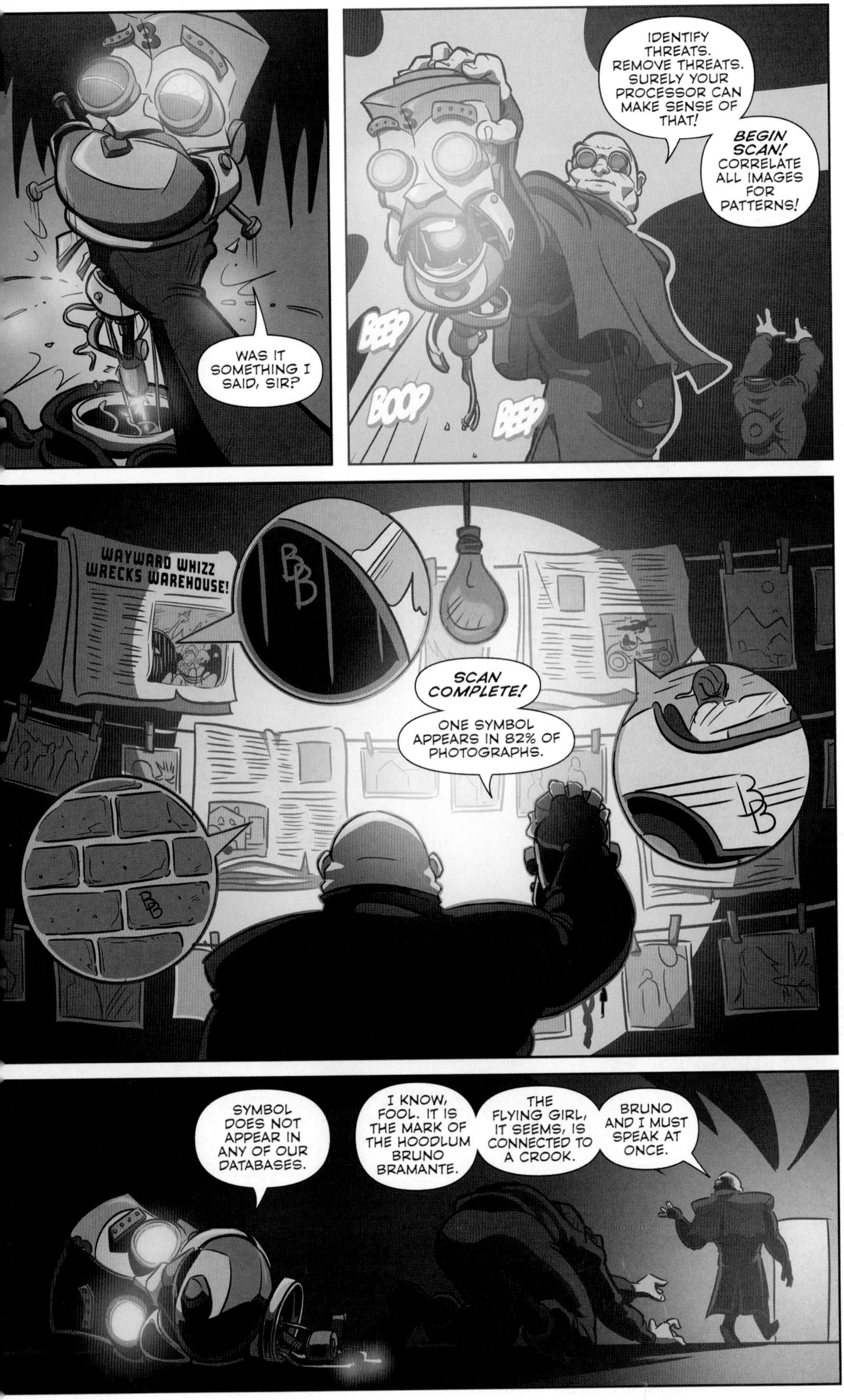
WAS IT SOMETHING I SAID, SIR?
IDENTIFY THREATS. REMOVE THREATS. SURELY YOUR PROCESSOR CAN MAKE SENSE OF THAT!
BEGIN SCAN! CORRELATE ALL IMAGES FOR PATTERNS!
BEEP
BOOP
BEEP
WAYWARD WHIZZ WRECKS WAREHOUSE!
SCAN COMPLETE!
ONE SYMBOL APPEARS IN 82% OF PHOTOGRAPHS.
SYMBOL DOES NOT APPEAR IN ANY OF OUR DATABASES.
I KNOW, FOOL. IT IS THE MARK OF THE HOODLUM BRUNO BRAMANTE.
THE FLYING GIRL, IT SEEMS, IS CONNECTED TO A CROOK.
BRUNO AND I MUST SPEAK AT ONCE.

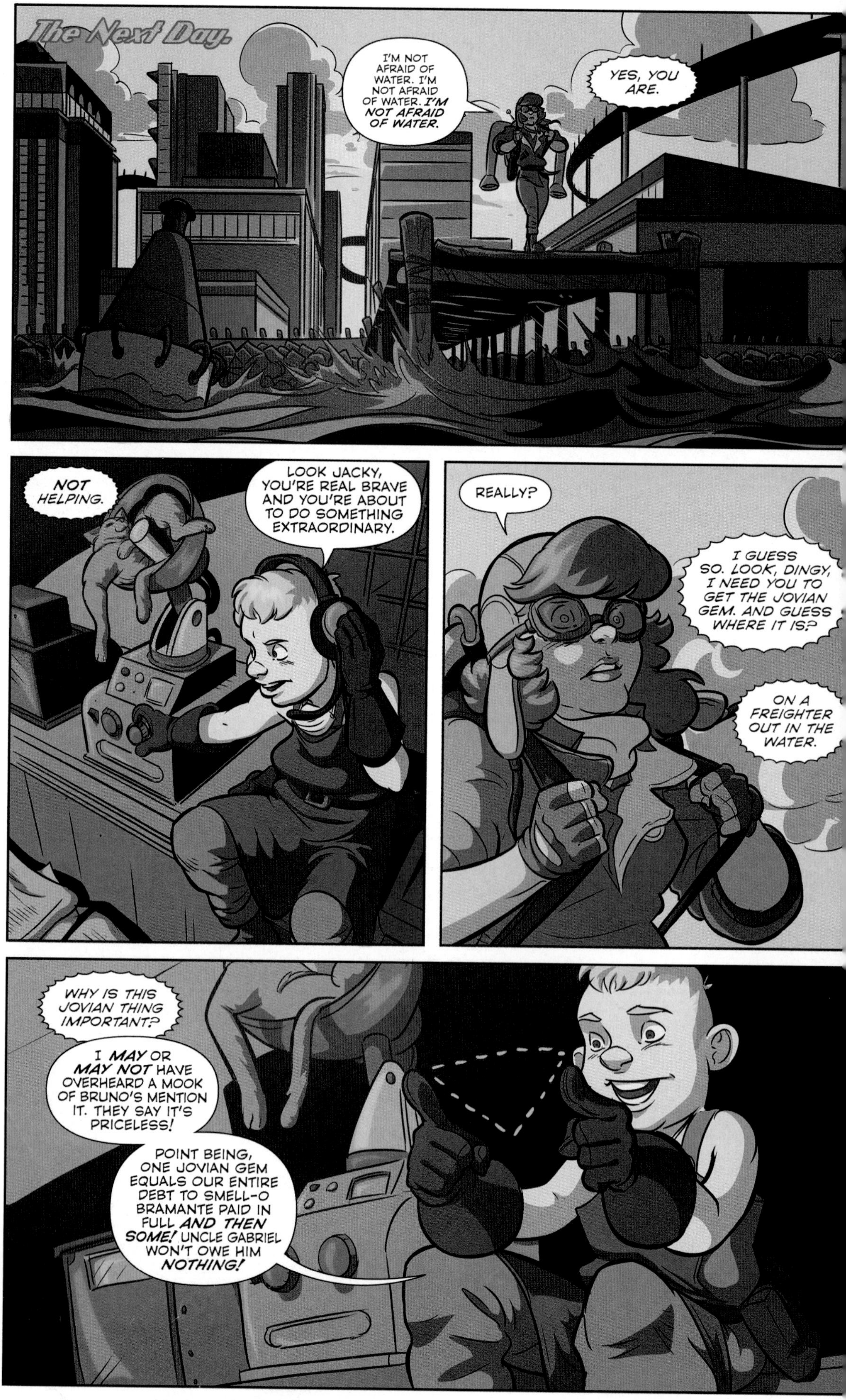

The Next Day.
I'M NOT AFRAID OF WATER. I'M NOT AFRAID OF WATER. *I'M NOT AFRAID OF WATER.*
YES, YOU ARE.
NOT HELPING.
LOOK JACKY, YOU'RE REAL BRAVE AND YOU'RE ABOUT TO DO SOMETHING EXTRAORDINARY.
REALLY?
I GUESS SO. LOOK, DINGY, I NEED YOU TO GET THE JOVIAN GEM. AND GUESS WHERE IT IS?
ON A FREIGHTER OUT IN THE WATER.
WHY IS THIS JOVIAN THING IMPORTANT?
I ***MAY*** OR ***MAY NOT*** HAVE OVERHEARD A MOOK OF BRUNO'S MENTION IT. THEY SAY IT'S PRICELESS!
POINT BEING, ONE JOVIAN GEM EQUALS OUR ENTIRE DEBT TO SMELL-O BRAMANTE PAID IN FULL ***AND THEN SOME!*** UNCLE GABRIEL WON'T OWE HIM ***NOTHING!***

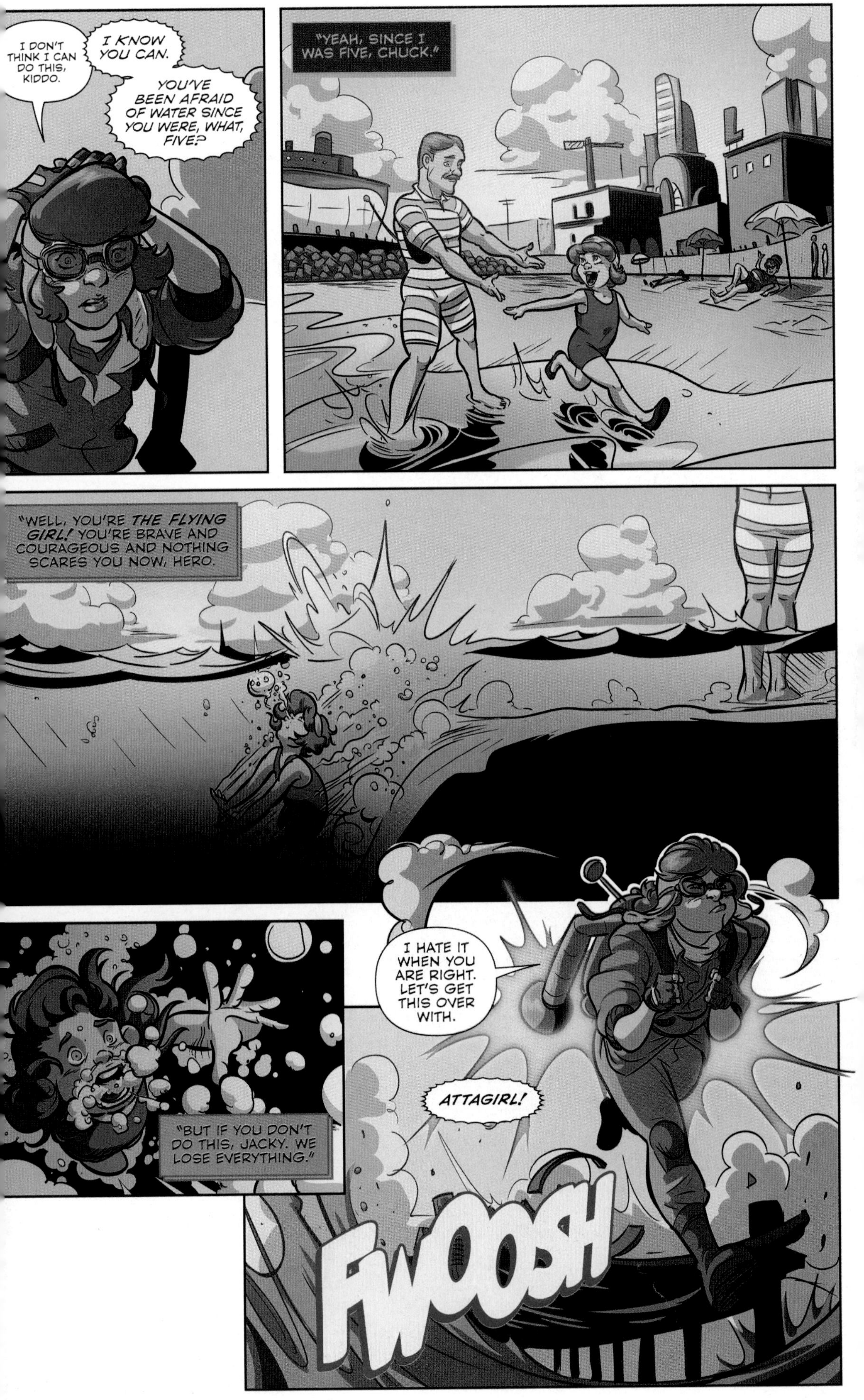

I DON'T THINK I CAN DO THIS, KIDDO.
I KNOW YOU CAN.
YOU'VE BEEN AFRAID OF WATER SINCE YOU WERE, WHAT, FIVE?
"YEAH, SINCE I WAS FIVE, CHUCK."
"WELL, YOU'RE THE FLYING GIRL! YOU'RE BRAVE AND COURAGEOUS AND NOTHING SCARES YOU NOW, HERO.
"BUT IF YOU DON'T DO THIS, JACKY. WE LOSE EVERYTHING."
I HATE IT WHEN YOU ARE RIGHT. LET'S GET THIS OVER WITH.
ATTAGIRL!
FWOOSH

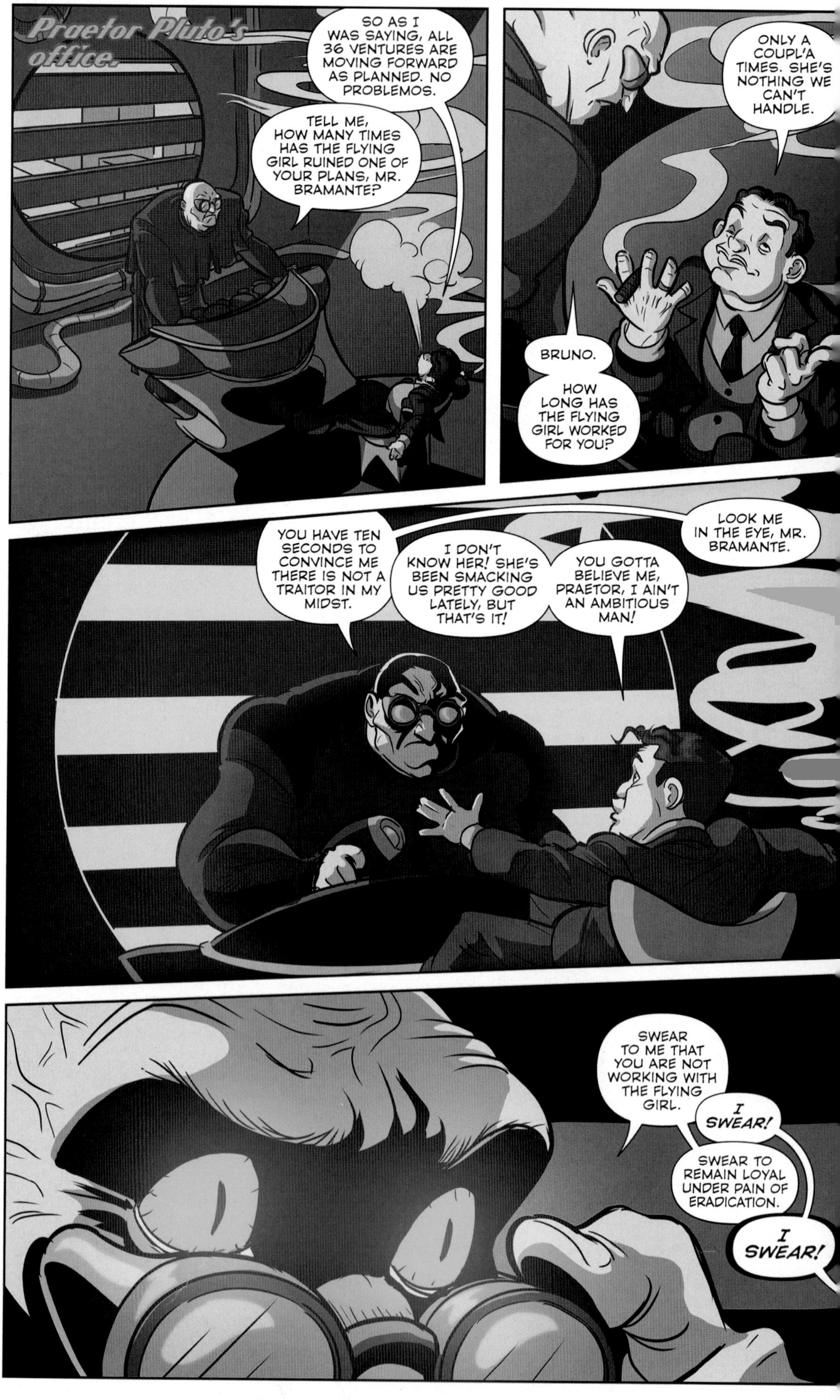
Praetor Pluto's office.
SO AS I WAS SAYING, ALL 36 VENTURES ARE MOVING FORWARD AS PLANNED. NO PROBLEMOS.
TELL ME, HOW MANY TIMES HAS THE FLYING GIRL RUINED ONE OF YOUR PLANS, MR. BRAMANTE?
ONLY A COUPL'A TIMES. SHE'S NOTHING WE CAN'T HANDLE.
BRUNO.
HOW LONG HAS THE FLYING GIRL WORKED FOR YOU?
LOOK ME IN THE EYE, MR. BRAMANTE.
YOU HAVE TEN SECONDS TO CONVINCE ME THERE IS NOT A TRAITOR IN MY MIDST.
I DON'T KNOW HER! SHE'S BEEN SMACKING US PRETTY GOOD LATELY, BUT THAT'S IT!
YOU GOTTA BELIEVE ME, PRAETOR, I AIN'T AN AMBITIOUS MAN!
SWEAR TO ME THAT YOU ARE NOT WORKING WITH THE FLYING GIRL.
I SWEAR!
SWEAR TO REMAIN LOYAL UNDER PAIN OF ERADICATION.
I SWEAR!

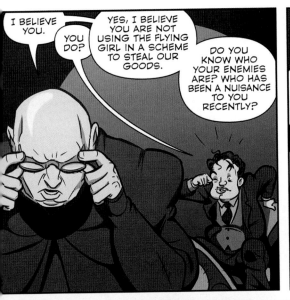

I BELIEVE YOU.

YOU DO?

YES, I BELIEVE YOU ARE NOT USING THE FLYING GIRL IN A SCHEME TO STEAL OUR GOODS.

DO YOU KNOW WHO YOUR ENEMIES ARE? WHO HAS BEEN A NUISANCE TO YOU RECENTLY?

NO ONE. EXCEPT THOSE JOHNSON KIDS.

AWE, BOSS, THEY'RE HELLHOUNDS! THE BOY DON'T KNOW WHEN TO KEEP HIS TRAP SHUT AND THE GIRL'S GOT RED HAIR--

--YOU CAN SEE SHE'S GOT THE DEVIL INSIDE HER BY THAT.

BUT, THEY'RE JUST RATTY KIDS WHO ARE LATE WITH MY MOOLA.

JOHNSON. I SHOULD HAVE KNOWN.

WHASSAT?

TAKE ME TO THE JOHNSON REPAIR SHOP AT ONCE!

WHY?

I KNOW WHO THE FLYING GIRL IS.

NIFTY! SO, WHO GETS TO BUMP HER OFF? ME OR YOU?

DON'T *EVER* TOUCH *ME*, YOU *TWIT!*

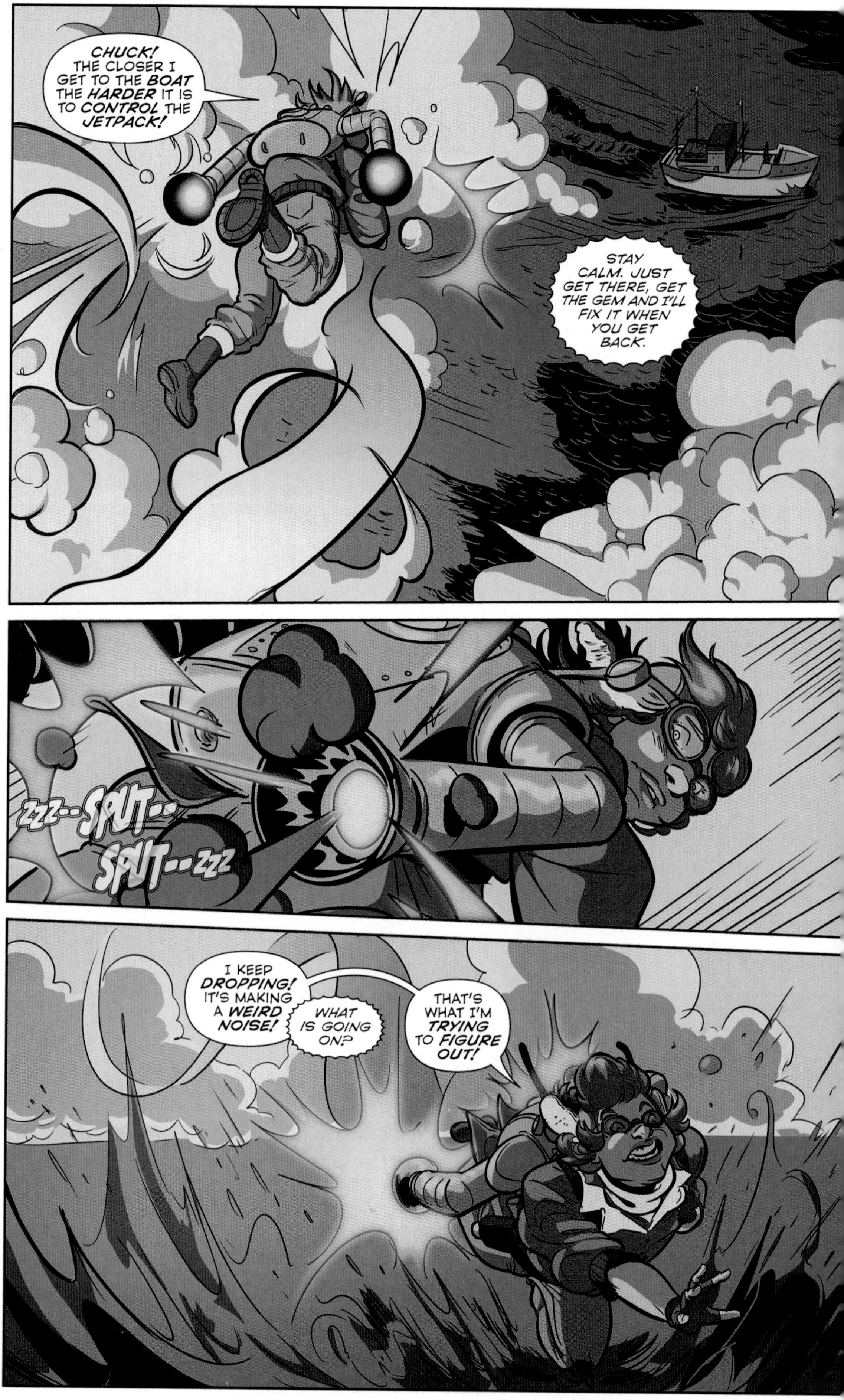

CHUCK! THE CLOSER I GET TO THE BOAT THE HARDER IT IS TO CONTROL THE JETPACK!
STAY CALM. JUST GET THERE, GET THE GEM AND I'LL FIX IT WHEN YOU GET BACK.
ZZZ--SPUT--
SPUT--ZZZ
I KEEP DROPPING! IT'S MAKING A WEIRD NOISE!
WHAT IS GOING ON?
THAT'S WHAT I'M TRYING TO FIGURE OUT!

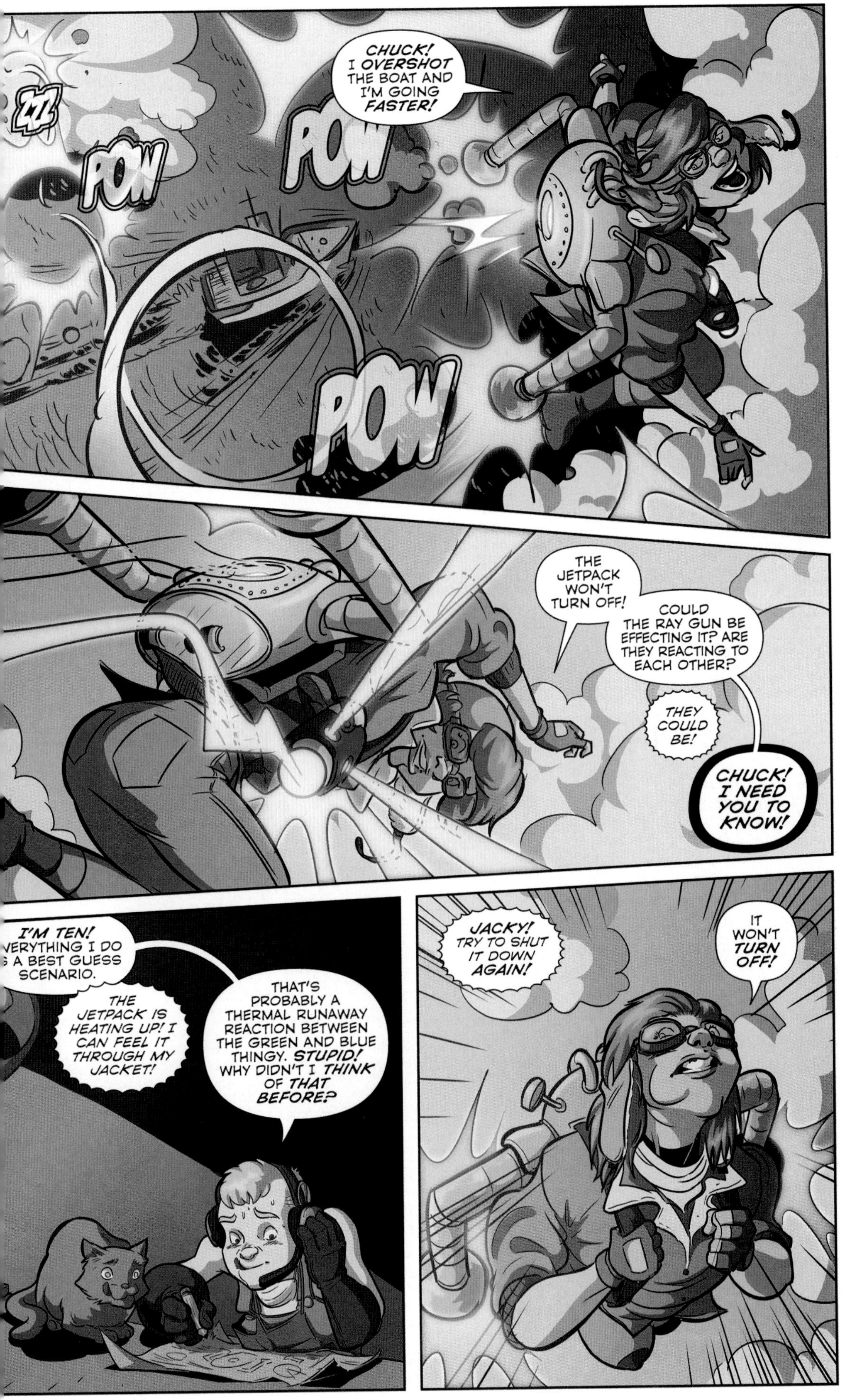
ZZZ
CHUCK! I OVERSHOT THE BOAT AND I'M GOING FASTER!
POW
POW
POW
THE JETPACK WON'T TURN OFF!
COULD THE RAY GUN BE EFFECTING IT? ARE THEY REACTING TO EACH OTHER?
THEY COULD BE!
CHUCK! I NEED YOU TO KNOW!
I'M TEN! VERYTHING I DO S A BEST GUESS SCENARIO.
THE JETPACK IS HEATING UP! I CAN FEEL IT THROUGH MY JACKET!
THAT'S PROBABLY A THERMAL RUNAWAY REACTION BETWEEN THE GREEN AND BLUE THINGY. STUPID! WHY DIDN'T I THINK OF THAT BEFORE?
JACKY! TRY TO SHUT IT DOWN AGAIN!
IT WON'T TURN OFF!

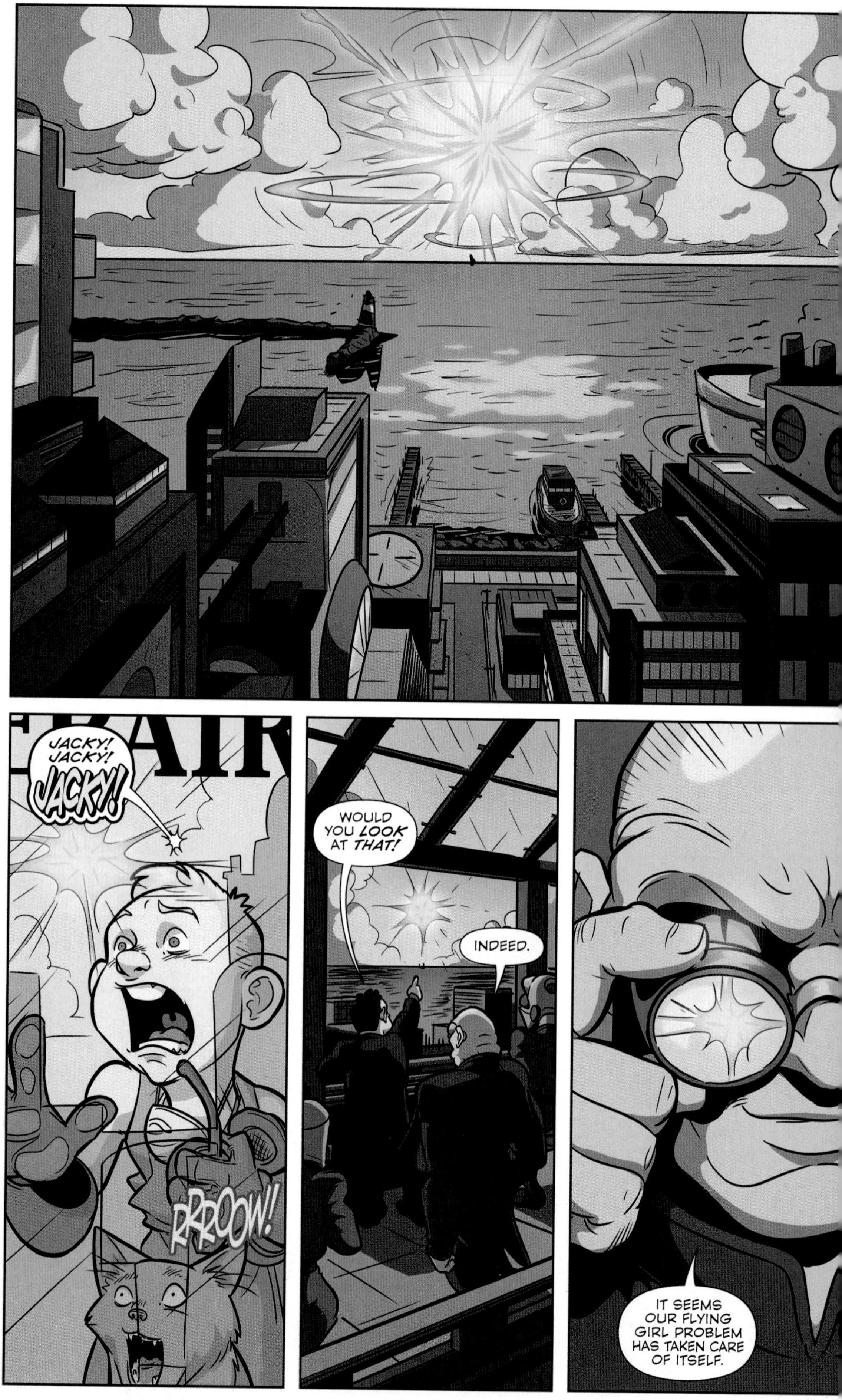

JACKY! JACKY! JACKY!
RRROOW!
WOULD YOU LOOK AT THAT!
INDEED.
IT SEEMS OUR FLYING GIRL PROBLEM HAS TAKEN CARE OF ITSELF.

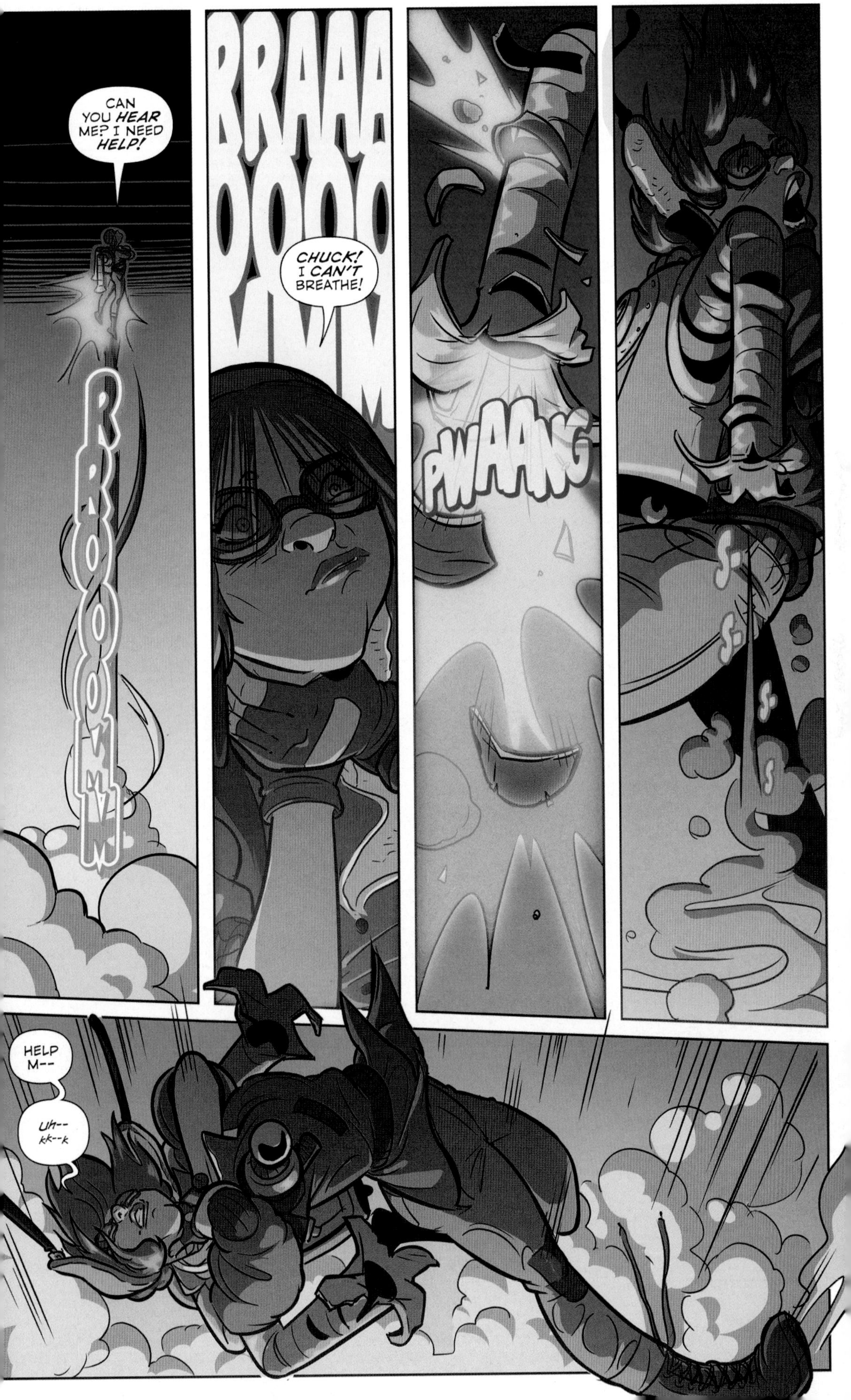
CAN YOU HEAR ME? I NEED HELP!
RROOOOOMMM
RRAAAOOOOMMM
CHUCK! I CAN'T BREATHE!
PWAANG
HELP M--
UH-- KK--K

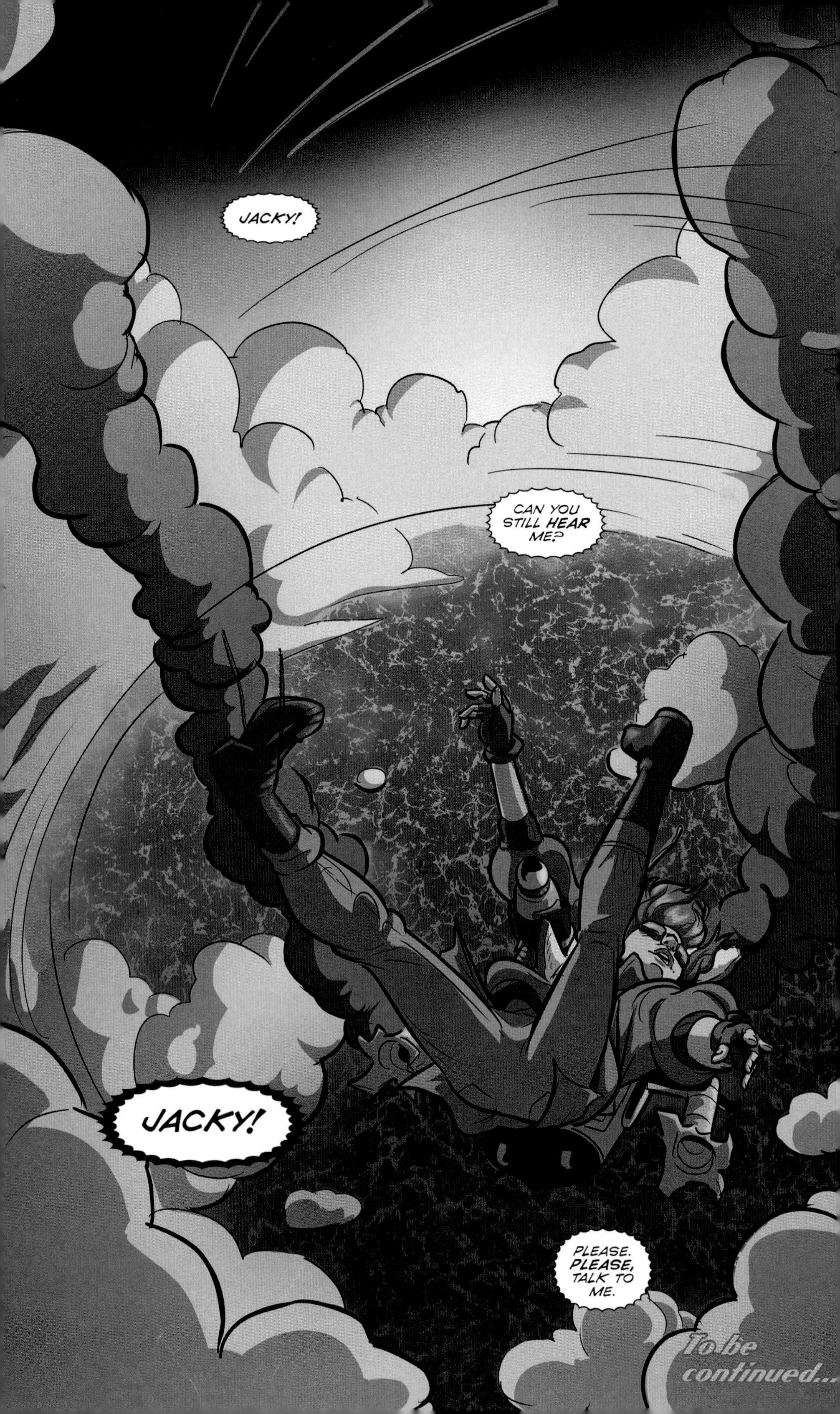
JACKY!
CAN YOU STILL HEAR ME?
JACKY!
PLEASE. PLEASE, TALK TO ME.
To be continued...

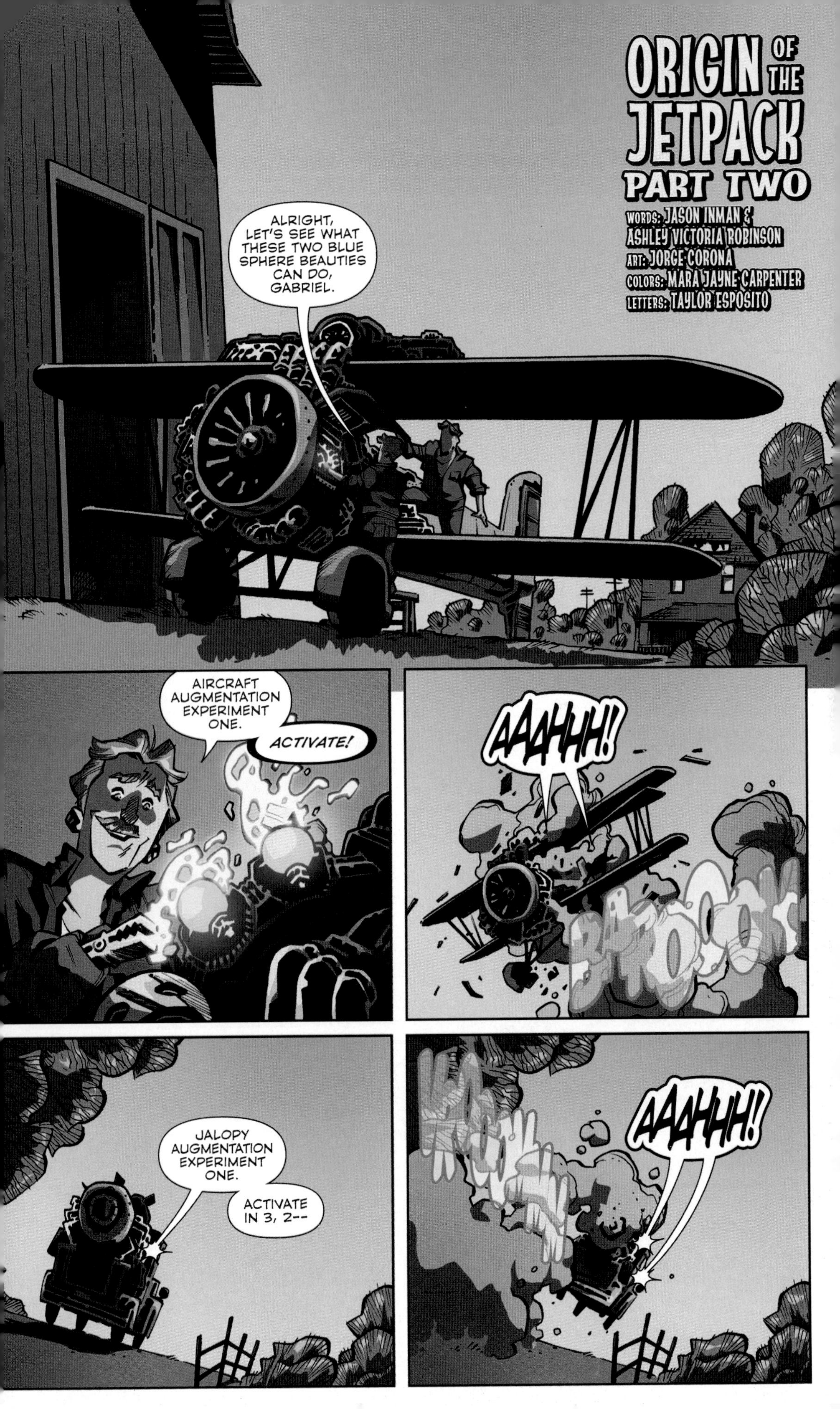
ORIGIN OF THE JETPACK
PART TWO
WORDS: JASON INMAN & ASHLEY VICTORIA ROBINSON
ART: JORGE CORONA
COLORS: MARA JAYNE CARPENTER
LETTERS: TAYLOR ESPOSITO
ALRIGHT, LET'S SEE WHAT THESE TWO BLUE SPHERE BEAUTIES CAN DO, GABRIEL.
AIRCRAFT AUGMENTATION EXPERIMENT ONE.
ACTIVATE!
AAAHHH!
BAROOOOM
JALOPY AUGMENTATION EXPERIMENT ONE.
ACTIVATE IN 3, 2--
AAAHHH!

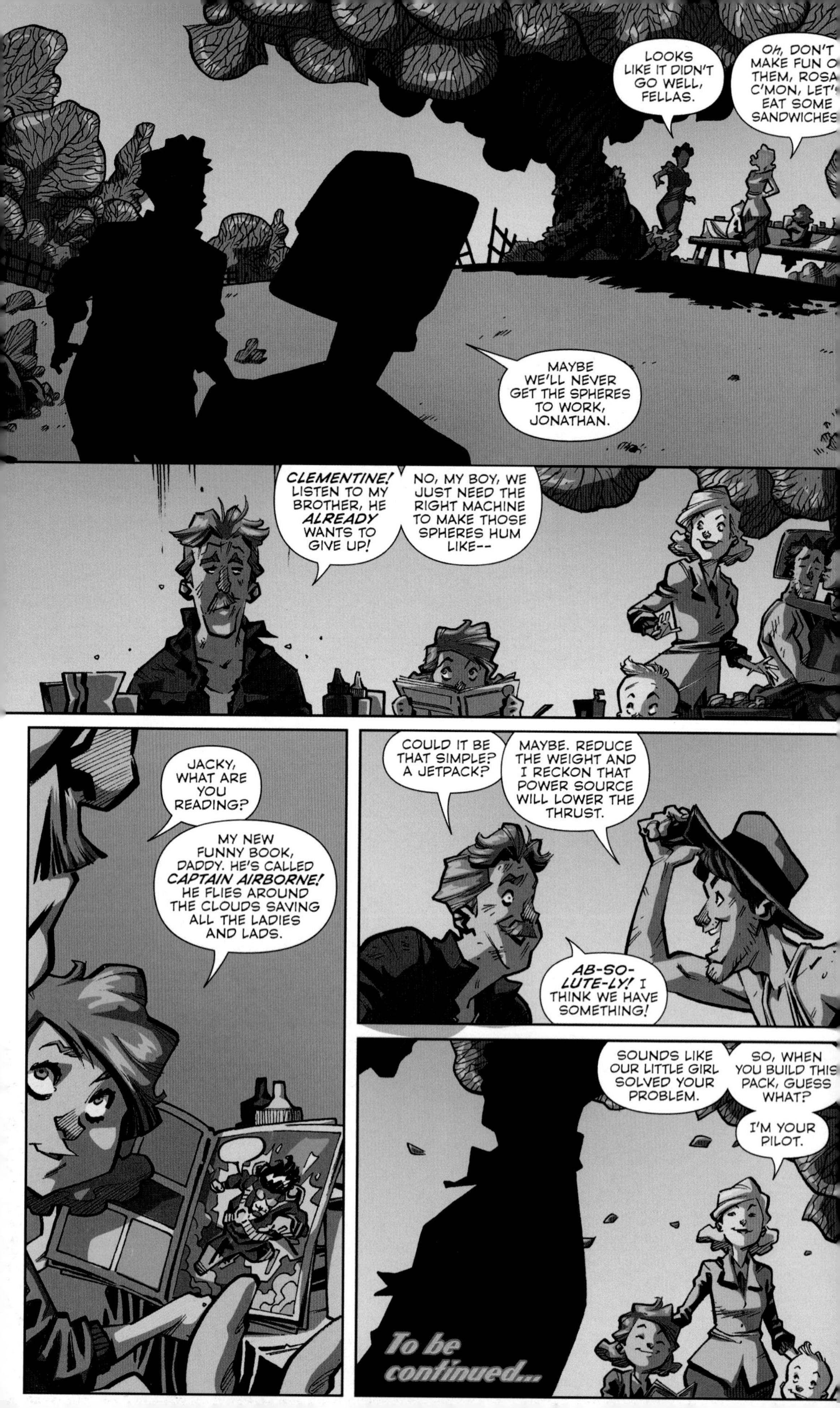
LOOKS LIKE IT DIDN'T GO WELL, FELLAS.
OH, DON'T MAKE FUN O THEM, ROSA C'MON, LET'S EAT SOME SANDWICHES
MAYBE WE'LL NEVER GET THE SPHERES TO WORK, JONATHAN.
CLEMENTINE! LISTEN TO MY BROTHER, HE ALREADY WANTS TO GIVE UP!
NO, MY BOY, WE JUST NEED THE RIGHT MACHINE TO MAKE THOSE SPHERES HUM LIKE--
JACKY, WHAT ARE YOU READING?
MY NEW FUNNY BOOK, DADDY. HE'S CALLED CAPTAIN AIRBORNE! HE FLIES AROUND THE CLOUDS SAVING ALL THE LADIES AND LADS.
COULD IT BE THAT SIMPLE? A JETPACK?
MAYBE. REDUCE THE WEIGHT AND I RECKON THAT POWER SOURCE WILL LOWER THE THRUST.
AB-SO-LUTE-LY! I THINK WE HAVE SOMETHING!
SOUNDS LIKE OUR LITTLE GIRL SOLVED YOUR PROBLEM.
SO, WHEN YOU BUILD THIS PACK, GUESS WHAT?
I'M YOUR PILOT.
To be continued...

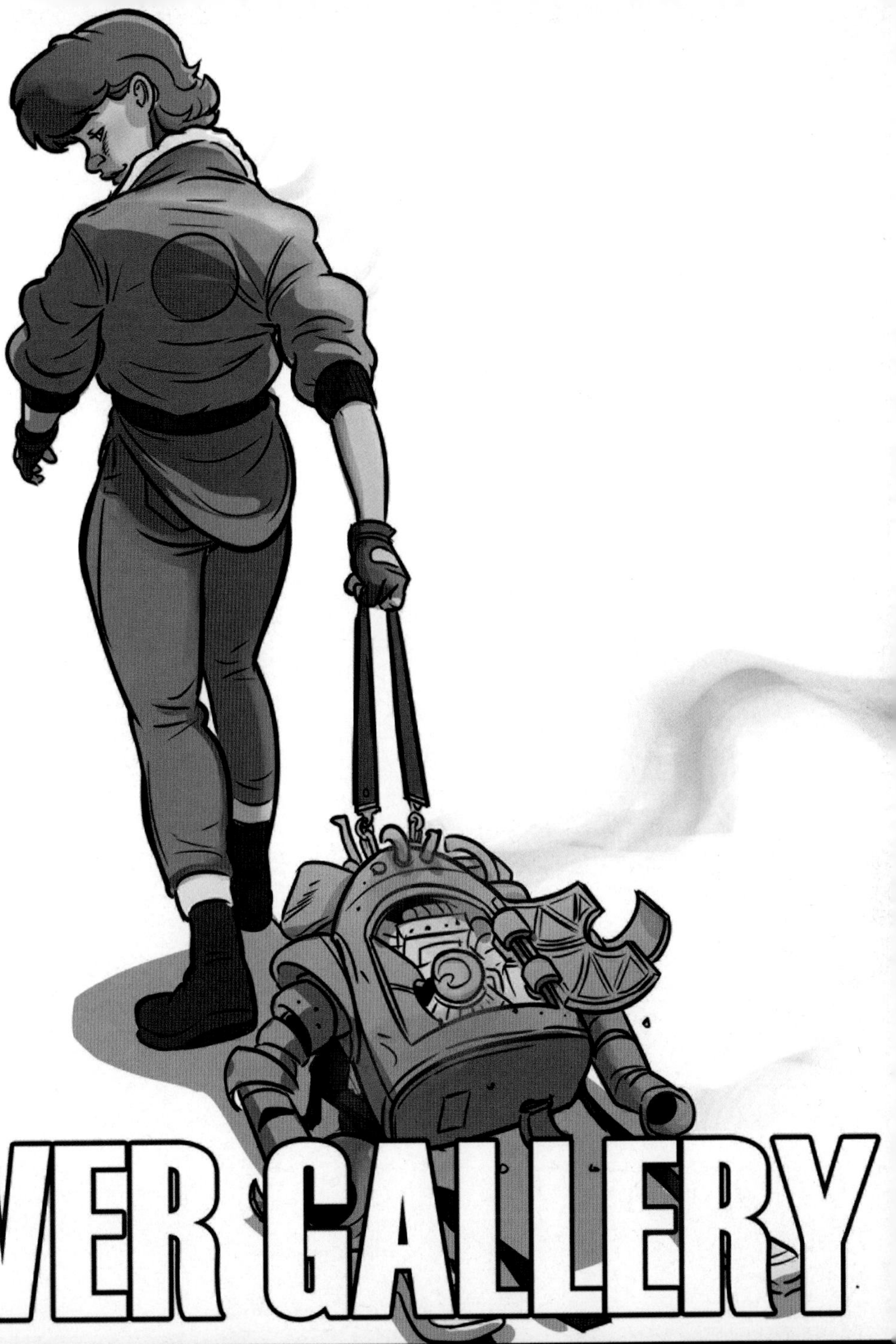

COVER GALLERY

COVER A - BEN MATSUYA
COVER B - JENN ST-ONGE

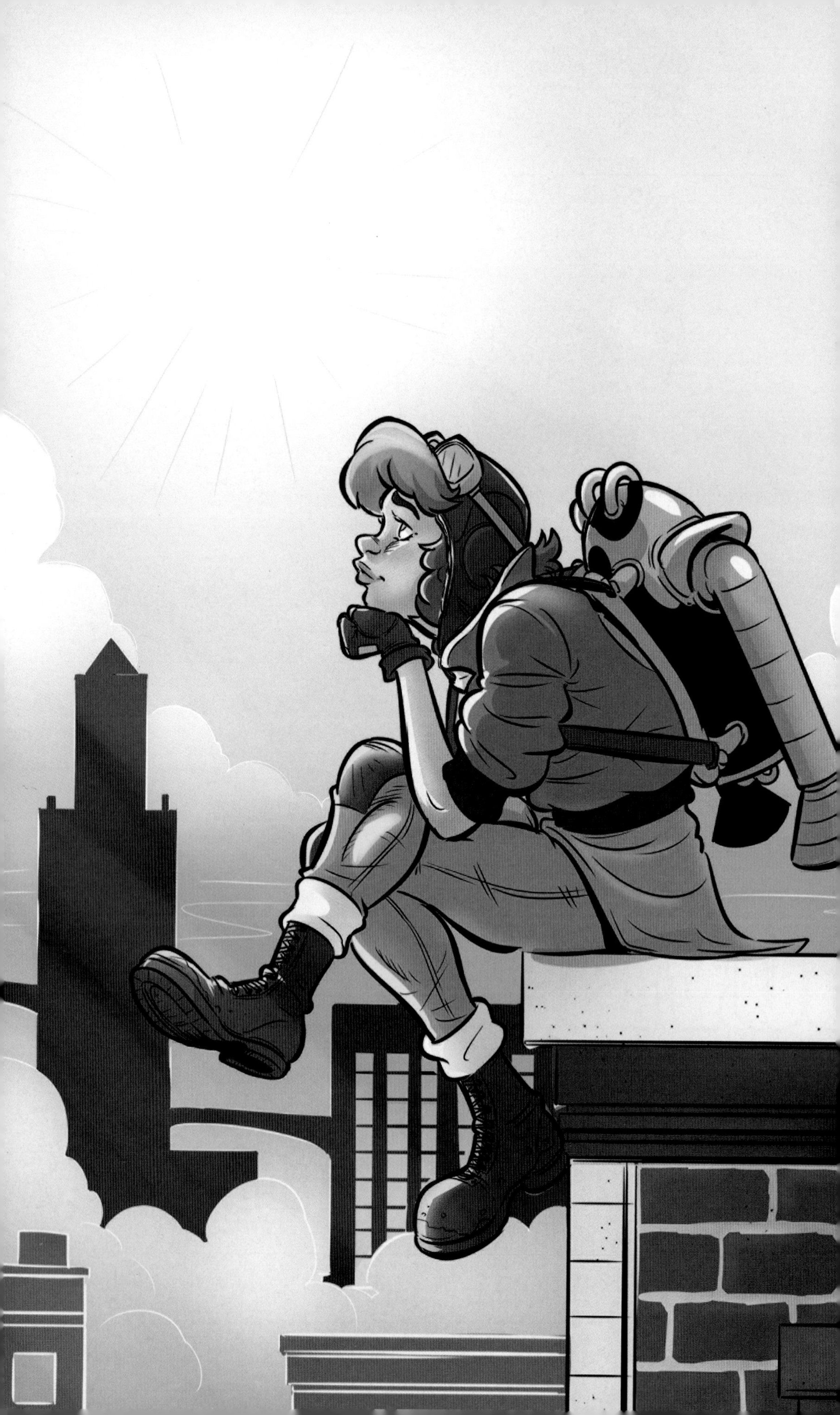

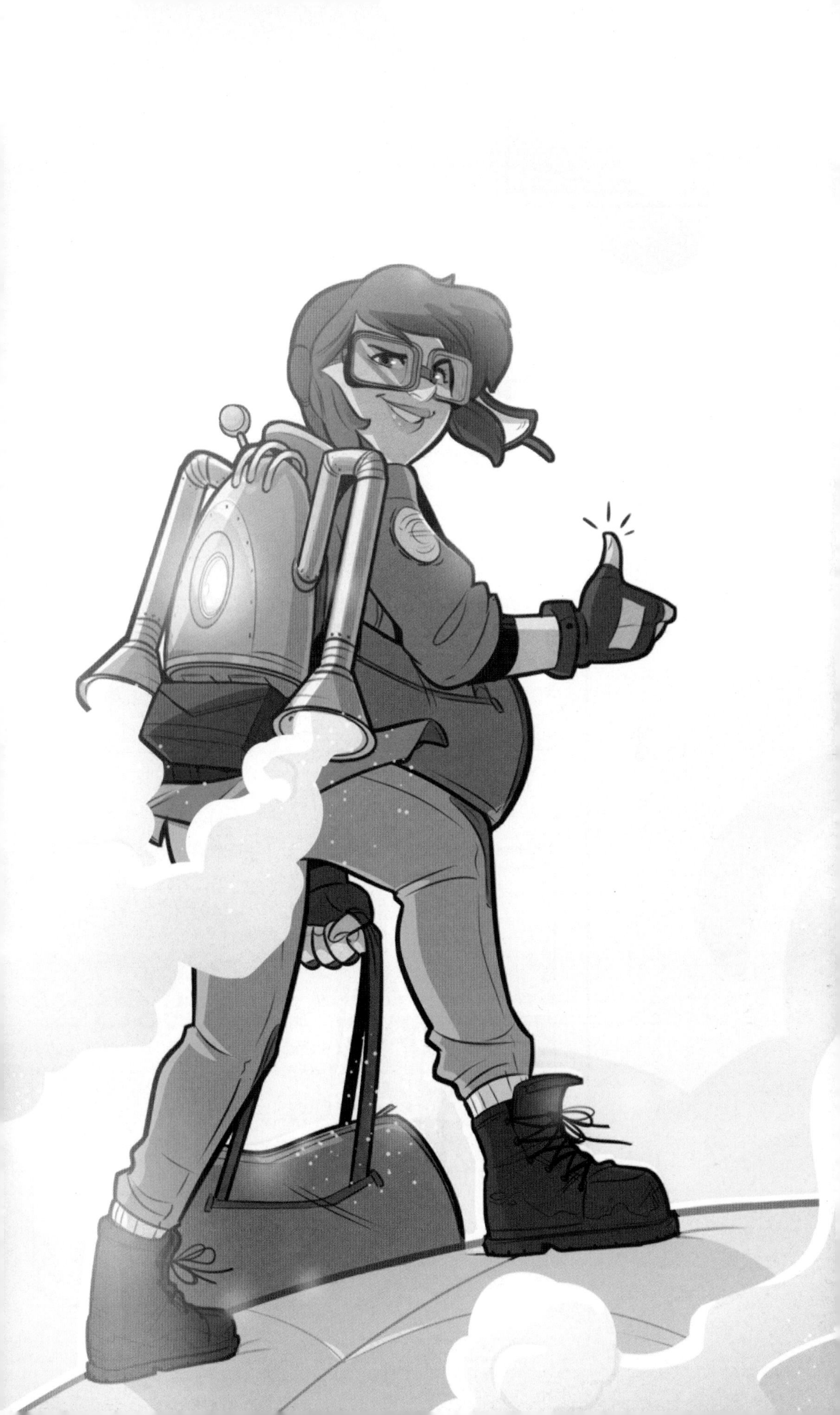

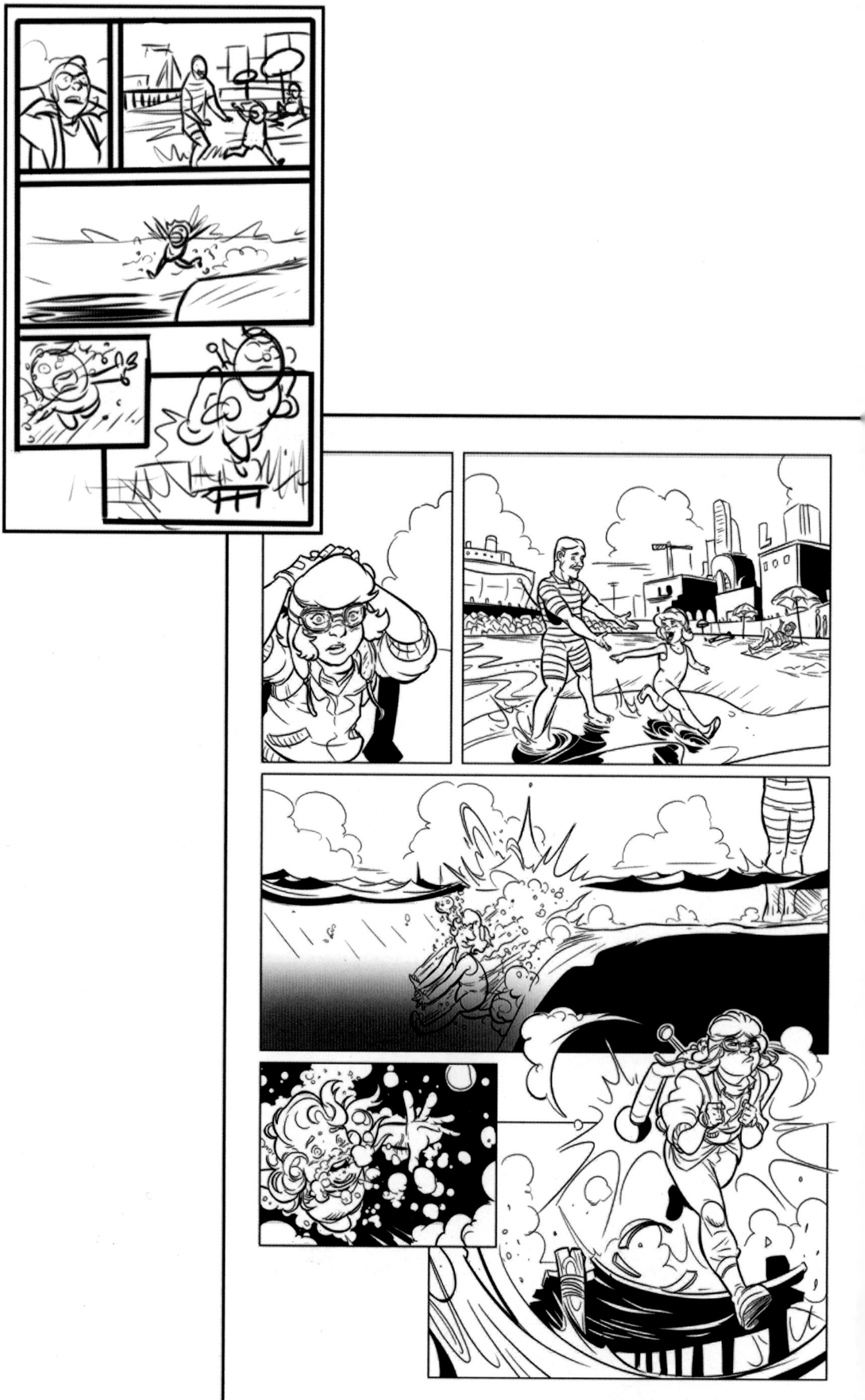

JUPITER JET #2, PAGE 13 ART PROCESS

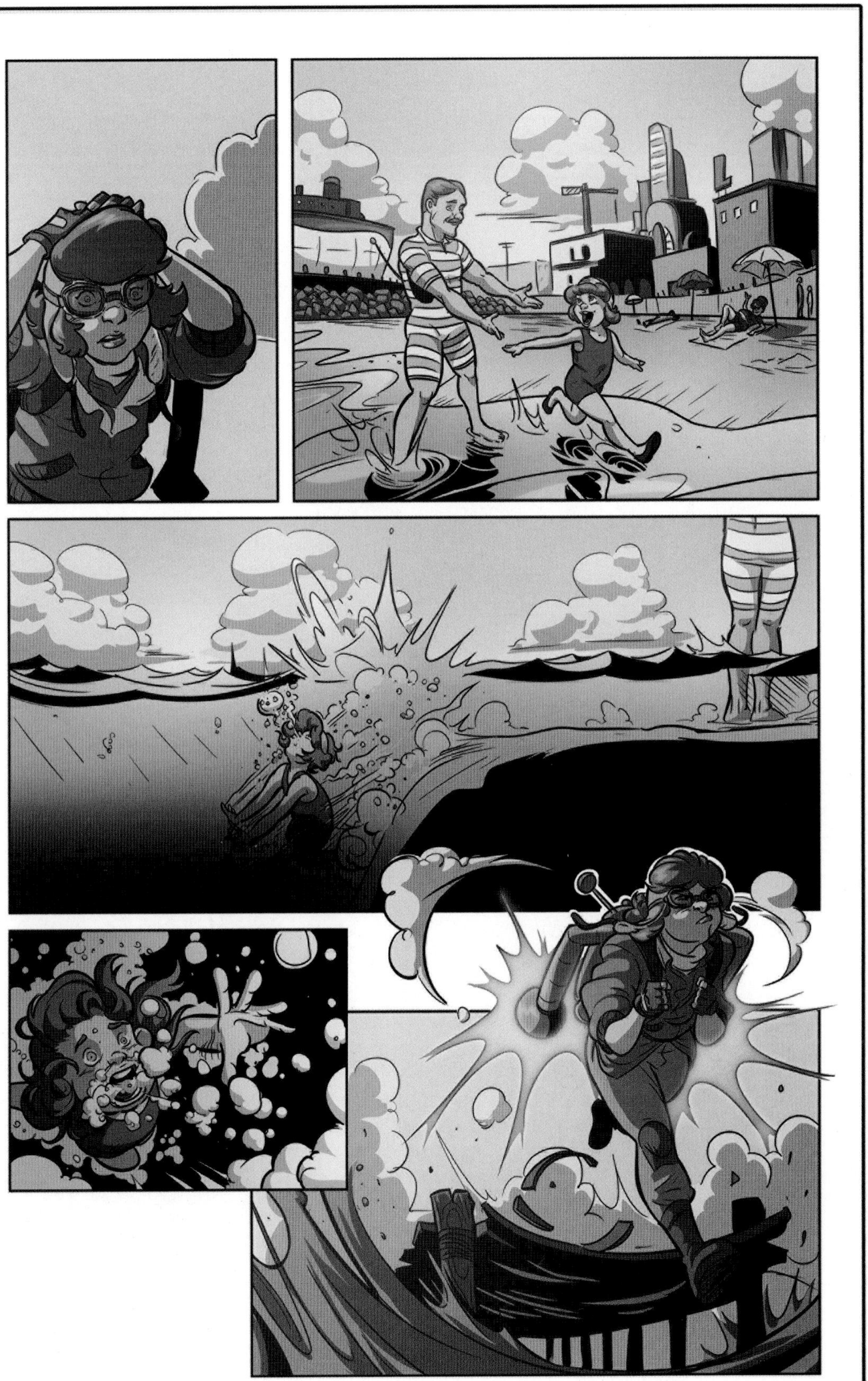

LAYOUTS & ARTWORK BY BEN MATSUYA
COLORS BY MARA JAYNE CARPENTER
COLOR FLATS BY SARA ALFAQEEH & TORI RIDLEY

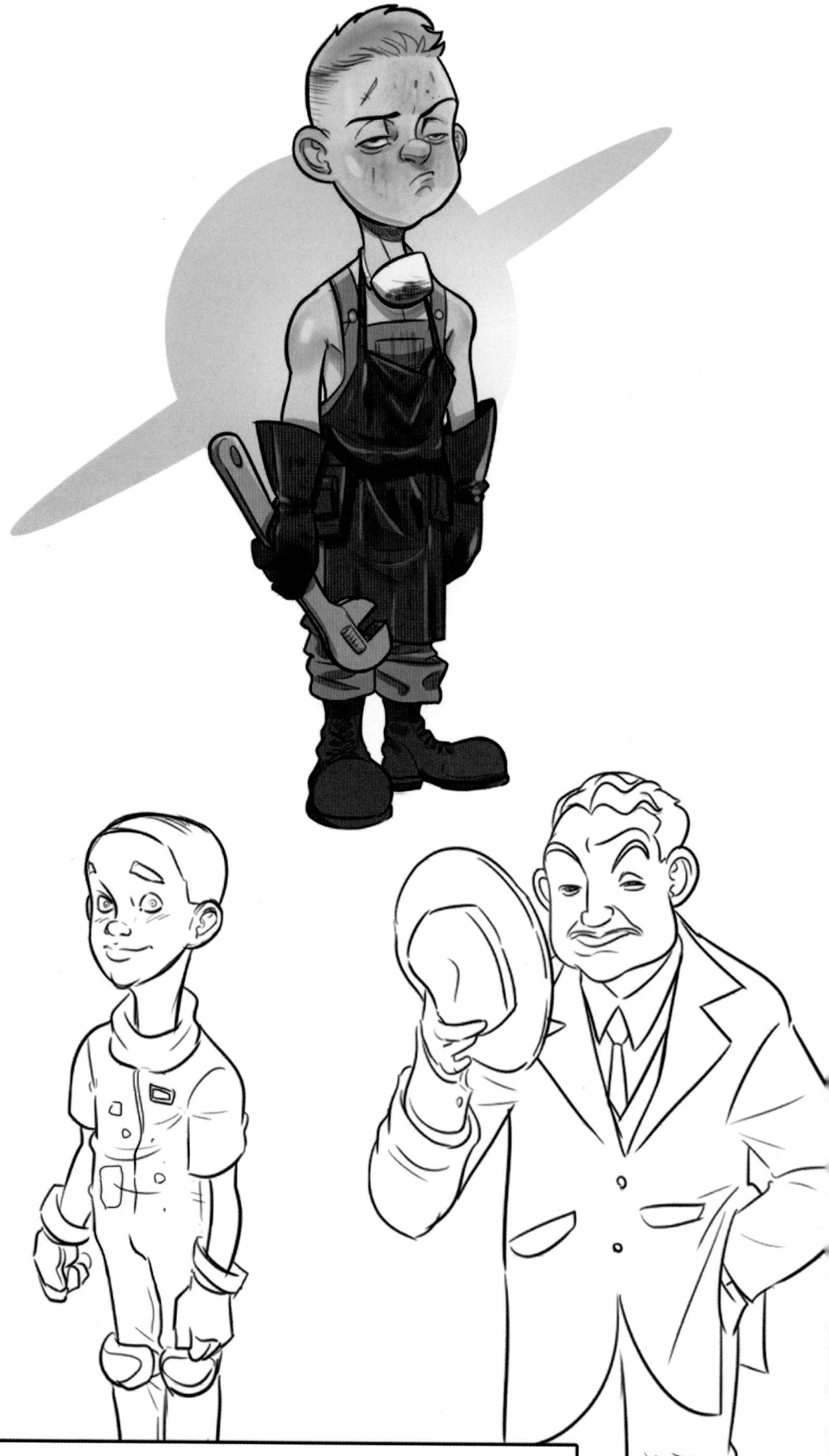

CHARACTER DESIGNS BY BEN MATSUYA

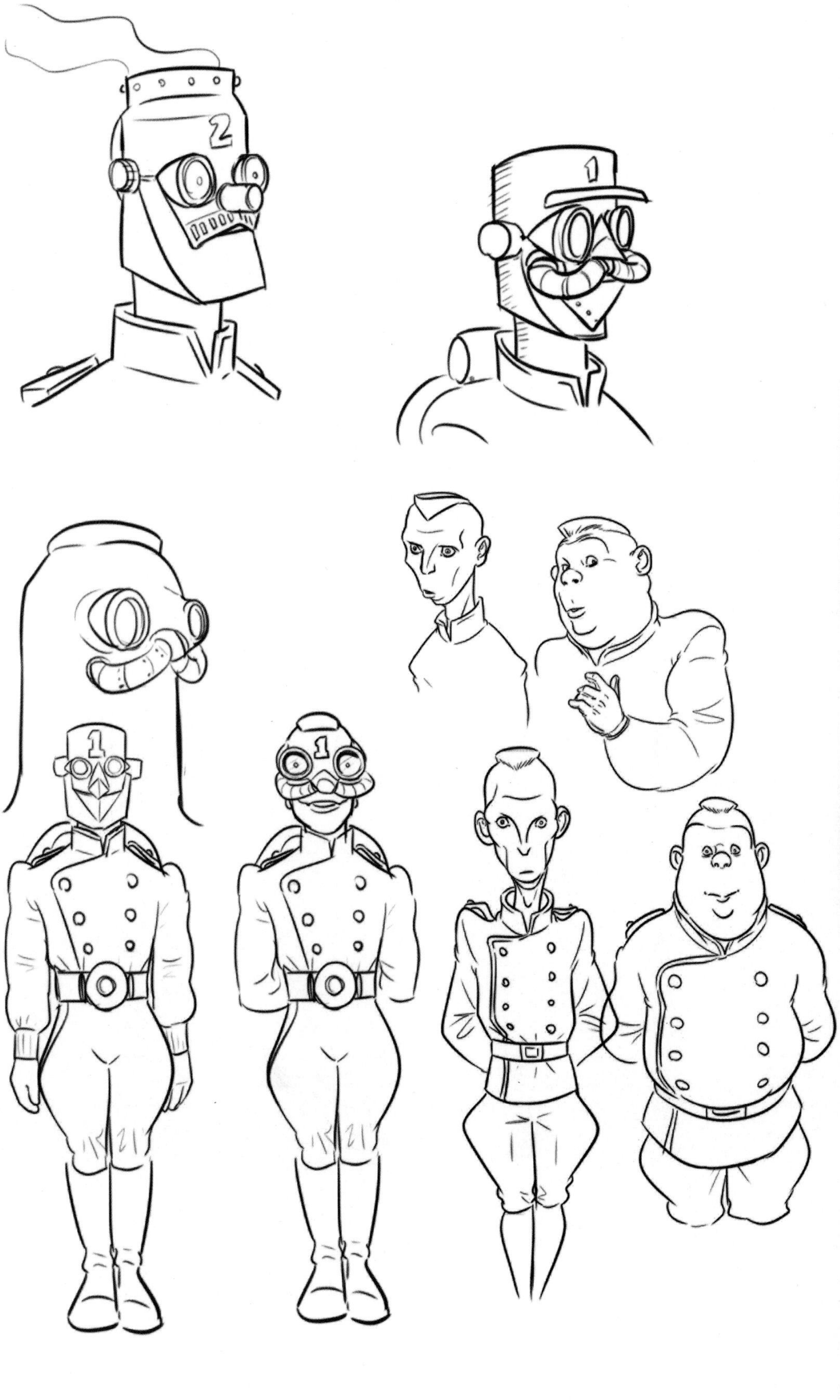
2
1
1
1

CHARACTER DESIGNS BY BEN MATSUYA

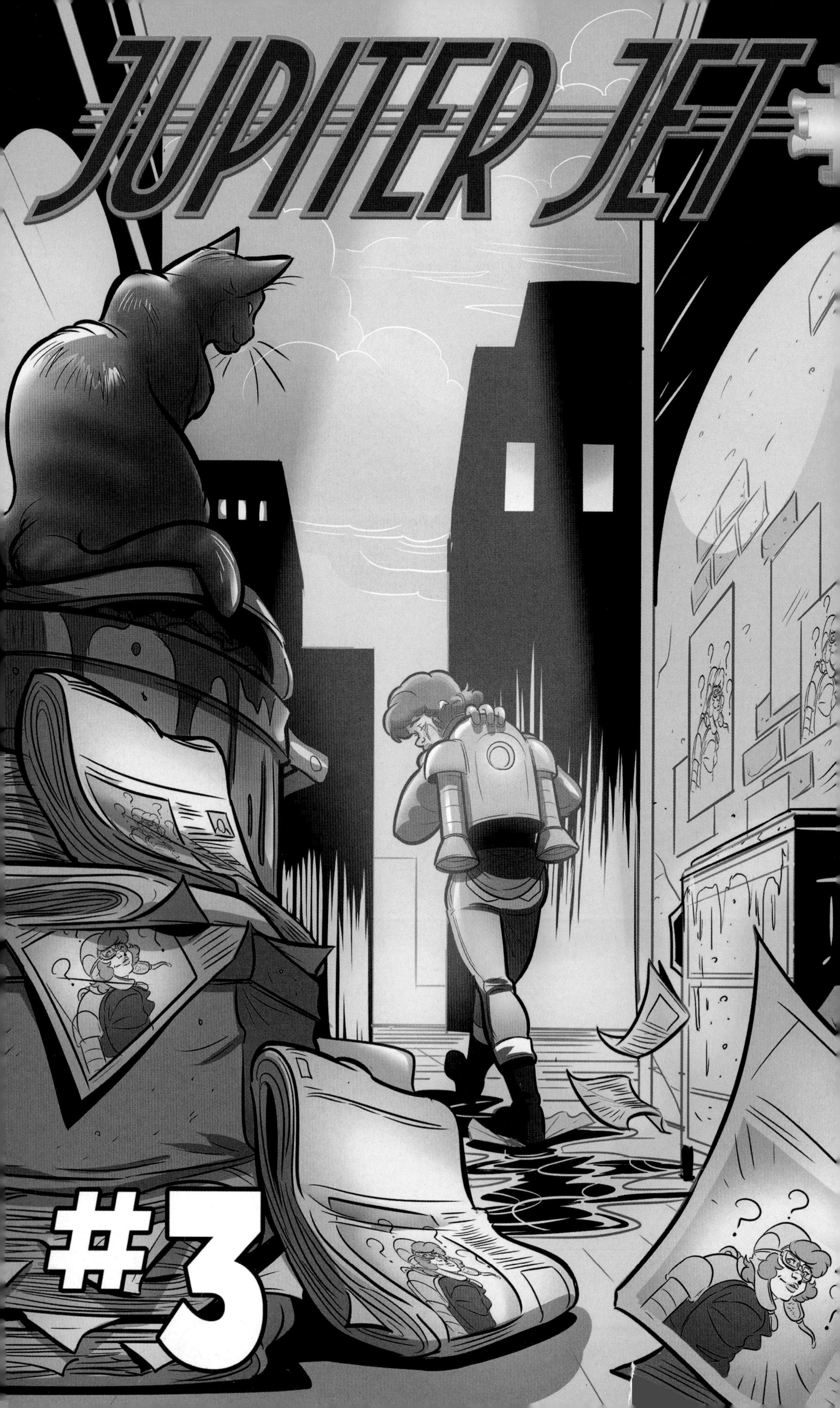
JUPITER JET
#3

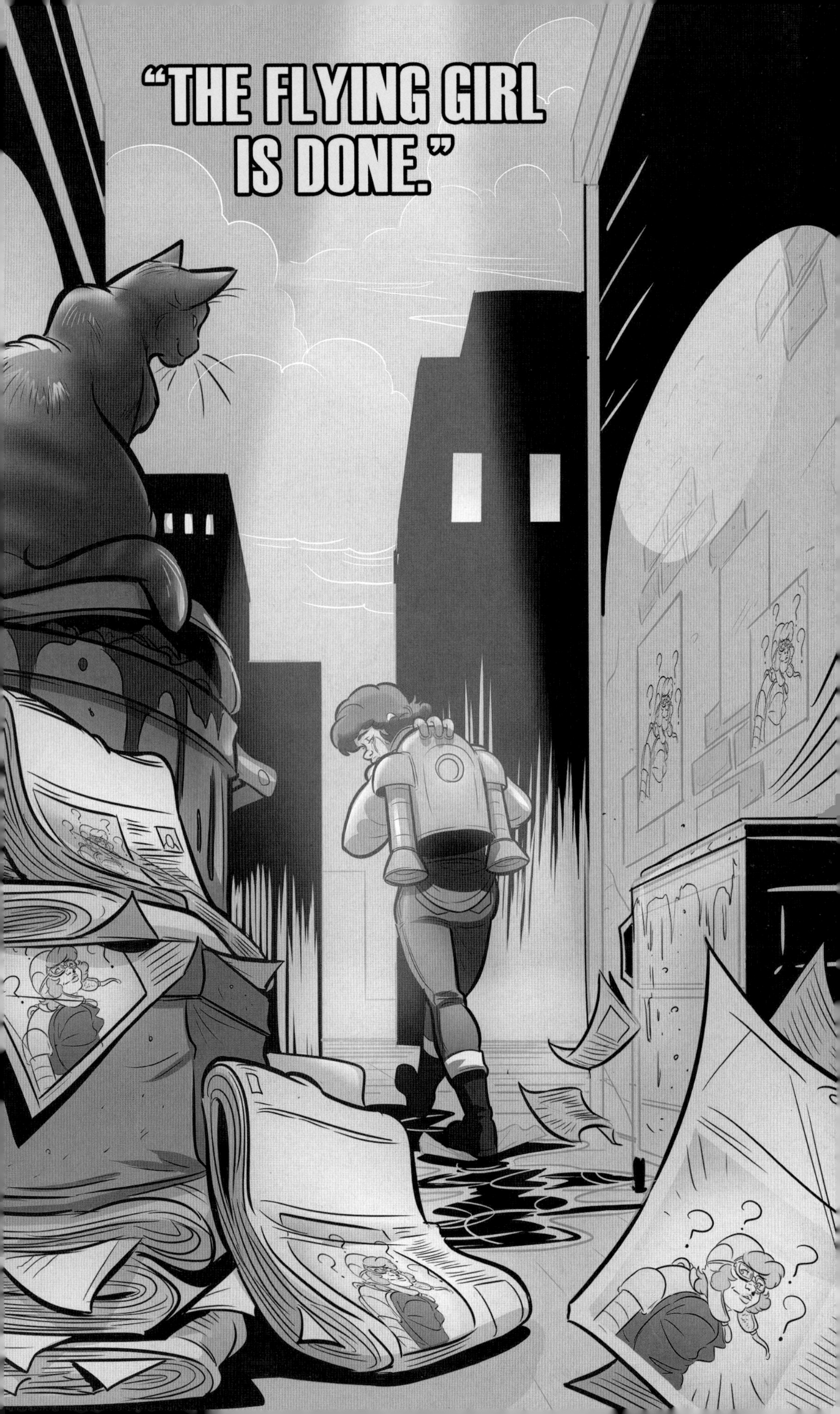
"THE FLYING GIRL IS DONE."

WRITTEN BY:
JASON INMAN &
ASHLEY VICTORIA ROBINSON

LINEART BY:
BEN MATSUYA

COLORS BY:
MARA JAYNE CARPENTER

COLOR FLATS BY:
TORI RIDLEY

LETTERS BY:
TAYLOR ESPOSITO OF GHOST GLYPH STUDIOS

COVER ARTIST:
BEN MATSUYA

PUBLISHER/ CEO: BRYAN SEATON • EDITOR IN CHIEF: SHAWN GABBORIN
PUBLISHER-DANGER ZONE: JASON MARTIN • MARKETING DIRECTOR/EDITOR: NICOLE D'ANDRIA
EXECUTIVE ADMINISTRATOR: DANIELLE DAVISON • TEST PILOT: CHAD CICCONI
PRESIDENT OF CREATOR RELATIONS: SHAWN PRYOR

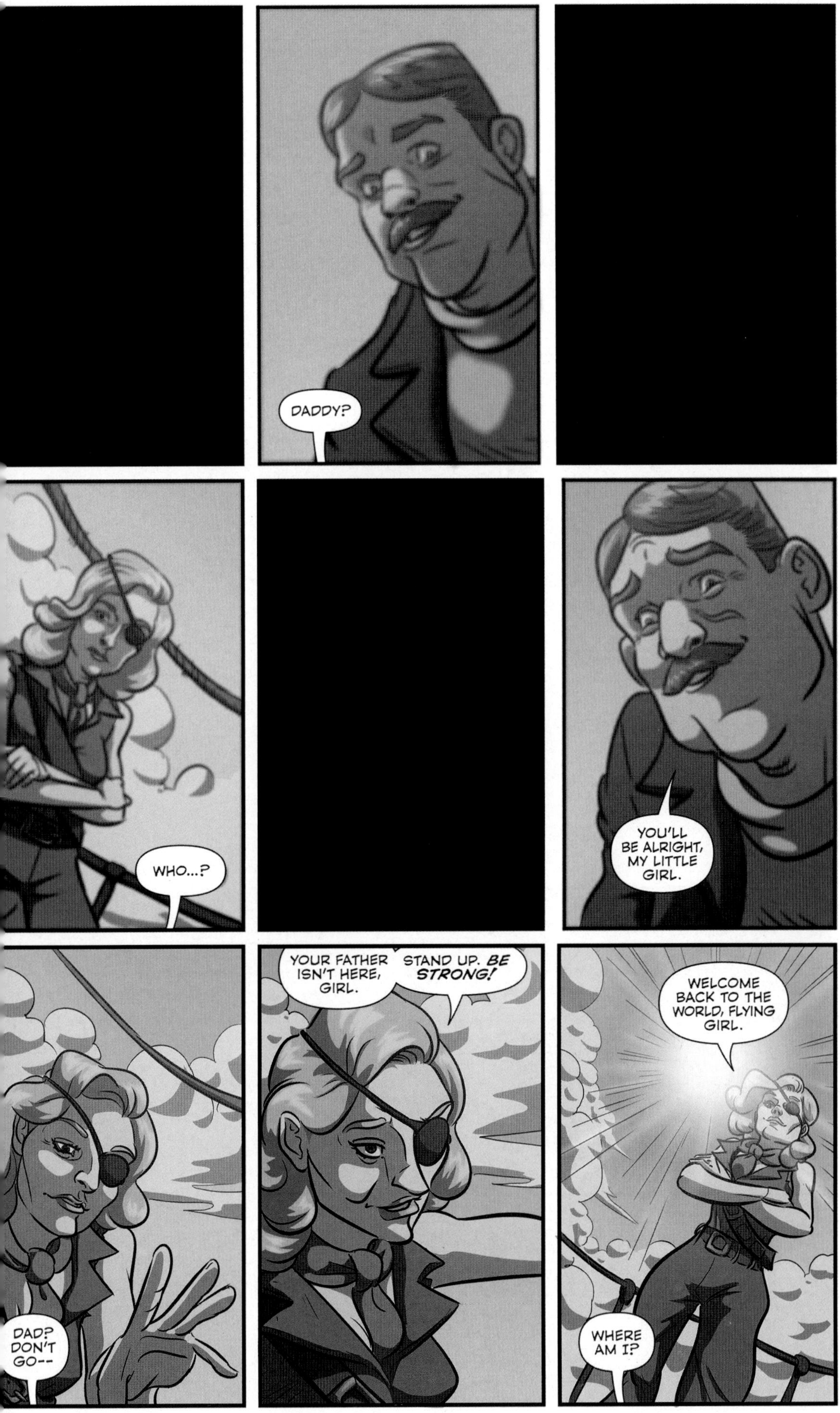
DADDY?
WHO...?
YOU'LL BE ALRIGHT, MY LITTLE GIRL.
DAD? DON'T GO--
YOUR FATHER ISN'T HERE, GIRL.
STAND UP. *BE STRONG!*
WELCOME BACK TO THE WORLD, FLYING GIRL.
WHERE AM I?

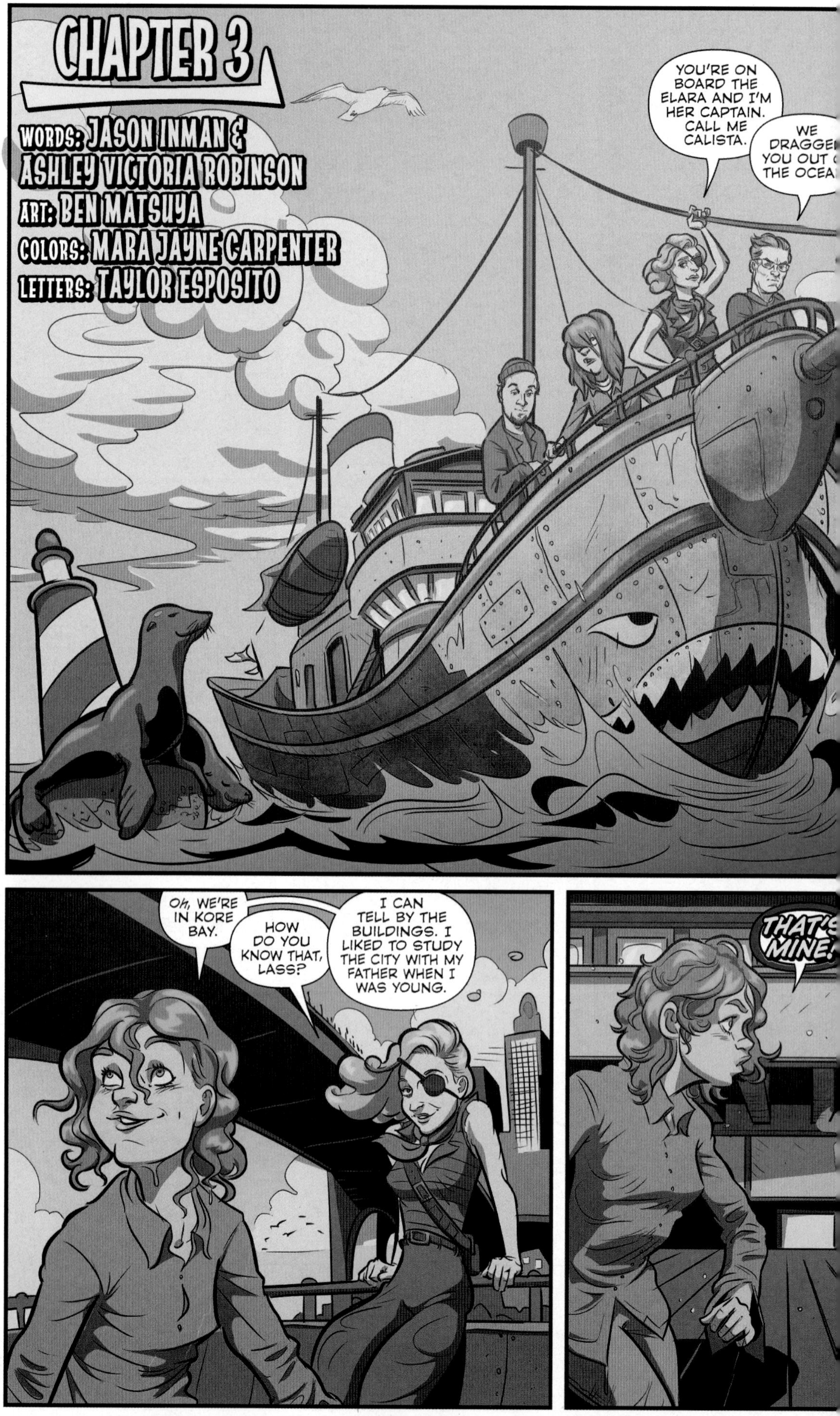
CHAPTER 3
WORDS: JASON INMAN & ASHLEY VICTORIA ROBINSON
ART: BEN MATSUYA
COLORS: MARA JAYNE CARPENTER
LETTERS: TAYLOR ESPOSITO
YOU'RE ON BOARD THE ELARA AND I'M HER CAPTAIN. CALL ME CALISTA.
WE DRAGGE YOU OUT THE OCEA
Oh, WE'RE IN KORE BAY.
HOW DO YOU KNOW THAT, LASS?
I CAN TELL BY THE BUILDINGS. I LIKED TO STUDY THE CITY WITH MY FATHER WHEN I WAS YOUNG.
THAT'S MINE!

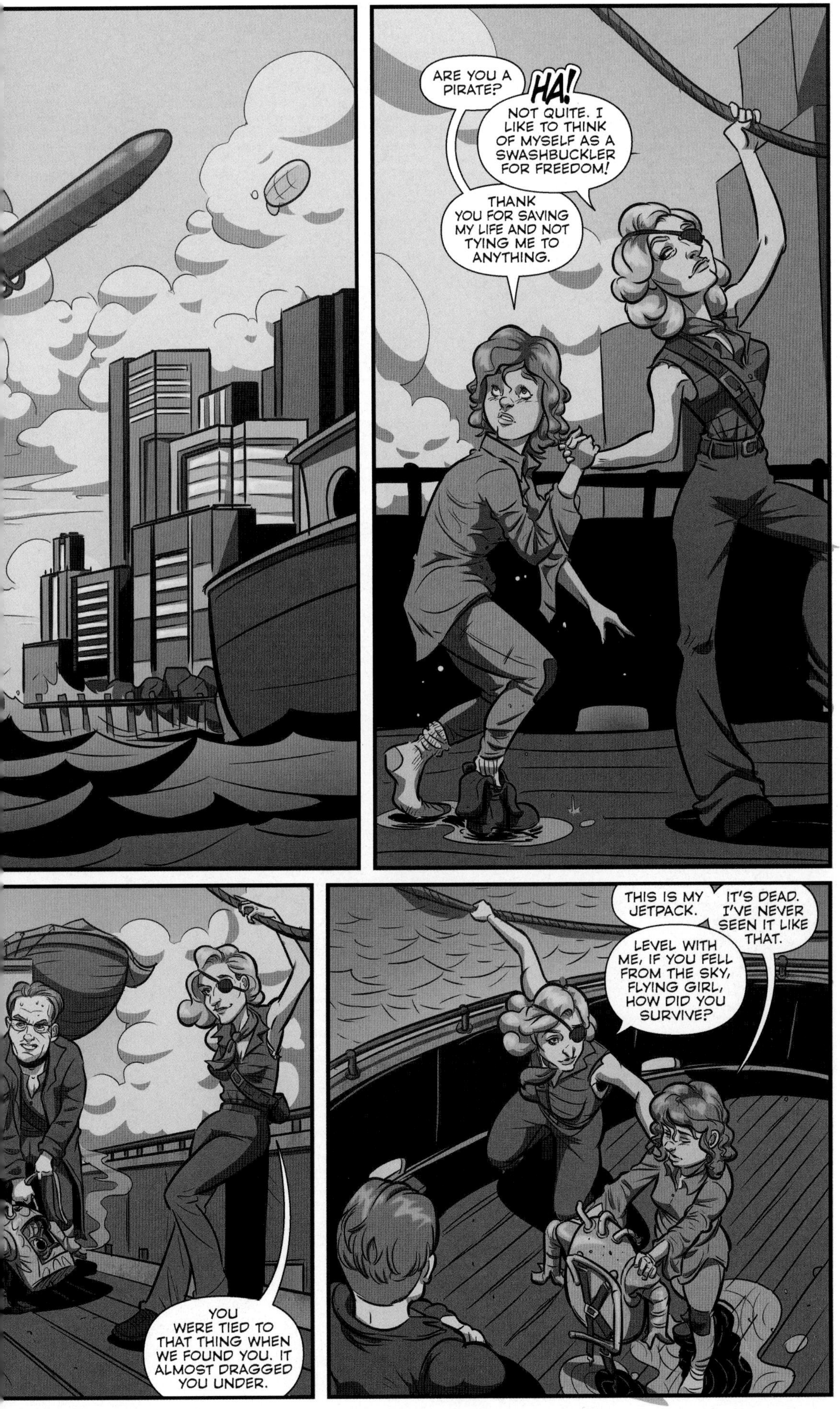
ARE YOU A PIRATE?
HA!
NOT QUITE. I LIKE TO THINK OF MYSELF AS A SWASHBUCKLER FOR FREEDOM!
THANK YOU FOR SAVING MY LIFE AND NOT TYING ME TO ANYTHING.
YOU WERE TIED TO THAT THING WHEN WE FOUND YOU. IT ALMOST DRAGGED YOU UNDER.
THIS IS MY JETPACK.
IT'S DEAD. I'VE NEVER SEEN IT LIKE THAT.
LEVEL WITH ME, IF YOU FELL FROM THE SKY, FLYING GIRL, HOW DID YOU SURVIVE?

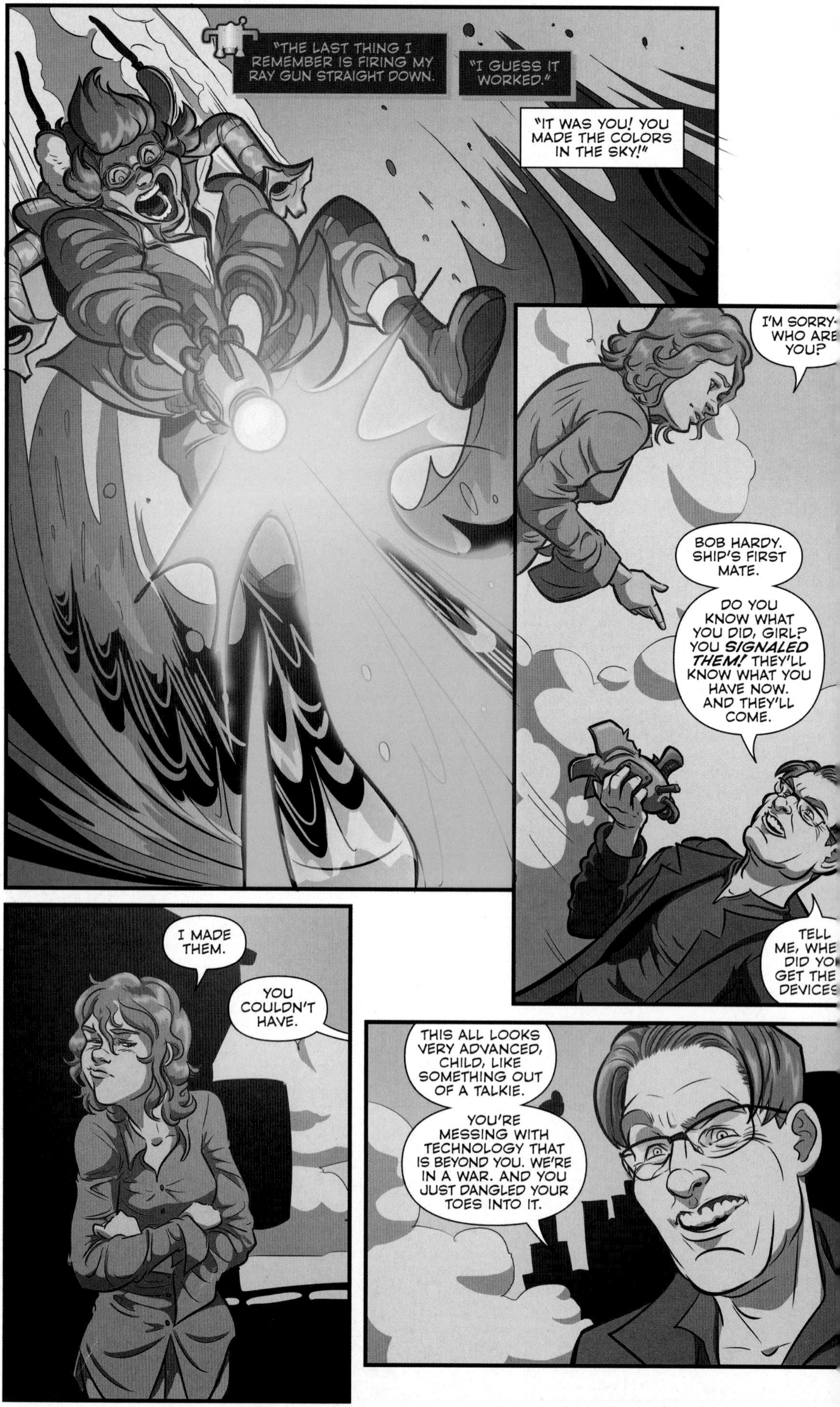
"THE LAST THING I REMEMBER IS FIRING MY RAY GUN STRAIGHT DOWN.
"I GUESS IT WORKED."
"IT WAS YOU! YOU MADE THE COLORS IN THE SKY!"
I'M SORRY-- WHO ARE YOU?
BOB HARDY. SHIP'S FIRST MATE.
DO YOU KNOW WHAT YOU DID, GIRL? YOU ***SIGNALED THEM!*** THEY'LL KNOW WHAT YOU HAVE NOW. AND THEY'LL COME.
TELL ME, WHE DID YO GET THE DEVICES
I MADE THEM.
YOU COULDN'T HAVE.
THIS ALL LOOKS VERY ADVANCED, CHILD, LIKE SOMETHING OUT OF A TALKIE.
YOU'RE MESSING WITH TECHNOLOGY THAT IS BEYOND YOU. WE'RE IN A WAR. AND YOU JUST DANGLED YOUR TOES INTO IT.

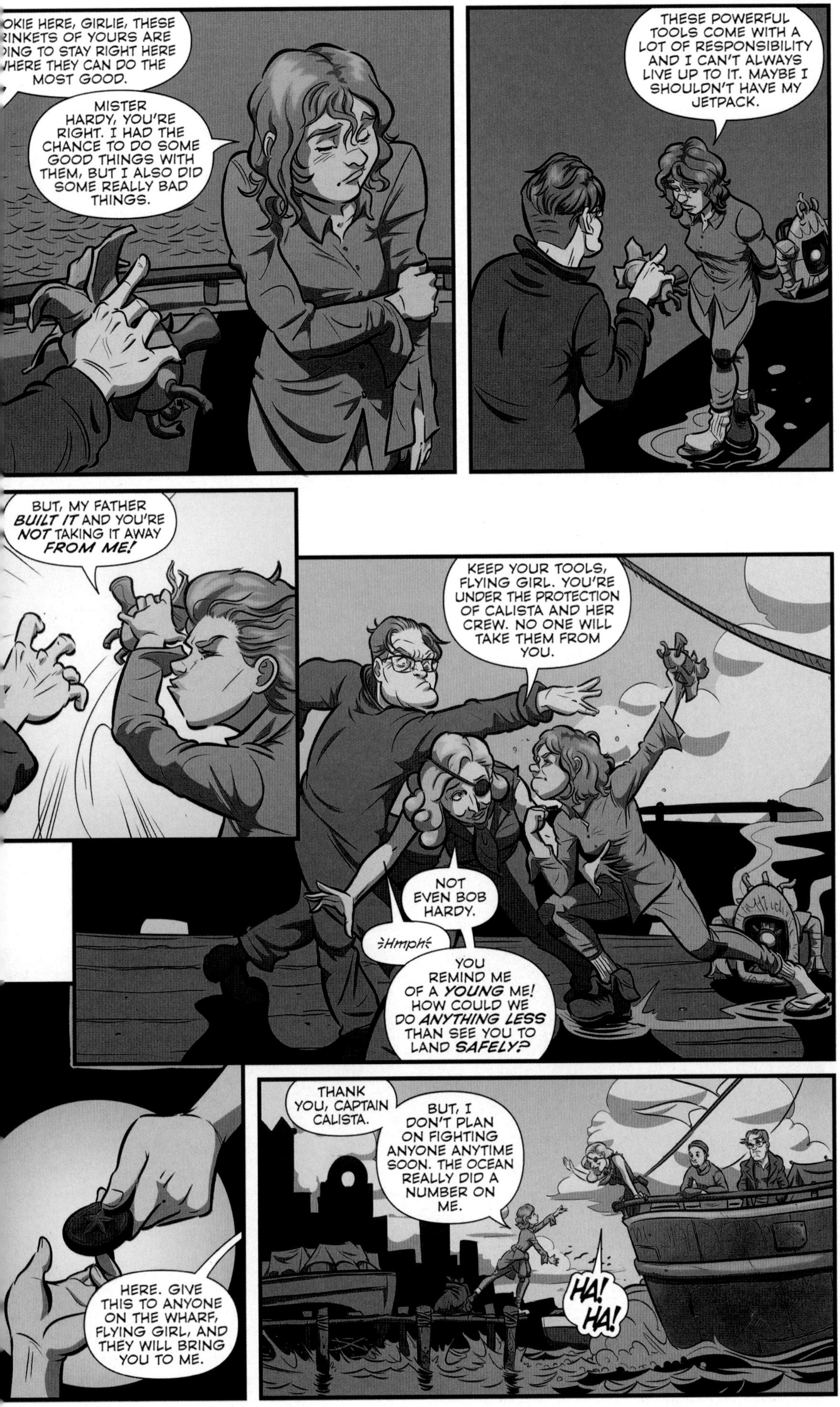
OKIE HERE, GIRLIE, THESE
RINKETS OF YOURS ARE
OING TO STAY RIGHT HERE
WHERE THEY CAN DO THE MOST GOOD.
MISTER HARDY, YOU'RE RIGHT. I HAD THE CHANCE TO DO SOME GOOD THINGS WITH THEM, BUT I ALSO DID SOME REALLY BAD THINGS.
THESE POWERFUL TOOLS COME WITH A LOT OF RESPONSIBILITY AND I CAN'T ALWAYS LIVE UP TO IT. MAYBE I SHOULDN'T HAVE MY JETPACK.
BUT, MY FATHER *BUILT IT* AND YOU'RE *NOT* TAKING IT AWAY *FROM ME!*
KEEP YOUR TOOLS, FLYING GIRL. YOU'RE UNDER THE PROTECTION OF CALISTA AND HER CREW. NO ONE WILL TAKE THEM FROM YOU.
NOT EVEN BOB HARDY.
Hmph
YOU REMIND ME OF A *YOUNG* ME! HOW COULD WE DO *ANYTHING LESS* THAN SEE YOU TO LAND *SAFELY?*
HERE. GIVE THIS TO ANYONE ON THE WHARF, FLYING GIRL, AND THEY WILL BRING YOU TO ME.
THANK YOU, CAPTAIN CALISTA.
BUT, I DON'T PLAN ON FIGHTING ANYONE ANYTIME SOON. THE OCEAN REALLY DID A NUMBER ON ME.
HA! HA!

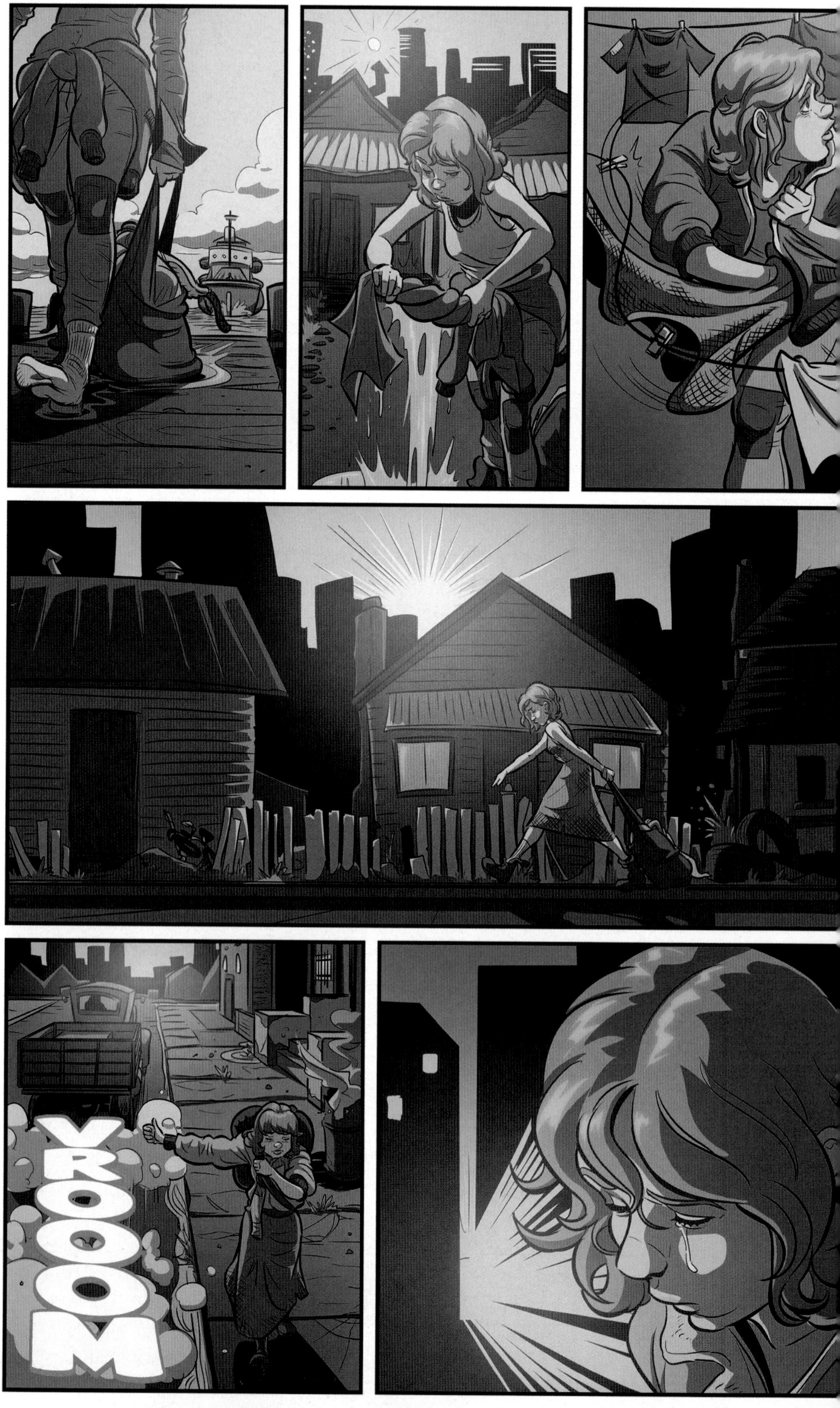
VROOOM

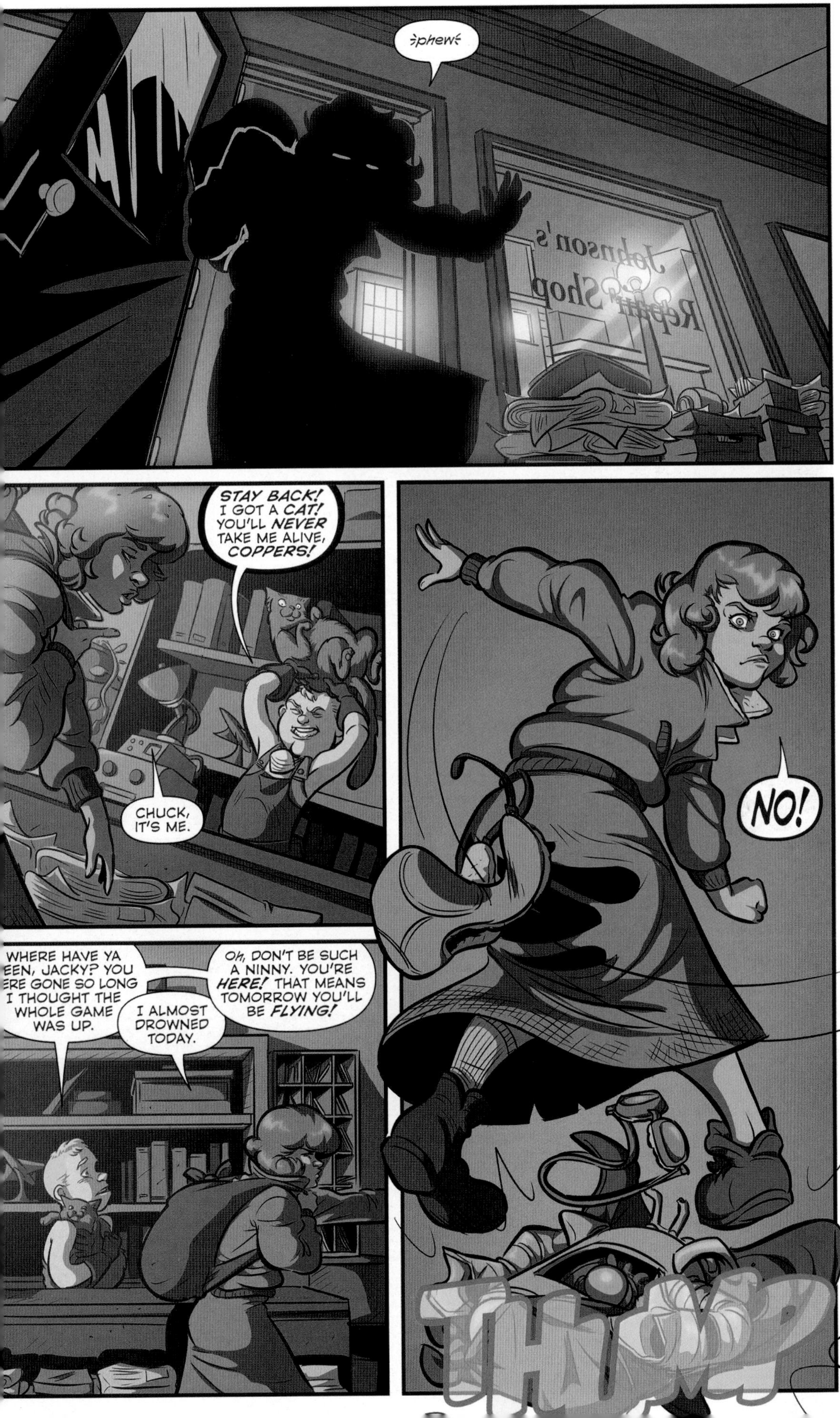
phew
Johnson's Repair Shop
STAY BACK! I GOT A CAT! YOU'LL NEVER TAKE ME ALIVE, COPPERS!
CHUCK, IT'S ME.
NO!
WHERE HAVE YA EEN, JACKY? YOU ERE GONE SO LONG I THOUGHT THE WHOLE GAME WAS UP.
I ALMOST DROWNED TODAY.
OH, DON'T BE SUCH A NINNY. YOU'RE HERE! THAT MEANS TOMORROW YOU'LL BE FLYING!
THUMP

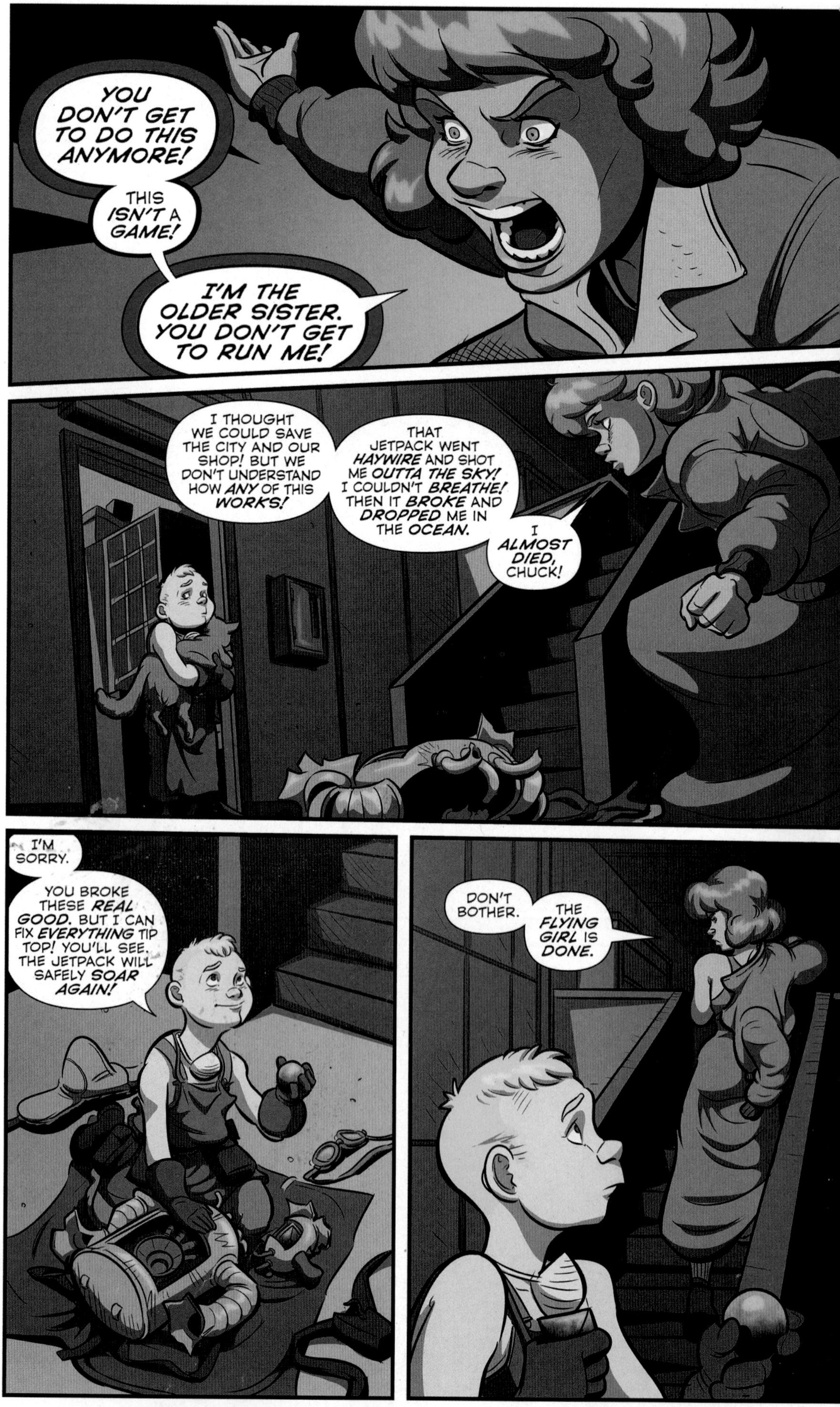

YOU DON'T GET TO DO THIS ANYMORE!
THIS ISN'T A GAME!
I'M THE OLDER SISTER. YOU DON'T GET TO RUN ME!
I THOUGHT WE COULD SAVE THE CITY AND OUR SHOP! BUT WE DON'T UNDERSTAND HOW ANY OF THIS WORKS!
THAT JETPACK WENT HAYWIRE AND SHOT ME OUTTA THE SKY! I COULDN'T BREATHE! THEN IT BROKE AND DROPPED ME IN THE OCEAN.
I ALMOST DIED, CHUCK!
I'M SORRY.
YOU BROKE THESE REAL GOOD. BUT I CAN FIX EVERYTHING TIP TOP! YOU'LL SEE. THE JETPACK WILL SAFELY SOAR AGAIN!
DON'T BOTHER.
THE FLYING GIRL IS DONE.

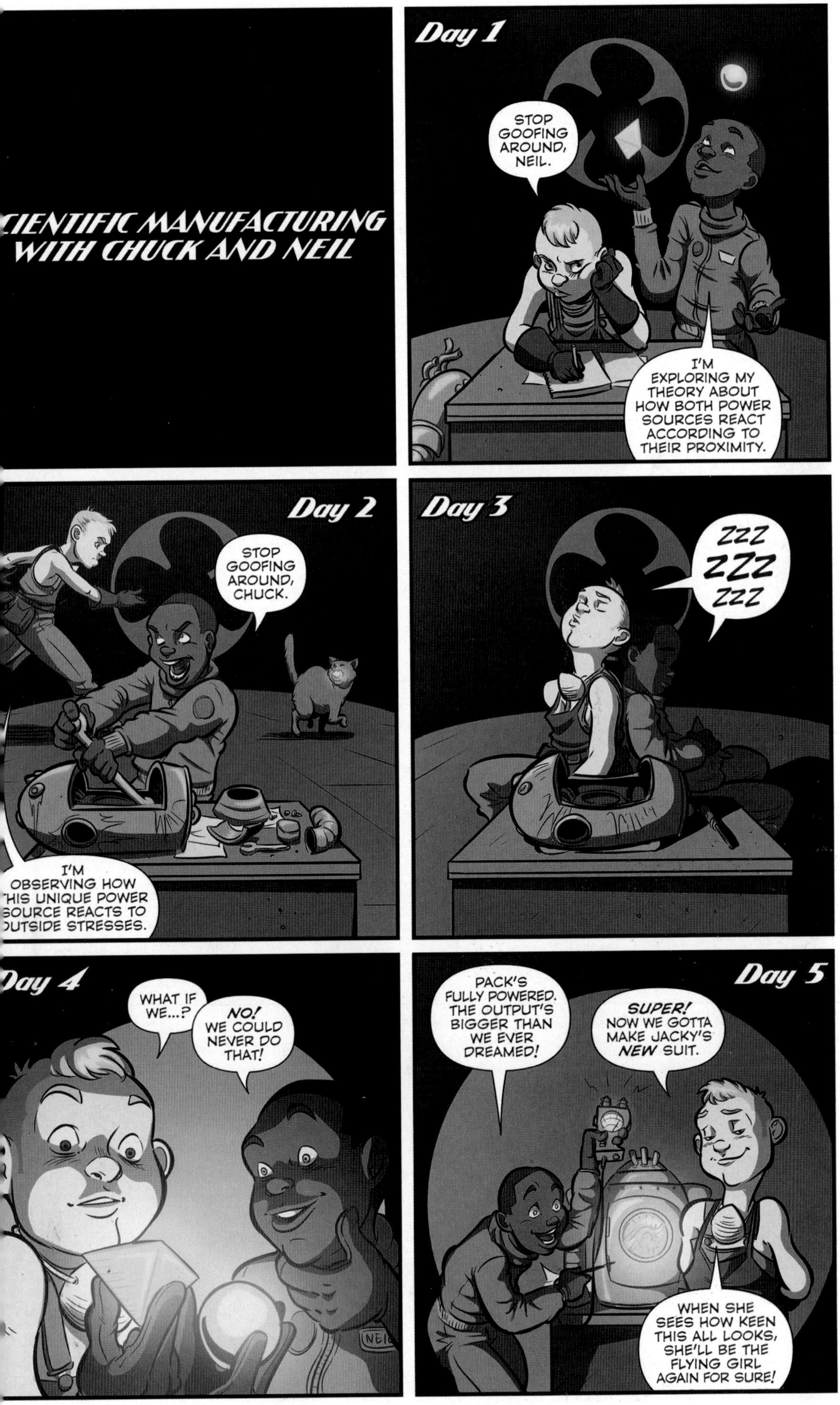
CIENTIFIC MANUFACTURING
WITH CHUCK AND NEIL
Day 1
STOP GOOFING AROUND, NEIL.
I'M EXPLORING MY THEORY ABOUT HOW BOTH POWER SOURCES REACT ACCORDING TO THEIR PROXIMITY.
Day 2
STOP GOOFING AROUND, CHUCK.
I'M OBSERVING HOW THIS UNIQUE POWER SOURCE REACTS TO OUTSIDE STRESSES.
Day 3
ZZZ
ZZZ
ZZZ
Day 4
WHAT IF WE...?
NO! WE COULD NEVER DO THAT!
Day 5
PACK'S FULLY POWERED. THE OUTPUT'S BIGGER THAN WE EVER DREAMED!
SUPER! NOW WE GOTTA MAKE JACKY'S NEW SUIT.
WHEN SHE SEES HOW KEEN THIS ALL LOOKS, SHE'LL BE THE FLYING GIRL AGAIN FOR SURE!

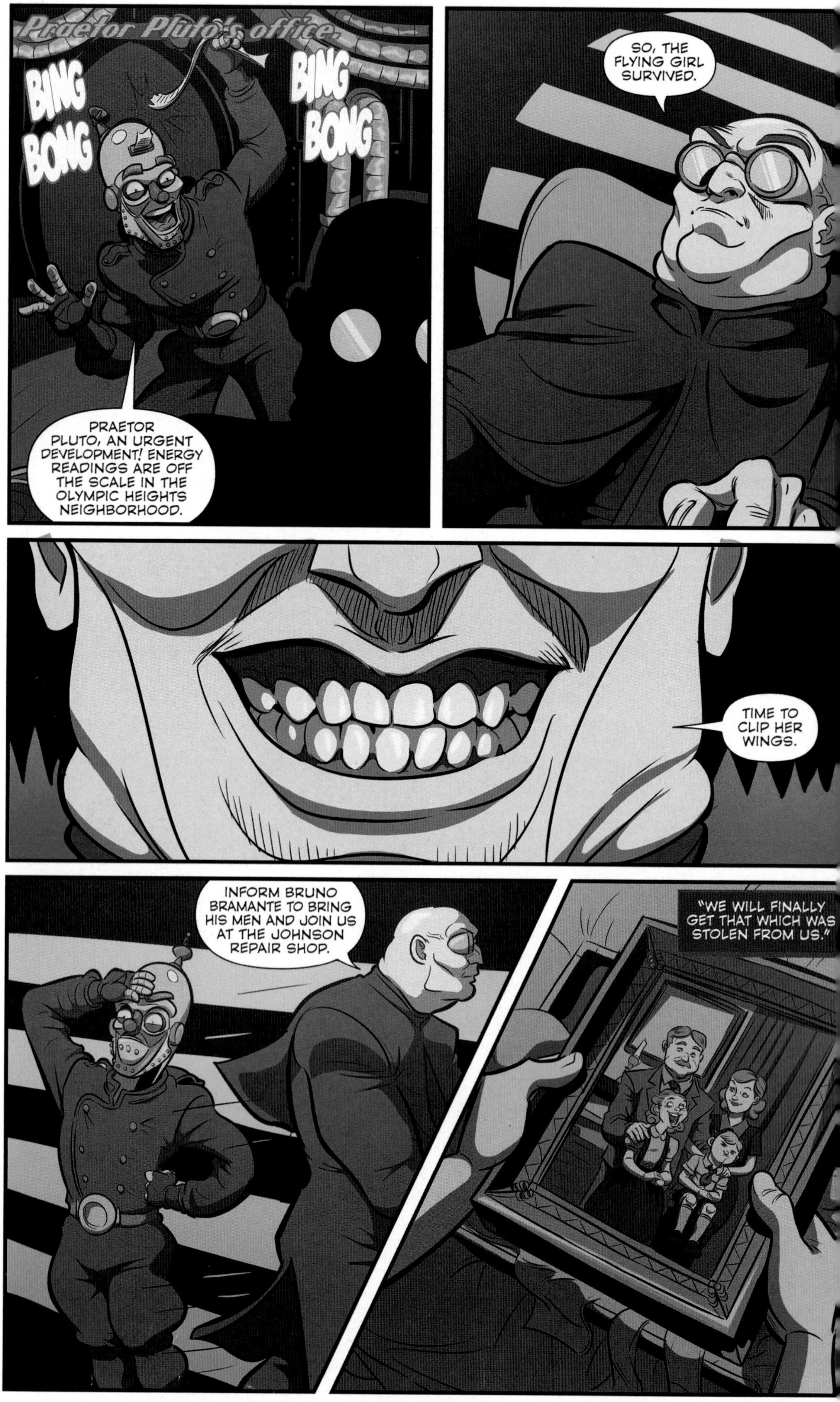
Praetor Pluto's office.
BING BONG
BING BONG
PRAETOR PLUTO, AN URGENT DEVELOPMENT! ENERGY READINGS ARE OFF THE SCALE IN THE OLYMPIC HEIGHTS NEIGHBORHOOD.
SO, THE FLYING GIRL SURVIVED.
TIME TO CLIP HER WINGS.
INFORM BRUNO BRAMANTE TO BRING HIS MEN AND JOIN US AT THE JOHNSON REPAIR SHOP.
"WE WILL FINALLY GET THAT WHICH WAS STOLEN FROM US."

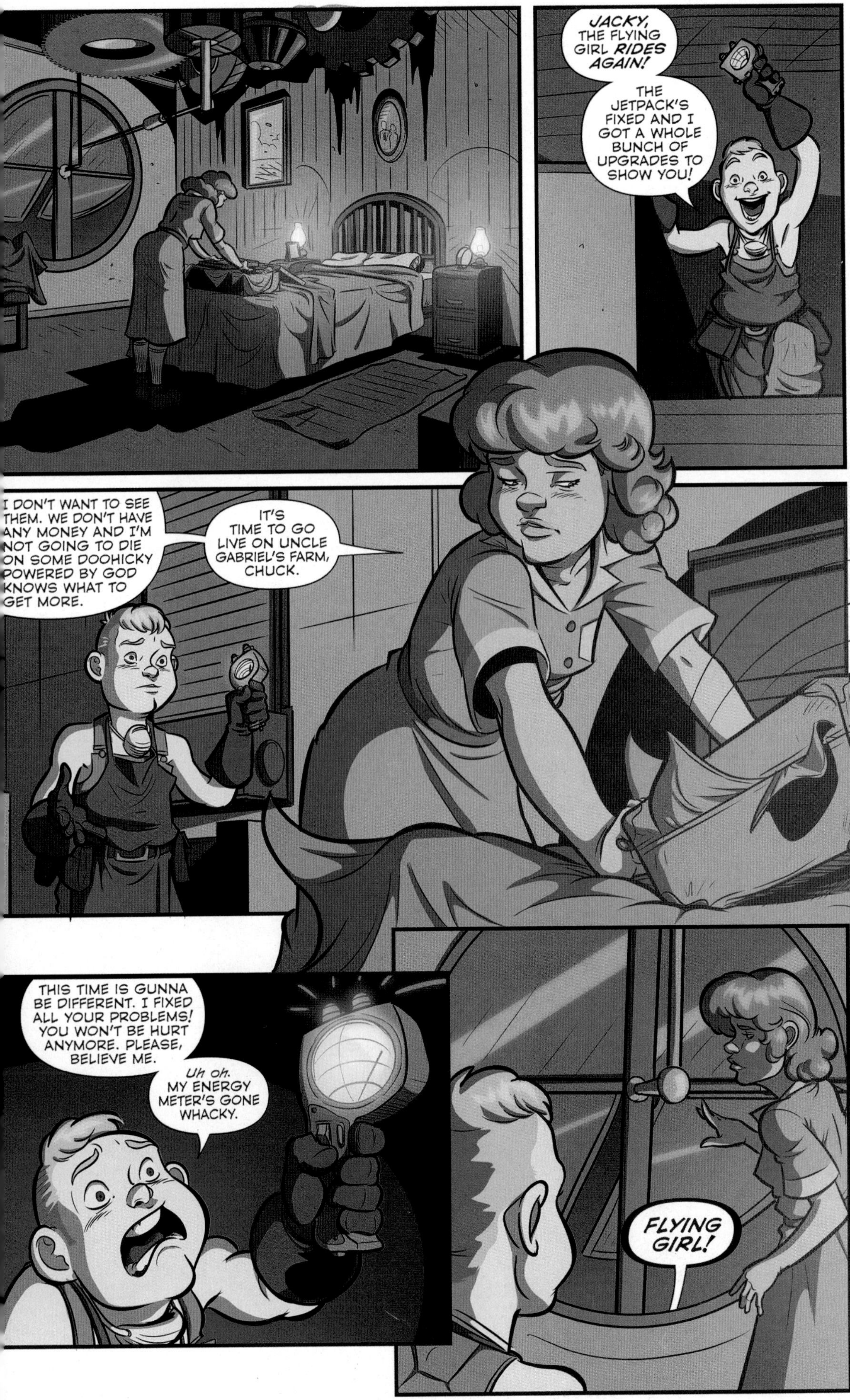

JACKY, THE FLYING GIRL ***RIDES AGAIN!***
THE JETPACK'S FIXED AND I GOT A WHOLE BUNCH OF UPGRADES TO SHOW YOU!
IT'S TIME TO GO LIVE ON UNCLE GABRIEL'S FARM, CHUCK.
I DON'T WANT TO SEE THEM. WE DON'T HAVE ANY MONEY AND I'M NOT GOING TO DIE ON SOME DOOHICKY POWERED BY GOD KNOWS WHAT TO GET MORE.
THIS TIME IS GUNNA BE DIFFERENT. I FIXED ALL YOUR PROBLEMS! YOU WON'T BE HURT ANYMORE. PLEASE, BELIEVE ME.
Uh oh. MY ENERGY METER'S GONE WHACKY.
FLYING GIRL!

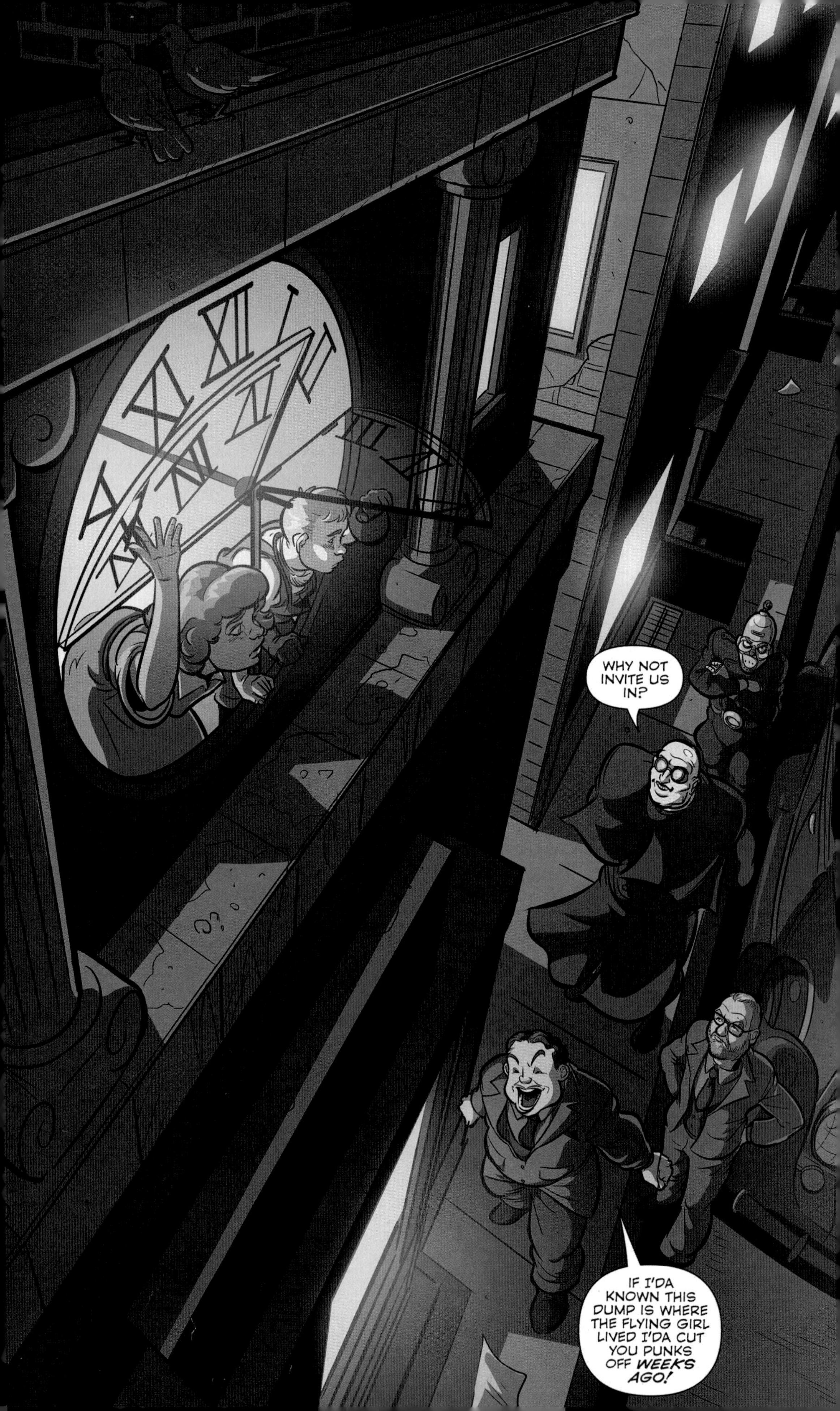
WHY NOT INVITE US IN?
IF I'DA KNOWN THIS DUMP IS WHERE THE FLYING GIRL LIVED I'DA CUT YOU PUNKS OFF *WEEKS AGO!*

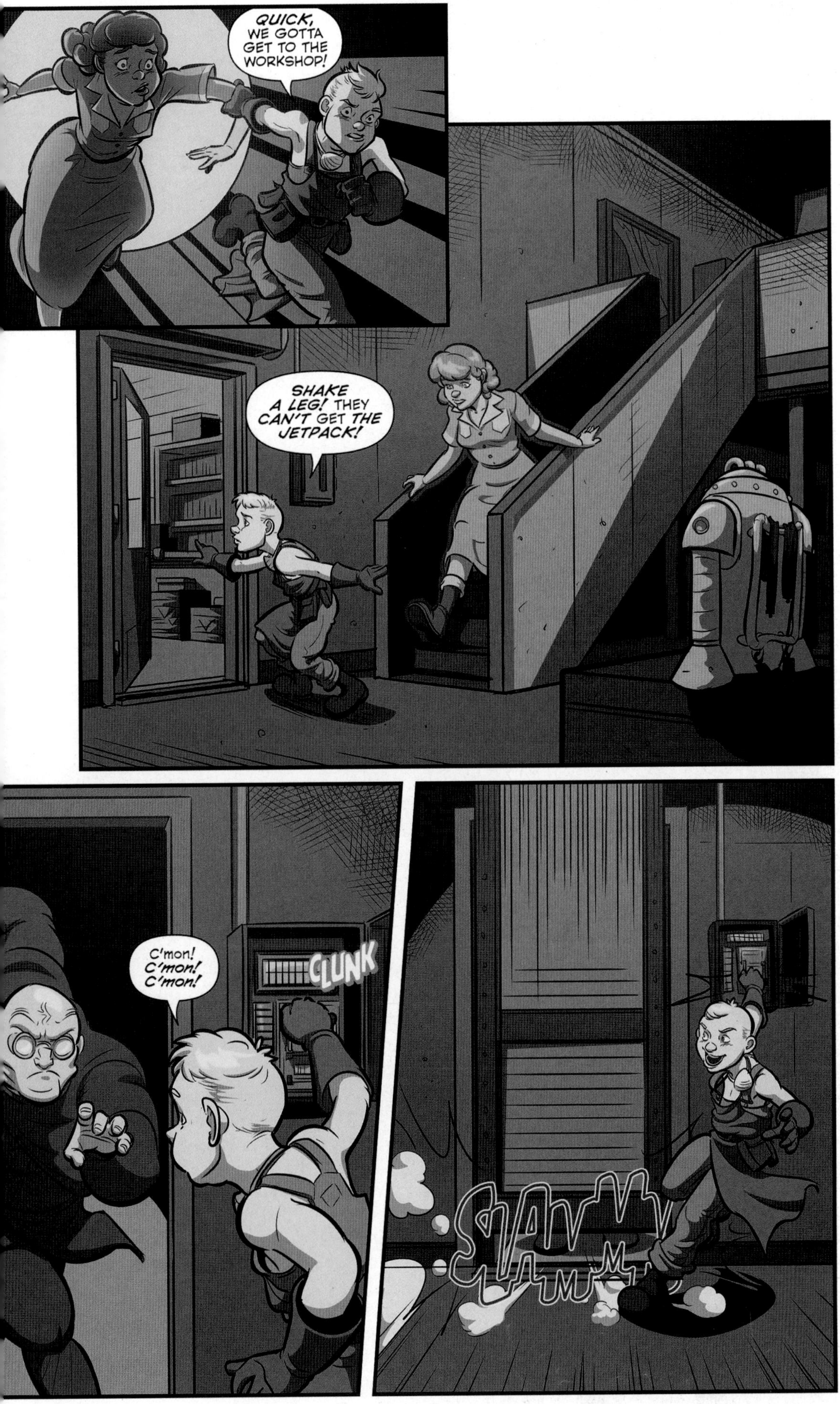
QUICK, WE GOTTA GET TO THE WORKSHOP!
SHAKE A LEG! THEY CAN'T GET THE JETPACK!
C'mon! C'mon! C'mon!
CLUNK

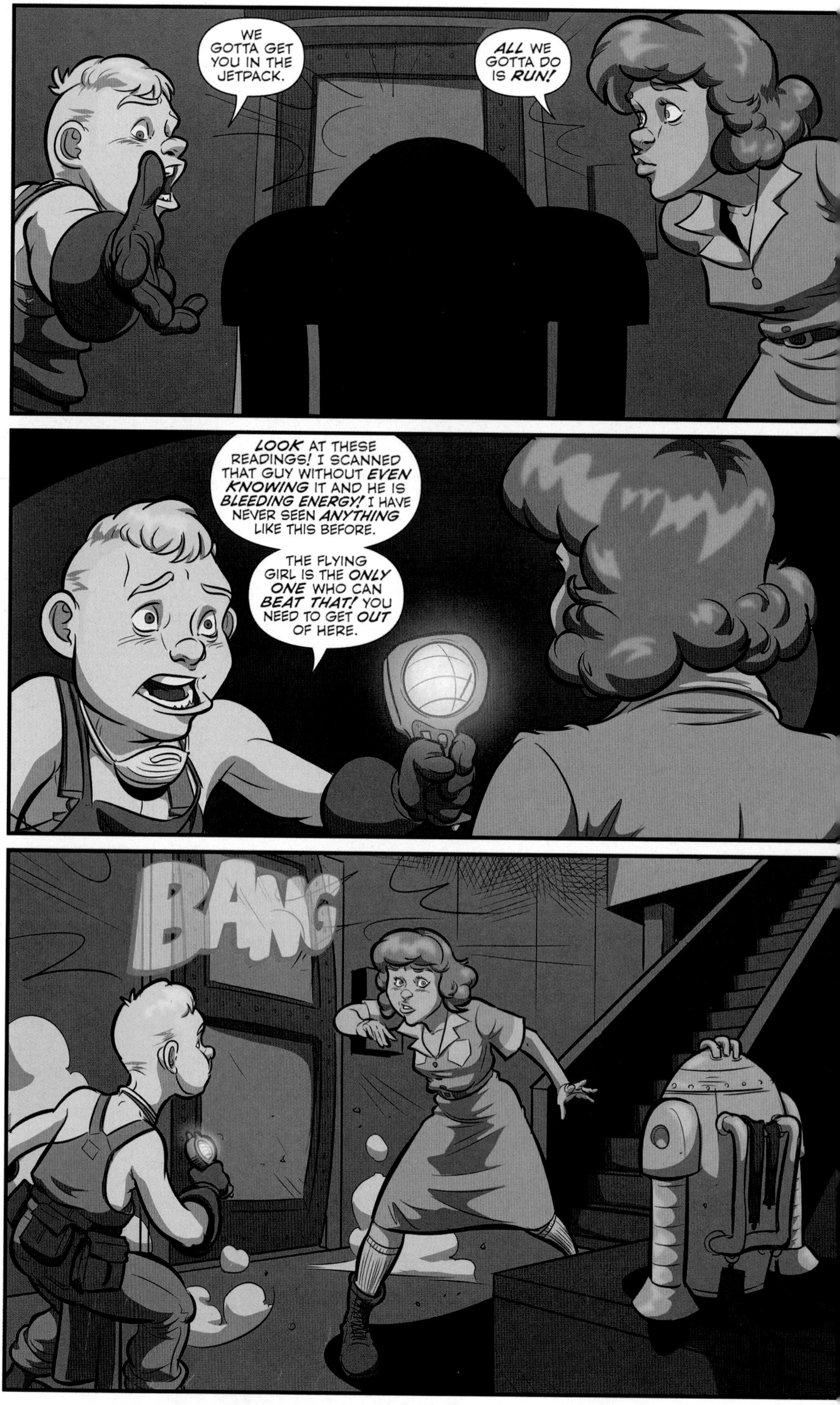

WE GOTTA GET YOU IN THE JETPACK.
ALL WE GOTTA DO IS RUN!
LOOK AT THESE READINGS! I SCANNED THAT GUY WITHOUT EVEN KNOWING IT AND HE IS BLEEDING ENERGY! I HAVE NEVER SEEN ANYTHING LIKE THIS BEFORE.
THE FLYING GIRL IS THE ONLY ONE WHO CAN BEAT THAT! YOU NEED TO GET OUT OF HERE.
BANG

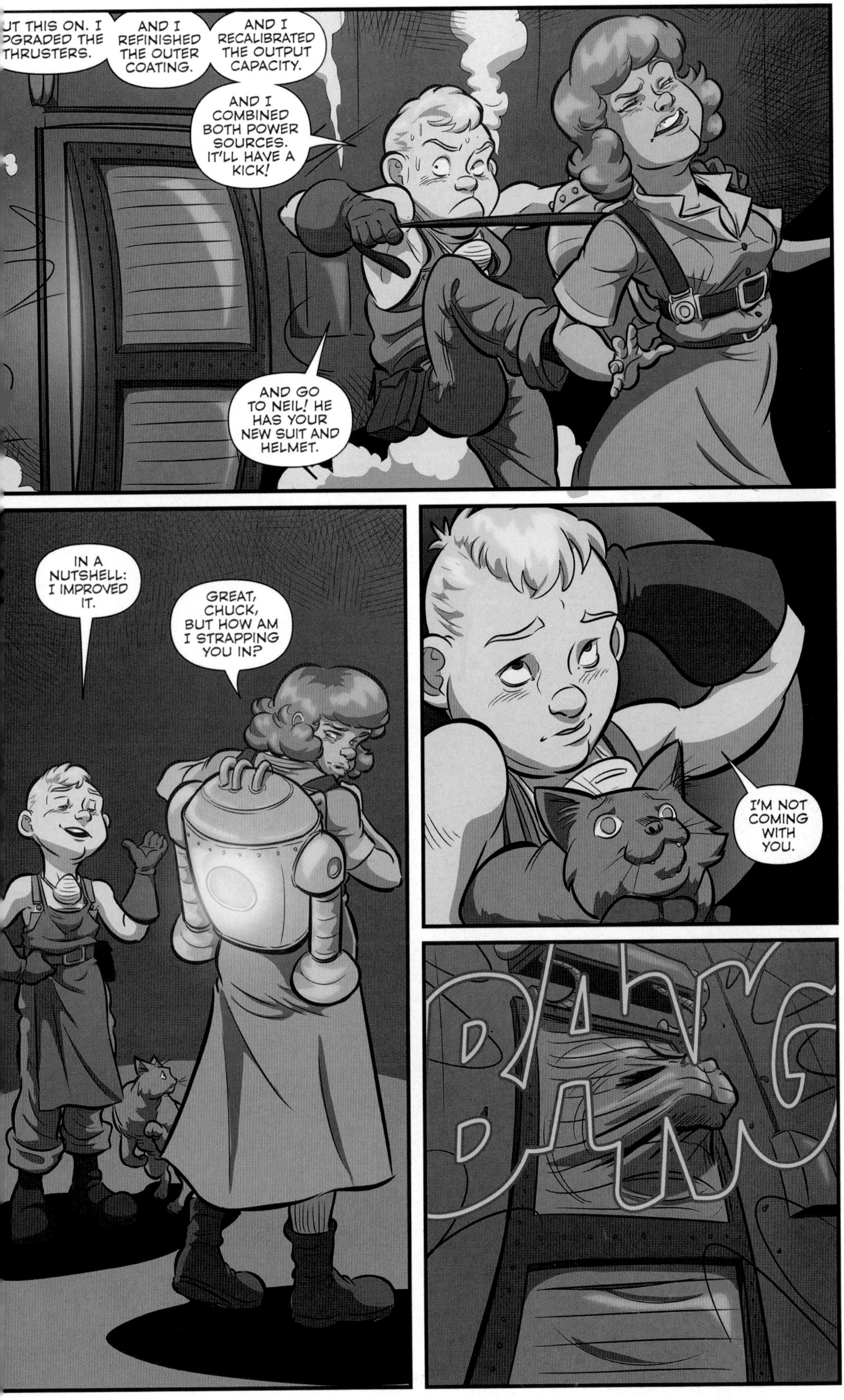
UT THIS ON. I PGRADED THE THRUSTERS.
AND I REFINISHED THE OUTER COATING.
AND I RECALIBRATED THE OUTPUT CAPACITY.
AND I COMBINED BOTH POWER SOURCES. IT'LL HAVE A KICK!
AND GO TO NEIL! HE HAS YOUR NEW SUIT AND HELMET.
IN A NUTSHELL: I IMPROVED IT.
GREAT, CHUCK, BUT HOW AM I STRAPPING YOU IN?
I'M NOT COMING WITH YOU.
BANG

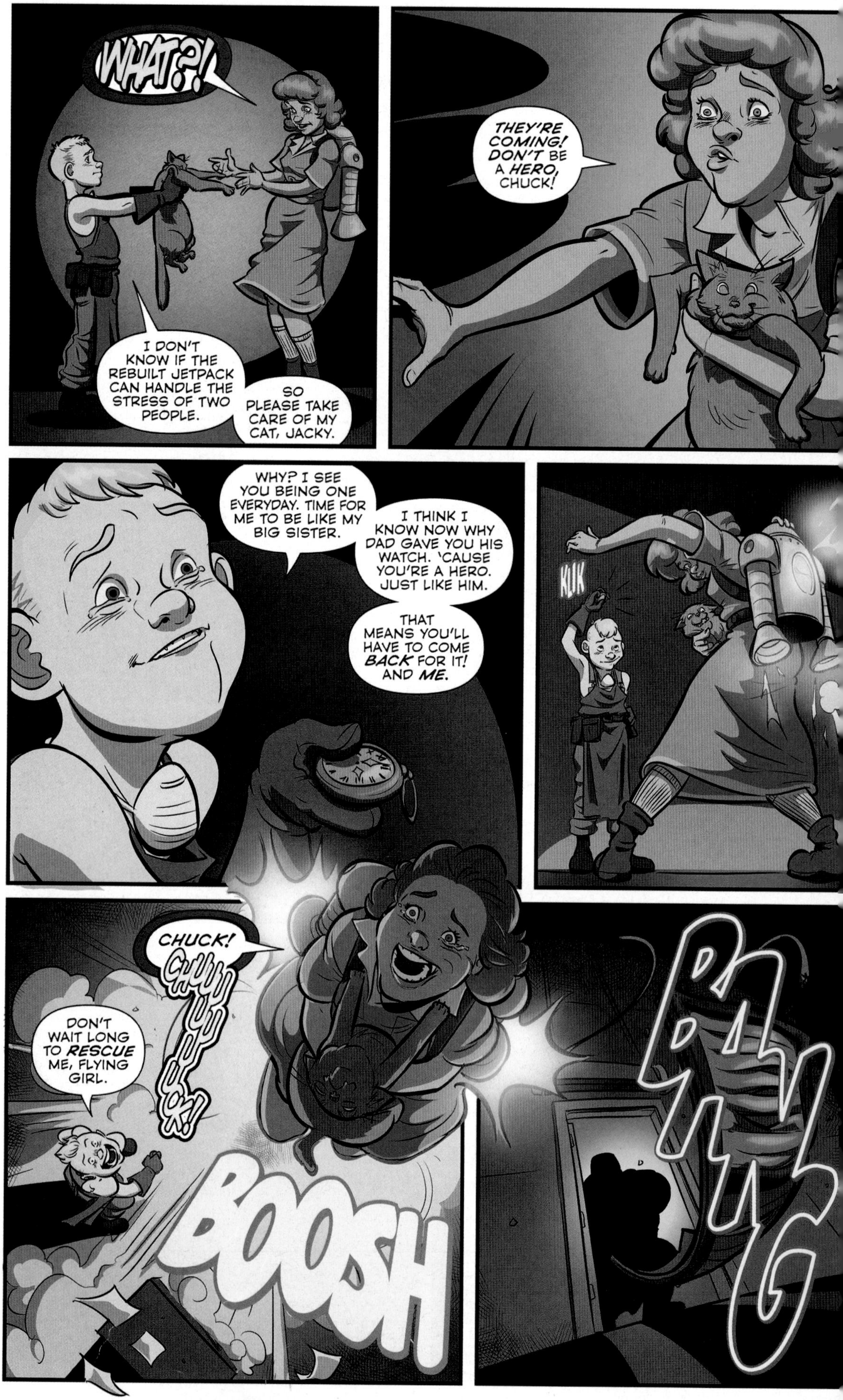
WHAT?!
I DON'T KNOW IF THE REBUILT JETPACK CAN HANDLE THE STRESS OF TWO PEOPLE.
SO PLEASE TAKE CARE OF MY CAT, JACKY.
THEY'RE COMING! DON'T BE A HERO, CHUCK!
WHY? I SEE YOU BEING ONE EVERYDAY. TIME FOR ME TO BE LIKE MY BIG SISTER.
I THINK I KNOW NOW WHY DAD GAVE YOU HIS WATCH. 'CAUSE YOU'RE A HERO. JUST LIKE HIM.
THAT MEANS YOU'LL HAVE TO COME BACK FOR IT! AND ME.
KLIK
CHUCK!
CHUUUUUCK!
DON'T WAIT LONG TO RESCUE ME, FLYING GIRL.
BOOSH
BLANG

SORRY, BOYS, FLYING GIRL TOURS ARE CLOSED FOR THE DAY. YOU MIGHT WANT TO TRY COMING BACK TOMORROW.

THOOM

WHERE DID YOUR SISTER GO, TWERP?

I DUNNO, BUT I KNOW YOU'LL NEVER CATCH HER. NOW, PUT ME DOWN BRUNO--I KNOW MY RIGHTS!

SLEEP, BOY.

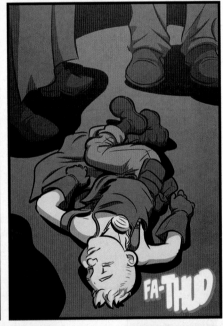

FA-THUD

WHAT'D YOU WANT US TO DO NOW, BOSS?

BURN IT DOWN.

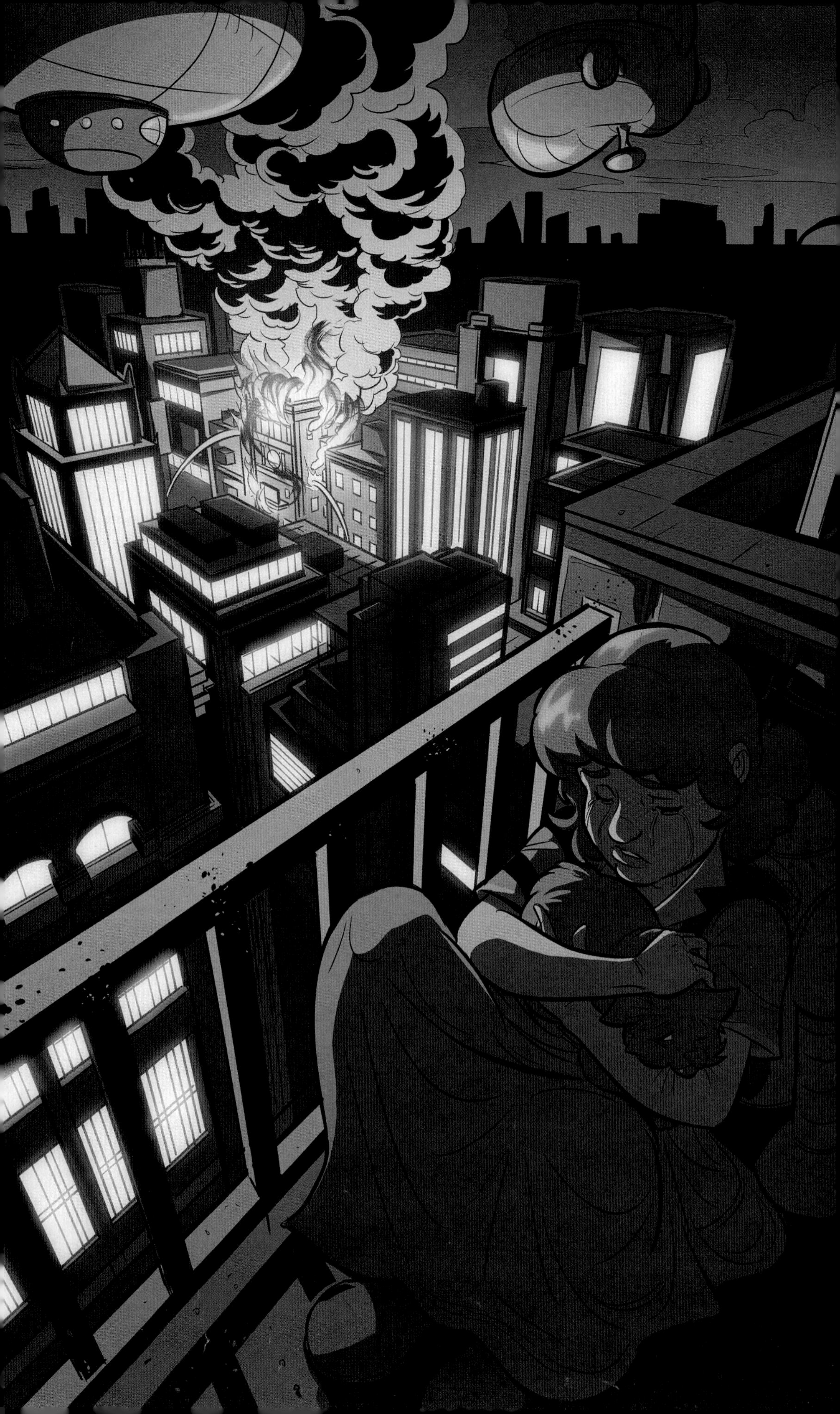

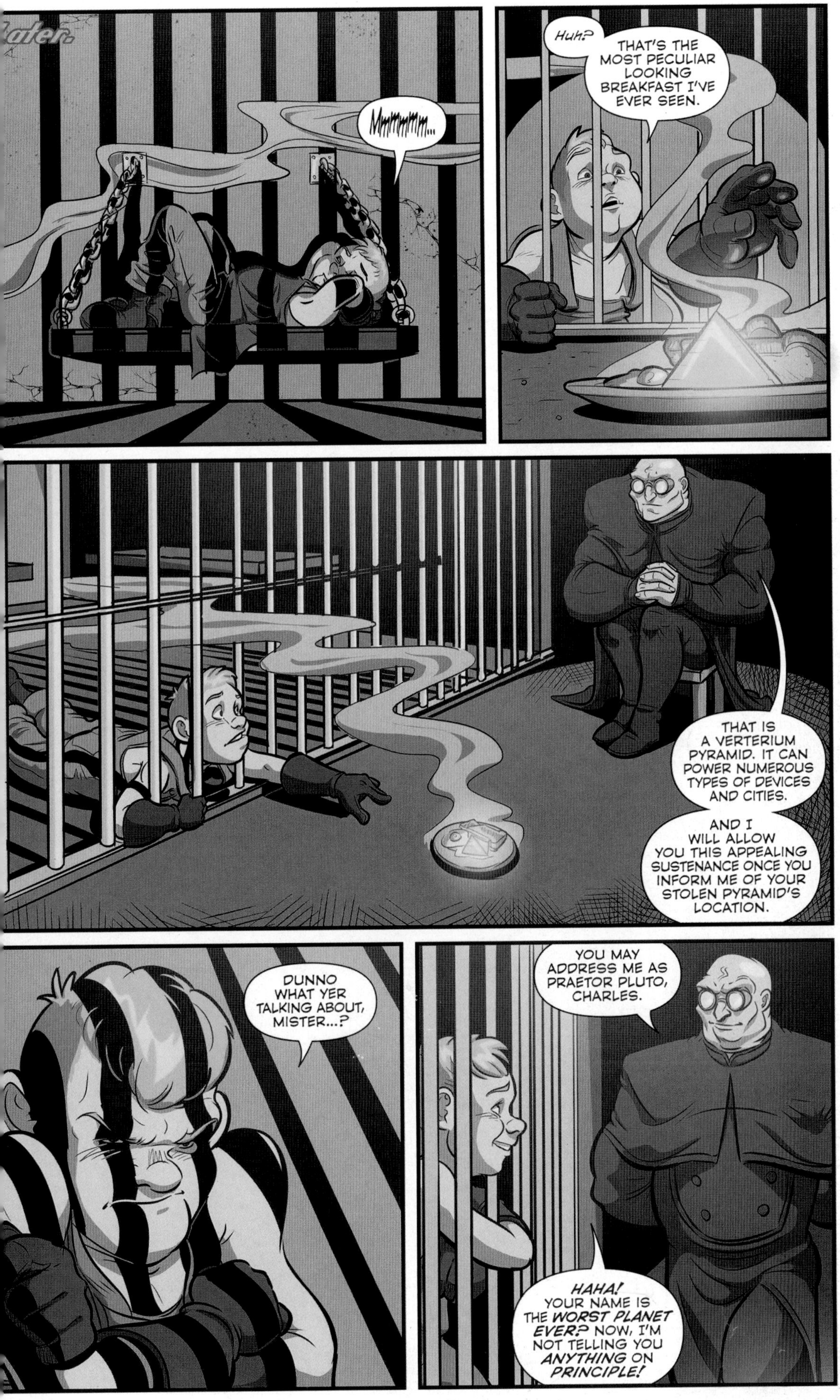
Later.
Mmmmmm...
Huh?
THAT'S THE MOST PECULIAR LOOKING BREAKFAST I'VE EVER SEEN.
THAT IS A VERTERIUM PYRAMID. IT CAN POWER NUMEROUS TYPES OF DEVICES AND CITIES.
AND I WILL ALLOW YOU THIS APPEALING SUSTENANCE ONCE YOU INFORM ME OF YOUR STOLEN PYRAMID'S LOCATION.
DUNNO WHAT YER TALKING ABOUT, MISTER...?
YOU MAY ADDRESS ME AS PRAETOR PLUTO, CHARLES.
HAHA! YOUR NAME IS THE WORST PLANET EVER? NOW, I'M NOT TELLING YOU ANYTHING ON PRINCIPLE!

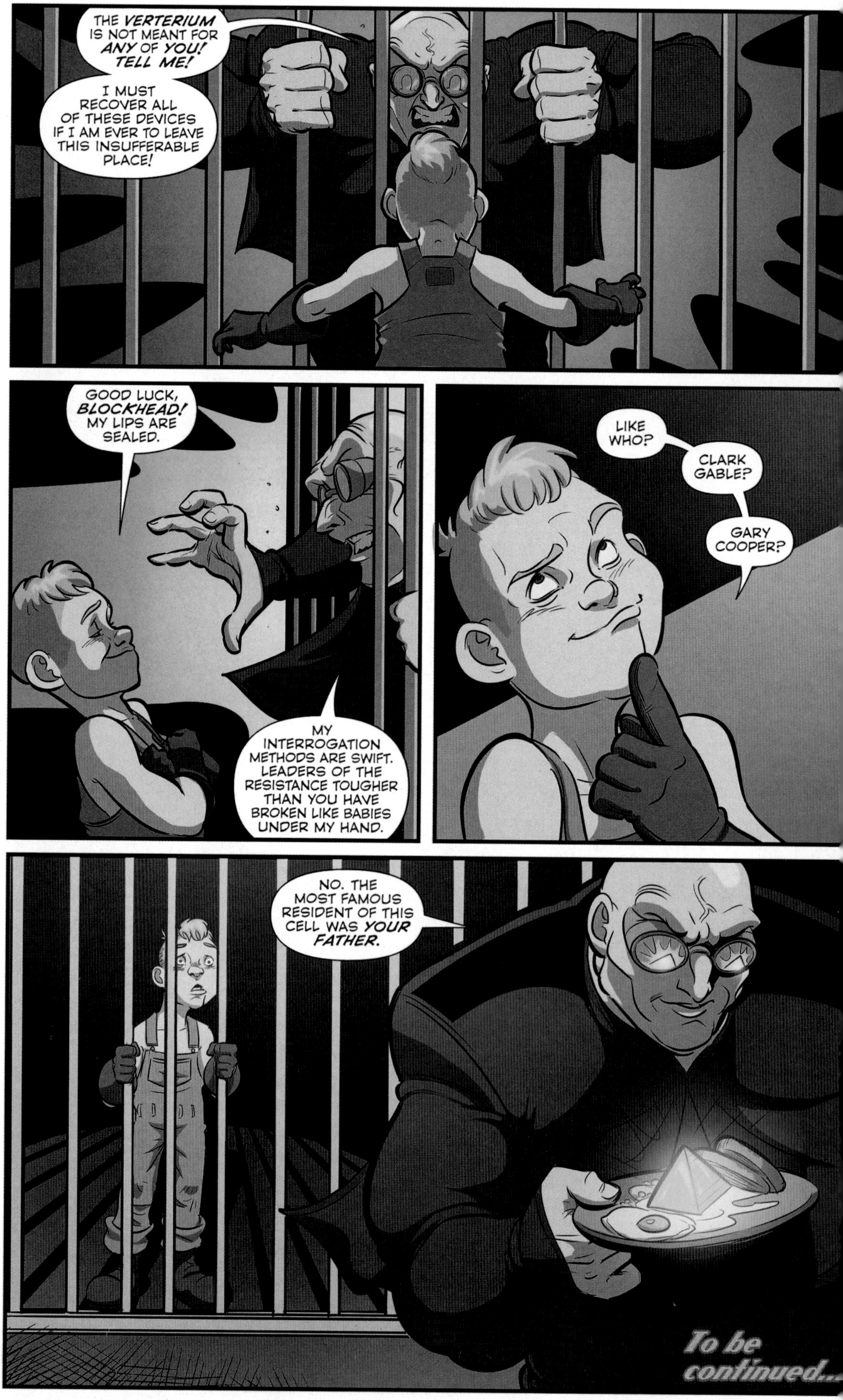
THE *VERTERIUM* IS NOT MEANT FOR *ANY* OF *YOU! TELL ME!*
I MUST RECOVER ALL OF THESE DEVICES IF I AM EVER TO LEAVE THIS INSUFFERABLE PLACE!
GOOD LUCK, *BLOCKHEAD!* MY LIPS ARE SEALED.
MY INTERROGATION METHODS ARE SWIFT. LEADERS OF THE RESISTANCE TOUGHER THAN YOU HAVE BROKEN LIKE BABIES UNDER MY HAND.
LIKE WHO?
CLARK GABLE?
GARY COOPER?
NO. THE MOST FAMOUS RESIDENT OF THIS CELL WAS *YOUR FATHER.*
To be continued...

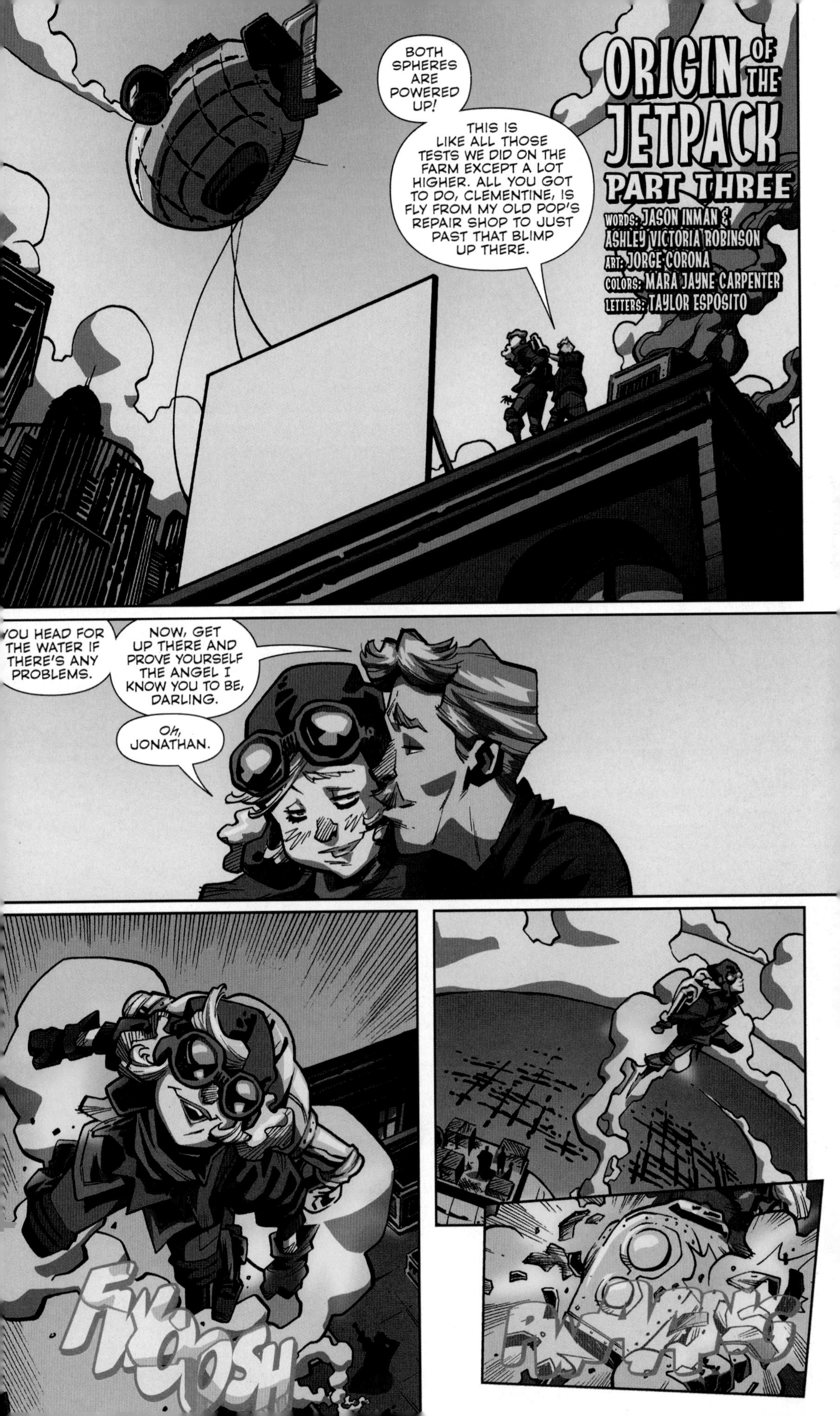
ORIGIN OF THE JETPACK
PART THREE
WORDS: JASON INMAN & ASHLEY VICTORIA ROBINSON
ART: JORGE CORONA
COLORS: MARA JAYNE CARPENTER
LETTERS: TAYLOR ESPOSITO
BOTH SPHERES ARE POWERED UP!
THIS IS LIKE ALL THOSE TESTS WE DID ON THE FARM EXCEPT A LOT HIGHER. ALL YOU GOT TO DO, CLEMENTINE, IS FLY FROM MY OLD POP'S REPAIR SHOP TO JUST PAST THAT BLIMP UP THERE.
YOU HEAD FOR THE WATER IF THERE'S ANY PROBLEMS.
NOW, GET UP THERE AND PROVE YOURSELF THE ANGEL I KNOW YOU TO BE, DARLING.
OH, JONATHAN.
FWOOSH

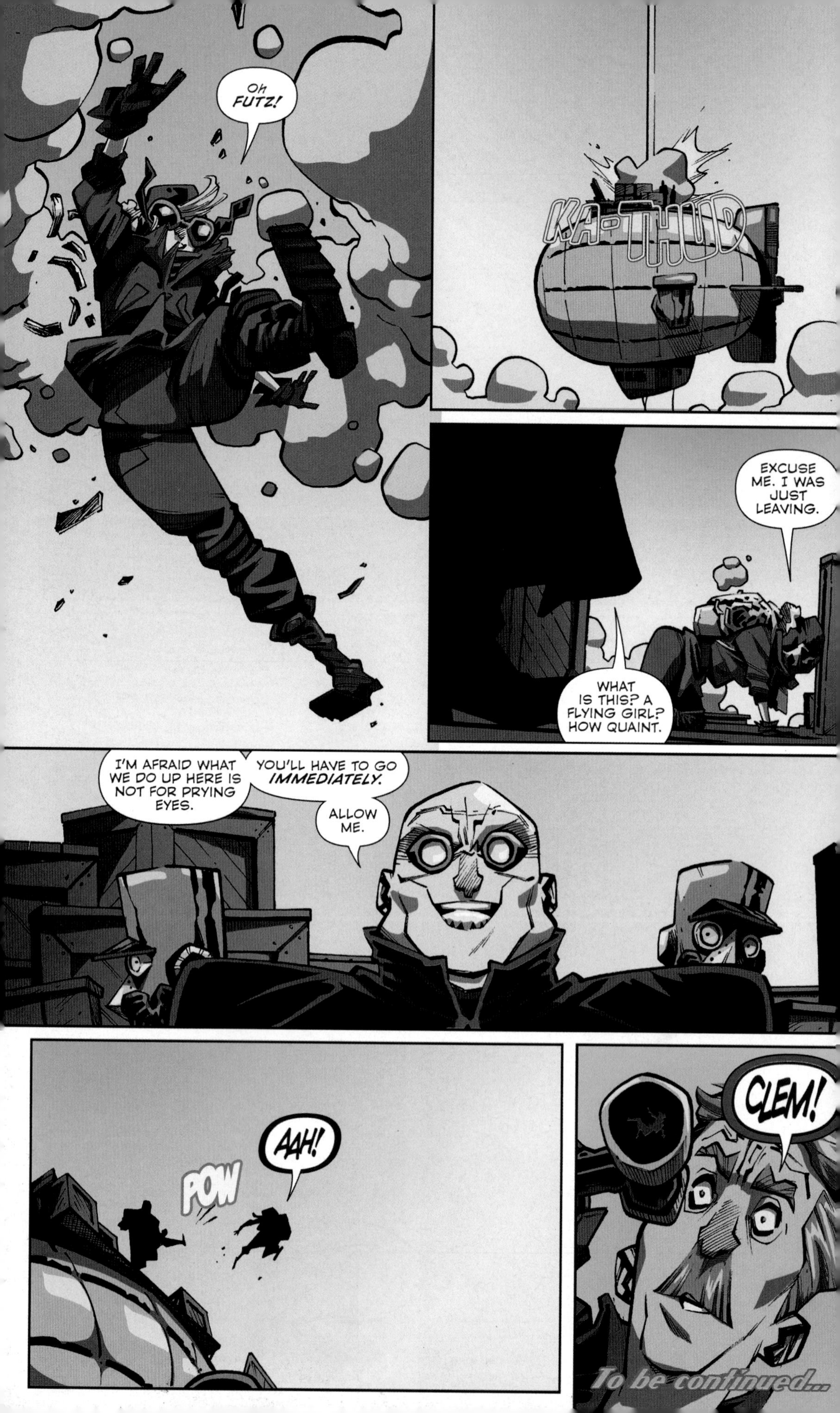

Oh FUTZ!
KA-THUD
EXCUSE ME. I WAS JUST LEAVING.
WHAT IS THIS? A FLYING GIRL? HOW QUAINT.
I'M AFRAID WHAT WE DO UP HERE IS NOT FOR PRYING EYES.
YOU'LL HAVE TO GO IMMEDIATELY.
ALLOW ME.
POW
AAH!
CLEM!
To be continued...

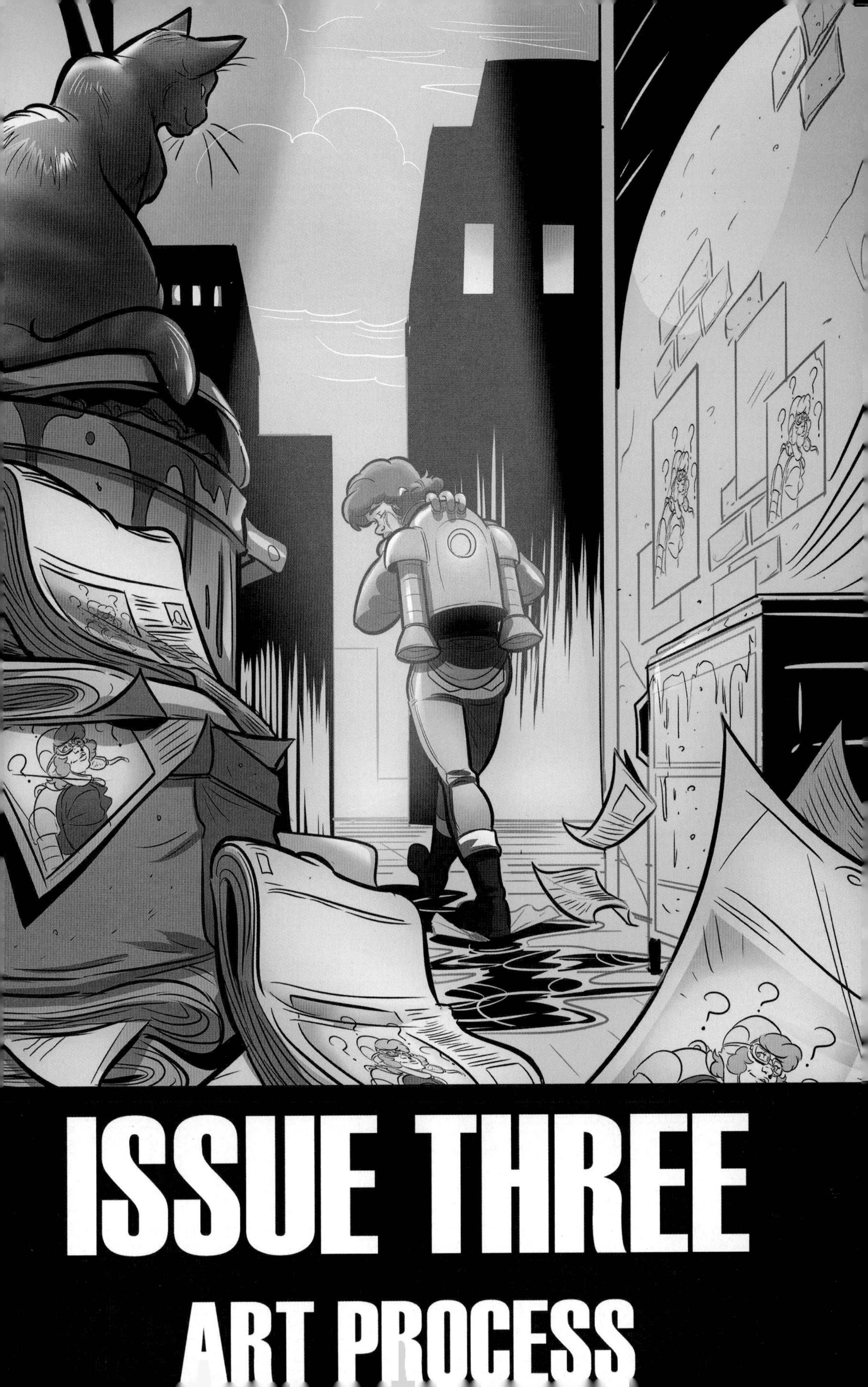

ISSUE THREE
ART PROCESS

ISSUE THREE THUMBNAILS BY BEN MATSUYA

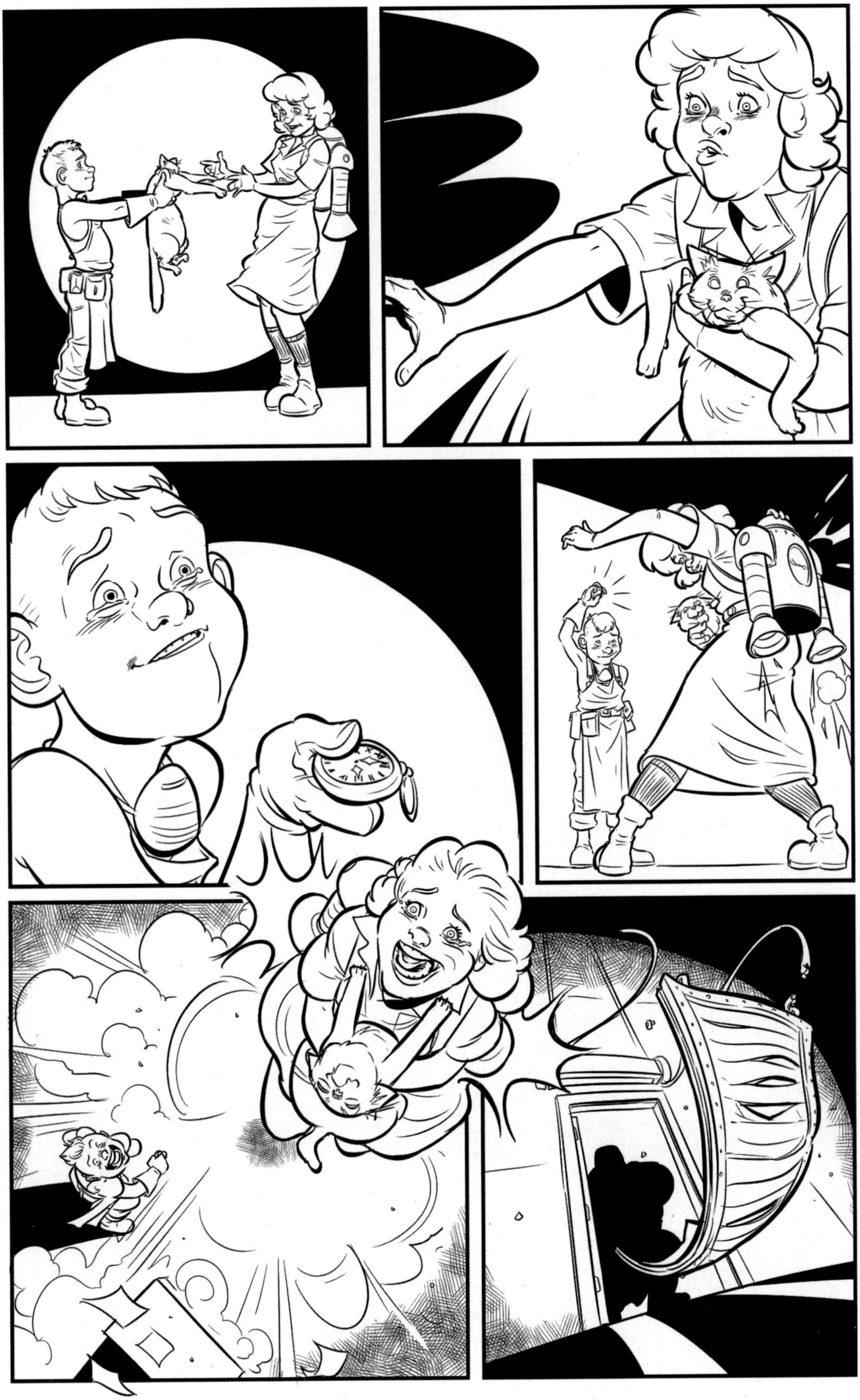

ISSUE 3 PAGE 16 PENCILS & INKS BY BEN MATSUYA

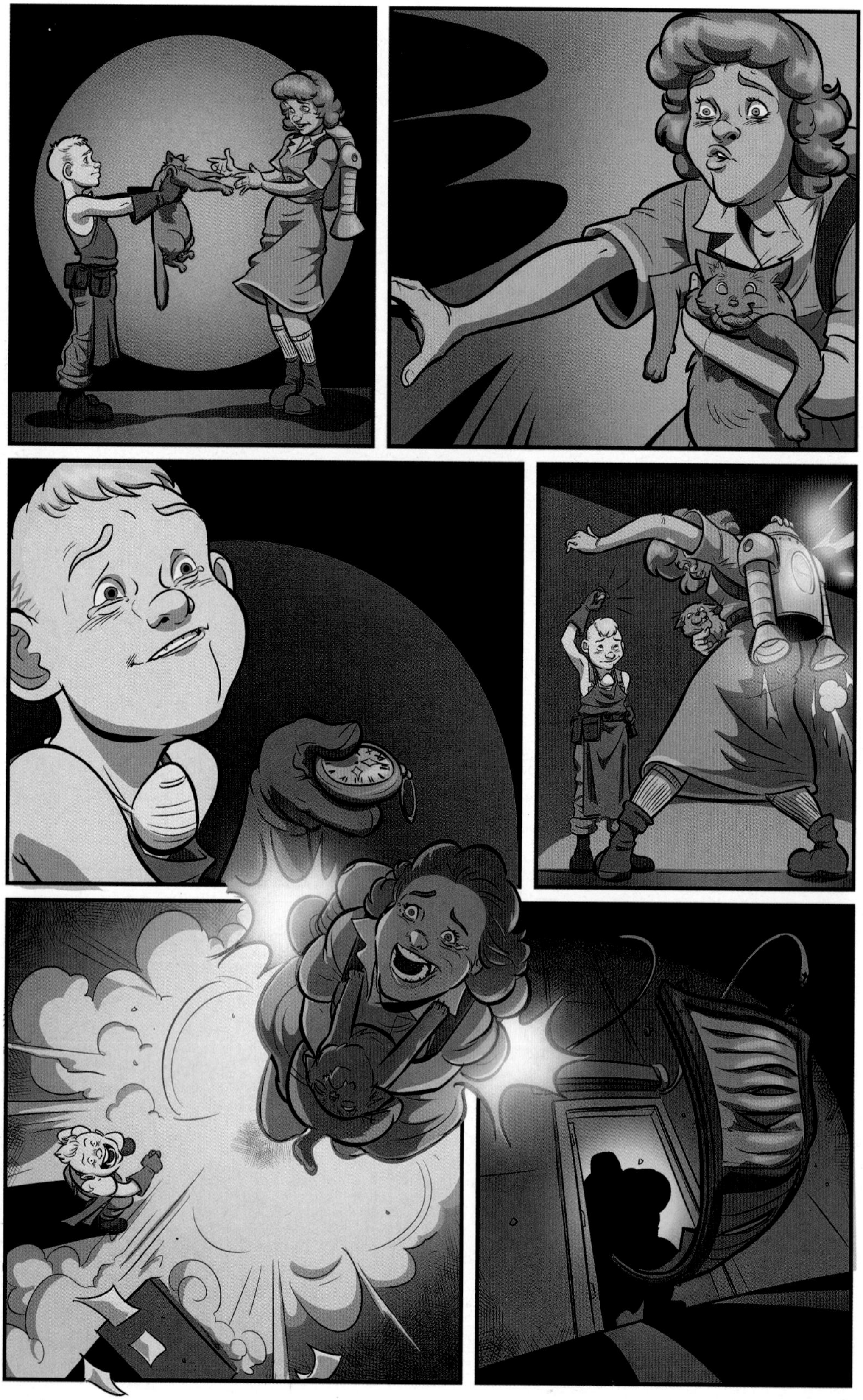

ISSUE 3 PAGE 16 COLORS BY MARA JAYNE CARPENTER

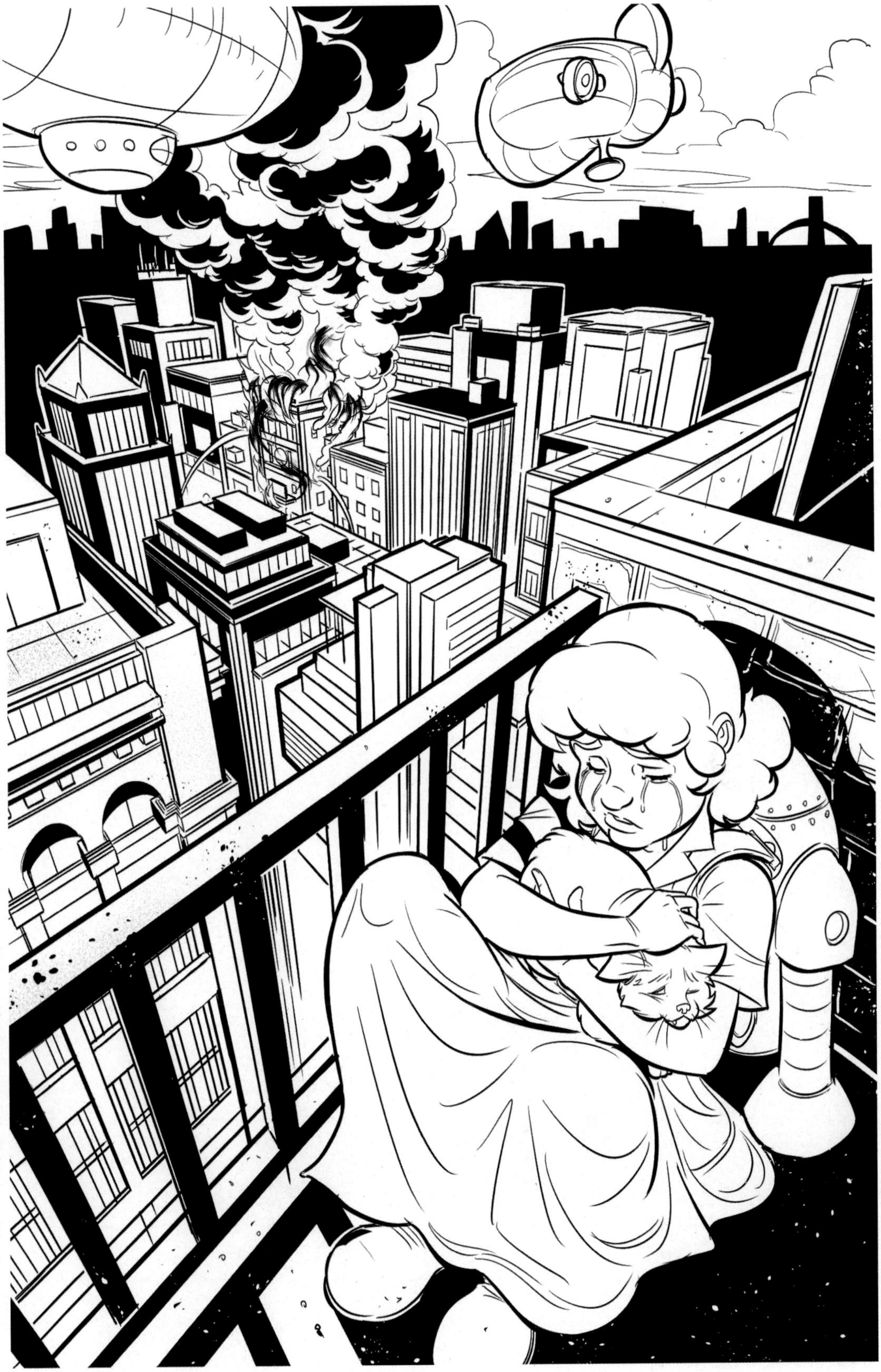

ISSUE 3 PAGE 18 PENCILS & INKS BY BEN MATSUYA

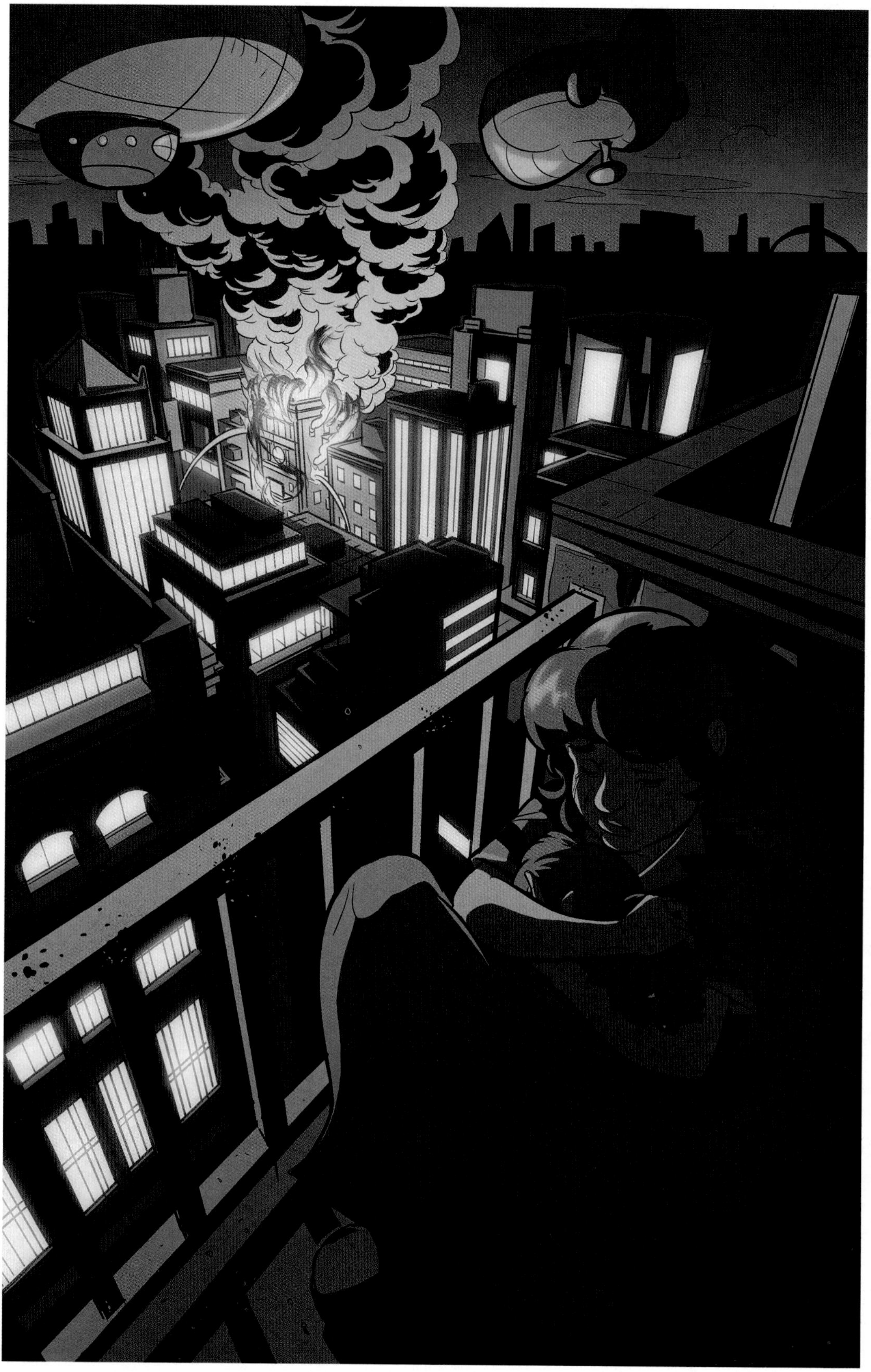

ISSUE 3 PAGE 18 COLORS BY MARA JAYNE CARPENTER

FOR EVERY ISSUE OF JUPITER JET ARTIST BEN MATSUYA CREATES MANY THUMBNAILS FOR POSSIBLE COVERS.

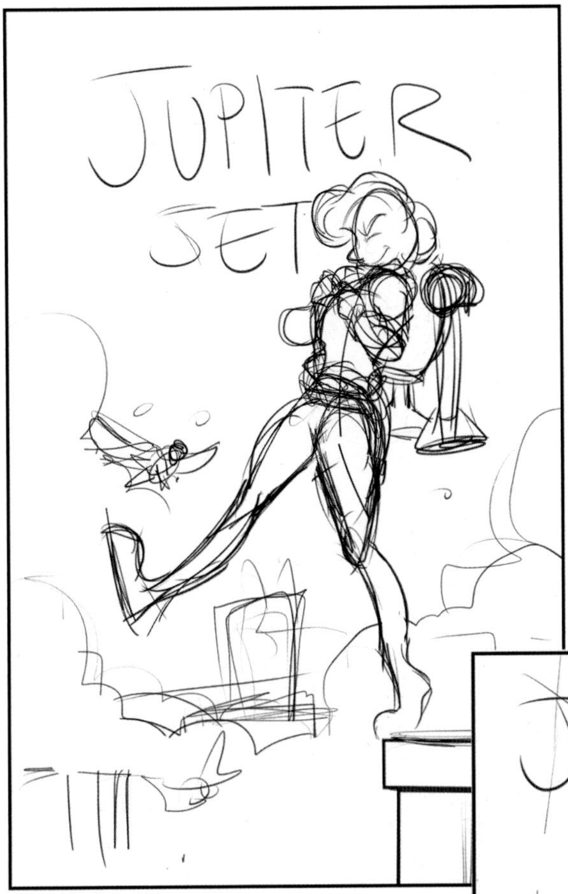
JUPITER
JET

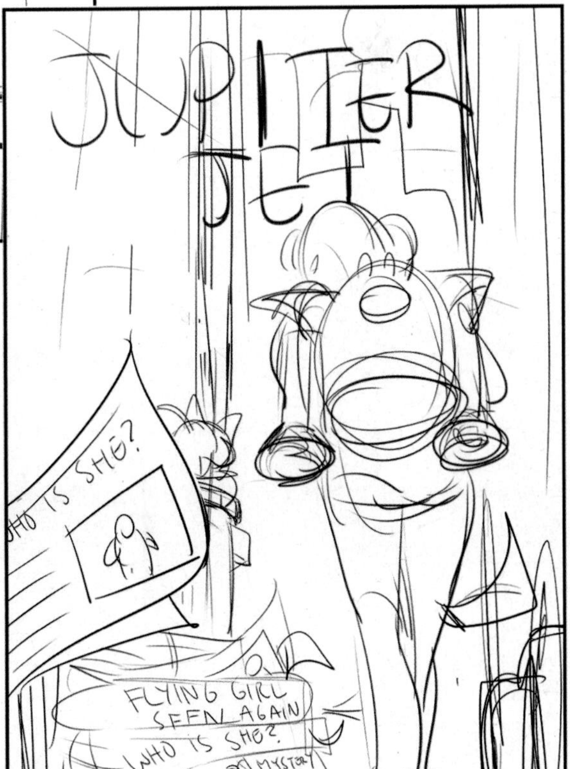
JUPITER
JET
HO IS SHE?
FLYING GIRL
SEEN AGAIN
WHO IS SHE?
MYSTERY
GIRL
SPOTTED.

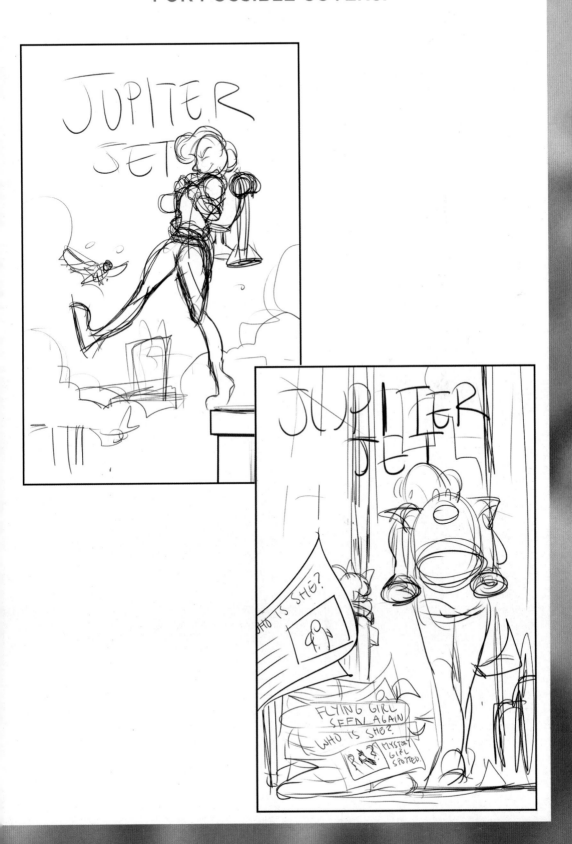

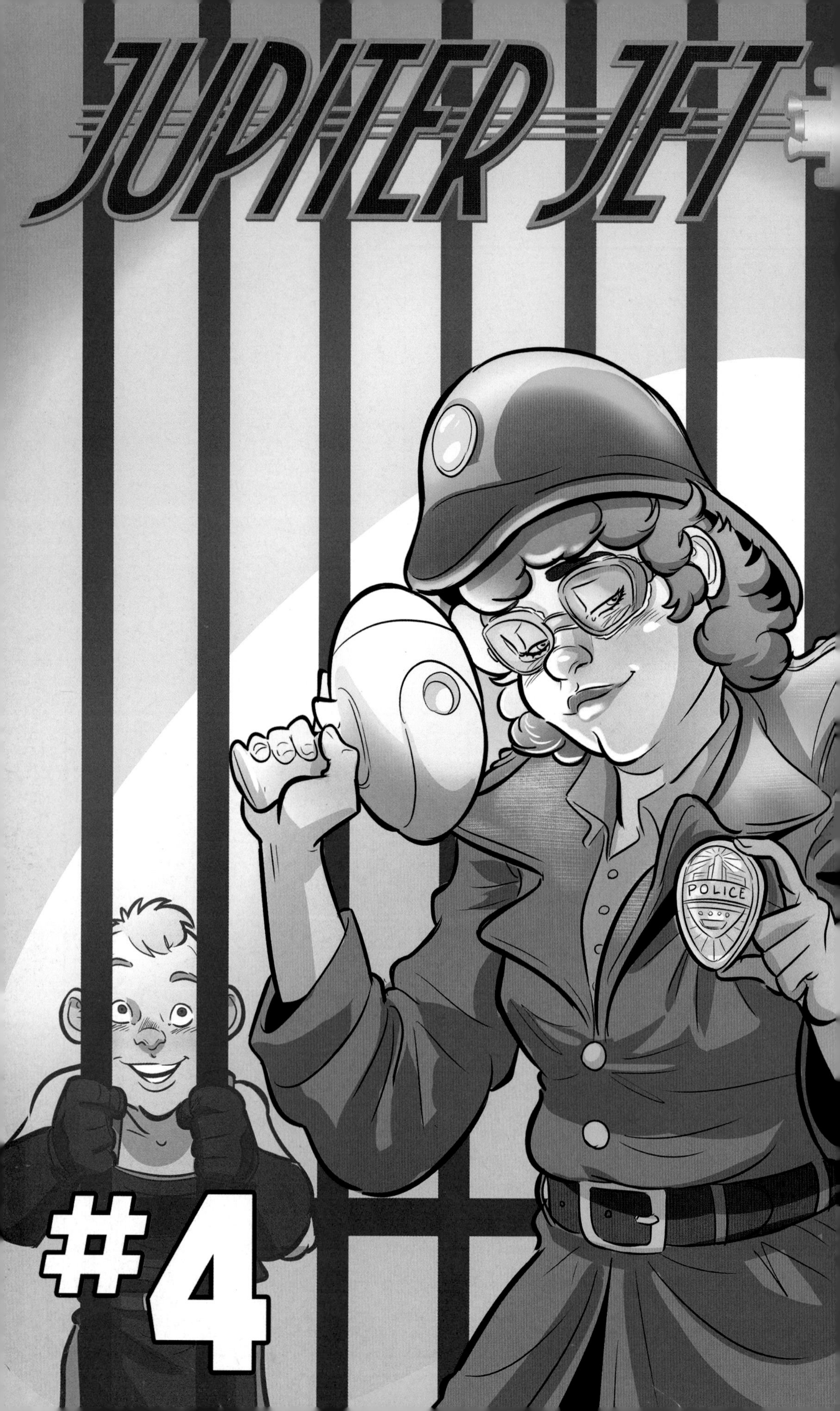

JUPITER JET
POLICE
#4

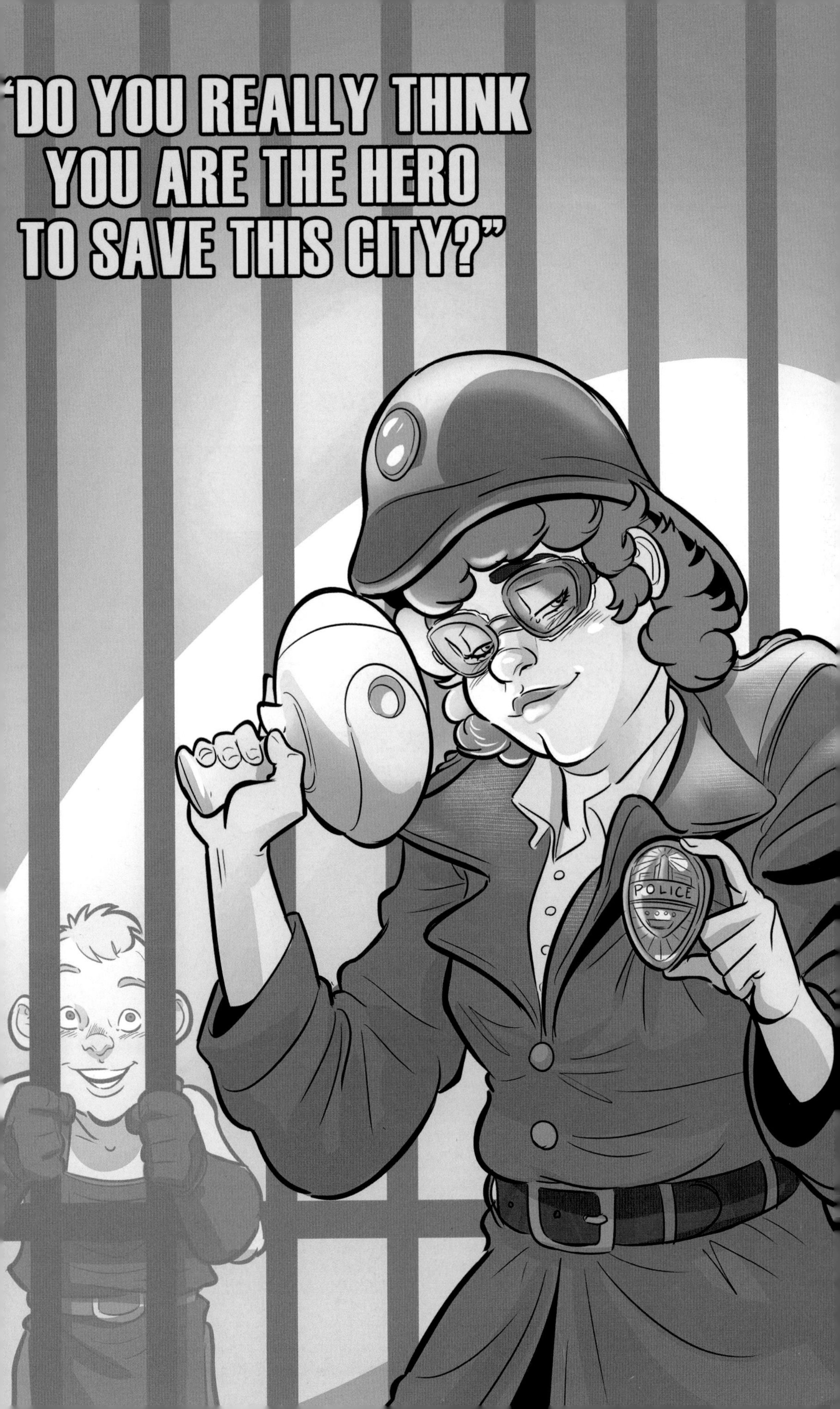
"DO YOU REALLY THINK YOU ARE THE HERO TO SAVE THIS CITY?"
POLICE

WRITTEN BY:
**JASON INMAN &
ASHLEY VICTORIA ROBINSON**

LINEART BY:
BEN MATSUYA

COLORS BY:
MARA JAYNE CARPENTER

COLOR FLATS BY:
TORI RIDLEY

LETTERS BY:
TAYLOR ESPOSITO OF GHOST GLYPH STUDIOS

COVER ARTIST:
BEN MATSUYA

**PUBLISHER/ CEO: BRYAN SEATON • EDITOR IN CHIEF: SHAWN GABBORIN
PUBLISHER-DANGER ZONE: JASON MARTIN • MARKETING DIRECTOR/EDITOR: NICOLE D'ANDRIA
EXECUTIVE ADMINISTRATOR: DANIELLE DAVISON • TEST PILOT: CHAD CICCONI
PRESIDENT OF CREATOR RELATIONS: SHAWN PRYOR**

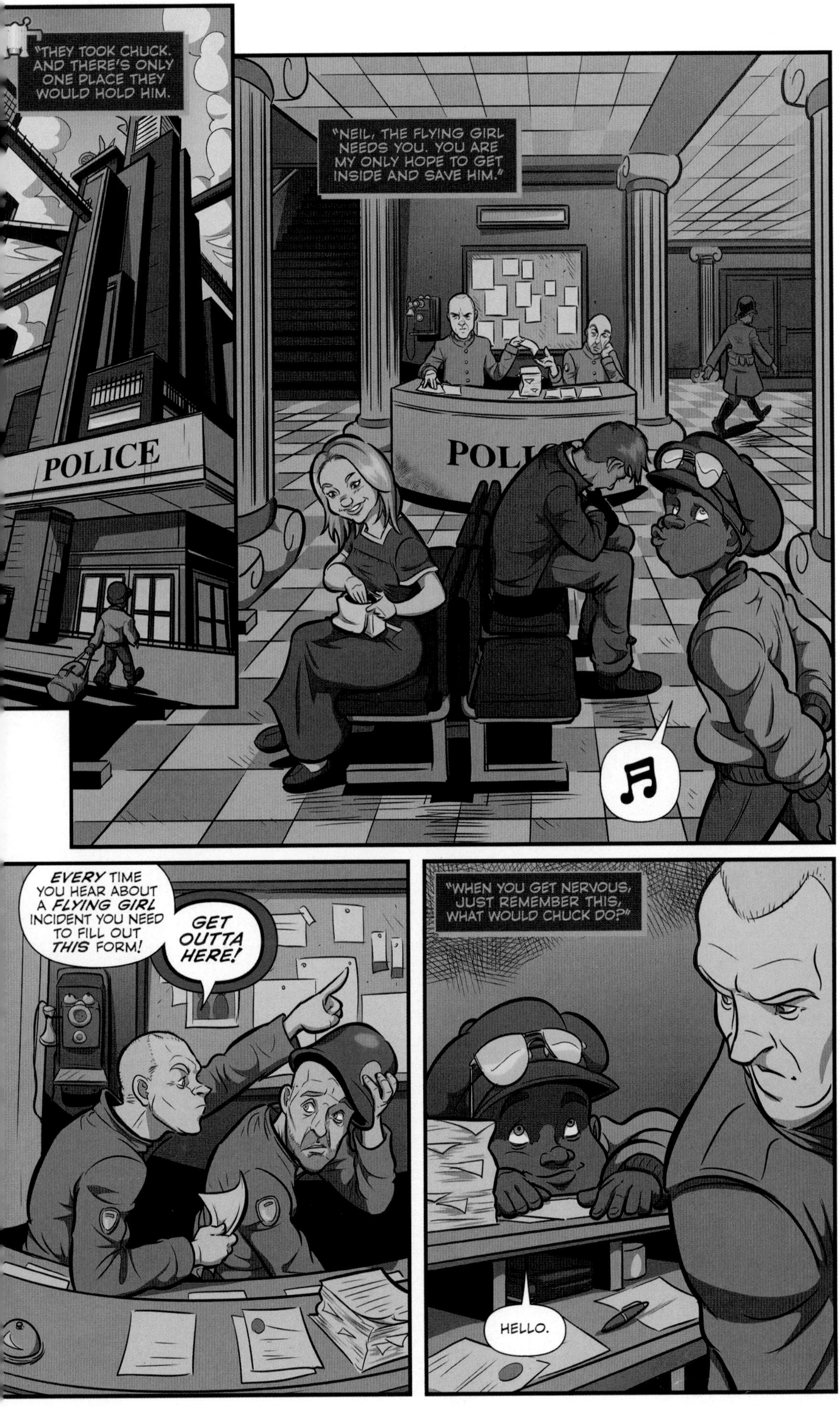
"THEY TOOK CHUCK. AND THERE'S ONLY ONE PLACE THEY WOULD HOLD HIM.
POLICE
"NEIL, THE FLYING GIRL NEEDS YOU. YOU ARE MY ONLY HOPE TO GET INSIDE AND SAVE HIM."
POLICE
♬
EVERY TIME YOU HEAR ABOUT A FLYING GIRL INCIDENT YOU NEED TO FILL OUT THIS FORM!
GET OUTTA HERE!
"WHEN YOU GET NERVOUS, JUST REMEMBER THIS, WHAT WOULD CHUCK DO?"
HELLO.

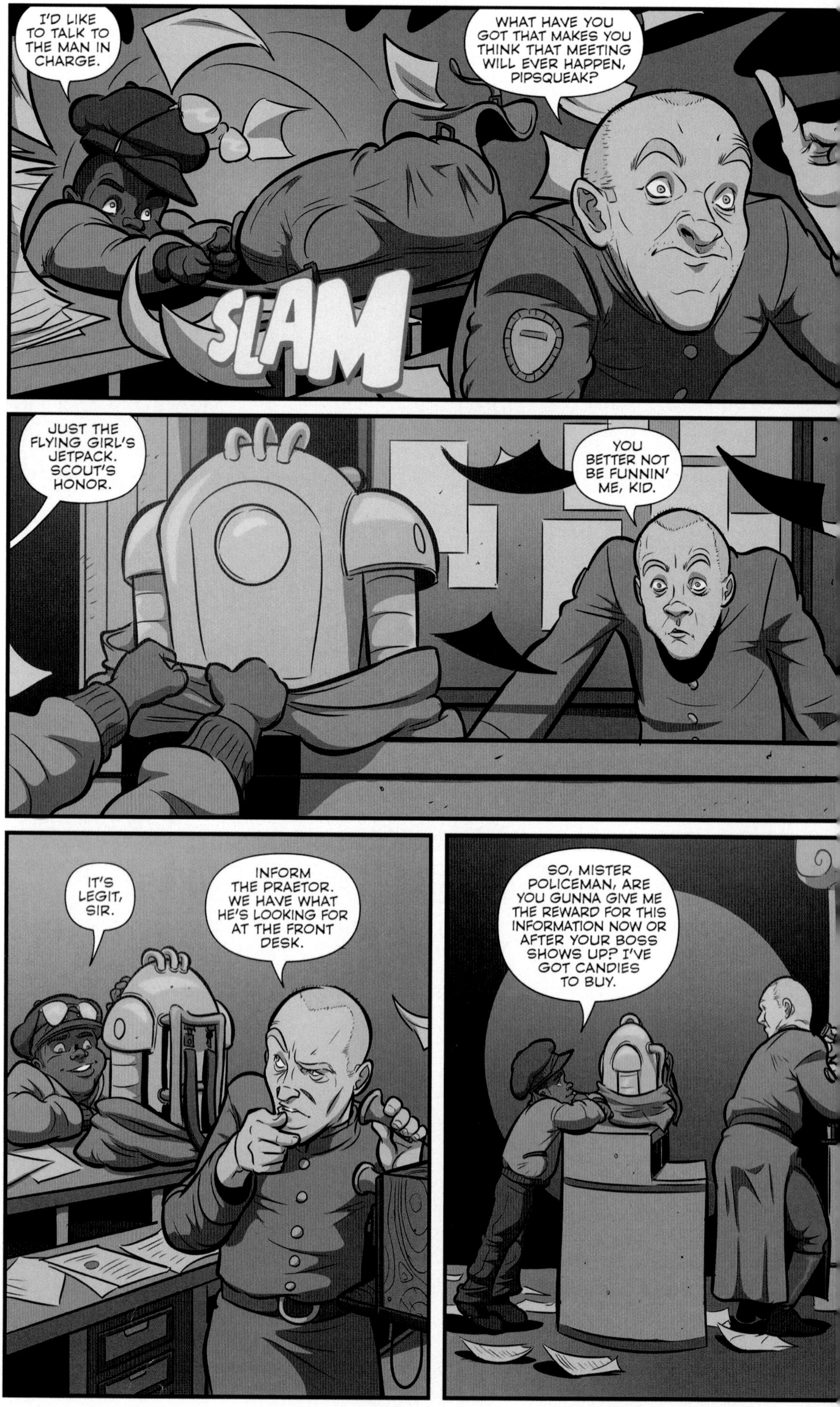
I'D LIKE TO TALK TO THE MAN IN CHARGE.
WHAT HAVE YOU GOT THAT MAKES YOU THINK THAT MEETING WILL EVER HAPPEN, PIPSQUEAK?
SLAM
JUST THE FLYING GIRL'S JETPACK. SCOUT'S HONOR.
YOU BETTER NOT BE FUNNIN' ME, KID.
IT'S LEGIT, SIR.
INFORM THE PRAETOR. WE HAVE WHAT HE'S LOOKING FOR AT THE FRONT DESK.
SO, MISTER POLICEMAN, ARE YOU GUNNA GIVE ME THE REWARD FOR THIS INFORMATION NOW OR AFTER YOUR BOSS SHOWS UP? I'VE GOT CANDIES TO BUY.

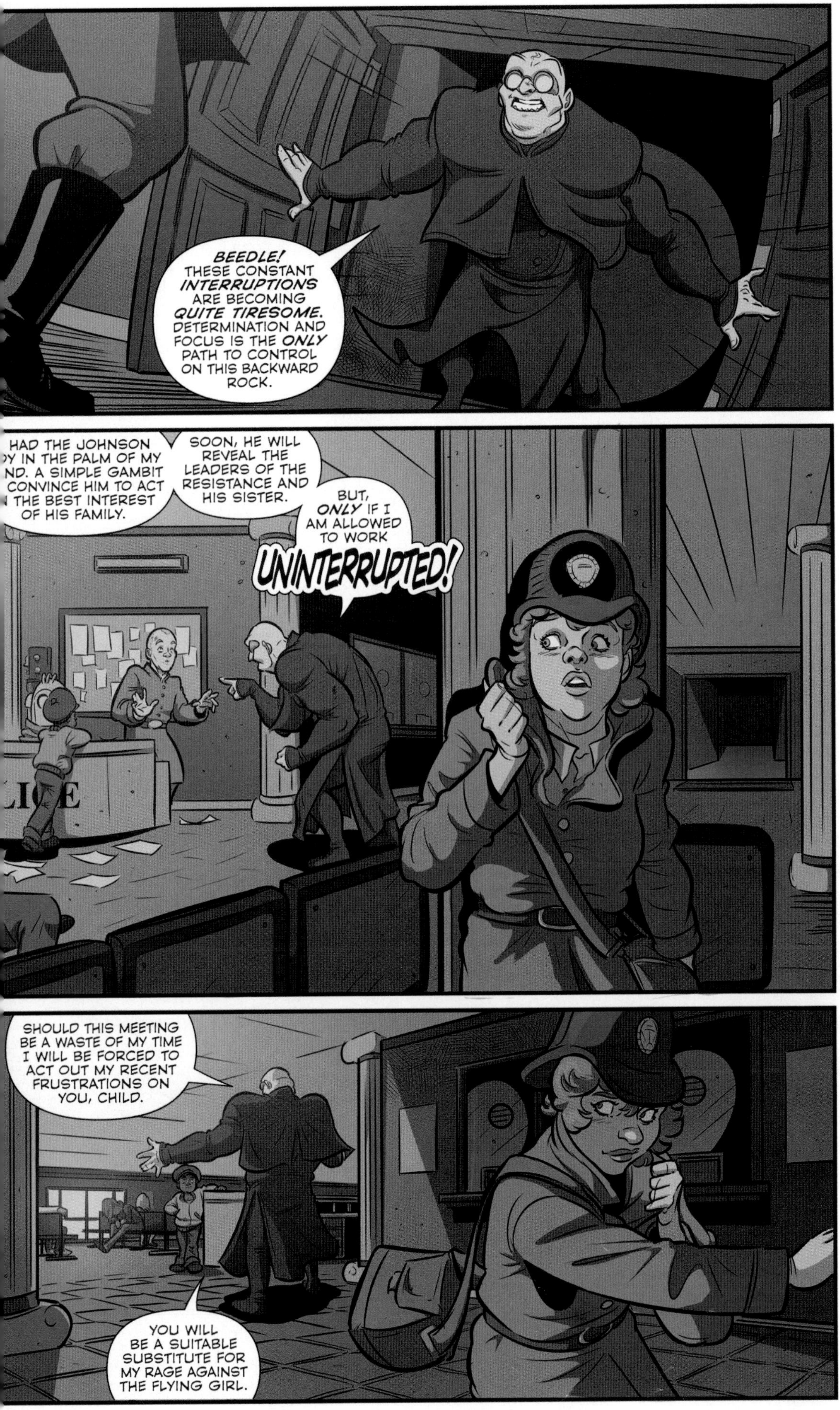
BEEDLE! THESE CONSTANT INTERRUPTIONS ARE BECOMING QUITE TIRESOME. DETERMINATION AND FOCUS IS THE ONLY PATH TO CONTROL ON THIS BACKWARD ROCK.
HAD THE JOHNSON DY IN THE PALM OF MY ND. A SIMPLE GAMBIT CONVINCE HIM TO ACT THE BEST INTEREST OF HIS FAMILY.
SOON, HE WILL REVEAL THE LEADERS OF THE RESISTANCE AND HIS SISTER.
BUT, ONLY IF I AM ALLOWED TO WORK
UNINTERRUPTED!
SHOULD THIS MEETING BE A WASTE OF MY TIME I WILL BE FORCED TO ACT OUT MY RECENT FRUSTRATIONS ON YOU, CHILD.
YOU WILL BE A SUITABLE SUBSTITUTE FOR MY RAGE AGAINST THE FLYING GIRL.

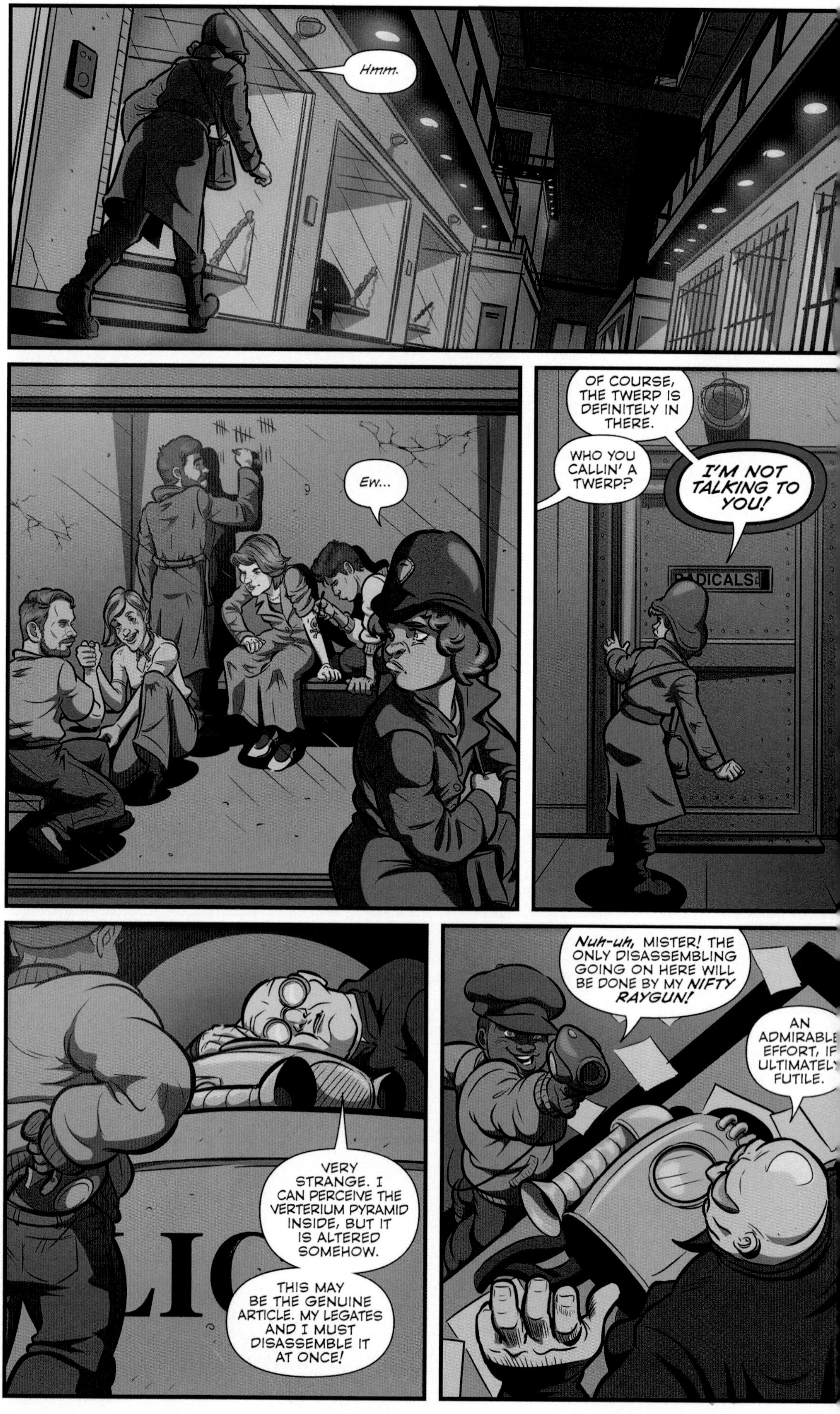

Hmm.
Ew...
OF COURSE, THE TWERP IS DEFINITELY IN THERE.
WHO YOU CALLIN' A TWERP?
I'M NOT TALKING TO YOU!
RADICALS
VERY STRANGE. I CAN PERCEIVE THE VERTERIUM PYRAMID INSIDE, BUT IT IS ALTERED SOMEHOW.
THIS MAY BE THE GENUINE ARTICLE. MY LEGATES AND I MUST DISASSEMBLE IT AT ONCE!
Nuh-uh, MISTER! THE ONLY DISASSEMBLING GOING ON HERE WILL BE DONE BY MY NIFTY RAYGUN!
AN ADMIRABLE EFFORT, IF ULTIMATELY FUTILE.

CHAPTER 4

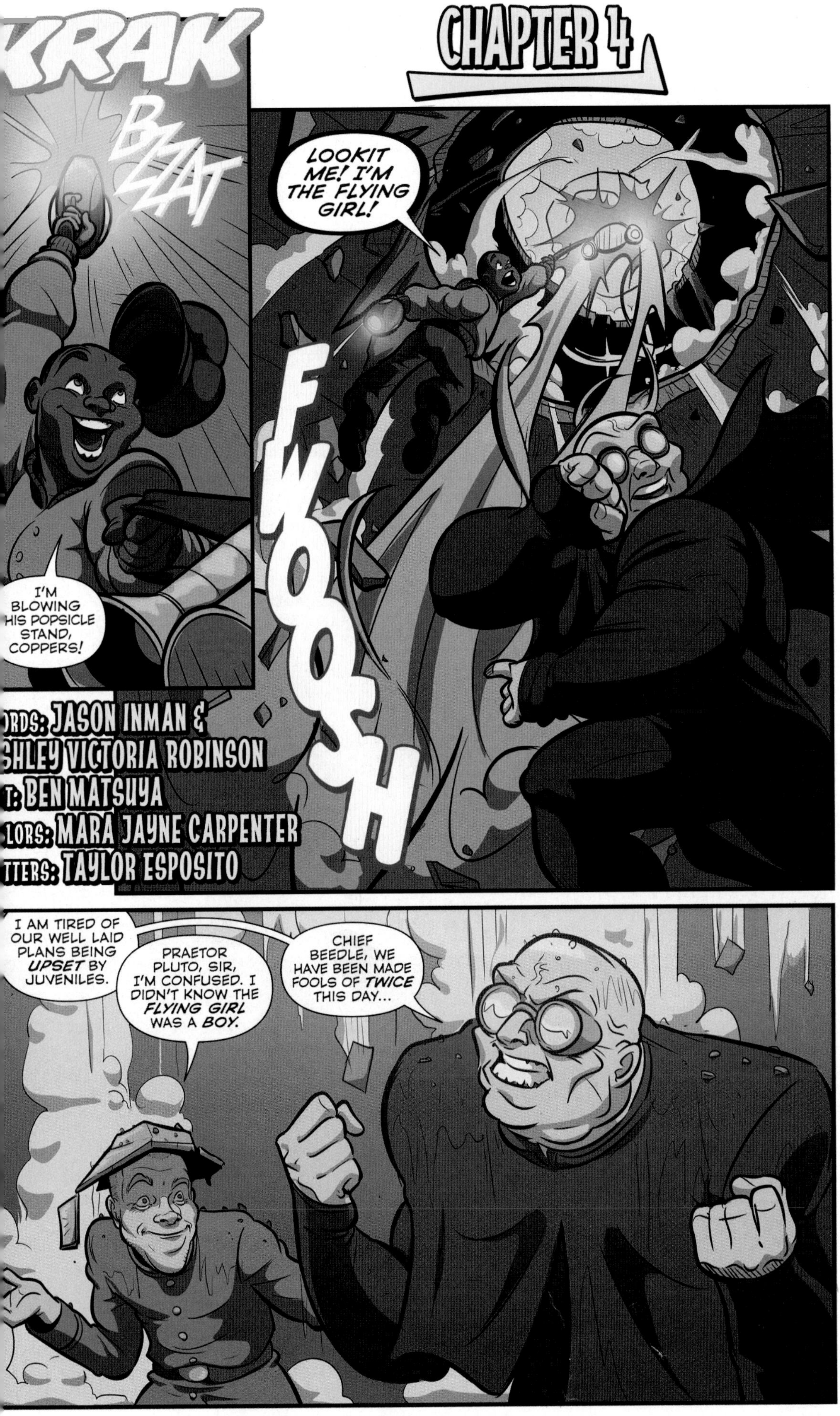
KRAK
BZZAT
I'M BLOWING HIS POPSICLE STAND, COPPERS!
LOOKIT ME! I'M THE FLYING GIRL!
FWOOSH
ORDS: JASON INMAN &
SHLEY VICTORIA ROBINSON
T: BEN MATSUYA
LORS: MARA JAYNE CARPENTER
TTERS: TAYLOR ESPOSITO
CHIEF BEEDLE, WE HAVE BEEN MADE FOOLS OF *TWICE* THIS DAY...
I AM TIRED OF OUR WELL LAID PLANS BEING *UPSET* BY JUVENILES.
PRAETOR PLUTO, SIR, I'M CONFUSED. I DIDN'T KNOW THE *FLYING GIRL* WAS A *BOY*.

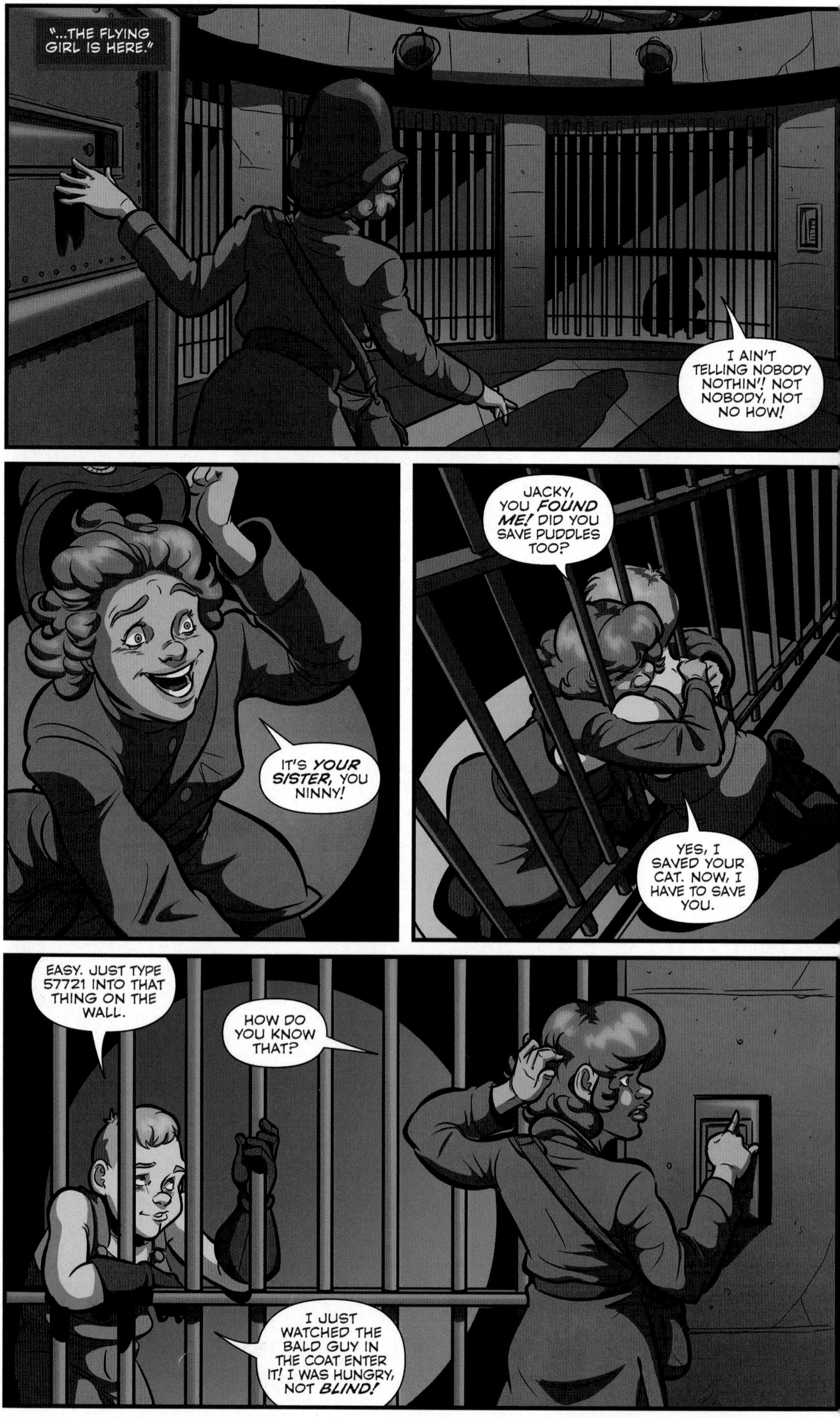
"...THE FLYING GIRL IS HERE."
I AIN'T TELLING NOBODY NOTHIN'! NOT NOBODY, NOT NO HOW!
IT'S YOUR SISTER, YOU NINNY!
JACKY, YOU FOUND ME! DID YOU SAVE PUDDLES TOO?
YES, I SAVED YOUR CAT. NOW, I HAVE TO SAVE YOU.
EASY. JUST TYPE 57721 INTO THAT THING ON THE WALL.
HOW DO YOU KNOW THAT?
I JUST WATCHED THE BALD GUY IN THE COAT ENTER IT! I WAS HUNGRY, NOT BLIND!

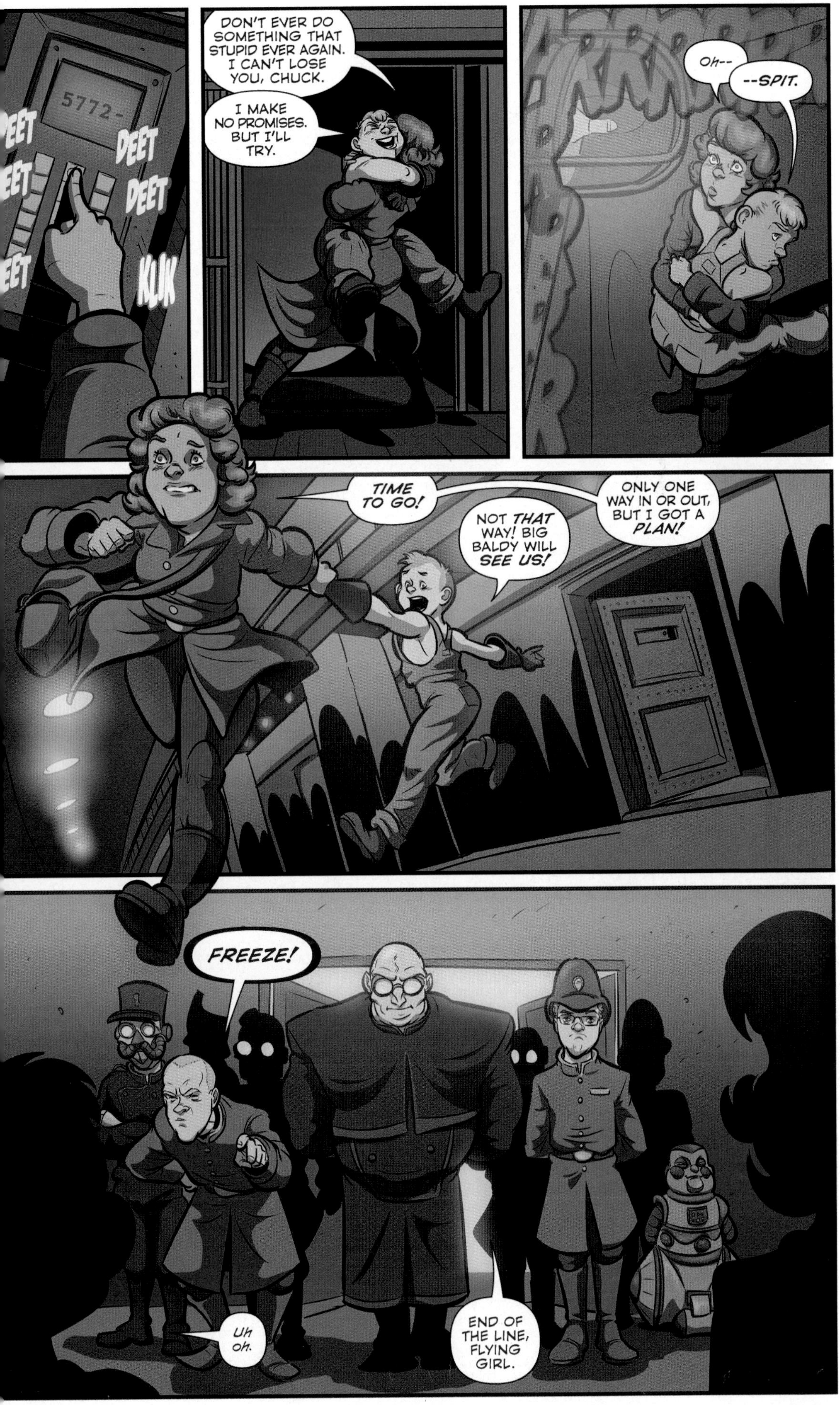
5772-
DEET
DEET
DEET
DEET
DEET
KLIK
DON'T EVER DO SOMETHING THAT STUPID EVER AGAIN. I CAN'T LOSE YOU, CHUCK.
I MAKE NO PROMISES. BUT I'LL TRY.
Oh--
--SPIT.
TIME TO GO!
ONLY ONE WAY IN OR OUT, BUT I GOT A PLAN!
NOT THAT WAY! BIG BALDY WILL SEE US!
FREEZE!
Uh oh.
END OF THE LINE, FLYING GIRL.

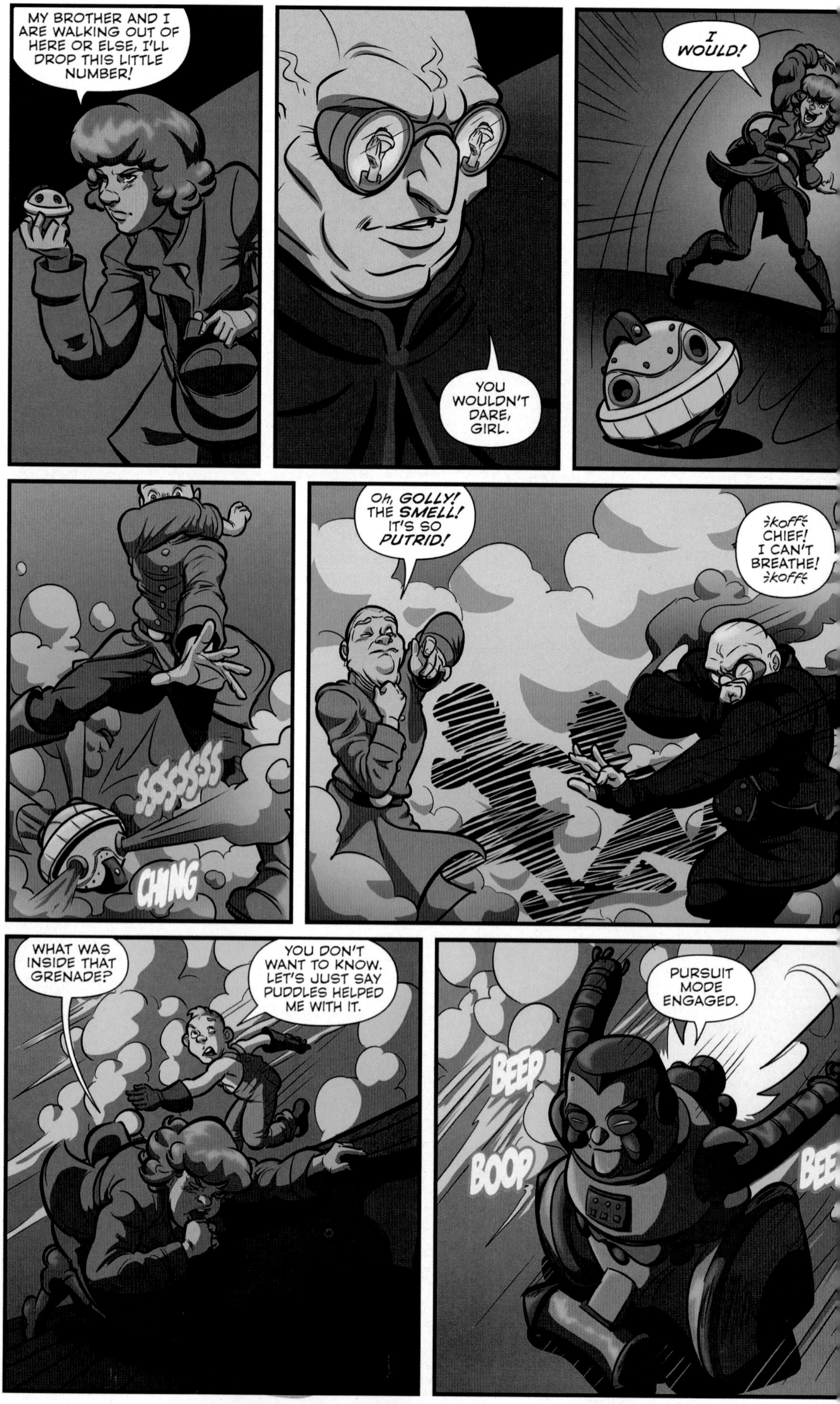
MY BROTHER AND I ARE WALKING OUT OF HERE OR ELSE, I'LL DROP THIS LITTLE NUMBER!
YOU WOULDN'T DARE, GIRL.
I WOULD!
SSSSSSSS
CHING
Oh, GOLLY! THE SMELL! IT'S SO PUTRID!
koff CHIEF! I CAN'T BREATHE! *koff*
WHAT WAS INSIDE THAT GRENADE?
YOU DON'T WANT TO KNOW. LET'S JUST SAY PUDDLES HELPED ME WITH IT.
PURSUIT MODE ENGAGED.
BEEP
BOOP

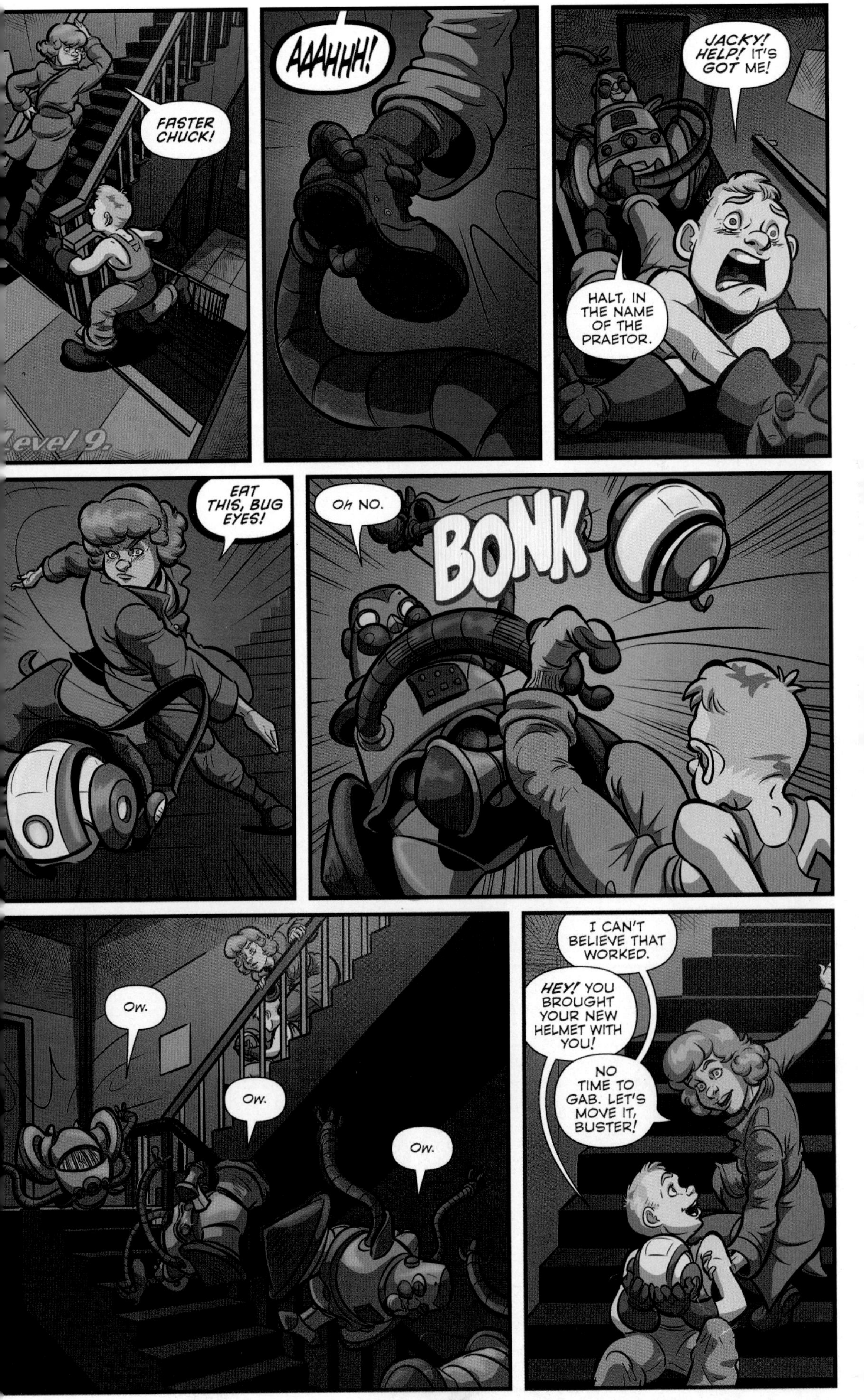

FASTER CHUCK!
Level 9.
AAAHHH!
JACKY! HELP! IT'S GOT ME!
HALT, IN THE NAME OF THE PRAETOR.
EAT THIS, BUG EYES!
Oh NO.
BONK
Ow.
Ow.
Ow.
I CAN'T BELIEVE THAT WORKED.
HEY! YOU BROUGHT YOUR NEW HELMET WITH YOU!
NO TIME TO GAB. LET'S MOVE IT, BUSTER!

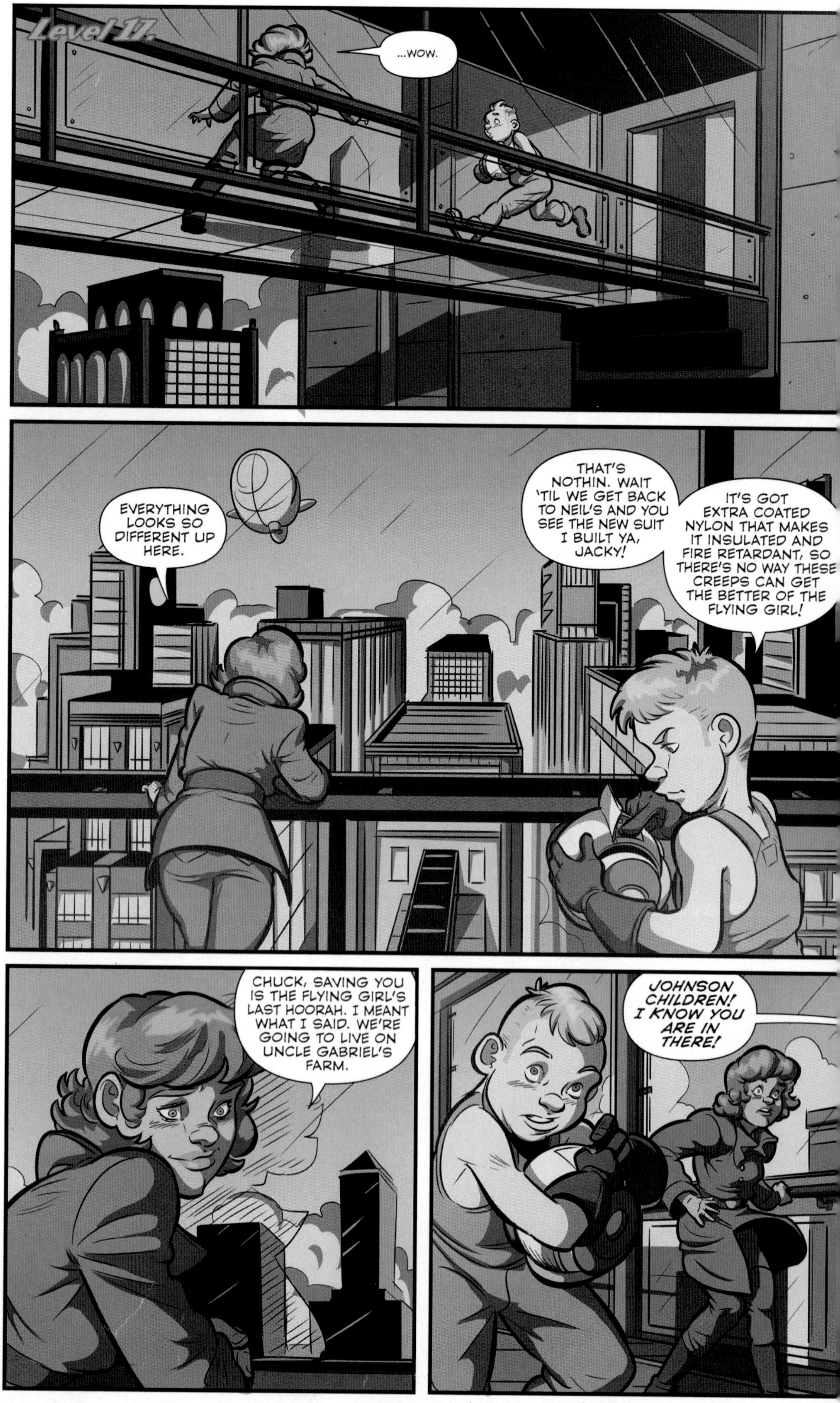
Level 17.
...WOW.
EVERYTHING LOOKS SO DIFFERENT UP HERE.
THAT'S NOTHIN. WAIT 'TIL WE GET BACK TO NEIL'S AND YOU SEE THE NEW SUIT I BUILT YA, JACKY!
IT'S GOT EXTRA COATED NYLON THAT MAKES IT INSULATED AND FIRE RETARDANT, SO THERE'S NO WAY THESE CREEPS CAN GET THE BETTER OF THE FLYING GIRL!
CHUCK, SAVING YOU IS THE FLYING GIRL'S LAST HOORAH. I MEANT WHAT I SAID. WE'RE GOING TO LIVE ON UNCLE GABRIEL'S FARM.
JOHNSON CHILDREN! I KNOW YOU ARE IN THERE!

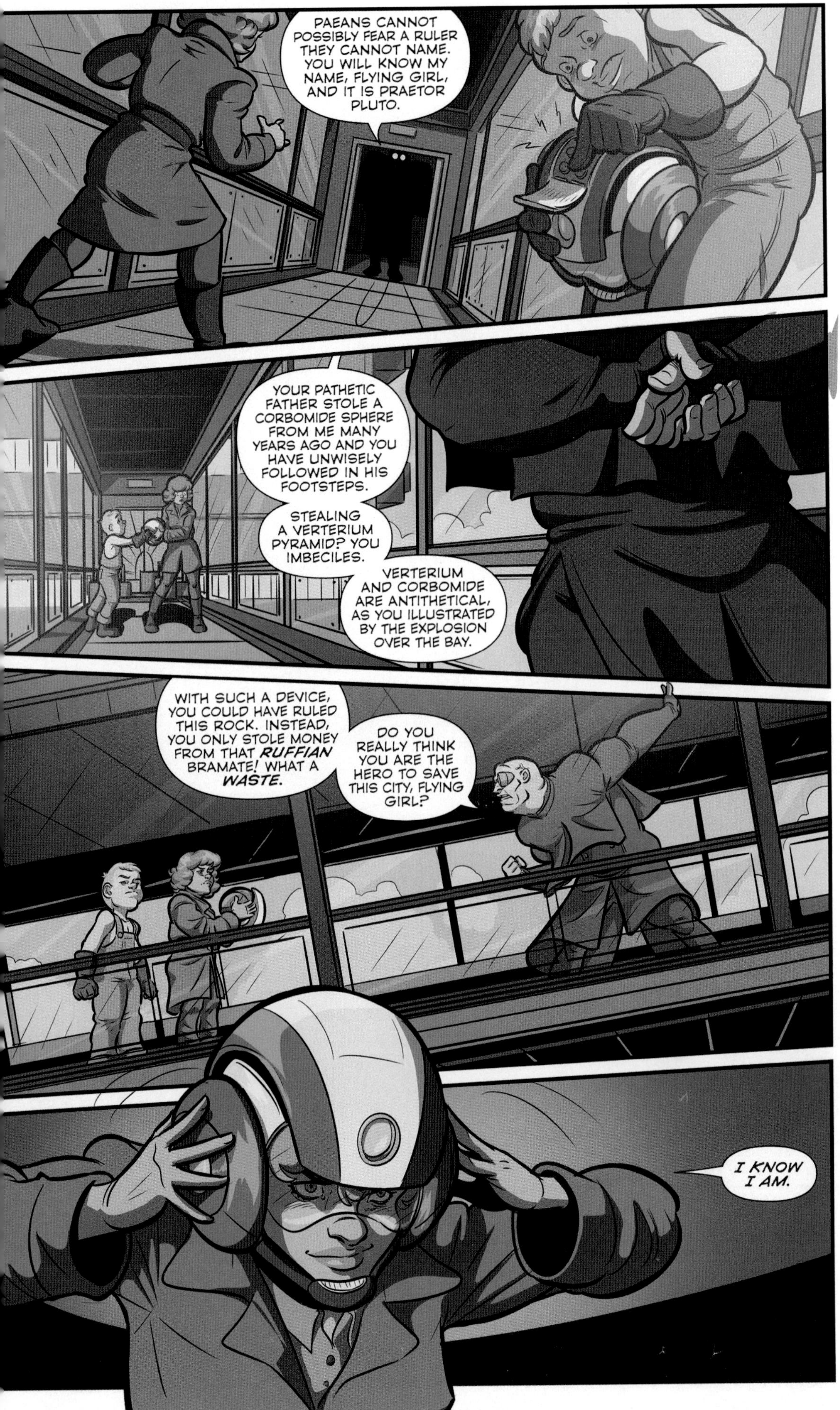
PAEANS CANNOT POSSIBLY FEAR A RULER THEY CANNOT NAME. YOU WILL KNOW MY NAME, FLYING GIRL, AND IT IS PRAETOR PLUTO.
YOUR PATHETIC FATHER STOLE A CORBOMIDE SPHERE FROM ME MANY YEARS AGO AND YOU HAVE UNWISELY FOLLOWED IN HIS FOOTSTEPS.
STEALING A VERTERIUM PYRAMID? YOU IMBECILES.
VERTERIUM AND CORBOMIDE ARE ANTITHETICAL, AS YOU ILLUSTRATED BY THE EXPLOSION OVER THE BAY.
WITH SUCH A DEVICE, YOU COULD HAVE RULED THIS ROCK. INSTEAD, YOU ONLY STOLE MONEY FROM THAT *RUFFIAN* BRAMATE! WHAT A ***WASTE.***
DO YOU REALLY THINK YOU ARE THE HERO TO SAVE THIS CITY, FLYING GIRL?
I KNOW I AM.

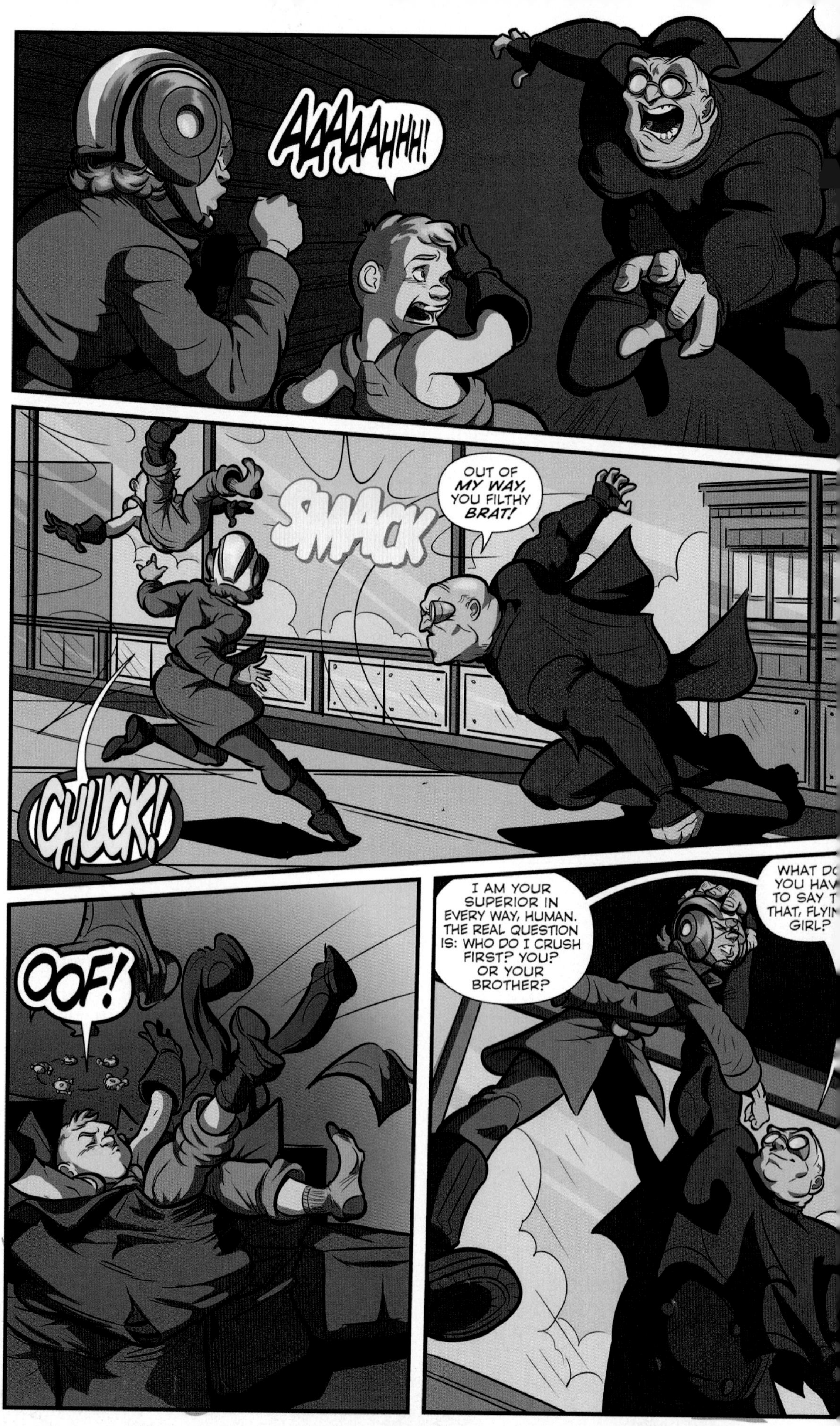
AAAAAHHH!
SMACK
OUT OF MY WAY, YOU FILTHY BRAT!
CHUCK!
OOF!
I AM YOUR SUPERIOR IN EVERY WAY, HUMAN. THE REAL QUESTION IS: WHO DO I CRUSH FIRST? YOU? OR YOUR BROTHER?

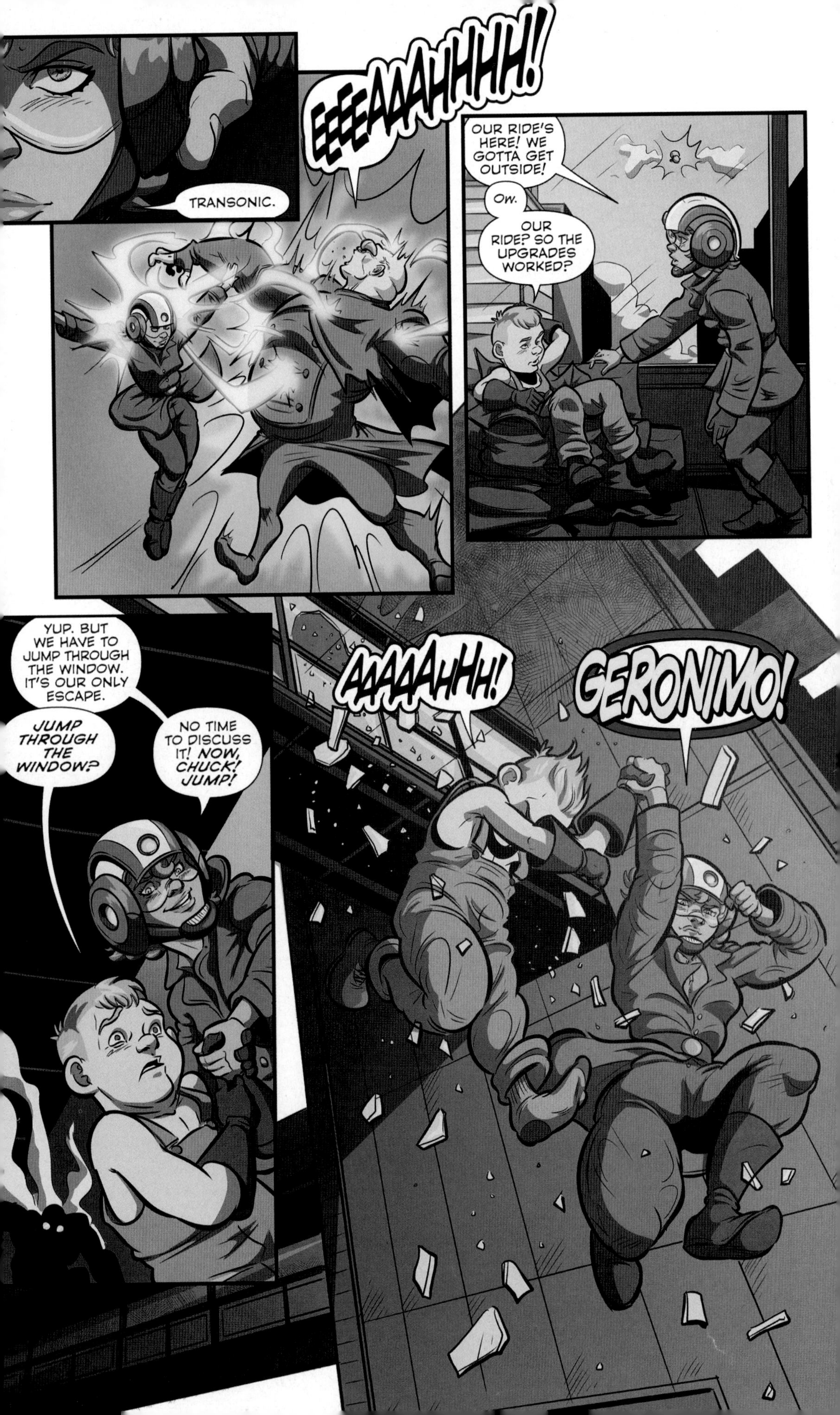
TRANSONIC.
EEEEAAAHHHH!
OUR RIDE'S HERE! WE GOTTA GET OUTSIDE!
Ow.
OUR RIDE? SO THE UPGRADES WORKED?
YUP. BUT WE HAVE TO JUMP THROUGH THE WINDOW. IT'S OUR ONLY ESCAPE.
JUMP THROUGH THE WINDOW?
NO TIME TO DISCUSS IT! NOW, CHUCK! JUMP!
AAAAAHHH!
GERONIMO!

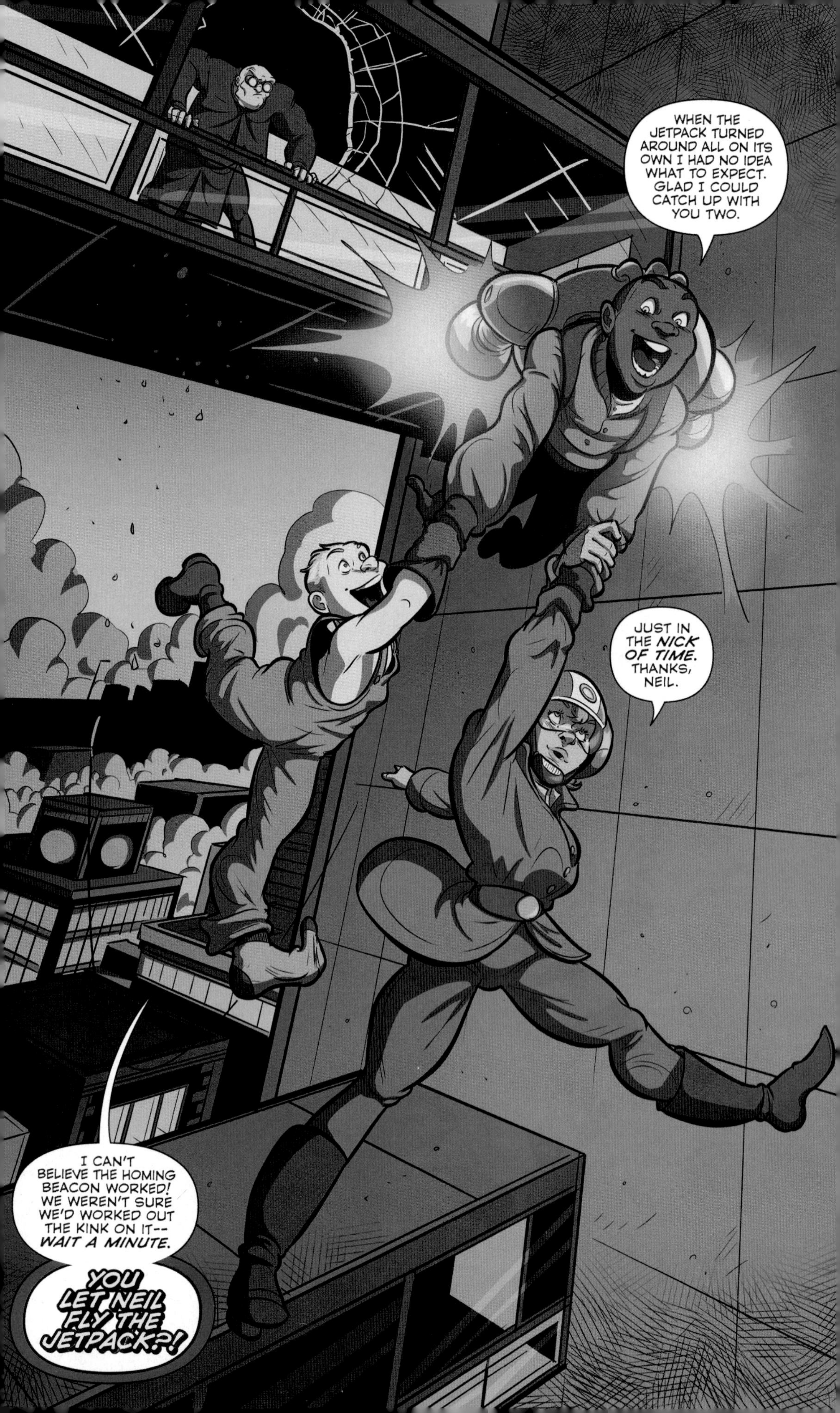
WHEN THE JETPACK TURNED AROUND ALL ON ITS OWN I HAD NO IDEA WHAT TO EXPECT. GLAD I COULD CATCH UP WITH YOU TWO.
JUST IN THE *NICK OF TIME.* THANKS, NEIL.
I CAN'T BELIEVE THE HOMING BEACON WORKED! WE WEREN'T SURE WE'D WORKED OUT THE KINK ON IT-- *WAIT A MINUTE.*
YOU LET NEIL FLY THE JETPACK?!

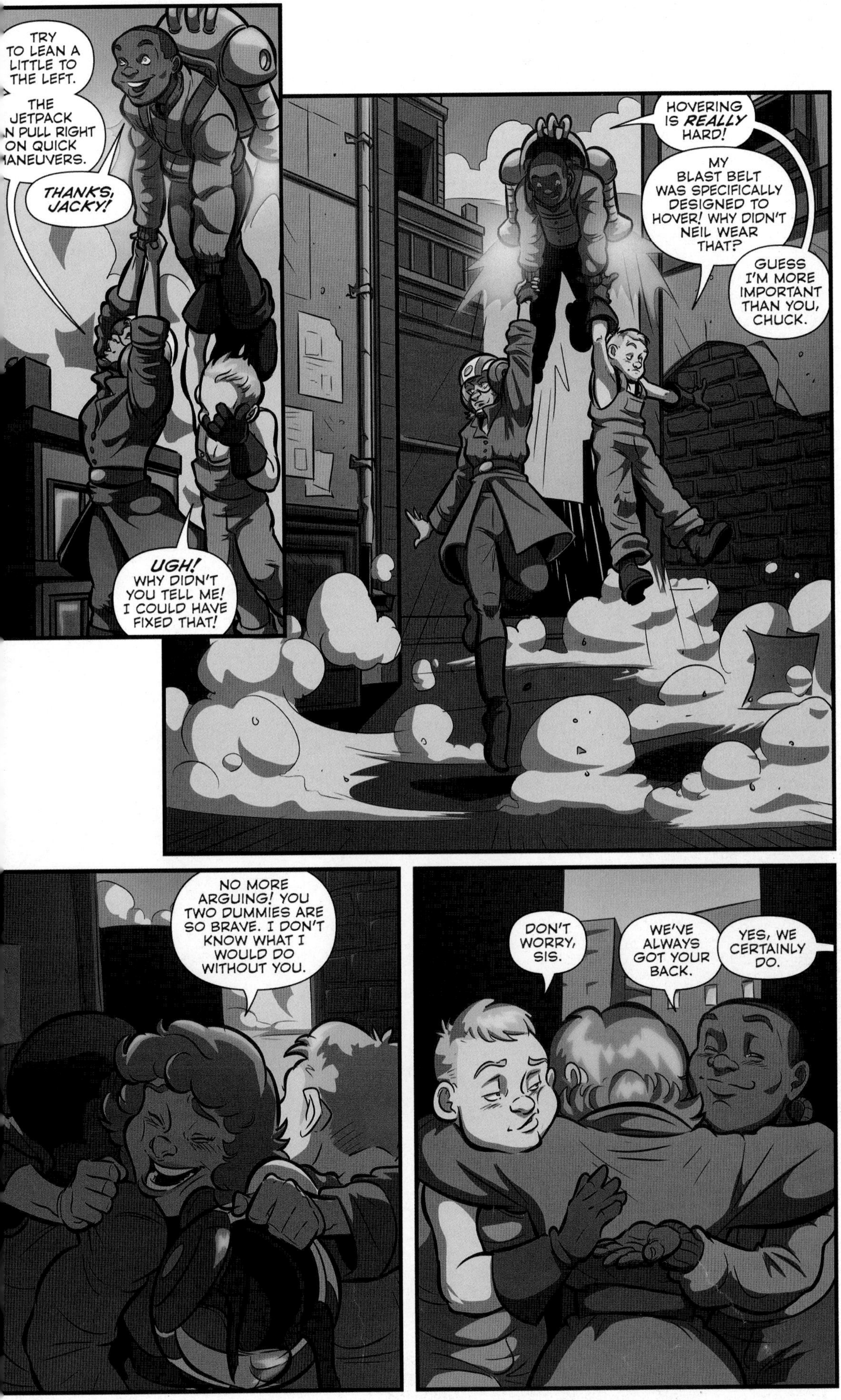
TRY TO LEAN A LITTLE TO THE LEFT.
THE JETPACK N PULL RIGHT ON QUICK ANEUVERS.
THANKS, JACKY!
UGH! WHY DIDN'T YOU TELL ME! I COULD HAVE FIXED THAT!
HOVERING IS REALLY HARD!
MY BLAST BELT WAS SPECIFICALLY DESIGNED TO HOVER! WHY DIDN'T NEIL WEAR THAT?
GUESS I'M MORE IMPORTANT THAN YOU, CHUCK.
NO MORE ARGUING! YOU TWO DUMMIES ARE SO BRAVE. I DON'T KNOW WHAT I WOULD DO WITHOUT YOU.
DON'T WORRY, SIS.
WE'VE ALWAYS GOT YOUR BACK.
YES, WE CERTAINLY DO.

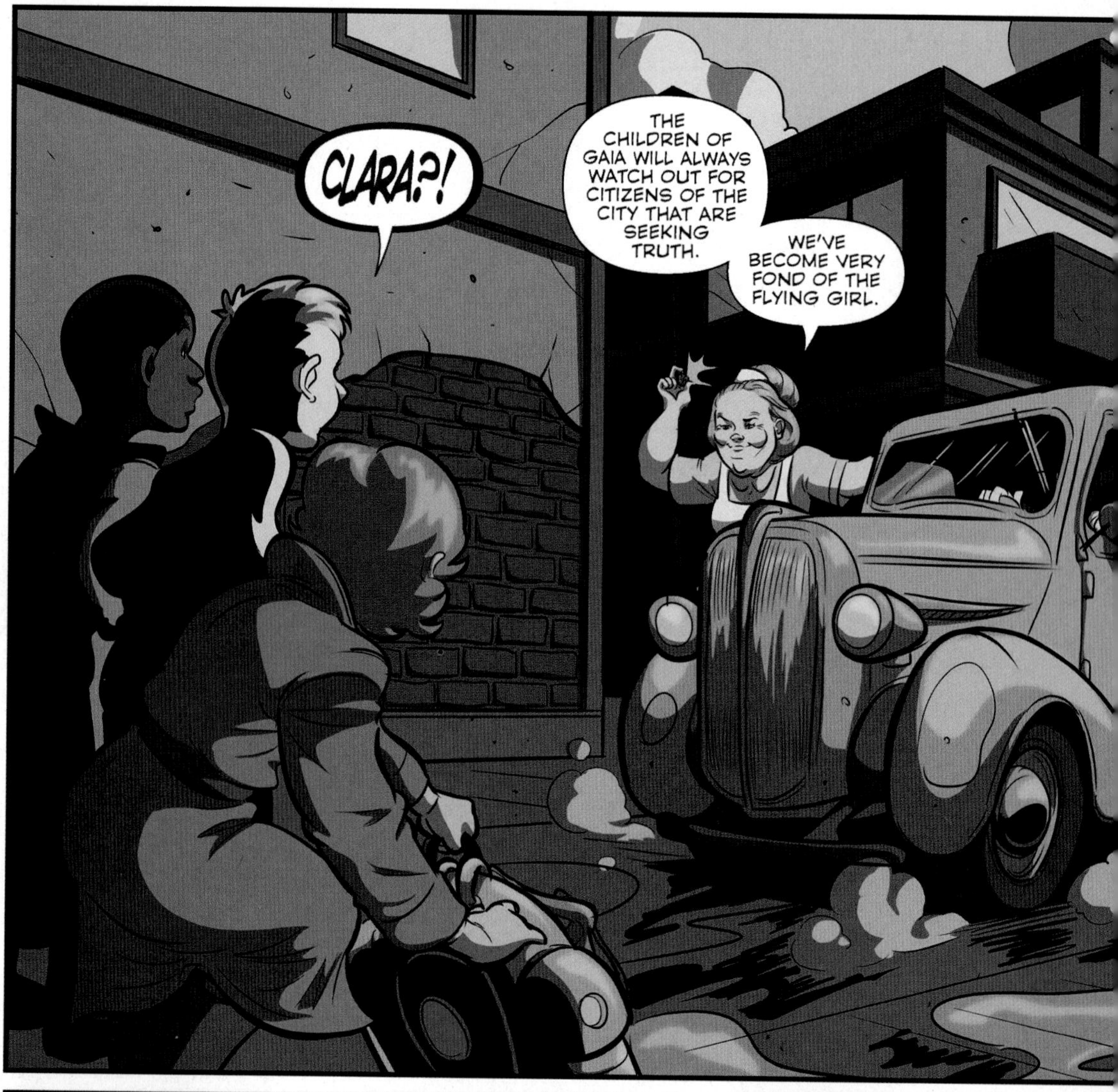
CLARA?!
THE CHILDREN OF GAIA WILL ALWAYS WATCH OUT FOR CITIZENS OF THE CITY THAT ARE SEEKING TRUTH.
WE'VE BECOME VERY FOND OF THE FLYING GIRL.

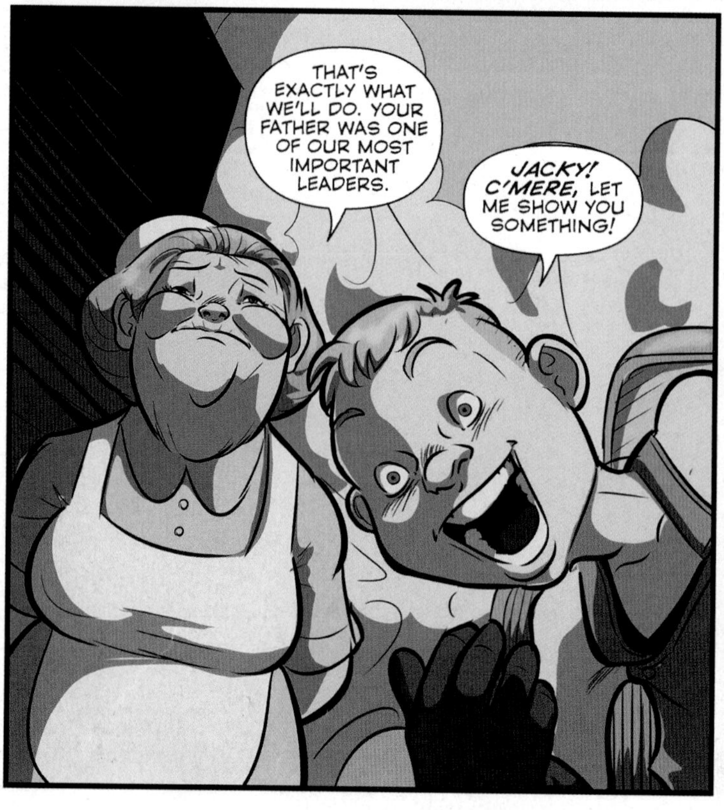
THAT'S EXACTLY WHAT WE'LL DO. YOUR FATHER WAS ONE OF OUR MOST IMPORTANT LEADERS.
JACKY! C'MERE, LET ME SHOW YOU SOMETHING!

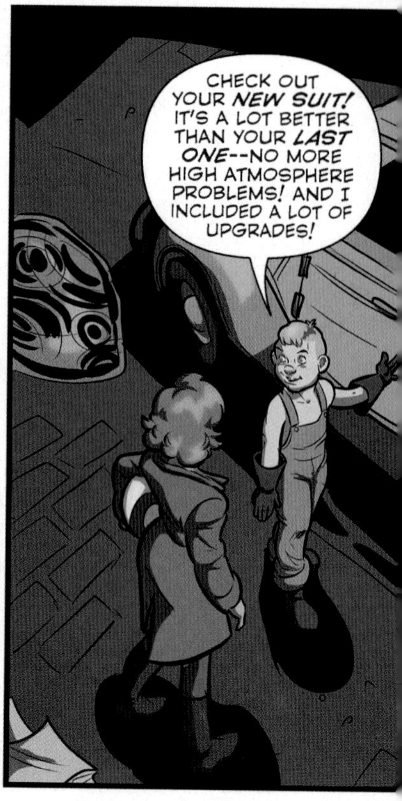
CHECK OUT YOUR NEW SUIT! IT'S A LOT BETTER THAN YOUR LAST ONE--NO MORE HIGH ATMOSPHERE PROBLEMS! AND I INCLUDED A LOT OF UPGRADES!

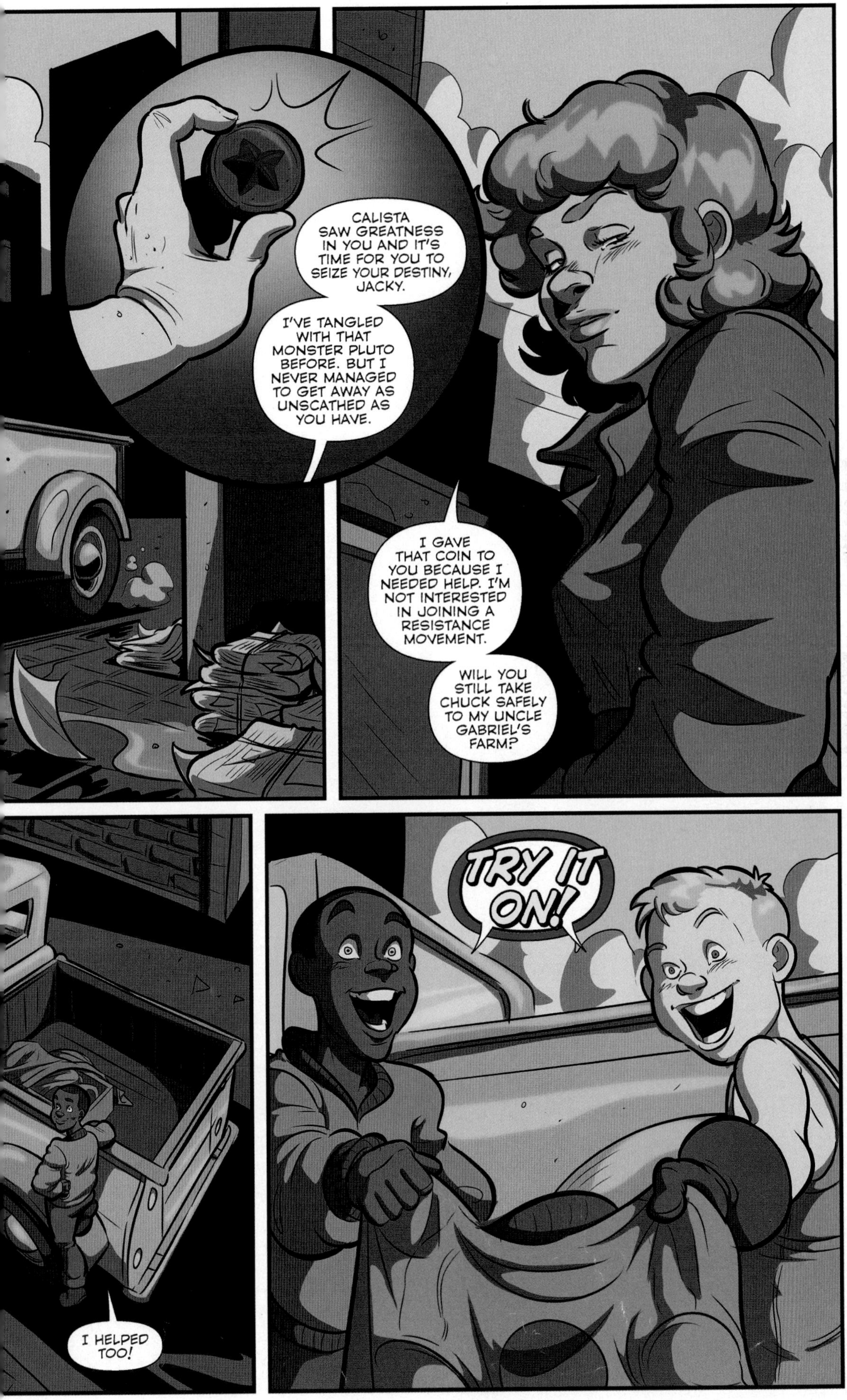
CALISTA SAW GREATNESS IN YOU AND IT'S TIME FOR YOU TO SEIZE YOUR DESTINY, JACKY.
I'VE TANGLED WITH THAT MONSTER PLUTO BEFORE. BUT I NEVER MANAGED TO GET AWAY AS UNSCATHED AS YOU HAVE.
I GAVE THAT COIN TO YOU BECAUSE I NEEDED HELP. I'M NOT INTERESTED IN JOINING A RESISTANCE MOVEMENT.
WILL YOU STILL TAKE CHUCK SAFELY TO MY UNCLE GABRIEL'S FARM?
I HELPED TOO!
TRY IT ON!

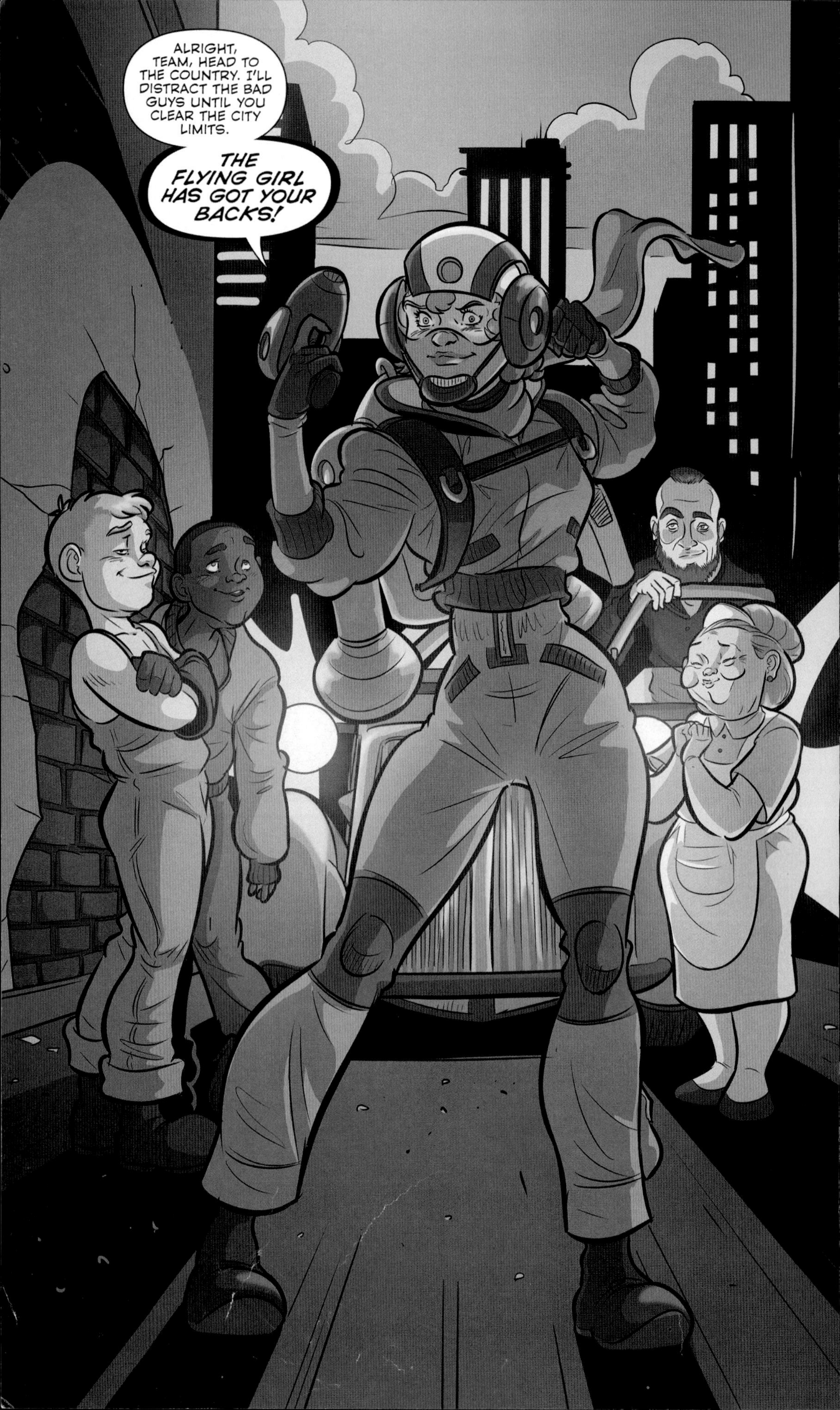
ALRIGHT, TEAM, HEAD TO THE COUNTRY. I'LL DISTRACT THE BAD GUYS UNTIL YOU CLEAR THE CITY LIMITS.
THE FLYING GIRL HAS GOT YOUR BACKS!

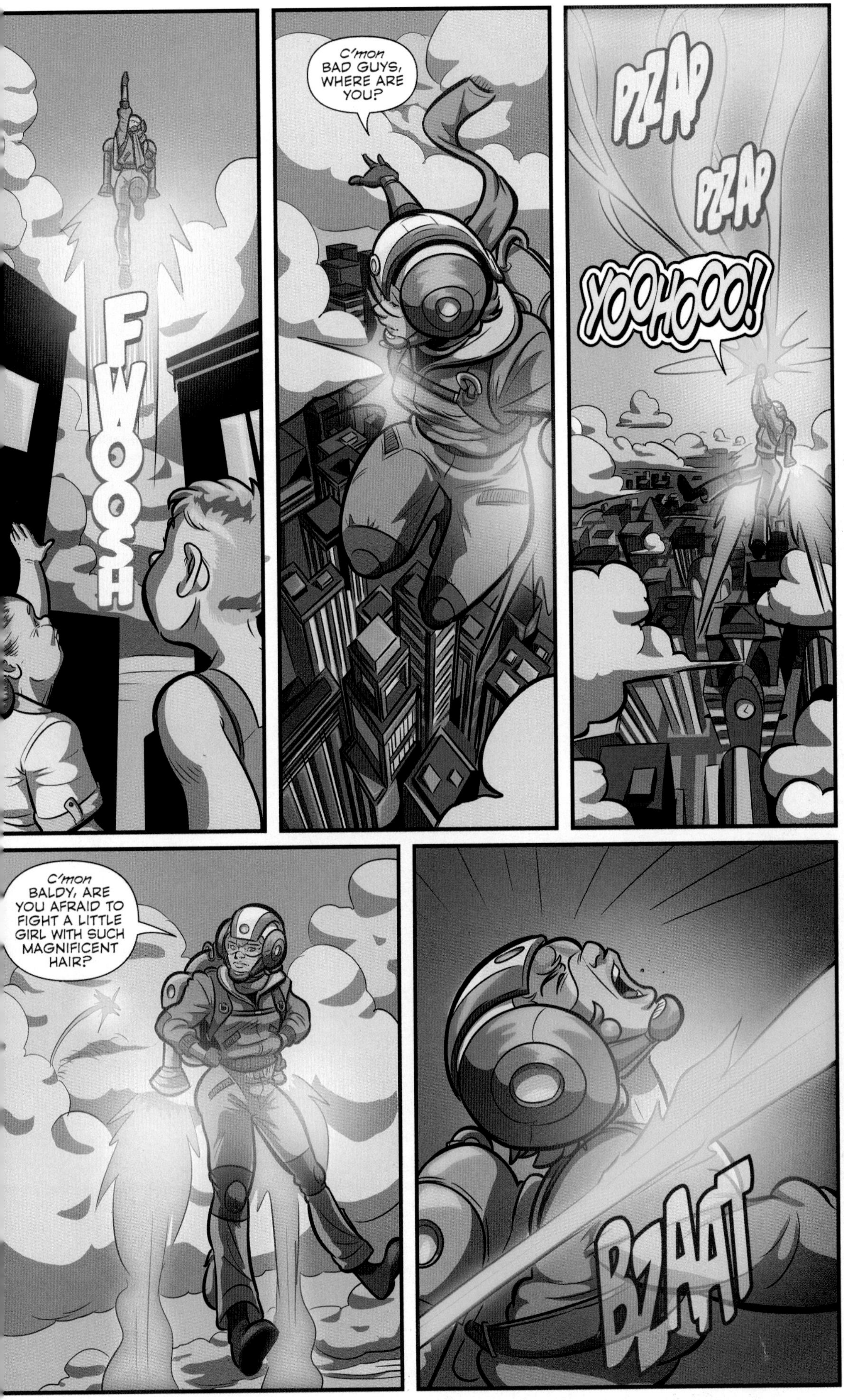
FWOOSH
C'mon BAD GUYS, WHERE ARE YOU?
PZZAP
PZZAP
YOOHOOO!
C'mon BALDY, ARE YOU AFRAID TO FIGHT A LITTLE GIRL WITH SUCH MAGNIFICENT HAIR?
BZAAT

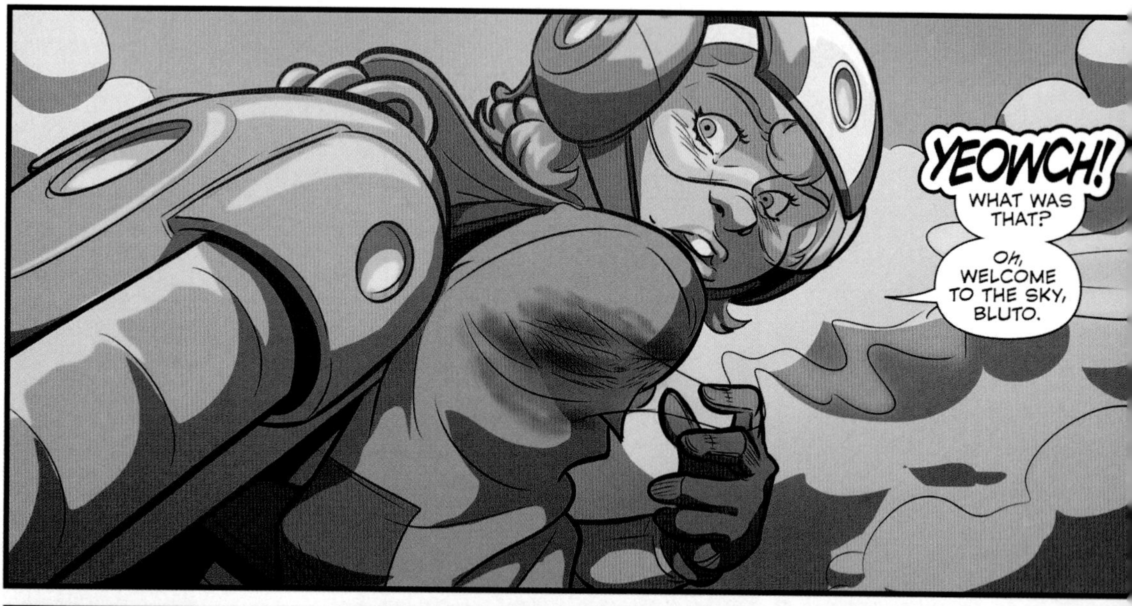
YEOWCH!
WHAT WAS THAT?
OH, WELCOME TO THE SKY, BLUTO.

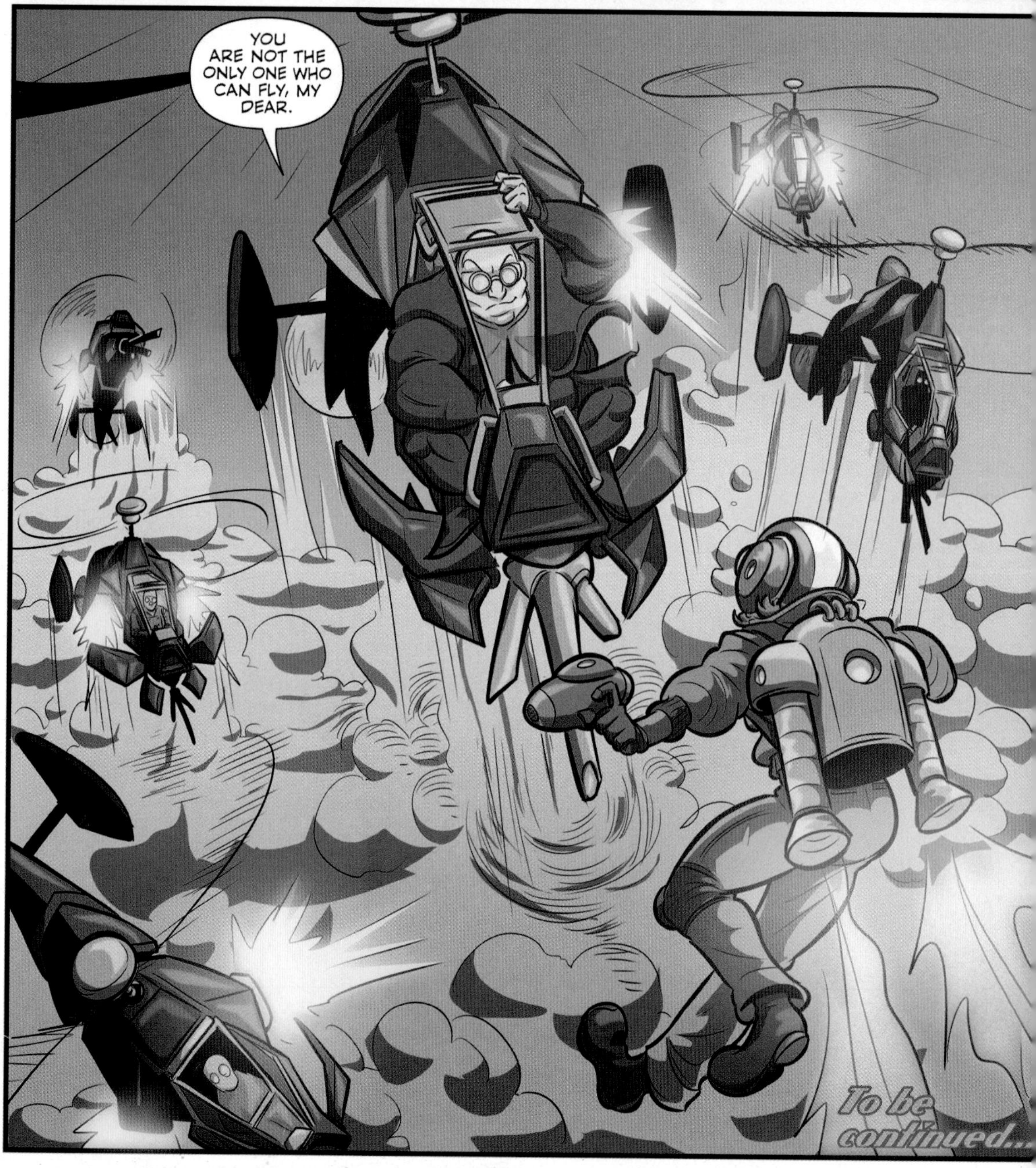
YOU ARE NOT THE ONLY ONE WHO CAN FLY, MY DEAR.
To be continued...

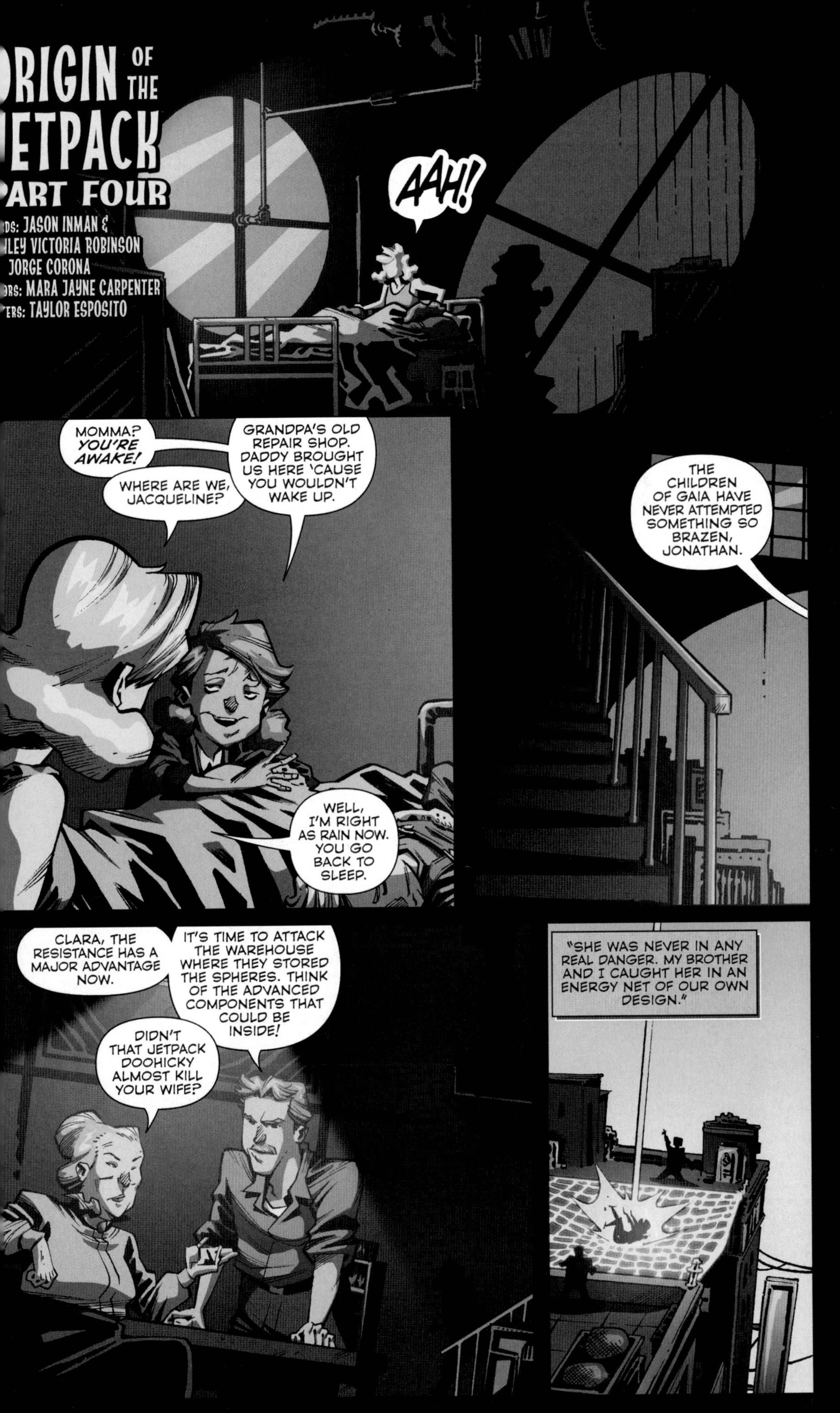
ORIGIN OF THE JETPACK
PART FOUR
DS: JASON INMAN &
ILEY VICTORIA ROBINSON
JORGE CORONA
DRS: MARA JAYNE CARPENTER
TERS: TAYLOR ESPOSITO
AAH!
MOMMA? YOU'RE AWAKE!
WHERE ARE WE, JACQUELINE?
GRANDPA'S OLD REPAIR SHOP. DADDY BROUGHT US HERE 'CAUSE YOU WOULDN'T WAKE UP.
WELL, I'M RIGHT AS RAIN NOW. YOU GO BACK TO SLEEP.
THE CHILDREN OF GAIA HAVE NEVER ATTEMPTED SOMETHING SO BRAZEN, JONATHAN.
CLARA, THE RESISTANCE HAS A MAJOR ADVANTAGE NOW.
IT'S TIME TO ATTACK THE WAREHOUSE WHERE THEY STORED THE SPHERES. THINK OF THE ADVANCED COMPONENTS THAT COULD BE INSIDE!
DIDN'T THAT JETPACK DOOHICKY ALMOST KILL YOUR WIFE?
"SHE WAS NEVER IN ANY REAL DANGER. MY BROTHER AND I CAUGHT HER IN AN ENERGY NET OF OUR OWN DESIGN."

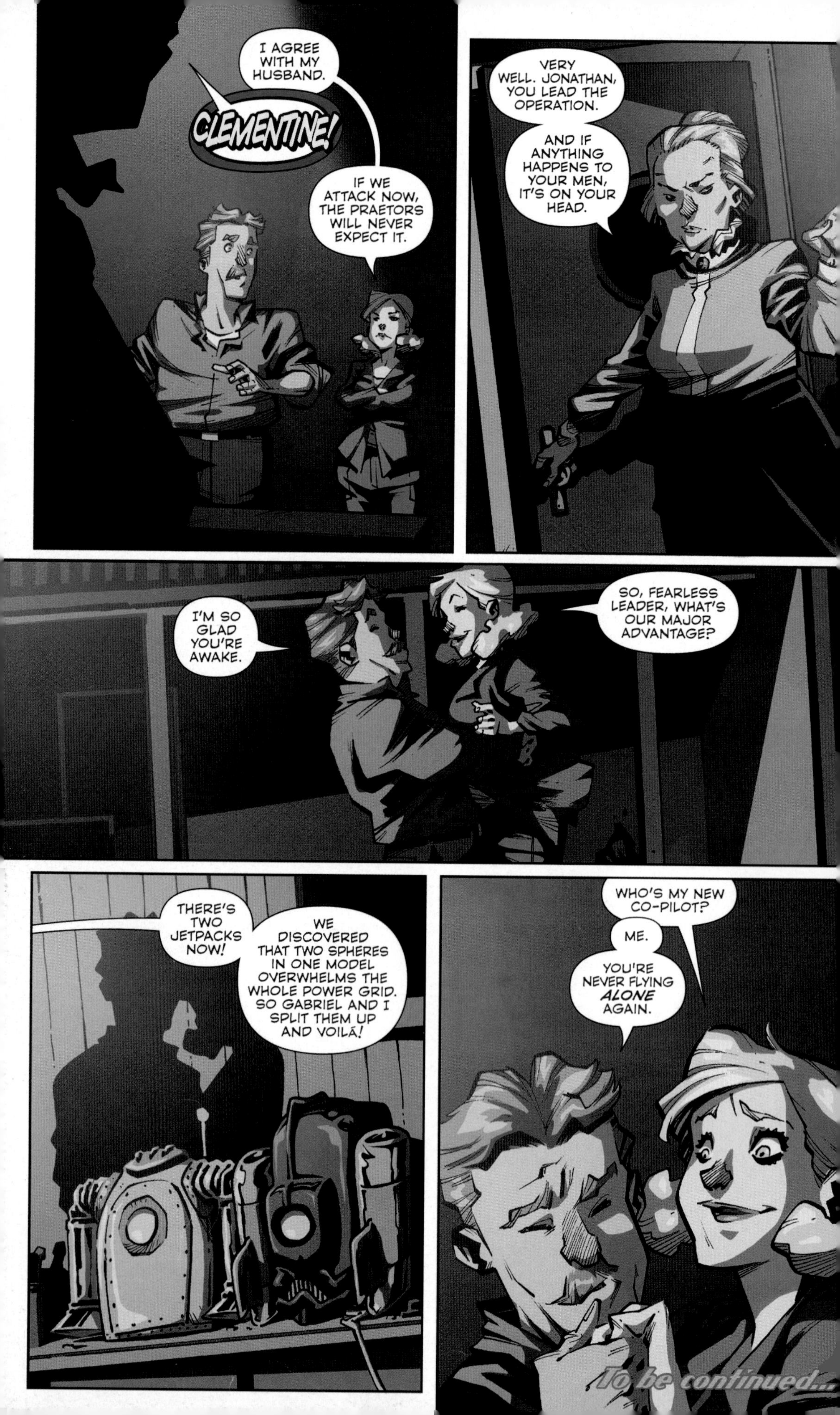
I AGREE WITH MY HUSBAND.
CLEMENTINE!
IF WE ATTACK NOW, THE PRAETORS WILL NEVER EXPECT IT.
VERY WELL. JONATHAN, YOU LEAD THE OPERATION.
AND IF ANYTHING HAPPENS TO YOUR MEN, IT'S ON YOUR HEAD.
I'M SO GLAD YOU'RE AWAKE.
SO, FEARLESS LEADER, WHAT'S OUR MAJOR ADVANTAGE?
THERE'S TWO JETPACKS NOW!
WE DISCOVERED THAT TWO SPHERES IN ONE MODEL OVERWHELMS THE WHOLE POWER GRID. SO GABRIEL AND I SPLIT THEM UP AND VOILÀ!
WHO'S MY NEW CO-PILOT?
ME.
YOU'RE NEVER FLYING ALONE AGAIN.
To be continued...

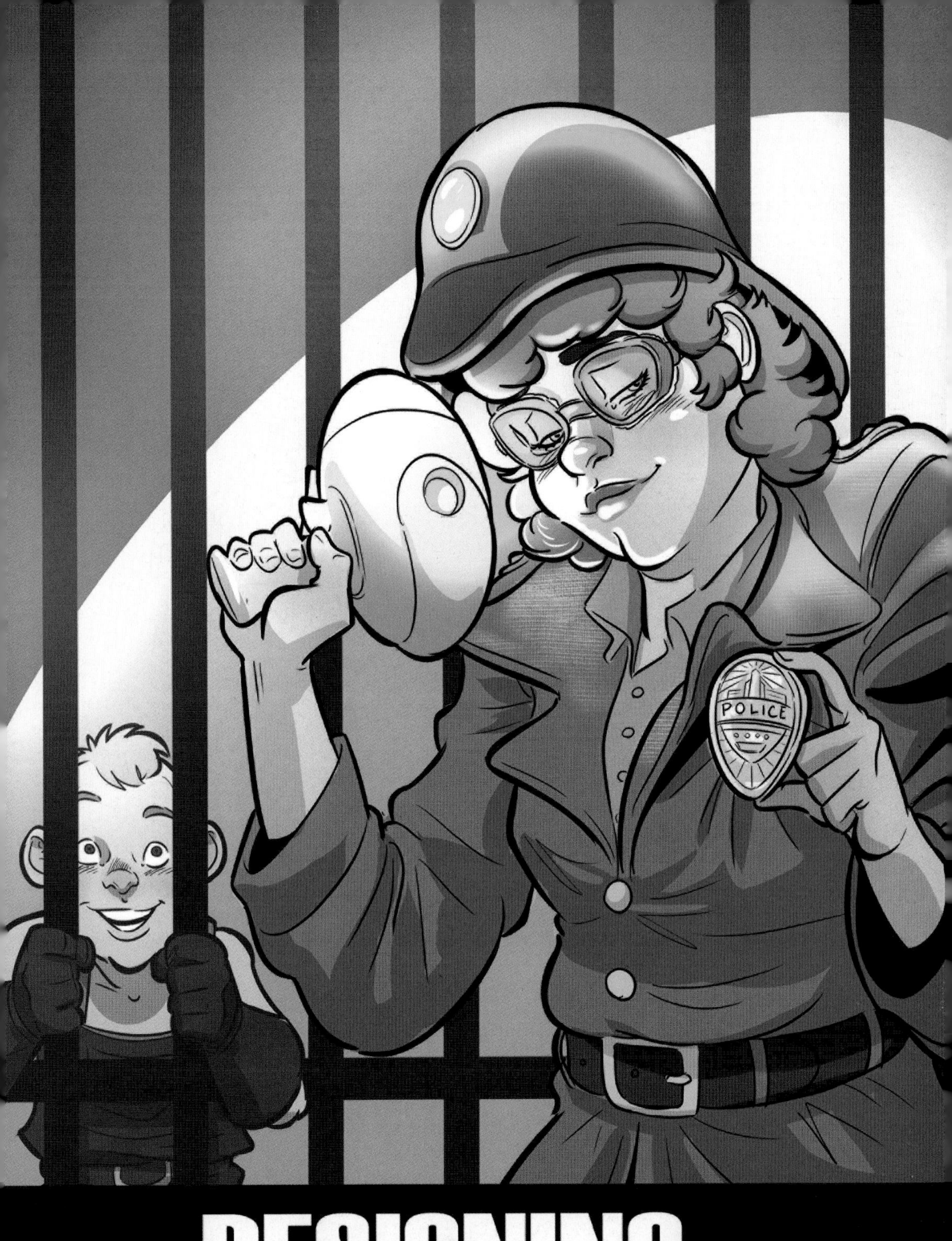
POLICE

DESIGNING JUPITER JET'S NEW COSTUME

JUPITER JET HAS A NEW COSTUME!
HERE'S A PEAK AT ARTIST BEN MATUSYA'S DESIGN PROCESS.

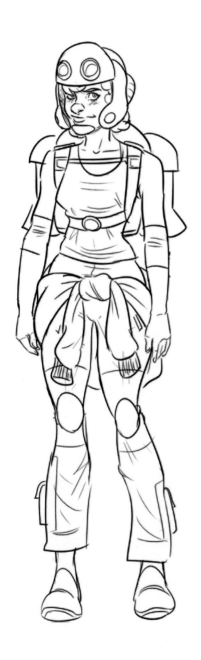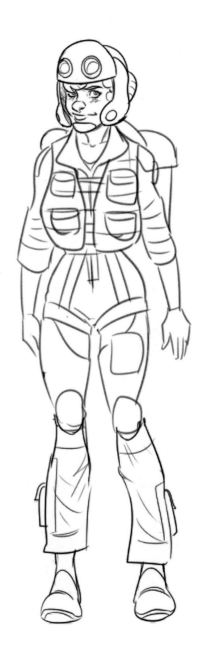

FINAL DESIGN

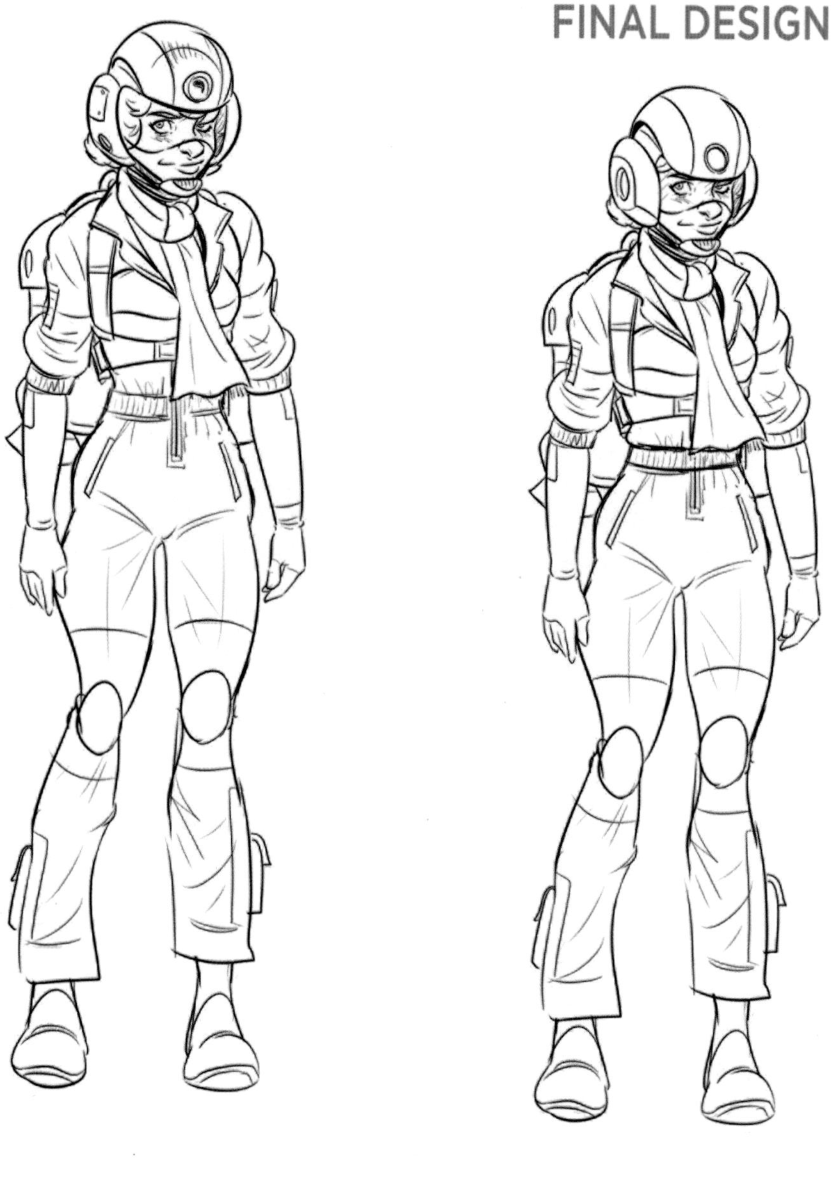

WRITER JASON INMAN'S CONTRIBUTION TO THE FINAL HELMET DESIGN

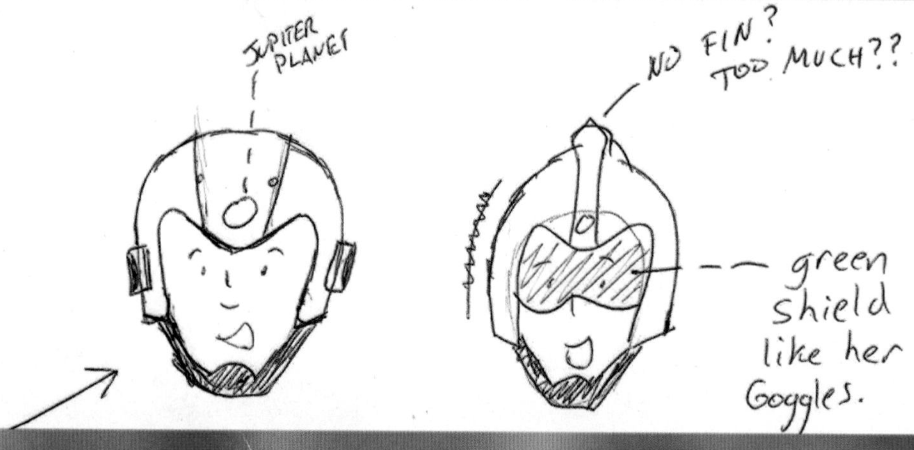

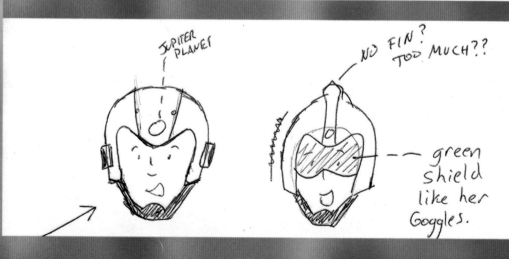

JUPITER PLANET
NO FIN? TOO MUCH??
green shield like her Goggles.

FINAL COLORS

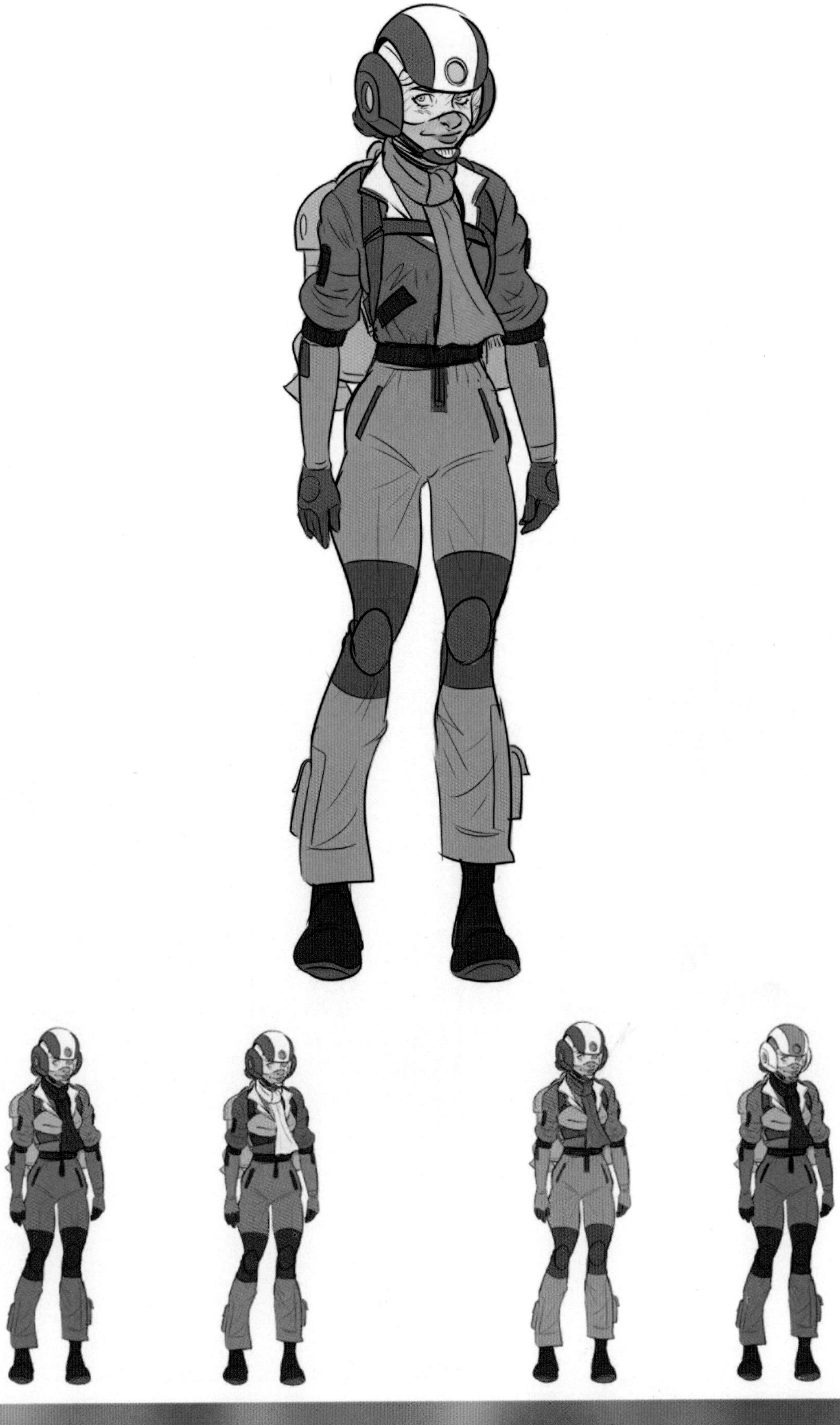

THE NEW COSTUME DEBUTS!

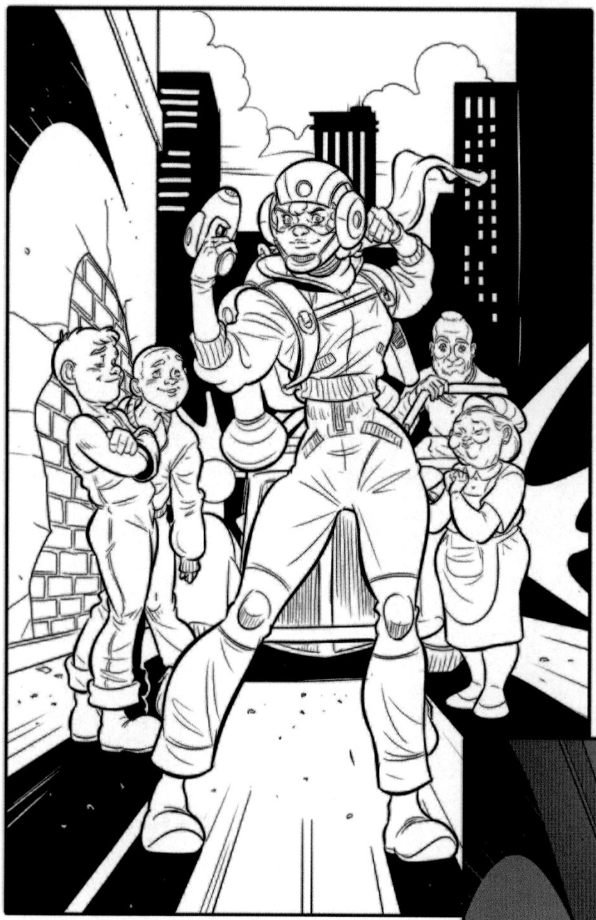

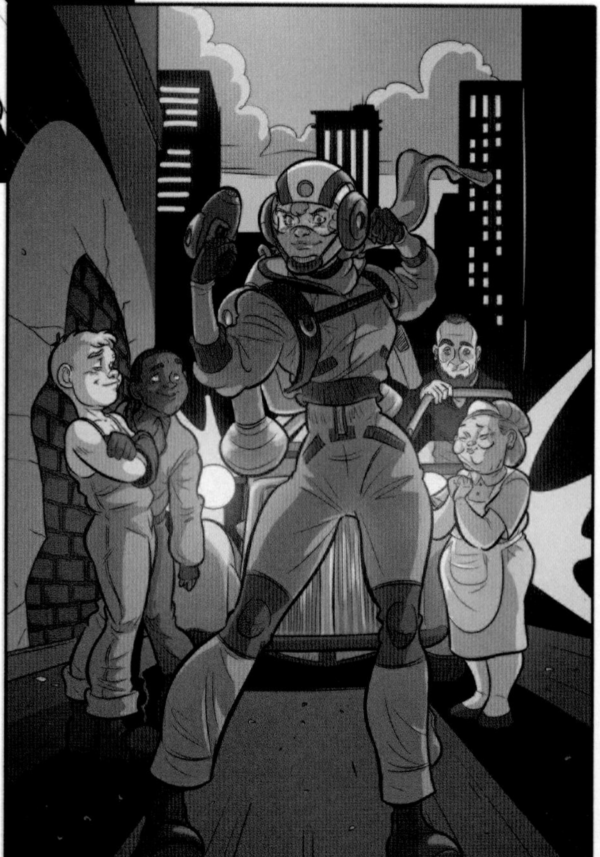

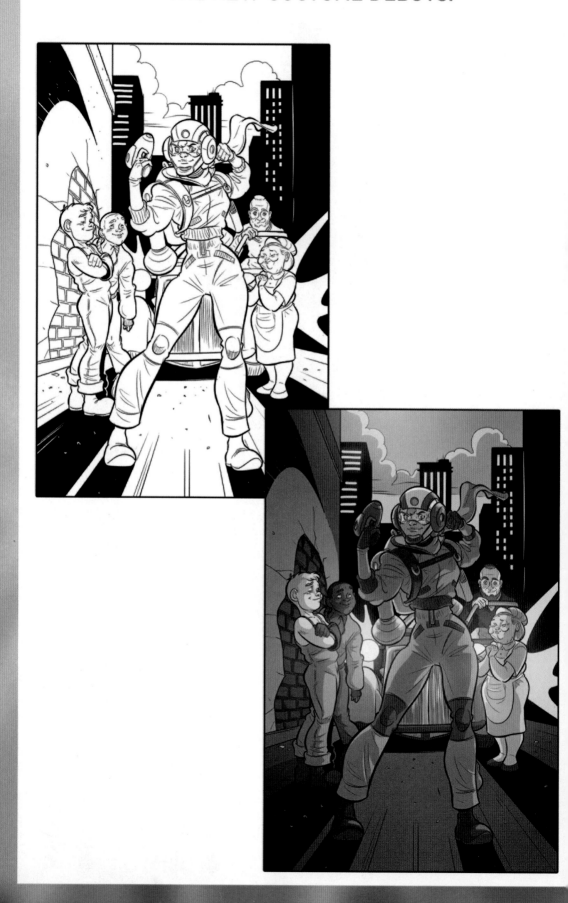

DID YOU MISS THE JUPITER JET CREATIVE TEAM'S CAMEO IN THIS ISSUE?

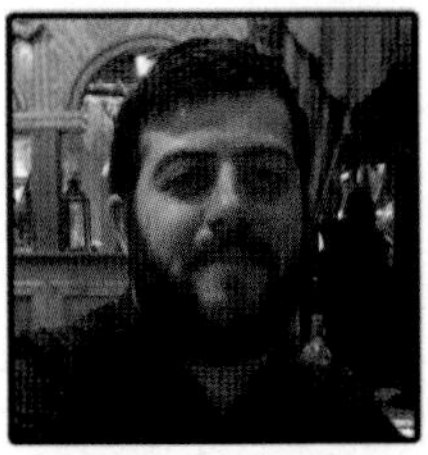

TAYLOR ESPOSITO
LETTERER

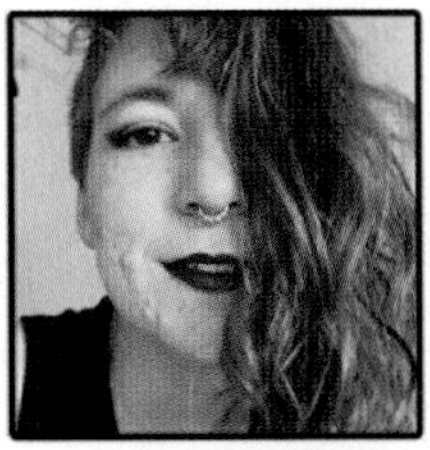

MARA JAYNE CARPENTER
COLORIST

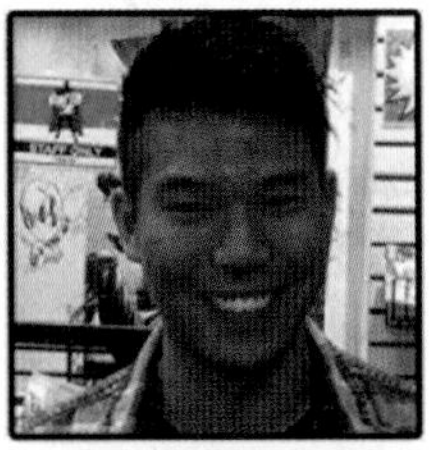

BEN MATSUYA
LINEART

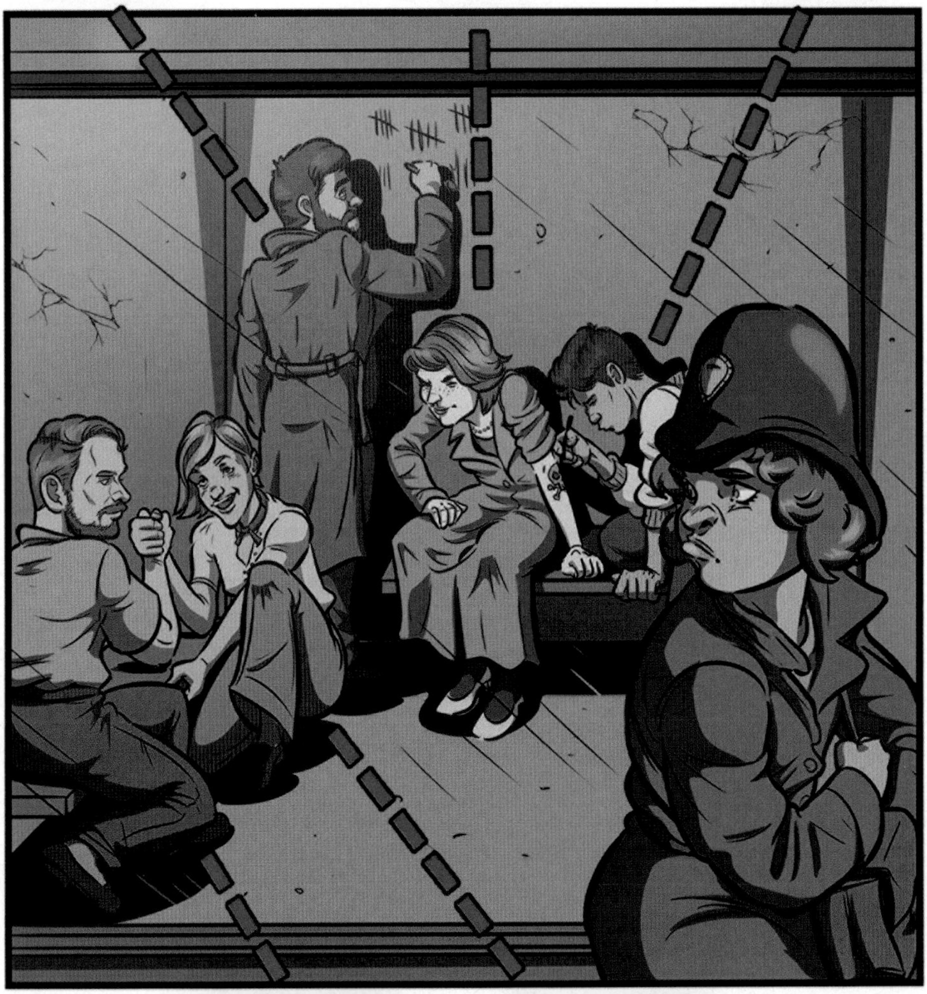

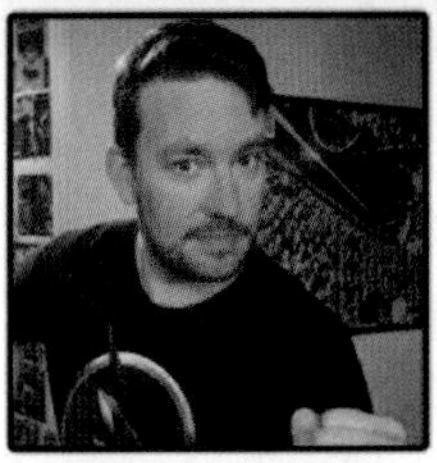

JASON INMAN
WRITER

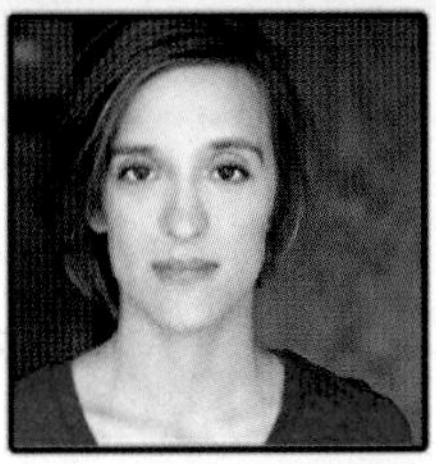

ASHLEY VICTORIA ROBINSON
WRITER

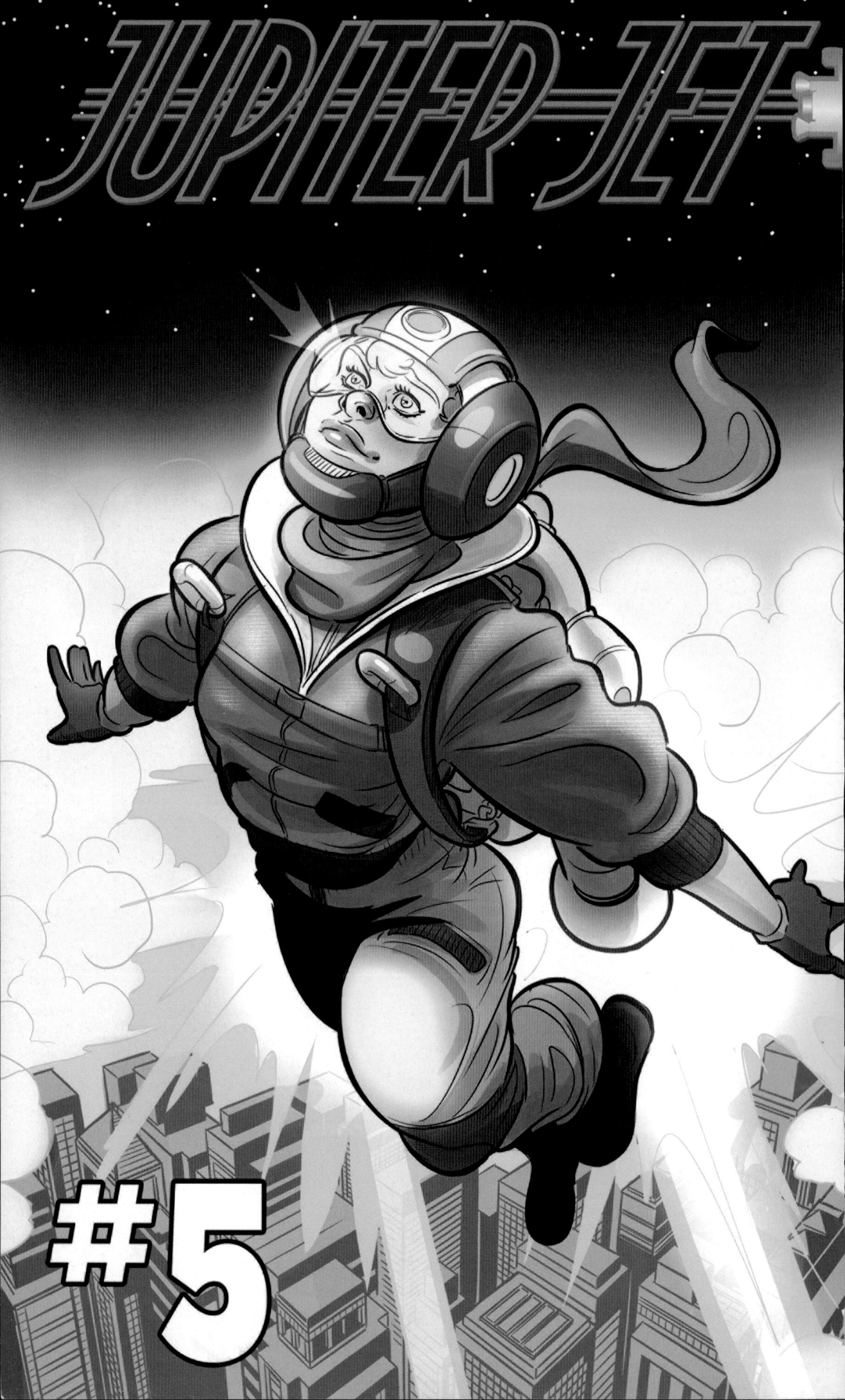
JUPITER JET
#5

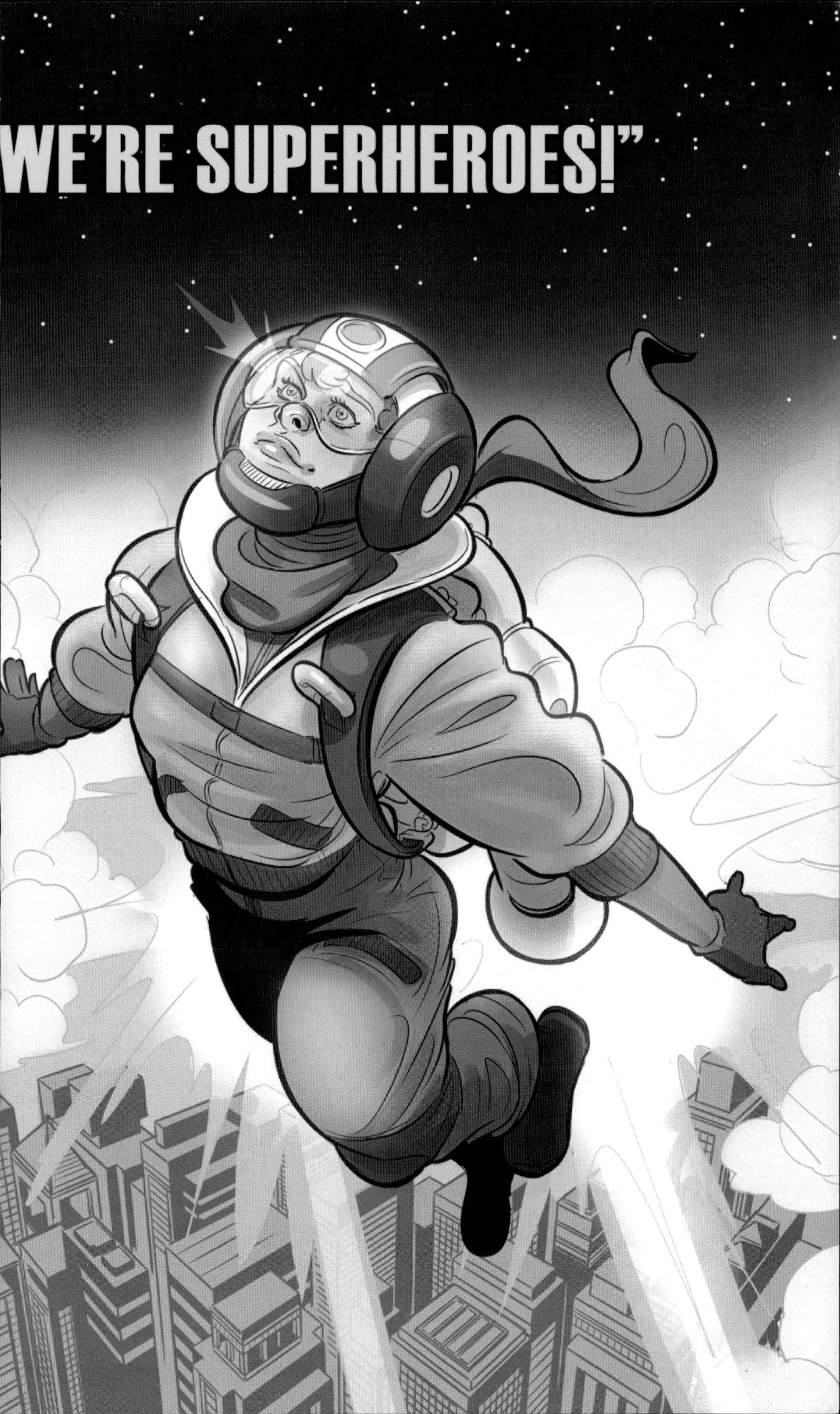
WE'RE SUPERHEROES!"

WRITTEN BY:
**JASON INMAN &
ASHLEY VICTORIA ROBINSON**

LINEART BY:
BEN MATSUYA

COLORS BY:
MARA JAYNE CARPENTER

COLOR FLATS BY:
TORI RIDLEY

LETTERS BY:
TAYLOR ESPOSITO OF GHOST GLYPH STUDIOS

COVER ARTIST (A):
BEN MATSUYA

COVER ARTIST (B):
ART BALTAZAR

**PUBLISHER/ CEO: BRYAN SEATON • EDITOR IN CHIEF: SHAWN GABBORIN
PUBLISHER-DANGER ZONE: JASON MARTIN • MARKETING DIRECTOR/EDITOR: NICOLE D'ANDRIA
EXECUTIVE ADMINISTRATOR: DANIELLE DAVISON • TEST PILOT: CHAD CICCONI
PRESIDENT OF CREATOR RELATIONS: SHAWN PRYOR**

SURRENDER NOW, FLYING GIRL AND I'LL LET YOUR BROTHER LIVE.

C'MON BOYS, THIS IS *NO TIME* FOR *HORSEPLAY!*

PLUS FIVE AGAINST ONE DOESN'T SEEM VERY *FAIR* TO ME.

LET'S *LEVEL* THE PLAYING FIELD!

PTANK

NO! CURSE YOU!

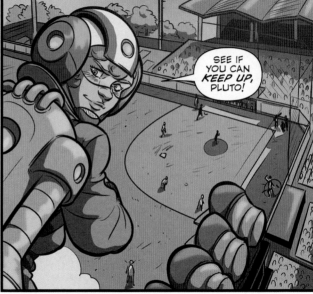

SEE IF YOU CAN *KEEP UP,* PLUTO!

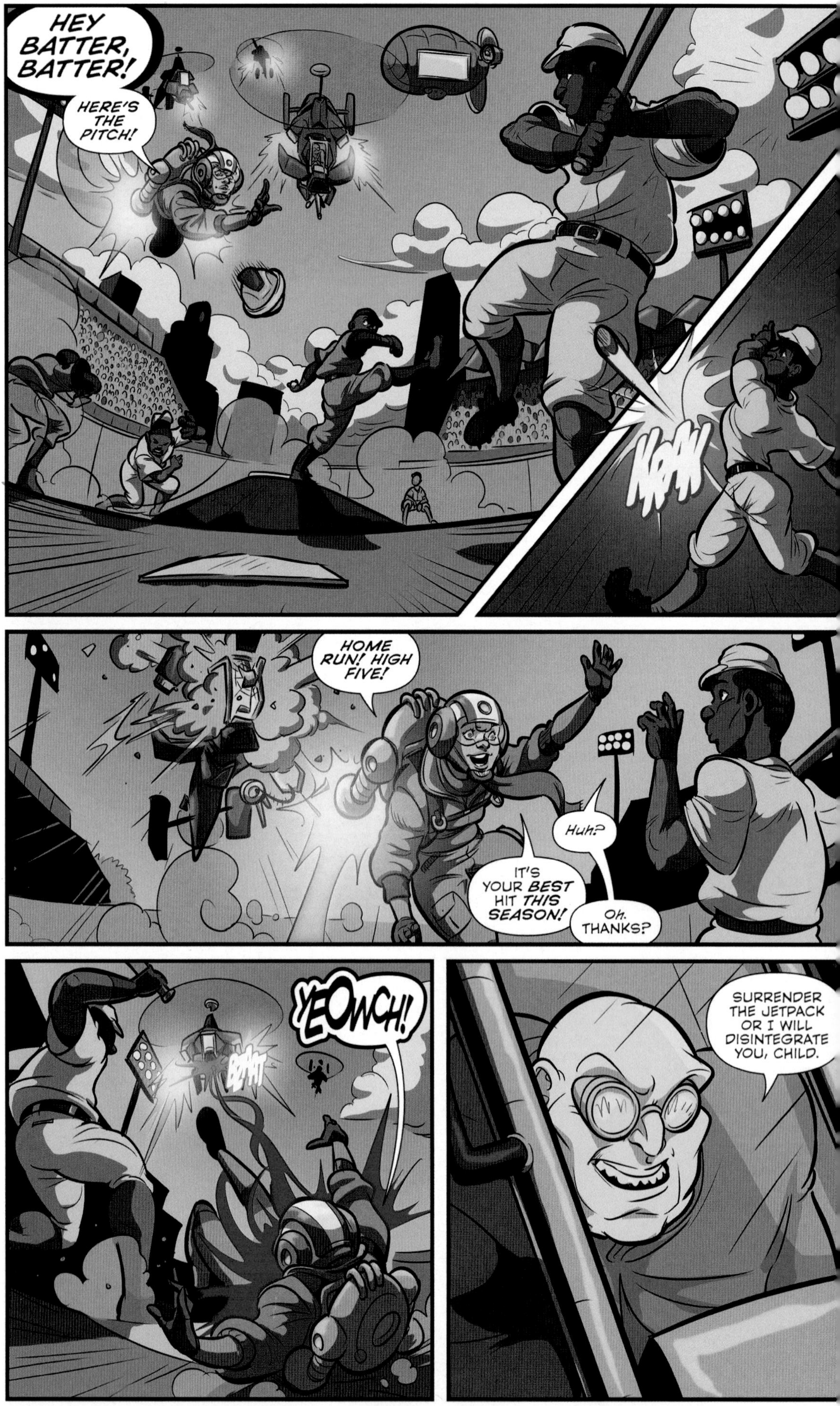
HEY BATTER, BATTER!
HERE'S THE PITCH!
HOME RUN! HIGH FIVE!
Huh?
IT'S YOUR BEST HIT THIS SEASON!
Oh. THANKS?
YEOWCH!
SURRENDER THE JETPACK OR I WILL DISINTEGRATE YOU, CHILD.

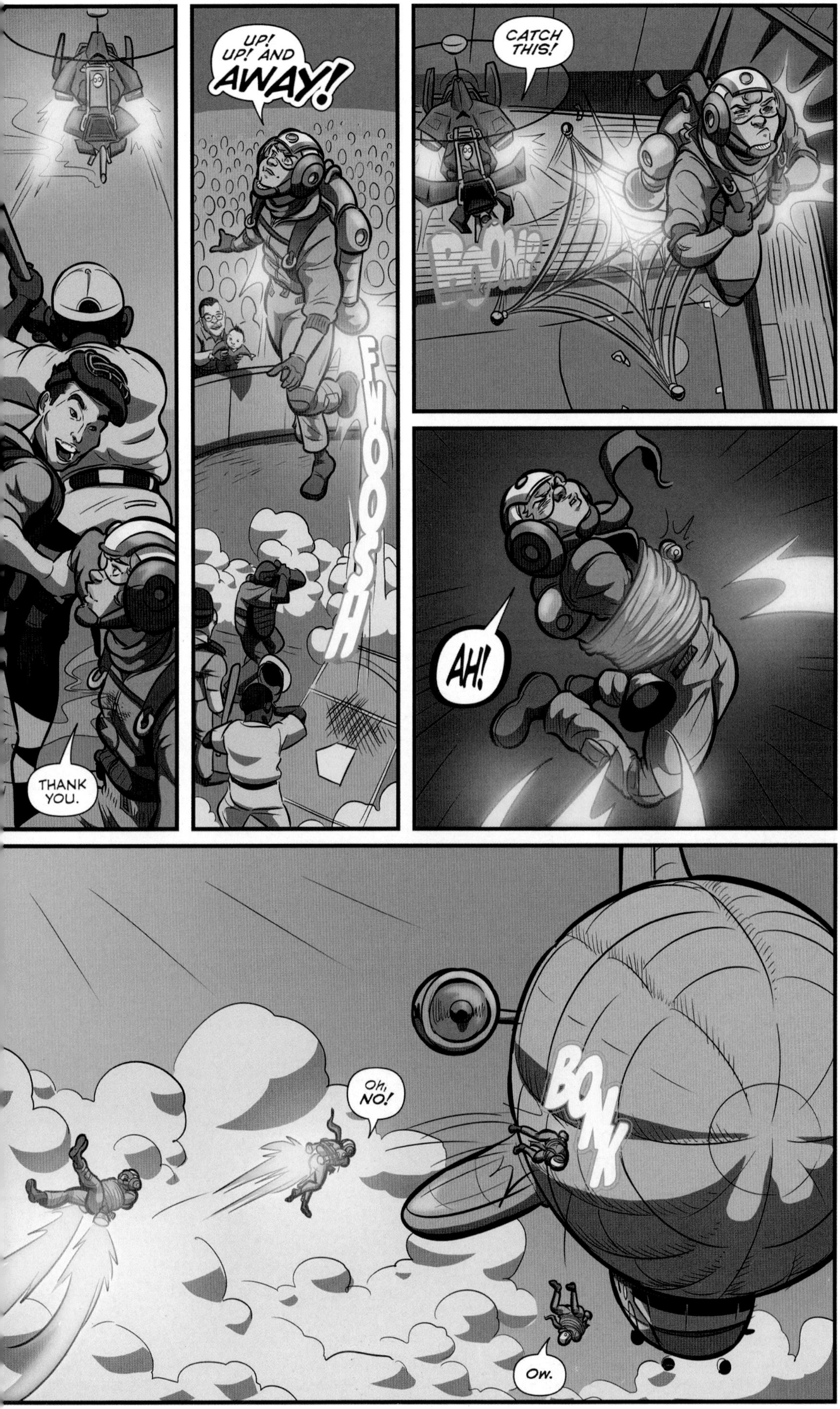
THANK YOU.
UP! UP! AND AWAY!
FWOOOSH
CATCH THIS!
BOOM
AH!
OH, NO!
BONK
OW.

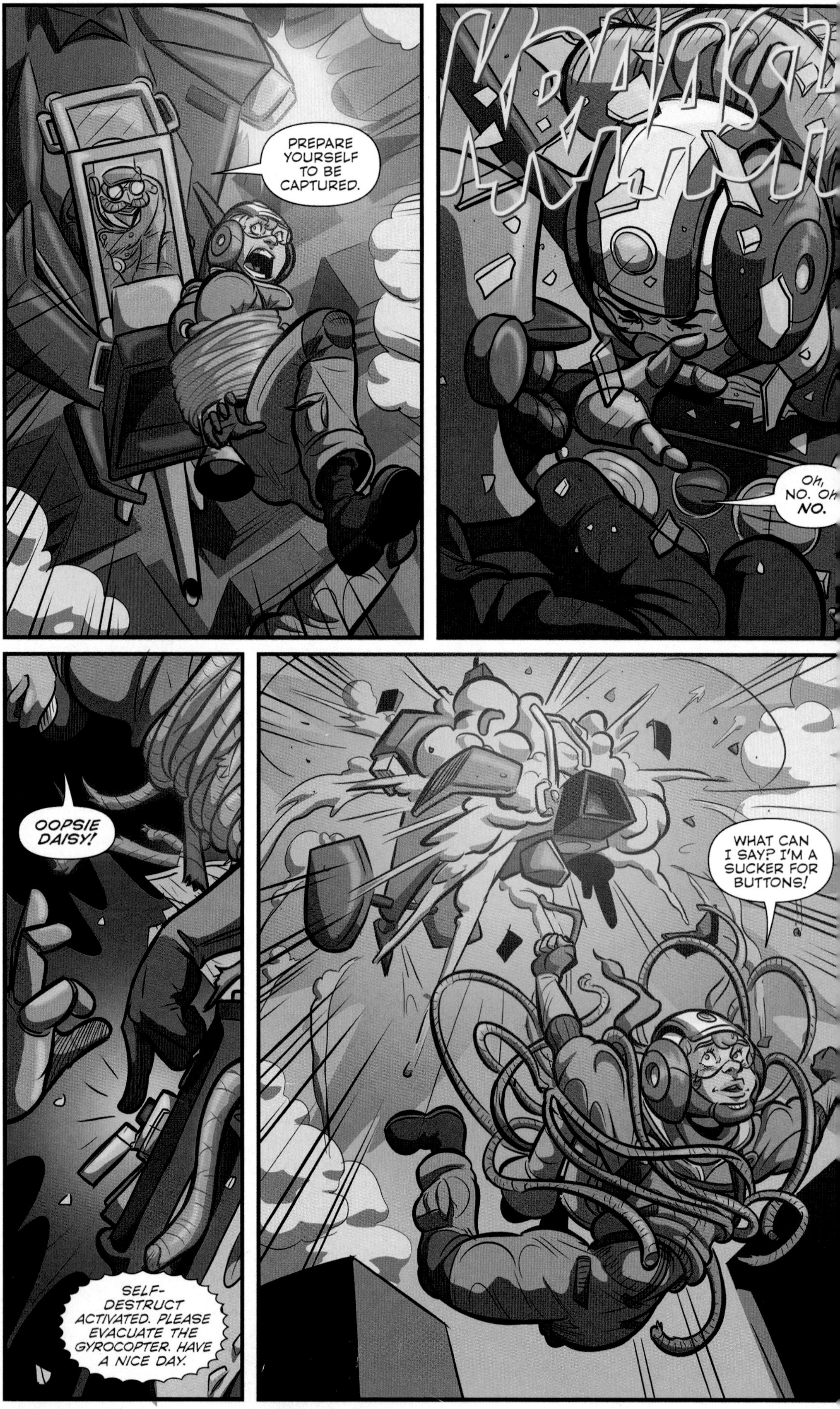
PREPARE YOURSELF TO BE CAPTURED.
Oh, NO. Oh NO.
OOPSIE DAISY!
SELF-DESTRUCT ACTIVATED. PLEASE EVACUATE THE GYROCOPTER. HAVE A NICE DAY.
WHAT CAN I SAY? I'M A SUCKER FOR BUTTONS!

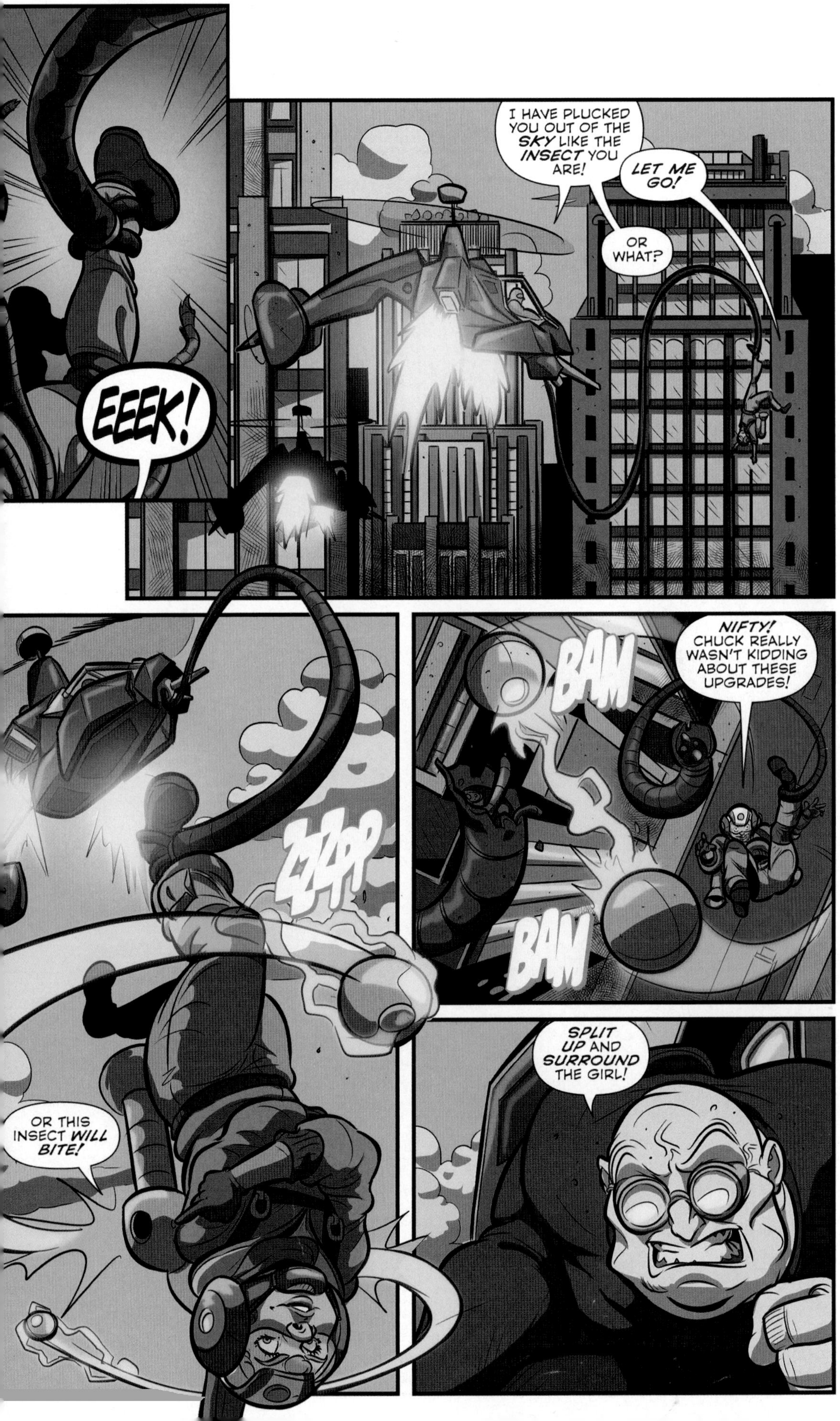
EEEK!
I HAVE PLUCKED YOU OUT OF THE SKY LIKE THE INSECT YOU ARE!
LET ME GO!
OR WHAT?
ZZZAP
OR THIS INSECT WILL BITE!
BAM
NIFTY! CHUCK REALLY WASN'T KIDDING ABOUT THESE UPGRADES!
BAM
SPLIT UP AND SURROUND THE GIRL!

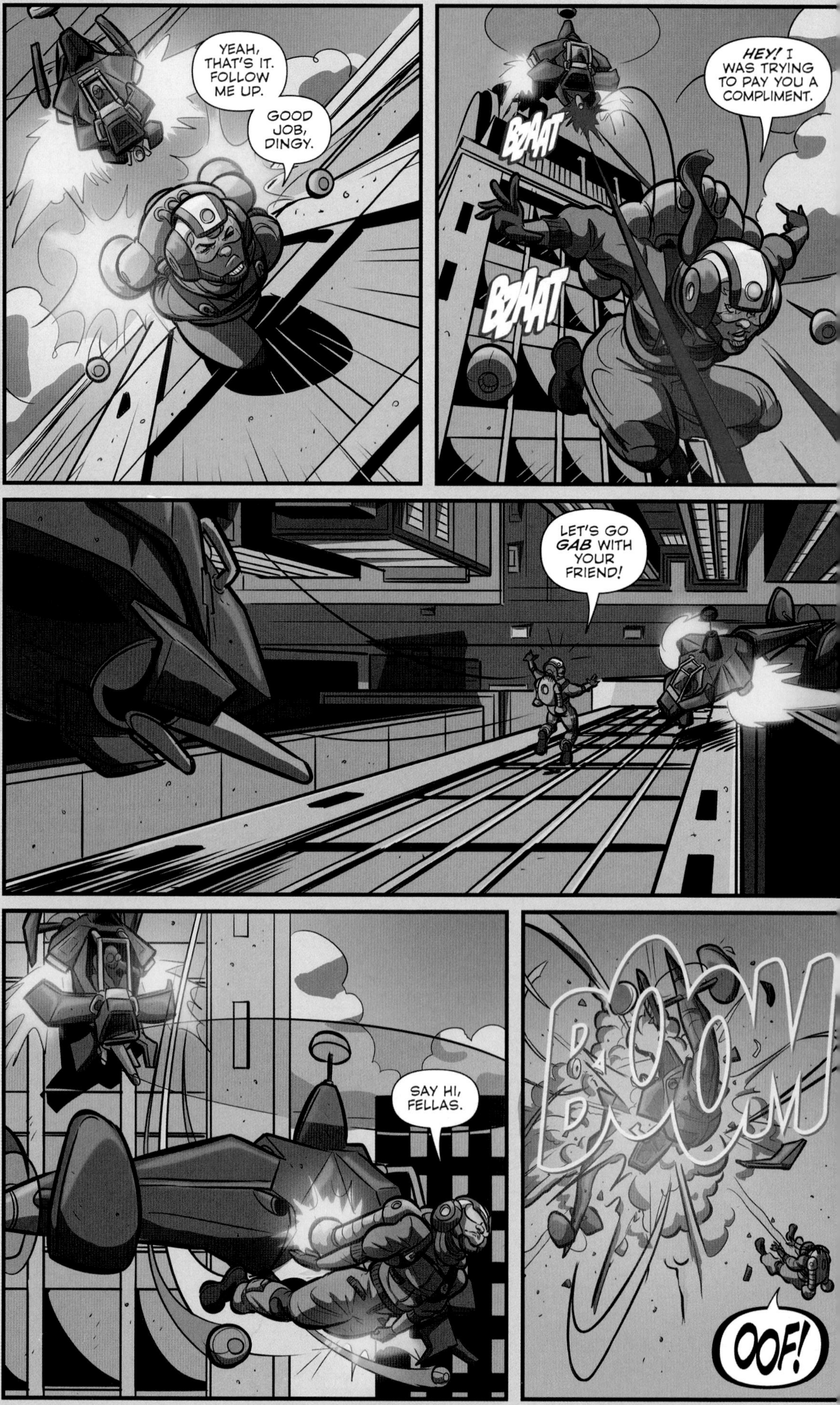
YEAH, THAT'S IT. FOLLOW ME UP.
GOOD JOB, DINGY.
BZAAT
BZAAT
HEY! I WAS TRYING TO PAY YOU A COMPLIMENT.
LET'S GO GAB WITH YOUR FRIEND!
SAY HI, FELLAS.
BOOM
OOF!

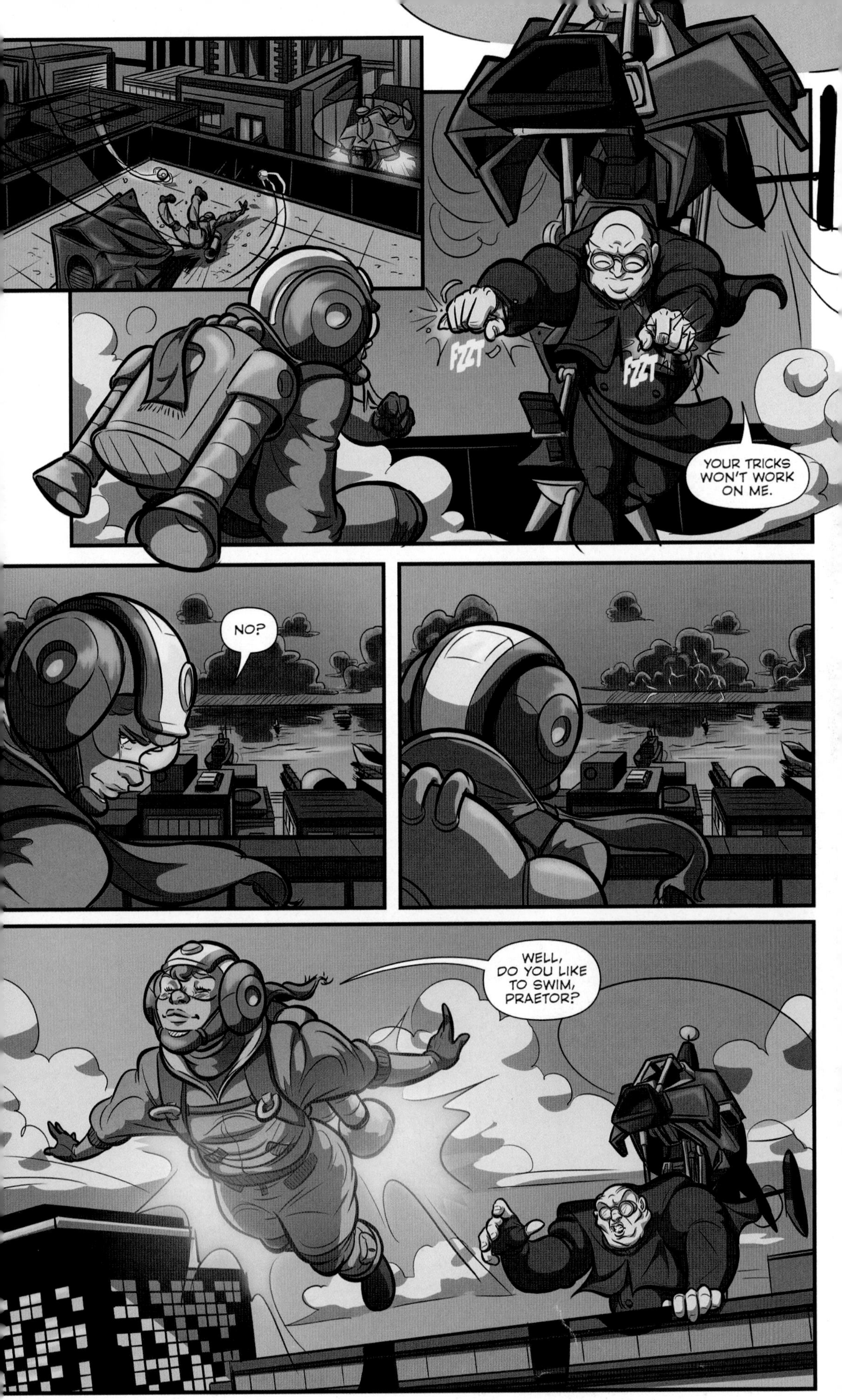
FZZT
FZZT
YOUR TRICKS WON'T WORK ON ME.
NO?
WELL, DO YOU LIKE TO SWIM, PRAETOR?

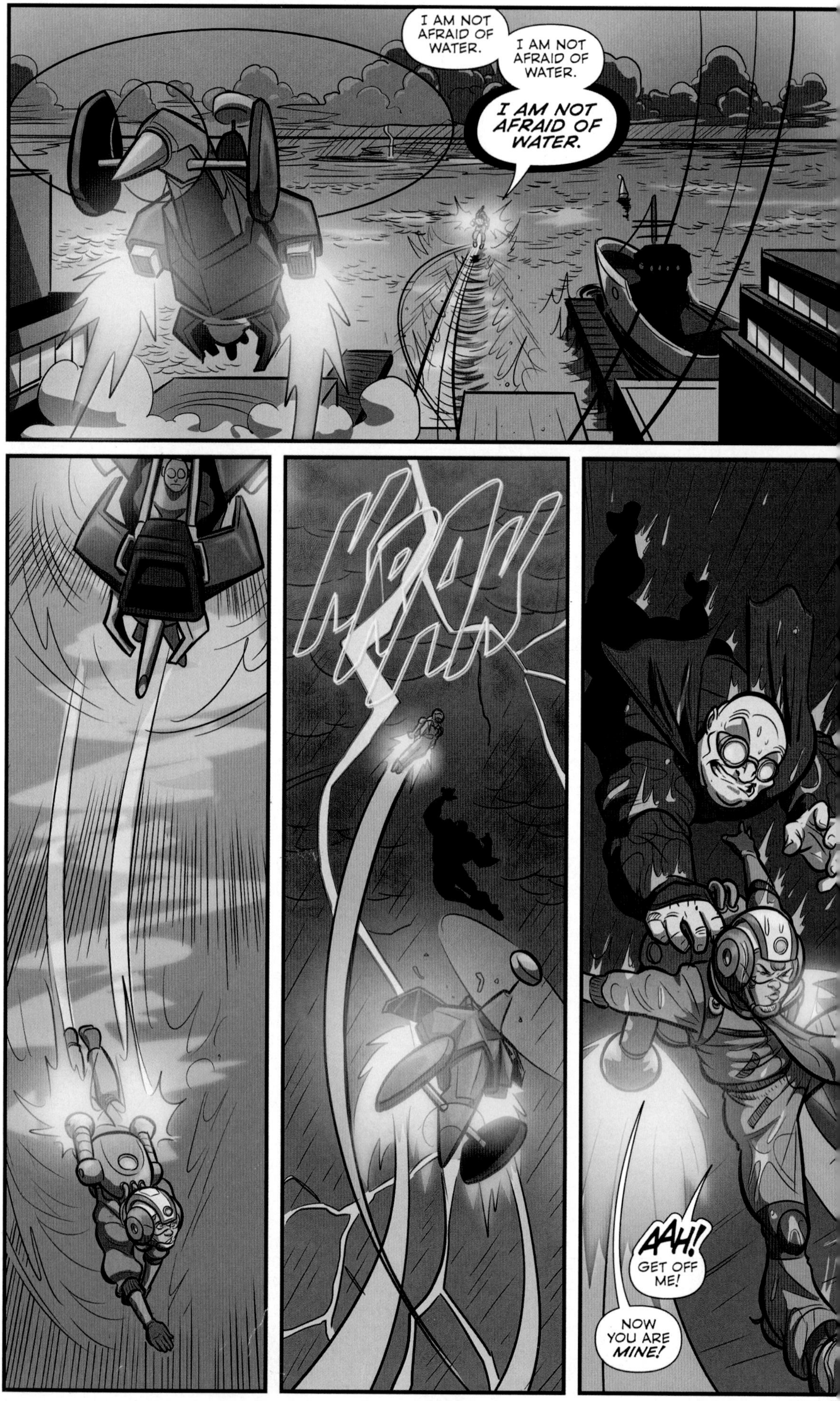
I AM NOT AFRAID OF WATER.
I AM NOT AFRAID OF WATER.
I AM NOT AFRAID OF WATER.
AAH! GET OFF ME!
NOW YOU ARE MINE!

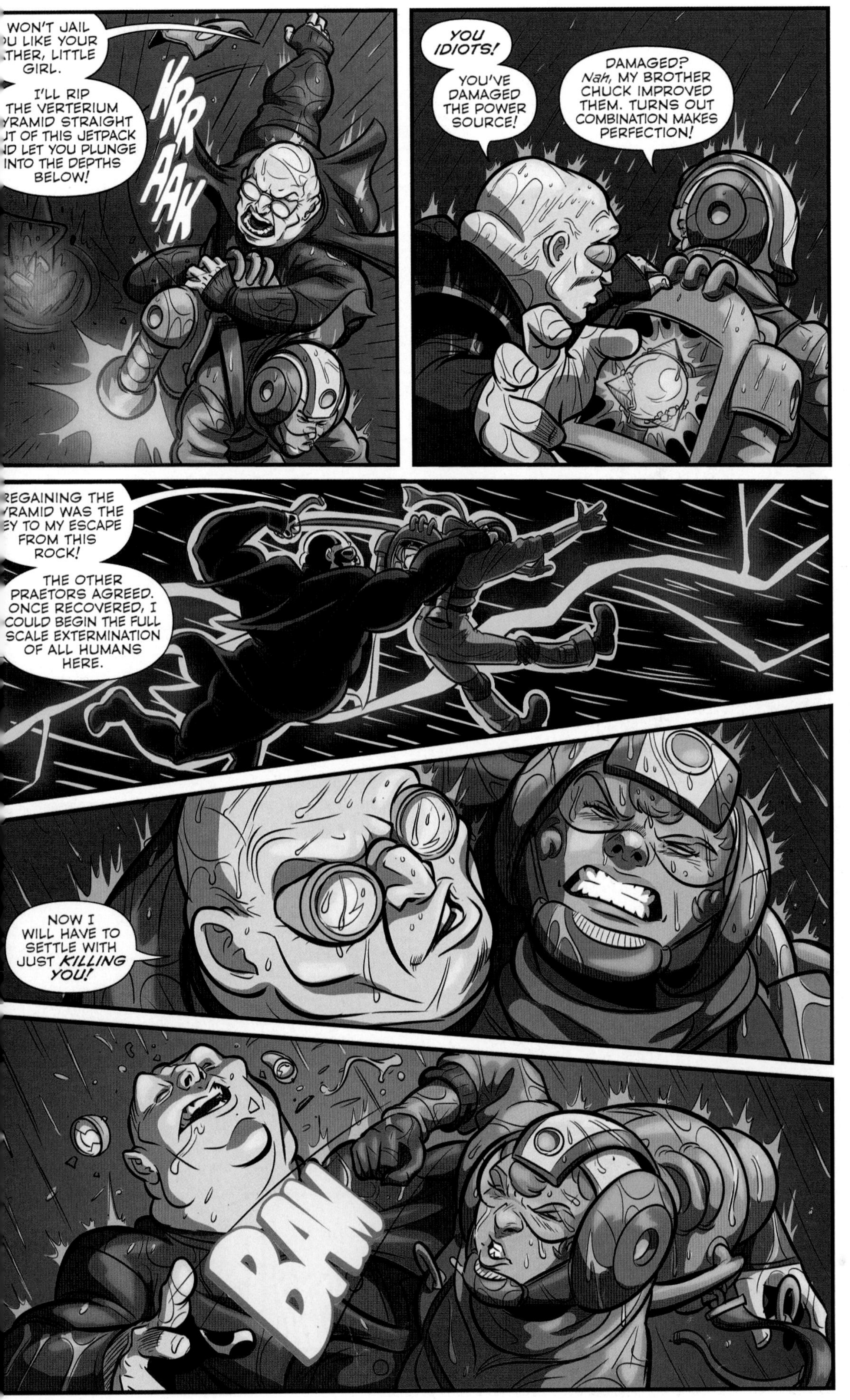
WON'T JAIL
OU LIKE YOUR
THER, LITTLE
GIRL.
I'LL RIP
THE VERTERIUM
YRAMID STRAIGHT
UT OF THIS JETPACK
ID LET YOU PLUNGE
INTO THE DEPTHS
BELOW!
HRRAAK
YOU IDIOTS!
YOU'VE DAMAGED THE POWER SOURCE!
DAMAGED? Nah, MY BROTHER CHUCK IMPROVED THEM. TURNS OUT COMBINATION MAKES PERFECTION!
REGAINING THE
YRAMID WAS THE
EY TO MY ESCAPE
FROM THIS
ROCK!
THE OTHER PRAETORS AGREED. ONCE RECOVERED, I COULD BEGIN THE FULL SCALE EXTERMINATION OF ALL HUMANS HERE.
NOW I WILL HAVE TO SETTLE WITH JUST KILLING YOU!
BAM

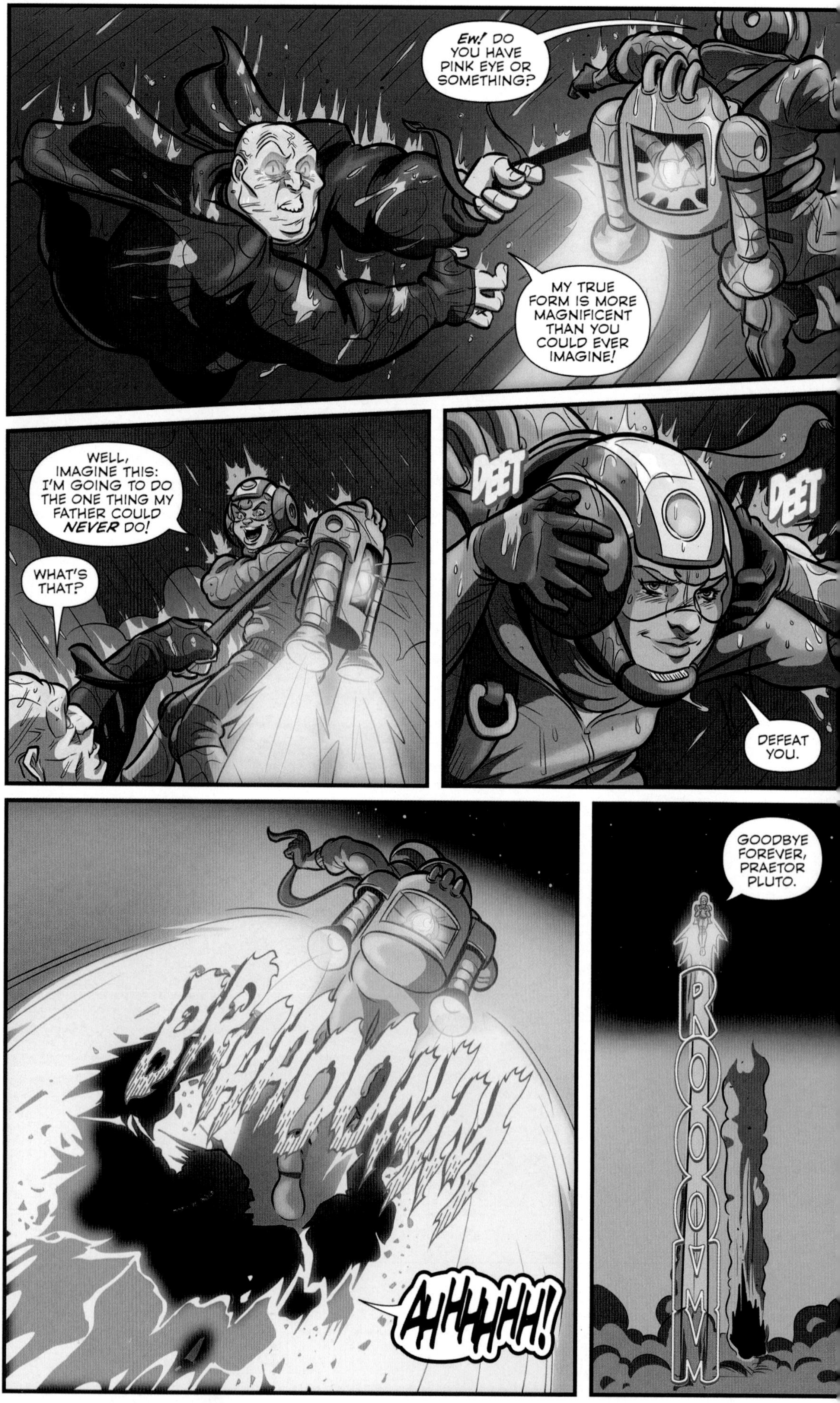
Ew! DO YOU HAVE PINK EYE OR SOMETHING?
MY TRUE FORM IS MORE MAGNIFICENT THAN YOU COULD EVER IMAGINE!
WELL, IMAGINE THIS: I'M GOING TO DO THE ONE THING MY FATHER COULD NEVER DO!
WHAT'S THAT?
DEET
DEET
DEFEAT YOU.
AHHHHHH!
GOODBYE FOREVER, PRAETOR PLUTO.
ROOOOM

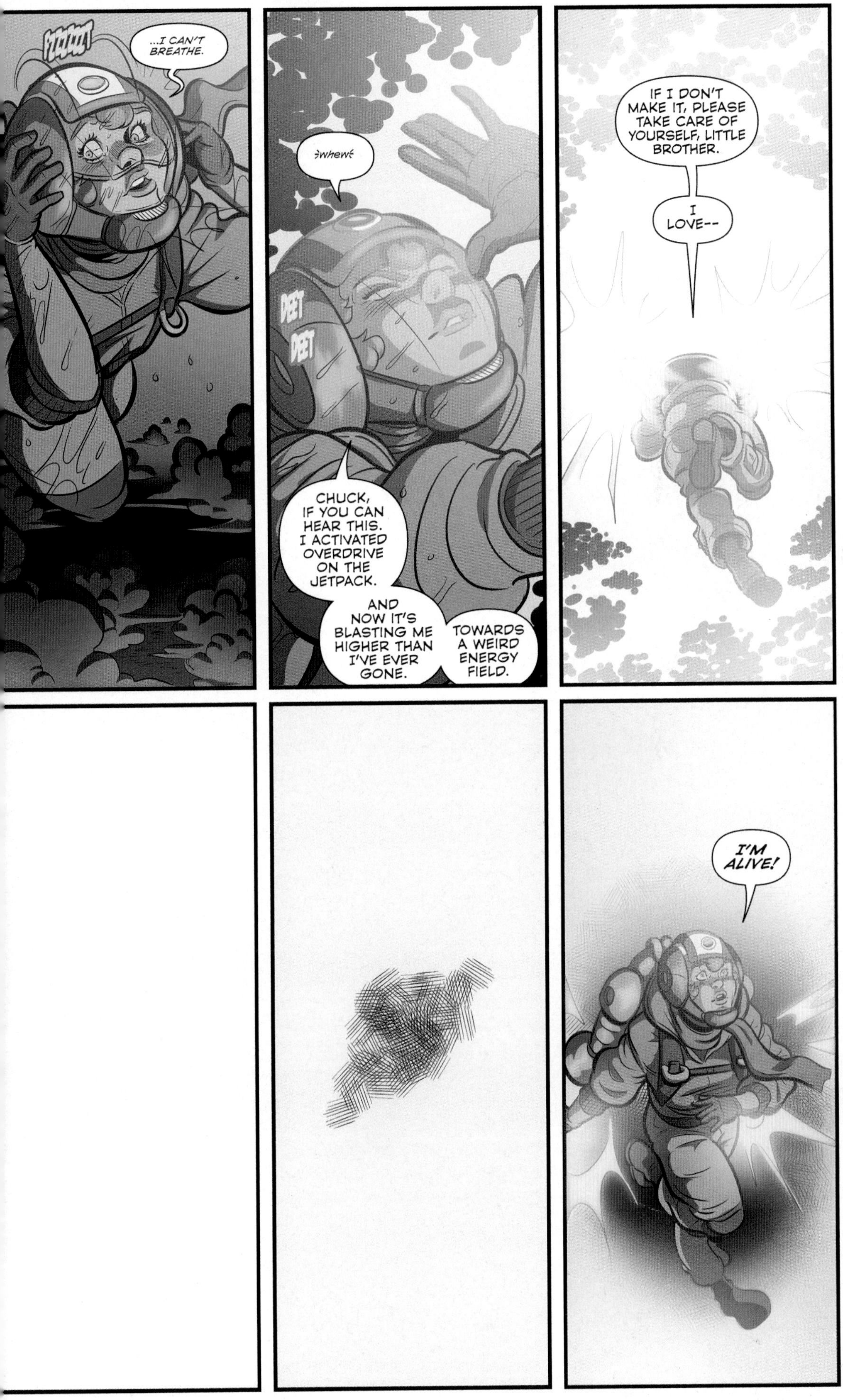
FZZZZZT
...I CAN'T BREATHE.
whew
DEET DEET
CHUCK, IF YOU CAN HEAR THIS. I ACTIVATED OVERDRIVE ON THE JETPACK.
AND NOW IT'S BLASTING ME HIGHER THAN I'VE EVER GONE.
TOWARDS A WEIRD ENERGY FIELD.
IF I DON'T MAKE IT, PLEASE TAKE CARE OF YOURSELF, LITTLE BROTHER.
I LOVE--
I'M ALIVE!

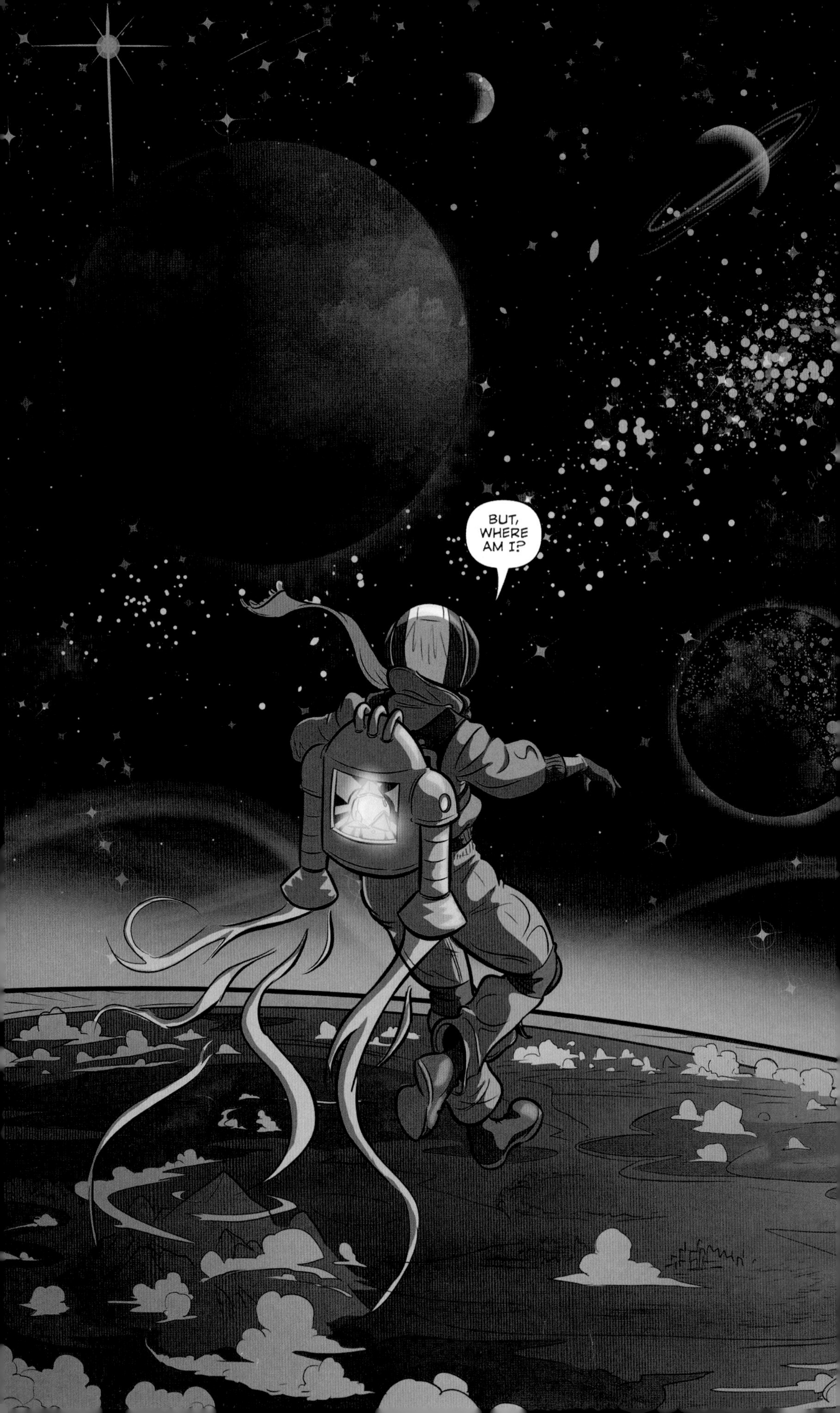
BUT, WHERE AM I?

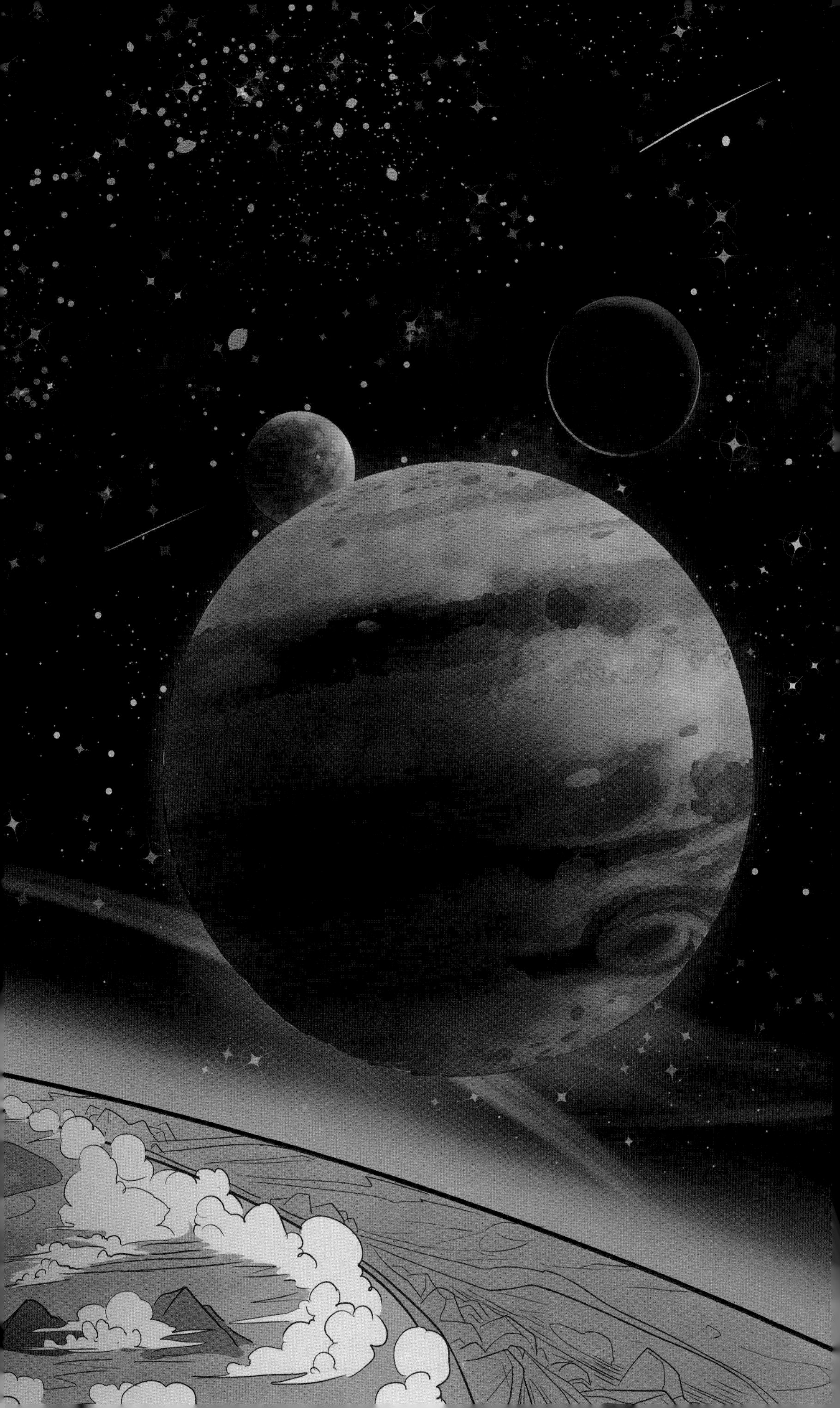

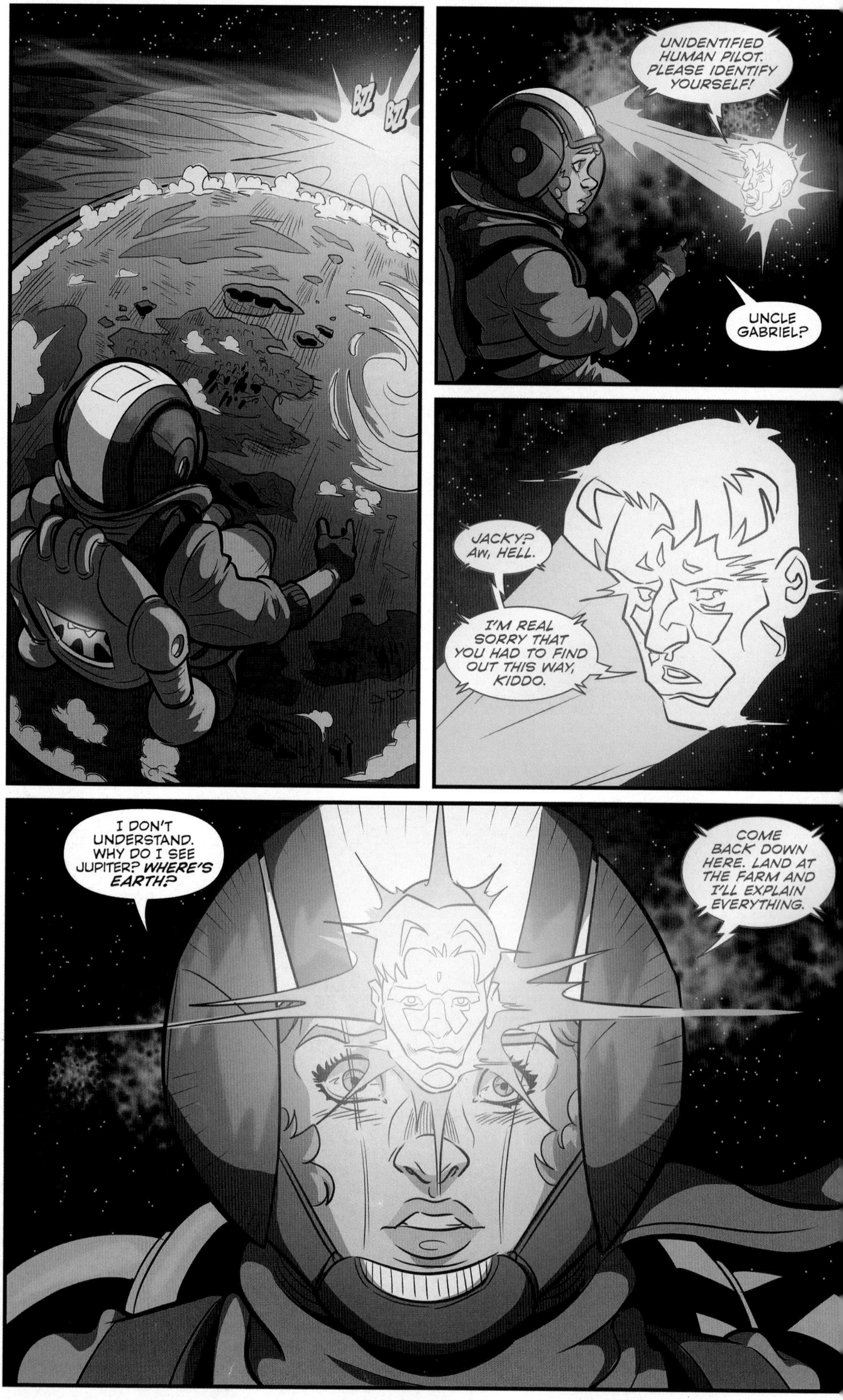
BZZ
BZZ
UNIDENTIFIED HUMAN PILOT. PLEASE IDENTIFY YOURSELF!
UNCLE GABRIEL?
JACKY? AW, HELL.
I'M REAL SORRY THAT YOU HAD TO FIND OUT THIS WAY, KIDDO.
I DON'T UNDERSTAND. WHY DO I SEE JUPITER? WHERE'S EARTH?
COME BACK DOWN HERE. LAND AT THE FARM AND I'LL EXPLAIN EVERYTHING.

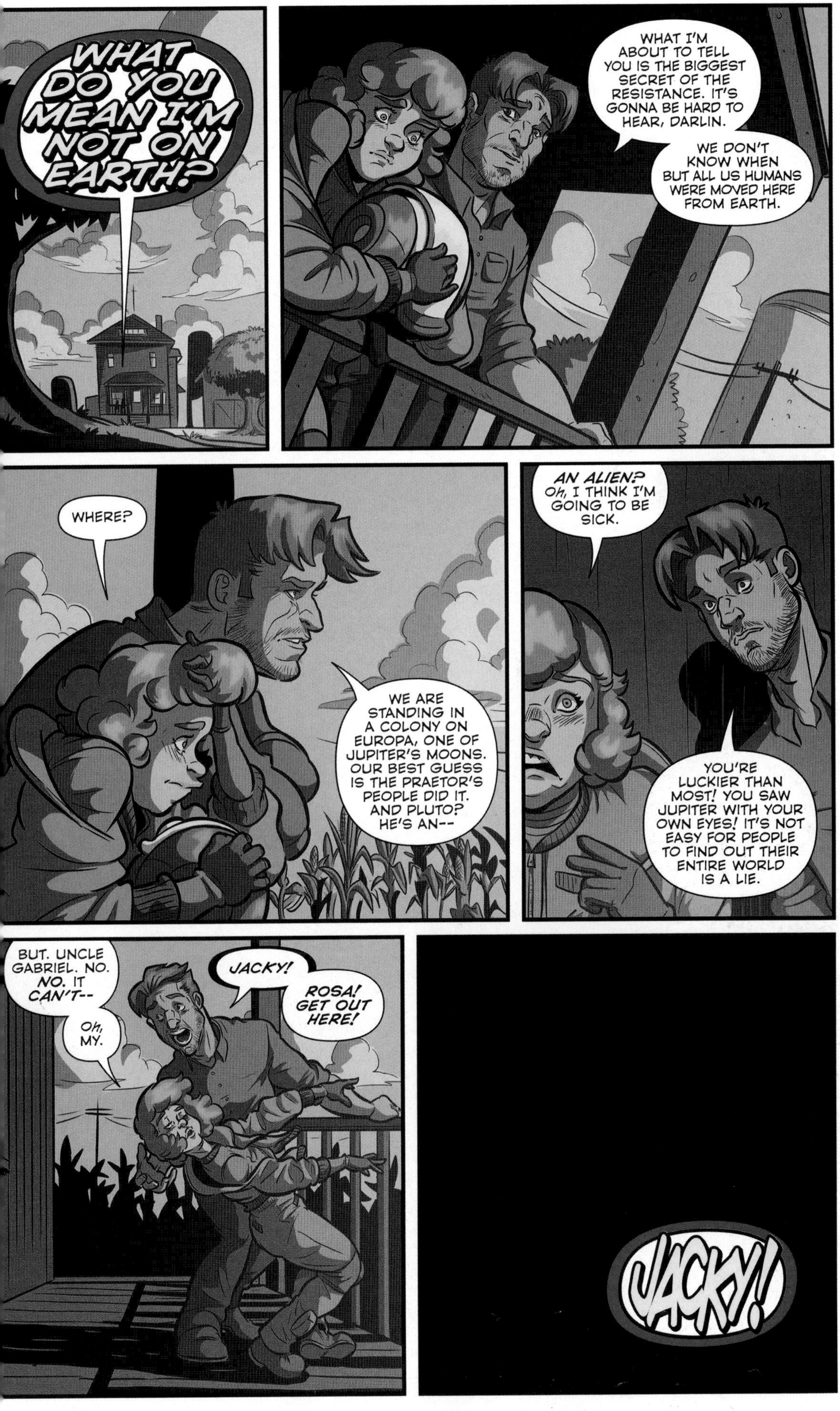
WHAT DO YOU MEAN I'M NOT ON EARTH?
WHAT I'M ABOUT TO TELL YOU IS THE BIGGEST SECRET OF THE RESISTANCE. IT'S GONNA BE HARD TO HEAR, DARLIN.
WE DON'T KNOW WHEN BUT ALL US HUMANS WERE MOVED HERE FROM EARTH.
WHERE?
WE ARE STANDING IN A COLONY ON EUROPA, ONE OF JUPITER'S MOONS. OUR BEST GUESS IS THE PRAETOR'S PEOPLE DID IT. AND PLUTO? HE'S AN--
AN ALIEN? Oh, I THINK I'M GOING TO BE SICK.
YOU'RE LUCKIER THAN MOST! YOU SAW JUPITER WITH YOUR OWN EYES! IT'S NOT EASY FOR PEOPLE TO FIND OUT THEIR ENTIRE WORLD IS A LIE.
BUT. UNCLE GABRIEL. NO. NO. IT CAN'T--
Oh, MY.
JACKY!
ROSA! GET OUT HERE!
JACKY!

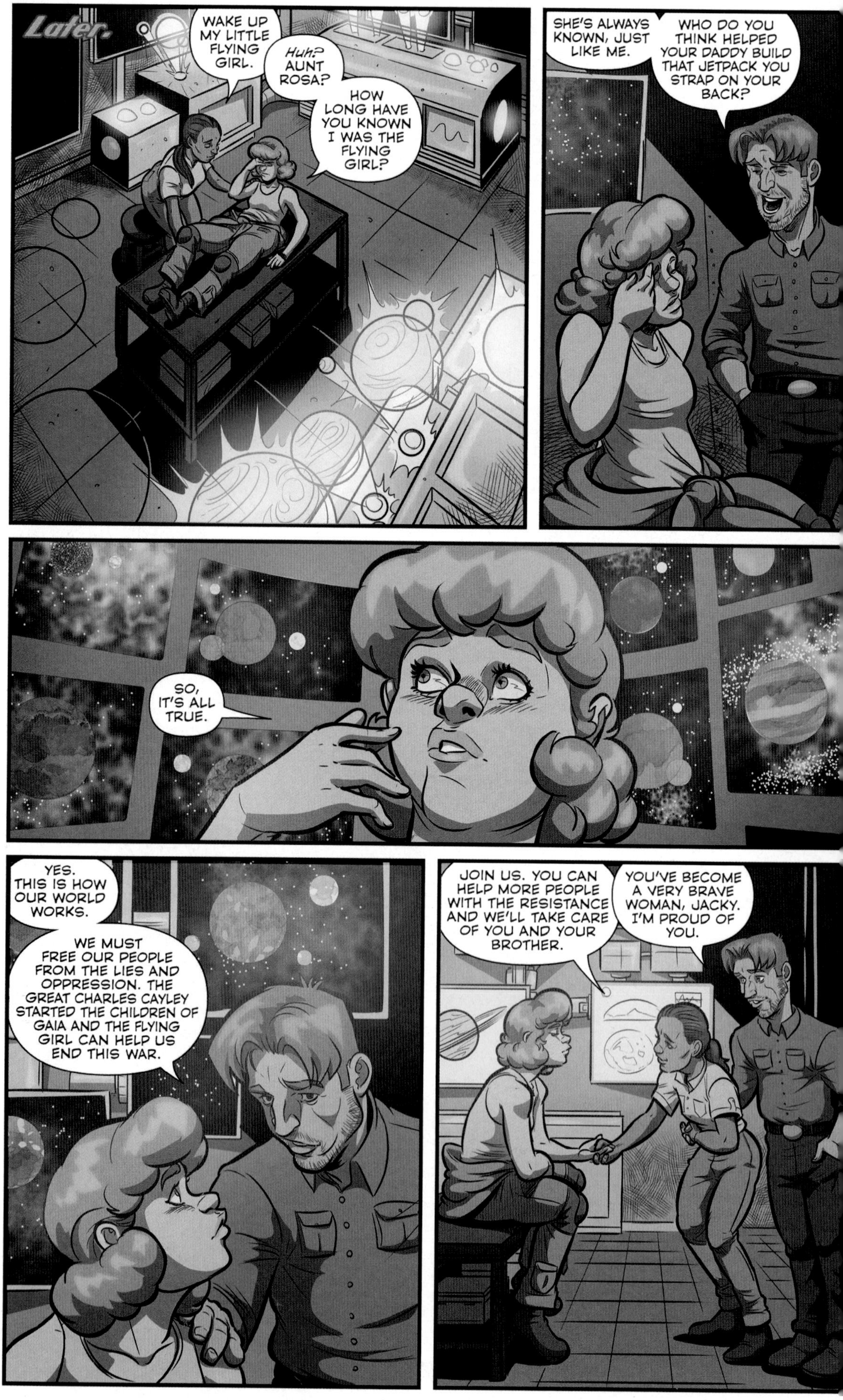
Later.
WAKE UP MY LITTLE FLYING GIRL.
Huh? AUNT ROSA?
HOW LONG HAVE YOU KNOWN I WAS THE FLYING GIRL?
SHE'S ALWAYS KNOWN, JUST LIKE ME.
WHO DO YOU THINK HELPED YOUR DADDY BUILD THAT JETPACK YOU STRAP ON YOUR BACK?
SO, IT'S ALL TRUE.
YES. THIS IS HOW OUR WORLD WORKS.
WE MUST FREE OUR PEOPLE FROM THE LIES AND OPPRESSION. THE GREAT CHARLES CAYLEY STARTED THE CHILDREN OF GAIA AND THE FLYING GIRL CAN HELP US END THIS WAR.
JOIN US. YOU CAN HELP MORE PEOPLE WITH THE RESISTANCE AND WE'LL TAKE CARE OF YOU AND YOUR BROTHER.
YOU'VE BECOME A VERY BRAVE WOMAN, JACKY. I'M PROUD OF YOU.

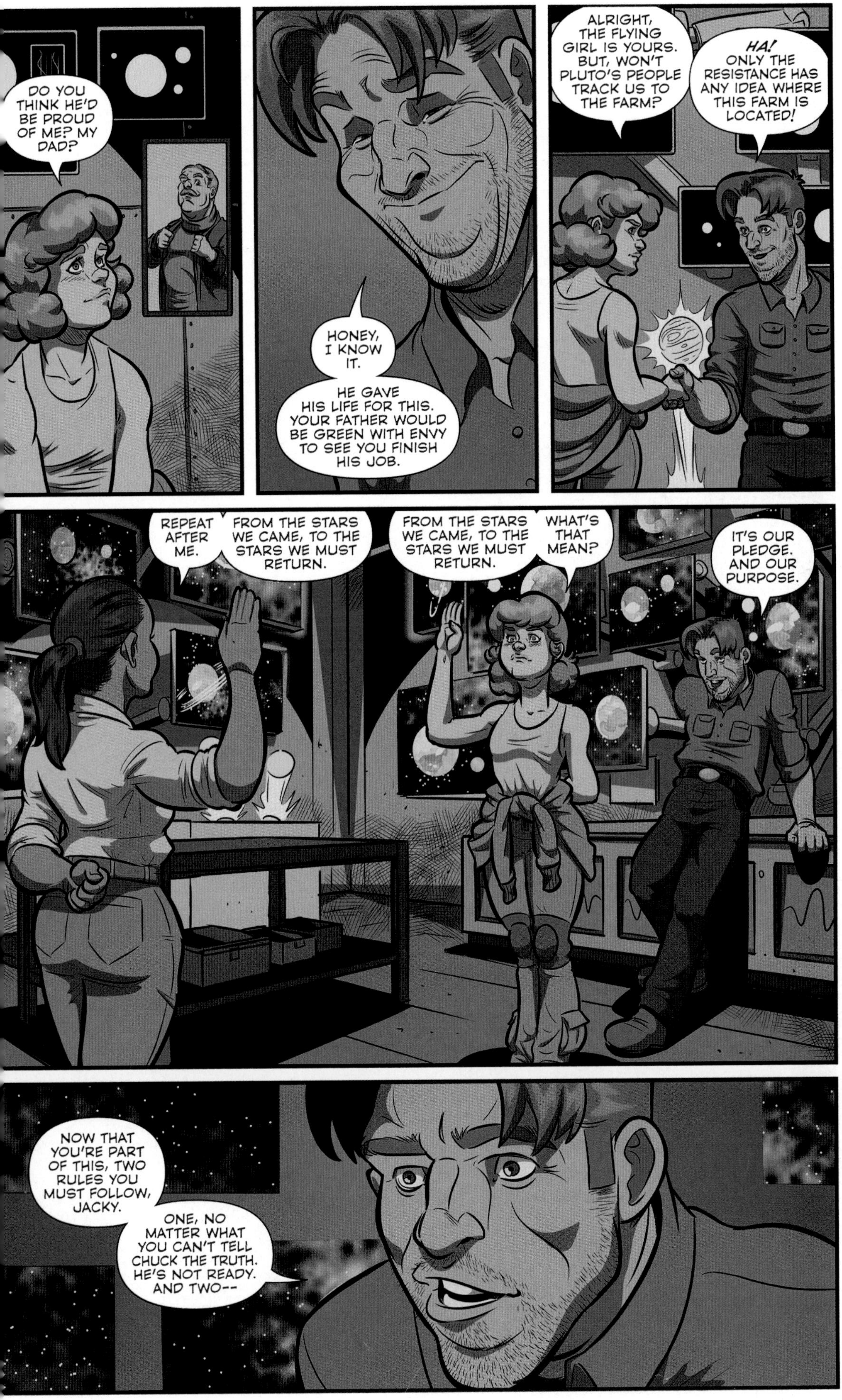
DO YOU THINK HE'D BE PROUD OF ME? MY DAD?
HONEY, I KNOW IT.
HE GAVE HIS LIFE FOR THIS. YOUR FATHER WOULD BE GREEN WITH ENVY TO SEE YOU FINISH HIS JOB.
ALRIGHT, THE FLYING GIRL IS YOURS. BUT, WON'T PLUTO'S PEOPLE TRACK US TO THE FARM?
HA! ONLY THE RESISTANCE HAS ANY IDEA WHERE THIS FARM IS LOCATED!
REPEAT AFTER ME.
FROM THE STARS WE CAME, TO THE STARS WE MUST RETURN.
FROM THE STARS WE CAME, TO THE STARS WE MUST RETURN.
WHAT'S THAT MEAN?
IT'S OUR PLEDGE. AND OUR PURPOSE.
NOW THAT YOU'RE PART OF THIS, TWO RULES YOU MUST FOLLOW, JACKY.
ONE, NO MATTER WHAT YOU CAN'T TELL CHUCK THE TRUTH. HE'S NOT READY. AND TWO--

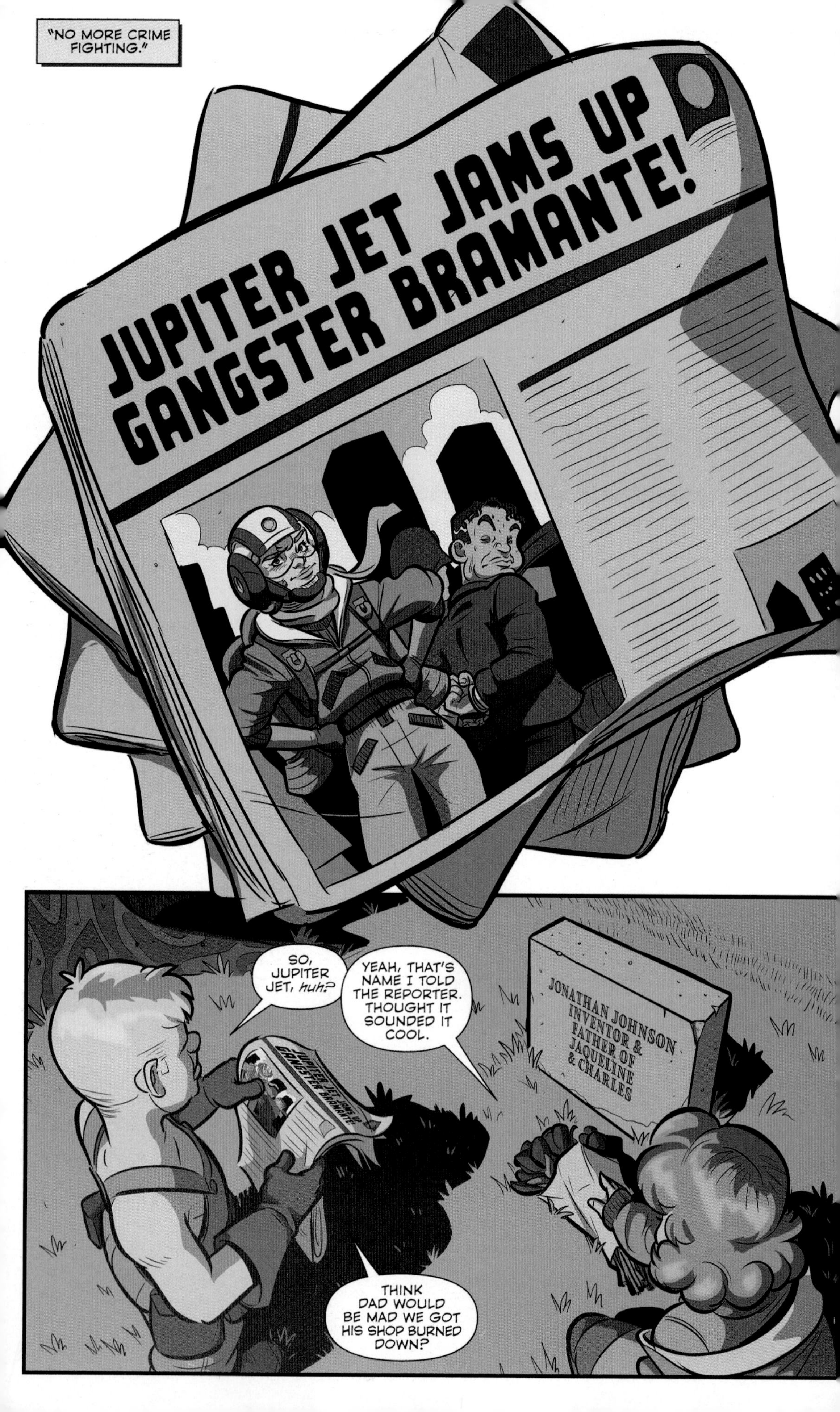
"NO MORE CRIME FIGHTING."
JUPITER JET JAMS UP GANGSTER BRAMANTE!
SO, JUPITER JET, *huh?*
YEAH, THAT'S NAME I TOLD THE REPORTER. THOUGHT IT SOUNDED IT COOL.
JONATHAN JOHNSON INVENTOR & FATHER OF JAQUELINE & CHARLES
THINK DAD WOULD BE MAD WE GOT HIS SHOP BURNED DOWN?

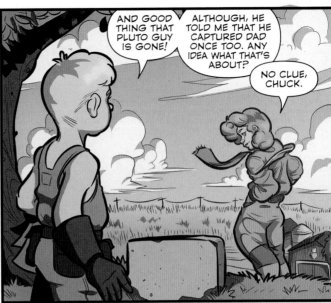

I THINK HE'D UNDERSTAND.

BRAMANTE IS GONE. THAT MEANS OLYMPIC HEIGHTS IS SAFE. THAT'S MORE IMPORTANT.

AND GOOD THING THAT PLUTO GUY IS GONE!

ALTHOUGH, HE TOLD ME THAT HE CAPTURED DAD ONCE TOO. ANY IDEA WHAT THAT'S ABOUT?

NO CLUE, CHUCK.

OH! I ALMOST FORGOT.

I GOT YOU A NEW WATCH, JACKY!

PLUTO TOOK THE ORIGINAL FROM ME. SORRY.

BUT, I BUILT THIS FROM MEMORY! IT'S AN EXACT REPLICA. MOSTLY.

THIS IS THE NICEST THING YOU'VE EVER GIVEN ME. THANK YOU.

THINK YOU'LL BE OK LIVING ON A FARM AND NOT THE CITY?

Oh YES! PLENTY OF ROOM FOR ME TO MAKE EVEN CRAZIER INVENTIONS!

C'MON. LET'S FLY AROUND FOR A BIT.

REALLY?

REALLY.

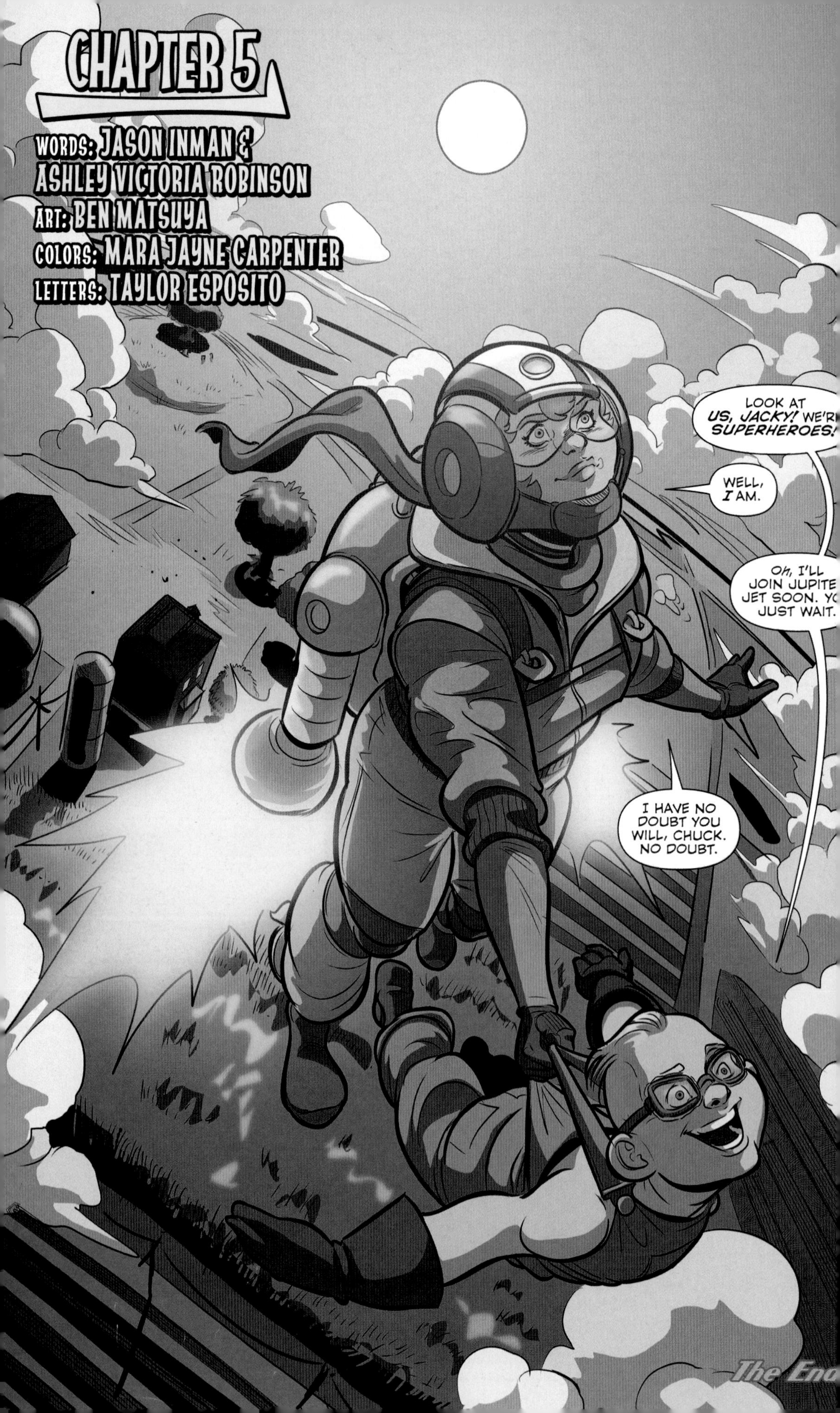
CHAPTER 5
WORDS: JASON INMAN & ASHLEY VICTORIA ROBINSON
ART: BEN MATSUYA
COLORS: MARA JAYNE CARPENTER
LETTERS: TAYLOR ESPOSITO
LOOK AT US, JACKY! WE'R SUPERHEROES!
WELL, I AM.
OH, I'LL JOIN JUPITE JET SOON. YO JUST WAIT.
I HAVE NO DOUBT YOU WILL, CHUCK. NO DOUBT.
The End

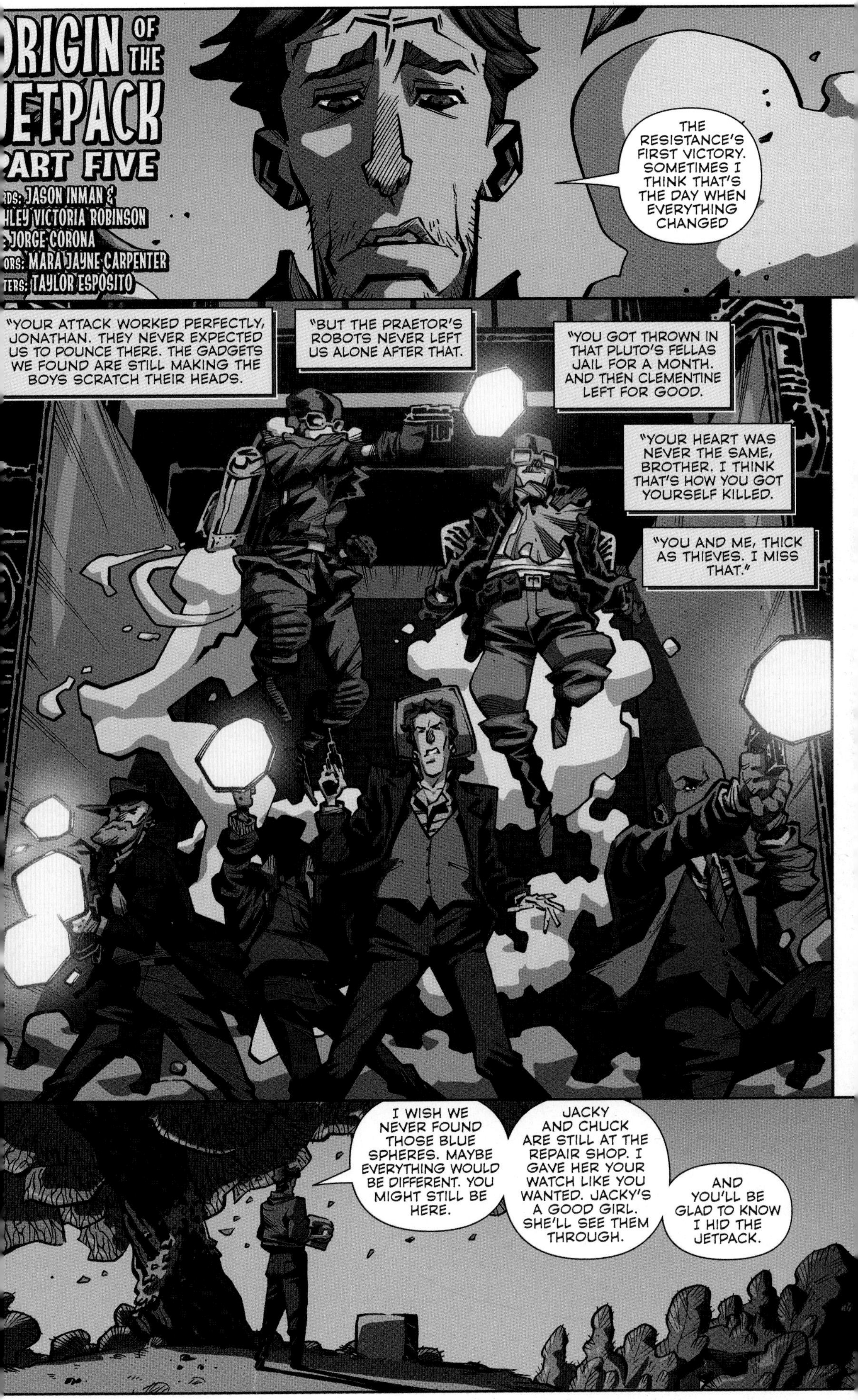
ORIGIN OF THE JETPACK
PART FIVE
WORDS: JASON INMAN & ASHLEY VICTORIA ROBINSON
ART: JORGE CORONA
COLORS: MARA JAYNE CARPENTER
LETTERS: TAYLOR ESPOSITO
THE RESISTANCE'S FIRST VICTORY. SOMETIMES I THINK THAT'S THE DAY WHEN EVERYTHING CHANGED
"YOUR ATTACK WORKED PERFECTLY, JONATHAN. THEY NEVER EXPECTED US TO POUNCE THERE. THE GADGETS WE FOUND ARE STILL MAKING THE BOYS SCRATCH THEIR HEADS.
"BUT THE PRAETOR'S ROBOTS NEVER LEFT US ALONE AFTER THAT.
"YOU GOT THROWN IN THAT PLUTO'S FELLAS JAIL FOR A MONTH. AND THEN CLEMENTINE LEFT FOR GOOD.
"YOUR HEART WAS NEVER THE SAME, BROTHER. I THINK THAT'S HOW YOU GOT YOURSELF KILLED.
"YOU AND ME, THICK AS THIEVES. I MISS THAT."
I WISH WE NEVER FOUND THOSE BLUE SPHERES. MAYBE EVERYTHING WOULD BE DIFFERENT. YOU MIGHT STILL BE HERE.
JACKY AND CHUCK ARE STILL AT THE REPAIR SHOP. I GAVE HER YOUR WATCH LIKE YOU WANTED. JACKY'S A GOOD GIRL. SHE'LL SEE THEM THROUGH.
AND YOU'LL BE GLAD TO KNOW I HID THE JETPACK.

"IT'S SAFE. NO ONE WILL EVER FIND IT."

JACKY!

I THINK THERE'S SOMETHING HIDDEN BEHIND THIS WALL!

WHAT COULD BE INSIDE THE WALL OF THE REPAIR SHOP, CHUCK?

MAYBE DAD *HID* SOMETHING!

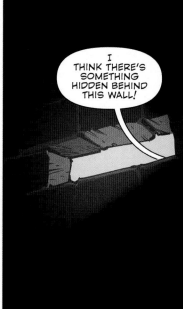

WOW! WHAT DO YOU THINK IT IS, JACKY?

SOMETHING GORGEOUS.

DO YOU THINK DAD LEFT IT FOR US?

I DON'T KNOW. LET'S GET IT RUNNING AND FIND OUT.

The end and the beginning.

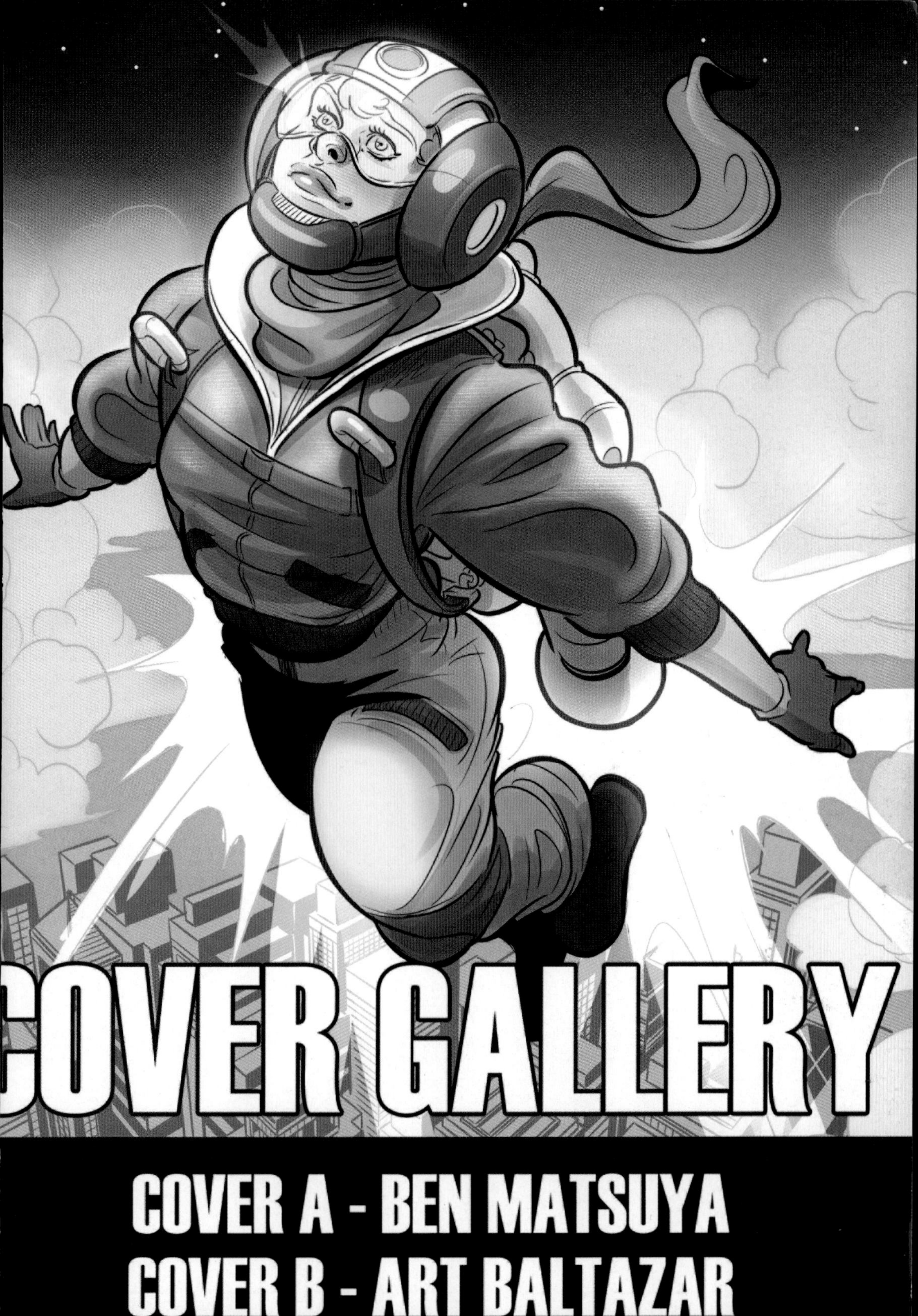

COVER GALLERY

COVER A - BEN MATSUYA
COVER B - ART BALTAZAR

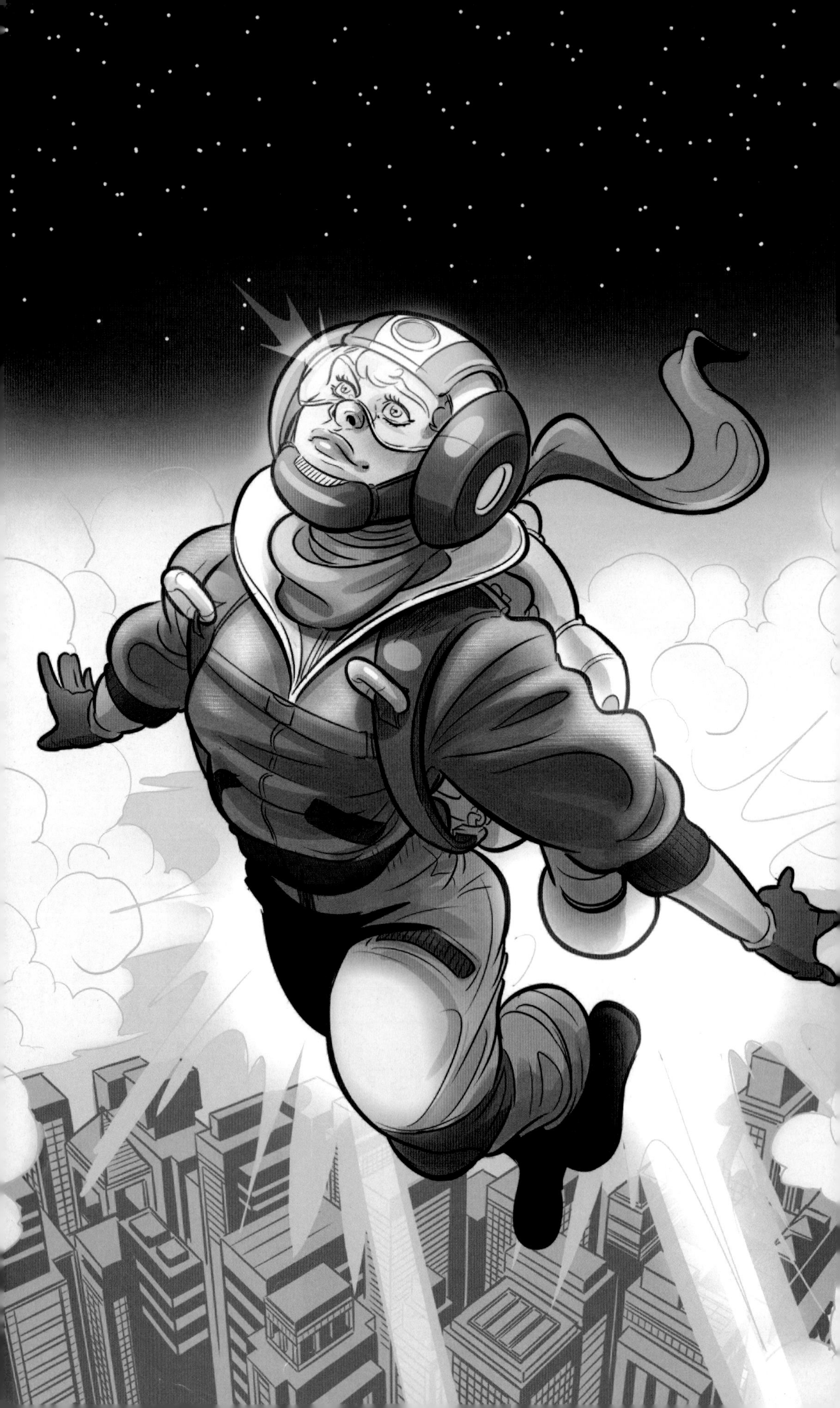

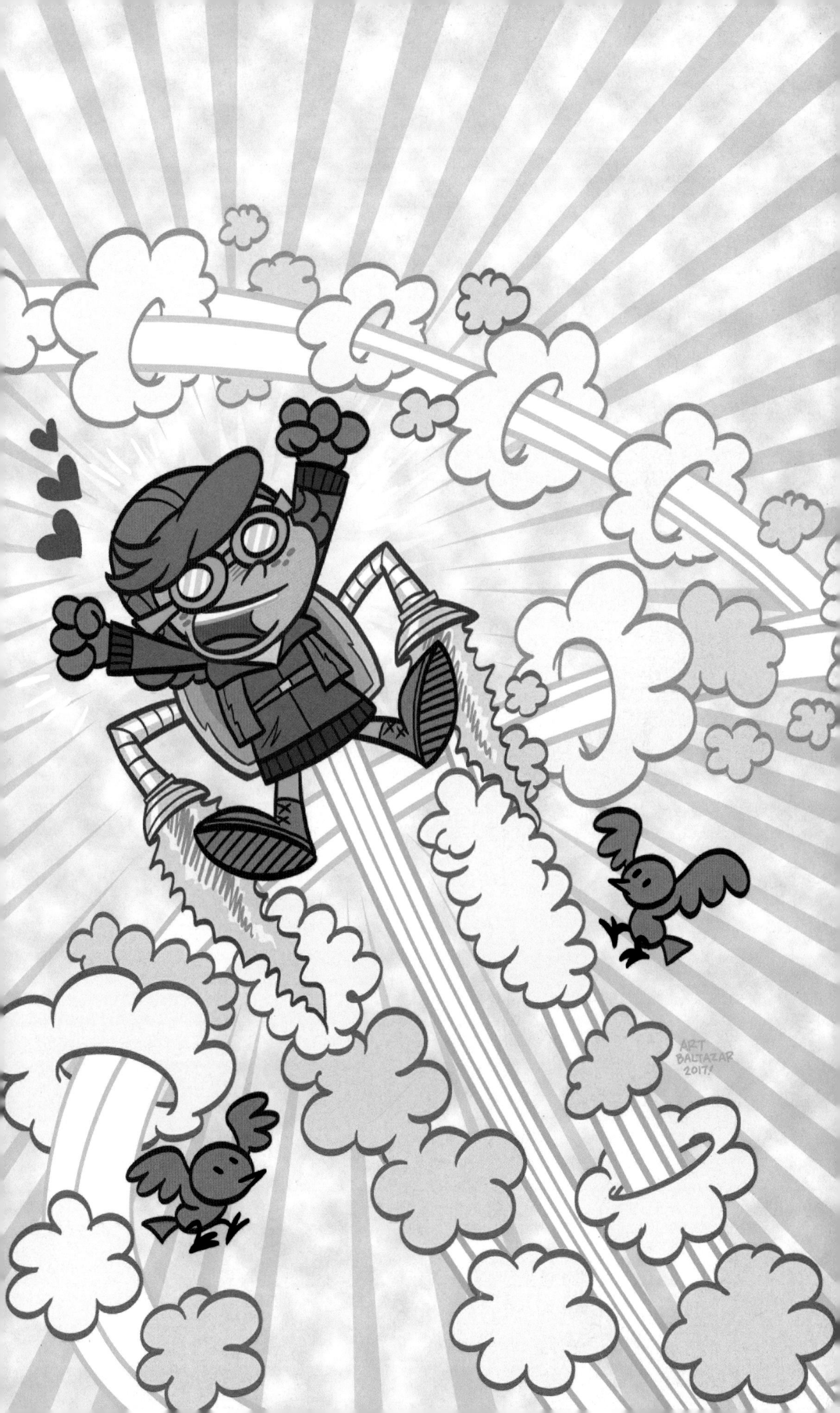
ART
BALTAZAR
2017!

SOME OF OUR JETSETTERS READING THEIR ISSUES OF JUPITER JET!

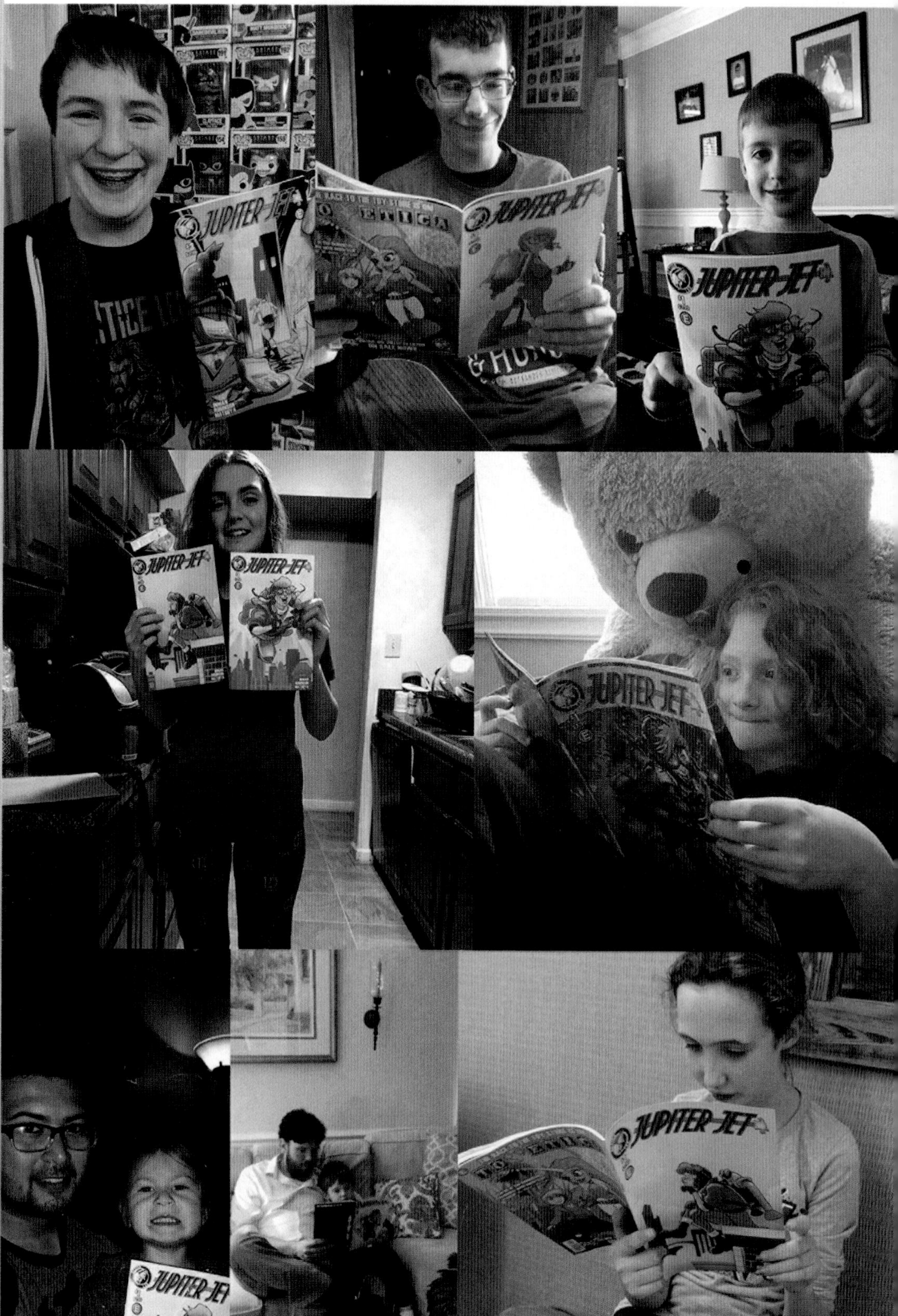

JUPITER JET

AFTERWORD BY JASON INMAN

If you're reading this, I want to thank you for sticking around to the end of Jupiter Jet! This has been an adventure through and through, and I can't thank you enough for being a part of it.

It's always been a dream of mine to create a comic book mini-series from the ground up and every step along the way was priceless.

As much as Jacky grew during these five issues, Ashley and I grew as writers. Jacky and Chuck are as real to us as our family, and Chuck won't shut up about when he's going to get his superhero name. (Next volume, Chuck!)

I could never have created this book all alone. Thank you to my mom for buying my comics all those years ago. Thanks to Ashley for coming up with the name that would change our lives. Thank you to Ben, Mara, and Taylor for being our regular jetpack flight crew, and thank you to Nicola, Jonboy, Jenn and Art for the high flying art.

Working on Jupiter Jet took me to the heights, and it's my hope that she isn't grounded anytime soon.
- - Jason

AFTERWORD BY ASHLEY VICTORIA ROBINSON

Jupiter Jet started out as a cool name I spoke over a diner table at lunch. From such humble beginnings you've given us the privilege of telling Jacky's story. I can't begin to express what an honor it has been sharing Jupiter Jet's ascension with you.

Thanks Ben, Taylor, Mara, Nicola, Jonboy, Jenn and Art for collaborating. Thanks Action Lab for putting us on shelves globally.

Thanks most of all to Jason, for never letting us shoot lower than the moon and to my parents - the first people to tell me stories.
Please know: it's my dream to tell more Jupiter Jet stories. I know Jacky and Chuck hope that you'll stick around the ride.

- - Ashley

THANK YOU, KICKSTARTER BACKERS!

Thanks to the generous support of everyone listed below, Jupiter Jet is now real!

5qu34k5
Aaron Kaiser
Aaron Kuder
Aaron Mefferd
Aaron Nabus from the Hall H Show podcast
Aaron Paolotto
Aaron Pressburg
Aaron Singh
Abhilash Sarhadi
Adam Drosin
Adrian Avina
Adrian Leverkuhn
Agent Q
Alan McDavid
Alan Webb
Alex Marzoña
Alex Segura
Alex Swickard
Alexander Attia
Alexander Tytan Jackson
Alexaundria Pagan
Allan "Boris" Fraser
Alok Baikadi
Anders Bolinder
Andres Valentin Lopez
Andrew Crump
Andrew Hash
Andrew Mrazik
Andrew Satu
Ann "Hood Up" Campea
Anneli Persson
Anthony Hill
Antonio J. Queipo Román
Ariana & Cody Collier
Arvin G.M.
Arvid Gregerson
Agustin Roman Jr
Audrey Lenhard
Austin C. Deutsch
Austin Singleton
B. Boese
Barbara Anderson
Barny Bong
Barry English
Ben Battistelli
Ben Said Scott
Benjamin G. Golub
Benjamin Goh
Benjamin Main
Benny the Comicstorian!
Bill Schweigart
Billy Craig
Blake Ortbring
Blake Phillips
Bobby Klaiber
Brad McAlpine
Brandon Monnett
Brandon Myers
Braulio Fernandez
Brendan Devlin
Brendan Edwards
Brenden Fulton
Brent
Brett Cruz
Brevin A. Smith Jr.
Brian
Brian Evans
Brian Groth
Brian Jaggers
Brian Raworth
Brian Richards
Bulent Hasan
Cassie Irons
Caitlin M. Riley
Carlos M. Mangual
Cat Broady
Cat Roberts
Charlie Szymanski (@MrMetlHed)
Charlotte James
Chase Perez
Chip Mosher
Chris Barnes
Chris Bramante
Chris Mays
Chris McKinnis
Christine "Button Tea" Tracy
Christine Gree
Christopher B
Christopher Dionisio
Chuck May
Clayton Galeski
Clayton Strain
Cody G.
Cole Sor
Colin Ngeow
Comics: The Gathering,
(comicsthegathering.com)
Corey Dolman
CP
Craig Borden
Crista Patrick
Dallas Moffitt
Dale Weaver
Damon-Eugene Rich
Dan Eyer
Dan Faust
Dan Kosonovich
Dan Patriss
Daniel Edmondson
Daniel Hill
Danny Miki
Dante Monaghan
Daryl Basarte
David A Garcia
David and Lexi Bovensiep
David Badrov
David C Williams UK
David Hagy
David Hamatake
David Holsinger
David J Sowers
David McLeod
David Schechter
Dean Gaston
Deanna Brigman
Derek Devereaux Smith
Derek Harder
Derek Outwater
Derrick Szymanski Jr
Diane Clark-Sutton
Dimos
DJ Wooldridge
Don, Beth & Meghan Ferris
Don Ventura
Dondre Murray
Doug Connors
Dr. Bradley Will
Dusty Pearson
Dvalin Monkeysbane
Earth-2 Comics
Einar V. Másson
Eli Taitano Somerfleck
Elise "Ely" Pierre
Emanuel Verdejo
Emanuel Z Sanchez
Emily and Hannah Judkowitz
Emma S.
Emmanuel A. Batista
Enrique Matthew and
Elena Mackenzie Chumbes
Eph
Eric Bird
Eric Messex
Eric Moser
Erin Sayers
Erik Montgomery
Everybody's Hometown Geek (Making
A Scene Productions, LLC)
Folarin Akinmade
For Caye Piper, from the Goodmans
For Joey
Francesco Rodrigues
Frank J Michael
Fred Bushee
Garrick A. Dietze
Gary Gaines
Gary Krob
Gene Shaw
Genki
George Dimitropoulos
George Jackson
Gerry Tolbert
Good Nerd Bad Nerd
Gordhan Rajani
Graham "Flying Badger" Butler
Graham Steinke
Grant Russell Abernathy
Greene County Creative
Greg Wold
Hank Shiff
Hannah Rothman
Henry Barajas
Holly Hutchinson
Hungry For More Games, LLC
Iobst Family
India and Amara Schiedel-Foucher
IndieRed
Ingrid Lind-Jahn
Intergalactic Kicker of Butts, Jake Edwards
Iran Quijano
Isaac Horvat
Izzy S.
Jack Rocha
Jackson Lanzing
Jacob Minick
Jacob Palermo
Jacob Westfall
Jake Damon
Jake G
Jake Hefner

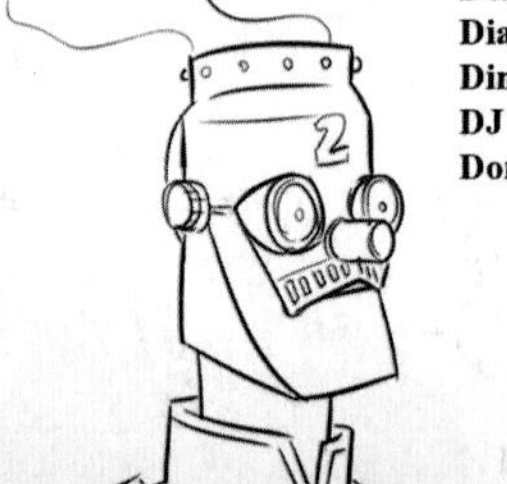

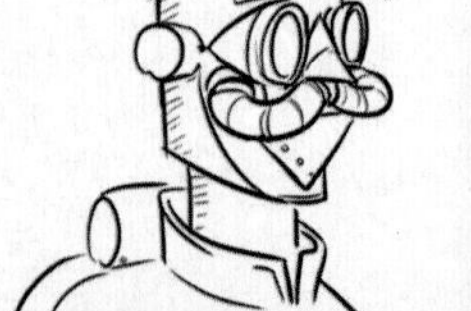
2

Jake Smith
Jalen C. Mathews
James Arnold Taylor
James Dooley
James Grasselli
James Matthew Smith
James Thatcher, Mary Kronenberger,
Samuel Thatcher, Joshua Thatcher,
& Gabriela Thatcher
Jamie and Jonathan Gilmour
Jarrad Butz
Jared Rose
Jason Bennett from PopCultHQ
Jason Crase
Jason G. Anderson
Jason LeGault
Jason Perrin
Jason Riddle
Jason Rodriguez
Jason Thomas
Jay Burrows
Jay D'Ici
Jay Lofstead
Jedi Knight Calon-Qwa Sage
Jeff F King
Jeff G Rack
Jeff Grantz (The Amazing Nerdiverse Podcast)
Jeff "JJ" Peterson
Jeffrey and Susan Bridges
Jeffrey T. Smith
Jennifer Fuglevand
Jennifer Smith
Jeremiah
Jeremie Lariviere
Jeremy Owen
Jeremy Skinner
Jerry Reece
Jessica Elliott
Jesus A. Sosa
Joe Chencharik @chendango1
Joe Jackson
JoelfromSD
Joel Jimenez
Johannes Schmidt
John Hardin
John Klais
John L. Beall
John Langevin
John MacLeod
John Roberts
John Roland
Johnathon Townsend
Jon G Mowoki
Jon Gauthier
Jonathan Bione
Jonathan Mortensen
Joost N
Jordan De Melo
Jordan Ferrill
Jordan Keeble!
Jordan "O-TRAIN" Oyer
Joris Vercammen
Josh Elder
Joshua Eskeets
Joshua Primrose
Joshua Tokuda
Joshua Williamson
Joshuah Galpin
JR Sanchez
J.T.
K. A. Diaz
Kaitlyn J Fleming,
Kat Kan
Kate Allred
Katie Binns
Kathy Ebright
Kaylen Miller
Kaz Tsuruoka
Kelly and Paul Peterson
Kelsey Knobloch
Ken Nagasako
Kenny Jackson
Kent Heidelman
Kevin Kiniry
Kevin Mahadeo
Kevin Scofield
Kieran Munro
Kijitsu
Kimberly Johnson
Kingsley Lu
Kirk Blackwood
Kirk, Mindy, Noah,
& Eli Spencer
Konrad Kedzior
Kristyn McDaniel
Ktdata | KickCast.Net
KVH
Kyle and Kristen Lewis
Kyle and Matty at Fringe Culture Blog
Kyle "@ClakyD" Clancy
Kyle Gardner
Kyle Snoke
Lance Pitt
Larry Potter
Lars Schiefelbein
Laura Kresse
Laticia Marshall
Lauren Daniels
Lauren Mayes
Lauren Weber
Laurent Frémont
Lee Singh
Leo "When Did I Get So Old" Kallis
Lindsey Hodges
Lisa Le
Lisette Osterloh
Liz Kramer
Lucas Burlock
Lucile Perkins-Wagel
Luke M. DeHon
Maite Acosta
Malcolm Jeffries
Marc 'GuildMaster' Specter
Marc Sinclair
Marcus Cook
Mark
Mark Harris
Mark Pexton for Ann Brook
Mark Rivera
Mark Scheetz
Mark "Thunderhowl" Brunsdon
Markus Olsson
Mat
Mat Shafer
Matt Coffeeman
Matt Fitz
Matt Hatcher
Matt Lord
Matt Waterman
Matt Z. Evans
Matthew Bach
Matthew Berner and Alyssa Dickerson
Matthew Foster
Matthew Goins
Matthew Robertson
Matthew Ryan Shoemaker
Matthew Z. Miliani
Matty P
Maxwell Martinez-Kratz
Megan Brett
Megan La Fayette
Mélissa Duncan
Melissa Posten
Meridith Stokes
Mgr. Radim Vrábel
Michael Alkire
Michael Beaver
Michael C. Falk
Michael Duong
Michael H. Sugarman
Michael K. Matsumoto
Michael O'Brien
Michael Penny
Mike Boyd/IceWarm
Mike Jones
Mike Krug
Mike Marlow
Mike Silva
Milena "Lady Man Lady, Sucka" Barone
Miles Ashcroft
Miss Movies
Mitch Gerads
Mohamad Badr
Mohamadreza Jafarof
Morgan Larsson
Nakiruna
Nancy Trickel
Nathan Marchand
Nelson Nantanapibul
Nicholas George
Nicholas J
Nicholas James Nowicki
Nick and Nicole Williams
Nick Bishop
Nick Fin
Nick Fischer
Nick Mundy
Nick Robles
Nikki McNeal
Nozomi Kobayashi
Olan Luttrell (Bluefront)
Owen Crabtree
Pablo (@KalPDG) Gonzalez
Patrick B.
Patrick "Biles" McMillan
Patrick Broome
Patrick Quinn
Paul Bentley
Paul Brian An
Paul H

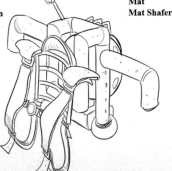

Paul Lawrence
Paul Malmont
Paul Santos
Paul y cod asyn Jarman
Paul Zeidman
Pete
Philip R. White
Phillip Thompson
Phillip White
Philipp Zbinden
Presley Reed III
Priscilla Song
Rachel Barnes
Rafa Rayes
Rafael P. Martinez
Ralph McFarlan
Raymond W Brooks
Raymundo Ortiz Jr
Ricardo Andrade
Ricardo Rodriguez Jr
Rich Proce
Rivas
Rob 'Bobbit' Dumic
Rob Cooper
Robert Ahn
Robert Chas Farley
Robert Foose
Robert Hicks
Robert L. Vaughn
Robert Stradley
Roberto M. Brijandez
Ron Peterson
Ruth Jenkins
Ryan Cady
Ryan Gray
Ryan M. McKenna
Ryan McDermott
Ryan Quint
Ryan Raines
Ryan "RTWolF" Finstad
Ryan Sands
S. Naomi Scott
Sal from ComicPOP
Sally Cummings
Sam Bashor
Sam Cretcher
Sam Martinez
Sam Shaw
Sam Wijaya
Scott Decker
Scott Greis
Scott Masters
Scott Mesar
Scott Niswander
Sean Janelle
Sean Krauss
Sean McCard
Sean Stewart
Shawn Craven
Sienna
Sohrab Tyrone Akhavein
Sophie Isabella
Spenser Starke
Stacy Fluegge
Steph
Stephen Grice

Stephen Leckbee
Sterling Gates
Steve & Erin Fekete
Steve A
Steve Davis
Steven Christopher Gregory
Steven M. Komas
Sunny 'CallMeMrKane' Chauhan
Sydney Jester
Takeshi
Tara Samek
Tasha Turner
Team Doctor - Carlos Falcon, MD
Thaddeus Hockenberry - @KalofKandor
Thanairy Gomez
Thank You Nerd Duke
The Cinema Squad
The Great NateO
The Joe on Joe Podcast
The Living Legend Will Lum Brogdon
The man, the myth, the legend... The Koller
Thomas N. Perkins IV
Thomas Zellers
Tim Beedle
Tim Dhanens
Tim Nguyen
Tim Robertson and Beverly Hope
Tiny E
TJ Bowdell
TJ Dexter
Tom Bacon
Tom Campbell
Tom Delfino
Tom Powers
Tom Taylor
Tom Trainor
Tony DeMarco
Tony "GManFromHeck" Guerrero
Tony Hendrix
T.R. Nordyke
Trace Hagemann
Travis W Bunch
Tyler Guza
Tyler Sexson
Vanessa Mosher
Vaulttechie
Veronica Baker
Victor Julio Rodriguez
Victor Rebella
Vince Bayless
Wael Binali
Wendy Lee Szany
Wes Morris
Wesley James
Whelpd
William Anderson
Willie Yip
Yair Miller
Yargith
Yaron Davidson
Yessenia Martinez
Yuri Lowenthal & Tara Platt
Zack Kaplan
Zackary Rall